CEMENT
DUST

CEMENT DUST

J. PETER BERGMAN

Cement Dust
A Novel

Copyright ©2019 by J. Peter Bergman
All rights reserved.

Published by
Silver Street Media, Inc.
www.silverstreetmedia.com

ISBN: 978-1-64339-932-4

Printed in the United States of America

To Faye Bastien,
some of whose stories
are included in this book, with relief.

CEMENT
DUST

1

Long before Billy Duncan's cousin Feyhe died, before the box of ash and rubble arrived in the mail from South Carolina, she had disappeared; Billy was forty-six, still called Billy, still living in New York. Not that death in itself isn't a disappearance, he ruminated, but Feyhe, who had been living at the Mary Magdalene Home on upper 5th Avenue, had actually, somehow, disappeared. She had been in residence there for seven months prior to her disappearance and, remarkably, no one had been able to account for her sudden, unscheduled departure. Technically she was too weak to leave on her own and too close to destitute to have gotten beyond the greening trees in Central Park any way other than on foot. She hadn't even had bus fare. It was a mystery, to be sure, how she had gotten up from her modified hospital bed, put on clothes that couldn't possibly fit her any longer, traveled down a long and windy corridor to the elevator, rode down three floors, passed by the front security desk, got out onto the circular drive that graced the old mansion the building had once been, down the walkway to the street and off to somewhere else. And on a rainy Thursday in May.

Billy could rattle off the many excuses he'd been given by the staff at the Mary Magdalene home. They ranged from the simplistic "we're sorry, nobody noticed her, I guess," to the more fantastic "perhaps she disguised herself as a nurse and walked out."

"She's a disagreeable, crippled, old bitch," he said to the head nurse,

1

"and she irritates the life out of you and your staff. How could you possibly not notice her absence? Every day I come here you, or someone, complains to me about her language, her attitude, her smell. And you think she cleaned up her act, put on a uniform, and strolled on by saying 'see ya, manana' or something!"

There had been no response.

Billy's own answer, easily distilled into one word, was "Feyhe." He could say this to himself out loud because he knew her, had made himself know her. He had taken to her when they first met the way a fly takes to a horse's ass. She had fascinated him, delighted him, and repulsed him as no other person in his family ever had done in the years before they met or the years afterward.

She was his mother's first cousin, a woman he had not known until he was in his mid-twenties. She had been a name, a couple of old photographs in a book of collected memorabilia of his mother's family. She had been a legend, a myth, a semi-saga, really. Feyhe was Miriam's cousin who dared things. That was his mother's description of her. "My cousin who dared things." Billy's mother had admired her cousin, Feyhe. She had recreated Feyhe as an idol, an adored sensibility. Billy had noted this, forgotten it, remembered it when it was time to recall such things.

"If I had left home the way Feyhe did," he summoned the memory of his mother saying to him one evening over cocoa as they went through her family album, "I'd have been a very different person, and so would you, Billy."

"I wouldn't be Billy, Momma," he remembered replying. He was ten at the time.

She had laughed and tousled his hair and hugged him close to her, kissing the top of his head, the tip of his nose, his brow in between them. "You'd always be Billy," she said, and they had gone back to looking at the photos, her telling him the names of the people in the pictures and their stories.

A lot of those old tales had been about "the sisters," three cousins who had been named for fruit. There was Peachie, the eldest; Prunella, the middle sister; and Nana, which was supposedly short for Banana, but practically no one ever called her that except Billy's mother, Miriam. Other stories relating to the photographs of relatives had to do with two brothers who were also his mother's first cousins. Morris and Ozzie were their names; their pictures were odd. The two always stood together, very close together, supporting one another, holding each other upright. When Billy turned twelve Miriam told him that Morris had been born with brain damage and his younger brother, Ozzie, had cared for him his whole life. Billy remembered them both as old men, always standing the way that they did in the pictures, except they weren't really holding each other up any longer. Ozzie had never married because he was caring for Morris and Morris could not be left alone. Billy understood this point and he remembered it so many years later when Feyhe disappeared. It was clear that she couldn't be left alone any longer either.

There was a picture of Feyhe in the book with her own brother who had been killed when he was only nine years old. Billy knew the boy's name, knew it well, because he had been named for this long-dead cousin. Feyhe's brother was William, called Billy, dead at age nine. And Billy himself had never been called anything but Billy, and he was alive and age six. He thought about being nine, wondered if he too would be dead at that age. He tried to put that thought out of his mind, but it kept returning in spite of all he tried to do to keep it at bay.

There was another photo of Feyhe, this time alone, wearing a very sexy dress, with a spiral stripe that ran from the hemline up and around and across her breasts and on over her right shoulder. She stood up straight as a flagpole and stared right into the camera lens, defying the photographer, or anyone else for that matter, to say anything derogatory about her appearance. She was not a beauty, but you couldn't tear your eyes away from her face, once the corkscrew pattern allowed you to look at her face.

She had deep set eyes and a long, thin nose. Her mouth was wide; her lower lip was deep and curved while her upper lip looked strange, separating in the middle and coming back together almost at the point where the lip joined the teeth. Her hair was light and curly, cut short and close to her head. Her arms were long and slender and so were her legs. She wore very high heeled shoes.

"What color was the dress, Momma," Billy had asked when he was nearly seven.

"Why do you want to know that?"

"I just want to know."

"Well, that dress was satin. The dark swirl that swam upward around it was a rich purple, I think, and the lighter section of the dress was the same color as Feyhe's hair, a pale, pale yellow."

He ducked his head and lowered his voice. "That sounds pretty."

Just as quietly, almost sadly, Miriam had said, "It was."

"Was her hair really a pale, pale yellow?"

"No. It was brown, like mine."

Twenty years later, at 9:30 in the morning on a sunny May Sunday, Billy, now twenty-six, had been at home working on designs for a new client when his phone rang. Billy did interiors. He did them so well, he had called his independent business "Billy Does Interiors," and that frankness, combined with his talents, had worked well for him. This was a job he had ached for, a complex set of rooms in a totally rebuilt brownstone. The Greenwich Village house, built in 1868, had been renovated and reconstructed many times in its one-hundred-and-eight-year history, but had just been converted back to a private home. He was designing seven of the rooms and hoping to get the garden as well, which would be his first garden design. This was important to him. He didn't want any interruptions as he pored over his plans and charts and diagrams.

He hesitated, then picked up the phone receiver. He always hesitated now, at twenty-six, because he hated to be interrupted by his mother when he was working and she was the only person likely to call him on a Sunday morning. Still, he generally picked up because she always knew when he was home, somehow she always knew.

"Feyhe's here," were the first words out of her mouth.

"Fay?" His voice must have sounded confused, he knew, because he was confused.

"My cousin, Feyhe, you know, from the pictures."

"My God, how did that happen?" Billy was actually as surprised as he sounded.

"We went to Banana's son's wedding last night, you know that miserable kid…Pricka," she said.

"Nana, and her son is Procco," he corrected her, but as usual she wouldn't be corrected. She was the only one in the family who actually referred to her cousin by her given name rather than by the shortened version.

"Your father and I were dancing the Cha-Cha-Cha when a woman came up to me and tapped me on the shoulder and said to me, 'I didn't get to dance with him at your wedding, Miriam, so maybe I could dance with him now?' Well, I looked at her and looked at her and suddenly it hit me who she was. Feyhe."

"So did Dad dance with her?"

"Nobody dances with your father except me. You know that."

Billy did indeed know how that worked. His mother could dance with anyone she liked, but his father could only dance with her. For years Billy had assumed that this was his mother's rule, but he had learned that in this, at least, his father had made the decision.

"So what was she like?"

"Why don't you come and see for yourself."

"I'm working, Momma, I can't just—"

"You work for yourself. Give yourself a day off. Come out and meet her."

"You mean she's there, with you at the house?"

"We brought her home with us and we talked all night."

"How great!"

"So come out and meet her. She wants to meet you. She's heard so much about you."

"She has? From whom?"

"Not whom. Me. That's whom." His mother laughed as she always did at such non-jokes that she thought were funny.

"What are you saying, Cousin Feyhe?" Billy wanted to know. "Drop the mystery stuff."

"We're all adults here," Duncan added.

She pulled herself upright into a broomstick-back straight-up position. Her head was touching the ceiling of the car's back seat. Billy watched as she grew into a towering beast. He saw his mother shrinking away at the same time into a small figure huddled in a corner. He sensed that something big was about to be said, something that would make them all feel small once it was out in the open.

"My Aunt Rose," Feyhe began, "*our* Aunt Rose, was a child molester, Billy. She would stick that big, sweaty chicken-feathered hand of hers up a skirt, or through an open fly, faster than you can blink an eye. There wasn't one child in our family that didn't suffer from that hand. Your mother knows this, if she'll just admit it. Your mother likes to think that everyone in our family, her family, is perfect and nice and sweet and loving. She likes that story. She always did. The truth is we've got some skeletons in our closet that still have flesh on those bones. Your Aunt Rose, or great-Aunt Rose actually, was personally responsible for the loss of my virginity, and probably your mother's as well. And what she did to her sons, I cannot begin to describe. She had such a thing about her oldest son, our cousin, Morris, that she wouldn't let him be. It wasn't enough to have a bris, like other boys, no. She had to examine him as he reached puberty. She had to examine him all the time. She didn't like a little foreskin. She had him cut again when he was nine and again when he was ten. Do you remember this, Miriam?"

Miriam nodded but said nothing. Billy was mesmerized. No one ever drove his mother to silence. No one ever had in his experience at least.

But Feyhe didn't stop there. "When he was thirteen, Billy, instead of preparing him for a bar mitzvah, his mother had him cut one more time. This time she had him castrated. She cut Morris's balls off. He was slow, not a crime in my book. He was slow at school, a slow-learner. He was probably too shy and too demoralized by that maniac of a mother, that's all. But she took him in to a doctor's office and had him declared "feeble," a word we didn't even know existed until then. I was fifteen and your mother was the same age as me then, although I don't think we're the same age any more, but I'm getting off the story. Aunt Rose had her oldest son declared mentally feeble and she had the doctor write a note that he shouldn't be allowed to marry and have children. Then she had Morris castrated. I don't think he was feeble or crazy or incompetent, Billy, but after that operation, after they cut off his balls, he was never a whole person again. He stopped talking and he stopped reading and he stopped joining in with us in anything we did. He hid all day and he hid all night, and Ozzie, who loved him, started to take care of him. He took care of him his whole life."

"That part is true," Miriam Duncan put in from her corner of the back seat.

"That's a terrible story," Billy said.

"And beautifully told, by the way," Angus chimed in from behind the steering wheel.

"You shut up, you crazy man, and drive," Feyhe called out to him, and then she laughed.

Angus joined in, more lustily than might have been expected. "It's nice to have you with us, Feyhe," he sang in a non-melodic manner.

"Shut up and drive." There was a short silence during which the scenery failed to distract them all. "Your mother never told you this story?" Feyhe asked Billy.

"No, never."

"I'm not surprised. Princess Miriam never paid much attention to what was going on around her."

"*Princess* Miriam?" Billy said, not too eagerly.

Feyhe laughed again, then said, "Not today, Billy. Some other time."

There was no more talk about Ozzie, the cousin who hadn't shown up at the wedding, or about Peachie or any of the others. West Point was looming on the horizon and there were cadets to watch. At least that was what Billy told himself as he sat in the Buick's wide front seat and stared out the window and down the road.

The walk around the academy grounds had yielded little but windburn and bleary eyes.

They had noshed rather than feasted, filling their bellies with hot dogs and their minds with fantasies about twenty-year-old career military men. Angus and Miriam had returned to the car while Feyhe and Billy had continued their walk, now arm in arm. They rested for a while against the old stone wall that topped the cliff overlooking the Hudson. The day was bright and clear and the view northward equaled its southerly opposite. A train plowed its way up the eastern bank of the river heading toward Poughkeepsie and points beyond.

"I love to watch the trains," Feyhe said. "I love to imagine the people on them going places they've been sent to see, not knowing what awaits them, not caring much either, probably."

"Why do you say that?" Billy asked her.

"I've taken those trains, kiddo. I've seen those people, talked with them, shared a meal with them. Most of them have been given a ticket, sold a destination, promised a future. Most of them have no idea what's really going on in their own lives. Most of them would rather die than face the reality that waits up there." She gestured wide, taking in everything to the north and the west. "When they find out how little there is in this world, they crumble inside, Billy. They just crumble and fade away. I've seen it. I've been with them."

"When? Where?" Billy said.

She was more silent than the bottom of the ocean. He was staring at her, looking into her eyes and finding nothing there, not even his own reflection. It was as if she had cut herself off from all possibilities, all reactions. Then she took his arm and moved him off again, back toward the parking lot, the car and his parents. She didn't speak again until they were almost on top of the Buick.

"Don't tell your mother what I said," she whispered.

"What did you say?"

"Good for you," and she smiled at him. It was a smile you could bask in, grow warm and tan in, and Billy did.

When Feyhe disappeared from the home on upper 5th Avenue on May 9, 1996, Billy was devastated. He was fairly sure he knew what had happened, but he had no way to prove it and no one to prove it to. His parents were long-gone. Ozzie was dead too. Peachie, Prunella and Banana didn't matter really. Their English cousins weren't involved any longer, and Feyhe's old friends had long since melted away into the deep shadows cast by New York City's smaller buildings. Joe was out of his life…sort of. There were only Feyhe's peculiar cousins on her father's side of the family to talk to about her disappearance. Billy had never liked them, any of them. They were impatient people, intolerant people, people who had never understood their own cousin. They wanted answers yesterday. They wanted to know about the money and the apartment and the "things." Billy had no answers for them. Billy knew what they knew and little else when it came to Feyhe's disappearance. He had his theories, as noted, but there was nothing he could do about them. They were locked inside the "inscrutables," the insular family of foreigners who would never answer his questions.

Besides himself, those nosy, grabby distant cousins were all there was. If they had no knowledge, no solutions, he could not help them.

"Feyhe is the cousin who does things—did things," Billy told them, double-quoting his mother's old saw. They seemingly agreed with the statement and added nothing to it. This was all there was, an agreement on a basic principle of the missing woman's life.

After all this time, she had managed to remove herself from his presence, from his care, somehow. After twenty years in his life—twenty years of Feyhe good and Feyhe bad, Feyhe giddy, sad, or angry, Feyhe at one extreme of the emotional scale or the other—she had disappeared and might be assumed dead. Or she might be alive somewhere doing who-knows-what with whomever.

"We're almost adult," he had said to her on his last sit-down visit with her at the home,

April 29, of that year. "We're almost an adult relationship, Feyhe, almost twenty-one years of involvement, friendship, battling, whatever." He recalled her laughter as she poked him in the shoulder, twisting her cigarette-smoke-stained nail into his flesh. She hadn't responded with words, but she had clearly enjoyed the idea of a relationship maturing into its own special adulthood. Or so it had seemed at the time. This much older cousin, his mother's nearest and dearest, his own best friend, really.

Words weren't always necessary. Feyhe had joined the "inscrutables" and had, herself, become more akin to them than to her own kind. She could express with just a gesture or a look what others needed—words, and lots of them—to relate. Everyone she left behind knew this about her in some way. Manic or depressive, Feyhe was expressive. Of course, Billy felt he knew it best of all, better than anyone, better than Owen, better than...

Of course, there was also Kim.

2

Feyhe wanted him for dinner. As usual he knew he'd change his plans, plans he'd made weeks earlier, to accommodate her. He didn't actually mind the change. Feyhe always had interesting people, good food and wine, interesting conversations at her dinner parties. They were good for contacts as well, and he and his cousin were both aware of that. His friendship with his mother's cousin had been good for his work.

"Who's coming?" he asked her hesitantly. Usually she didn't like to talk about her guests in advance, preferring to surprise him and probably anyone else she invited to her East Side apartment.

"You don't know them, so telling you won't help." She sounded slightly snippier than usual.

"Oh, come on, Feyhe," he said, turning his voice into the little boy voice she found hard to resist.

"You didn't say please, Billy."

"Why waste a word?" he asked her, snapping back, using her own verbal badinage.

Feyhe laughed. "You are getting to be incorrigible," she said.

"You don't even know what that means, Feyhe. I know you don't."

"Words mean whatever I want them to mean. You know that, Billy."

"Words aren't that mutable. If they were, you and I would have our very own language."

"Don't we?" she asked, and it was his turn to laugh.

It had been three years since West Point. Billy and Feyhe had been building a friendship ever since. She admired his work and he adored hers, buying several pieces from her for apartments he was designing. He liked the clean lines of her sculpture and the forms themselves. She was adventurous, turning a seemingly amorphous shape into something very different and specific when viewed from another angle. He could redefine her pieces for his clients, making them see through his eyes as they gazed at Feyhe's work. She was an artist and he was her interpreter.

She worked in clay and marble and bronze. Her sculptures were all human form, and yet they were anything but human. A face, an arm, or leg would emerge from something earth-grown, something ancient and unnameable. You could enter a room and be confronted by one of Feyhe's shapes, not really pay attention to it because it commanded no attention and then turn toward it and see the realization of the artist's vision of humanity in nature and be riveted by the juxtaposition of art and nature. Her work was different from anything he had seen before, and it was an exclusive for him, something unique he could incorporate into his design work. They both profited from this joint effort and they enjoyed the experience of enhancing one another, professionally.

On a personal level, their friendship took on other tones. Feyhe was fun at times, serious at others. She had a sense about people. She knew who would spark and who would most likely fall lifeless into a pit when placed in the same room at the same time. Sometimes she preferred the latter; it was fun for her to watch two people scramble for a topic of common interest or for a civil remark when an evening got too long and too boring to be tolerated.

Mostly, though, she liked the sparking. She loved to listen to Billy's youthful ripostes when someone from her generation would grapple with her younger cousin on a subject. It could be anything from current political affairs in the city to the latest trend in musical theatre. It could be books or food, art or design. Feyhe liked to place herself in one corner of her generous living room and start things, then lean back, very much the Empress, and listen to what would come from the conversation. Once Billy got started, she rarely interjected a thought until he was finished. Then she might add a word or two of her own, mightily skewering him on the rotisserie of youth. It was the sort of thing his own mother might try to do, but that was impossible without Billy striking out at her. Somehow when Feyhe did it, he didn't mind the shock and the pain. It was tolerable. He considered her his equal and knew she felt the same about him. That was the difference.

"So you're not going to tell me, I gather," he said before hanging up the phone.

"You'll see and you'll be surprised."

"Will I be delighted?"

"I'll tell you afterward," she whispered, and she dropped the receiver into its cradle. Billy held his own princess phone for a moment longer, then laid it to rest on his end table.

On his desk was the preliminary sketch for a combined living and dining room for a townhouse on East 83rd Street, one block away from Feyhe's apartment on East 84th. The client was a friend of hers, someone Billy had met a few months earlier at one of her dinners. The job was proving to be unique for him. The man was a "bachelor" in his early fifties. He was a publisher, although Billy still wasn't sure what sort of books the man produced. He had toured the apartment the same night they met and he had been struck by the volume of bare window in the rooms he might be designing. Looking west and south was a window corner consisting of nineteen windows. The windows took up all of the western wall and an additional seventeen feet on the southern side. The views were incredible, overwhelming. The building was relatively new and this apartment on the twenty-fifth floor had relatively unobstructed views through the distant harbor to the south and across Central Park to the west.

"Do you ever do anything in this room besides look at the view?" Billy had asked when he was first shown the room.

"Yes," Frederick Ostendorf replied. Billy waited for more, but that was the sum total of the man's response.

I think. I need some time to…"

Ostendorf had approached him quietly as they spoke and now he was standing in front of Billy, standing far too close for comfort.

"…time to give real consideration to the light and the colors, for one thing."

"Thank you, Billy, for giving so much thought to my flat."

"Yes, well, thank you, Frederick, for asking me to…to…" He grabbed Ostendorf's free hand, giving it a slight, but firm, shake, and then he was turning away, toward the apartment's front door. "I'll be in touch soon. Good night, Frederick."

"Good night, Billy," the man said and Billy could hear the amusement the man was feeling at his hasty and awkward retreat.

In the vestibule, Billy nervously slapped the elevator button. There were only two apartments per floor and the space between the doors was only three times the width of the elevator's double door. Ostendorf still stood in the doorway of his apartment watching Billy sweat.

"Remember, as you work, that I make love in this room."

"Yes, yes, I'll remember."

"Love," the man repeated.

Just then, the elevator door opened and Billy leaped in, startling the elevator operator. "Good night, Frederick, and thank you," he shouted as the door closed between them. He didn't notice for at least fifteen floors as the elevator descended that he was still holding the Mai Tai in his left hand.

Billy placed the sketch on its narrow edge behind the umbrella stand in Feyhe's apartment when he arrived. He could hear voices and assumed he was the last one to show up for the gathering. He called out to Feyhe, whose kitchen had two doors, one in the entryway and one in the rear hall close to the dining room. She didn't respond. He took a hasty look at himself in the mirror on the inside of the hall closet, realized that he had worn the wrong tie after his hesitant decision earlier at home, and took a deep breath. Then he walked into the living room.

There were three other people there. Frederick Ostendorf was one of them. He waved jauntily at Billy and Billy waved back. Ostendorf was chatting with a woman Billy had never seen before and there was a man, obviously with the woman, who stood just behind her, listening but not speaking.

Feyhe emerged from her bedroom at the end of the long corridor. She was wearing a dress of that same shade of purple that Billy's mother had once described to him in the corkscrew design of Feyhe's 1930s dress. She wasn't smiling. Billy raised one eyebrow in her direction, as if asking a question. She ignored his look but headed into the dining room. Billy moved off in that direction, hoping that the others wouldn't notice his instant absence.

Feyhe was adjusting silverware at the far end of the table. She didn't look up when Billy entered the room. Instead she made a point of ignoring him.

"What's the matter? What have I done?" Billy asked her.

"Nothing."

"What does that mean?"

"It means you've done nothing. Drop it."

"You're angry." Billy could always tell when Feyhe was in a non-responsive mood and when he was at the bottom of it.

"Frustrated, Billy, is what I am." She finally looked at him and he didn't like her eyes.

They were narrowed, staring, unappreciative. "That's a hideous tie, by the way."

"I know. I realized it too late, I'm afraid."

"I have some in my bedroom you could switch to."

"I'll take my chances, thanks, with this one. It's just dinner."

She came towards him swiftly, stopping only inches away from him. "My dinners are not just dinner, they are life. When an element is wrong in the life I present to my guests, then I am wrong in presenting it. You're late and you're in poor taste. Change the tie, Billy."

He hesitated for a moment, then nodded. "All right. I'll change."

They walked together to her room and she opened a drawer in her armoire, revealing a collection of men's ties. She looked at him, taking in the colors and patterns of his shirt, jacket, slacks. Then she pulled out a tie.

"It's a Marinska original," she said. "One drop of gravy and you're a dead man." She tossed him the tie and left the room.

He was alone with her things. Quickly he pulled off his own tie and reconfirmed his neck with hers. It was a good tie, a great tie, and absolutely right for him. He smiled his best smile as he finished off the knot, then went back to the living room. This time Feyhe smiled at him as he came among her other guests.

"Billy, nice to see you," Ostendorf said, greeting him. He leaned forward as if expecting a hug or a quick kiss. Billy extended his hand instead. Ostendorf took it and, rather than shaking it, pulled Billy into the small conversational circle. "Do you know Elena Yauger?"

"No, I don't. It's nice to meet you."

Elena Yauger studied Billy for what felt like a long, long time. Then she spoke. "I've heard about you," she said. "You're what I expected."

"I...I d-don't know how to take that."

"That's right," she said, then she turned back to speak with Ostendorf. The publisher smiled at Billy, then turned his back on the younger man, taking Elena Yauger on a short stroll to the far end of the room. Yauger's companion remained with Billy.

"She's like that," the man said, "pay no attention."

"She was rather abrupt, wasn't she?" Billy asked him.

"It's her way. Sometimes she's actually nice to people on a first meeting. You actually got off rather light."

"Really?" Billy said. Then he gave the other man some actual attention. "I'm Billy Duncan."

"Hello, Roger Johnson. I come with Elena. It's like a package deal." Billy laughed. Roger laughed along with him.

"You're not a couple, I take it."

"No, no," Roger said. "I'm just the escort. I get paid for my time. I don't get paid to take her guff and I don't get paid for anything other than bringing her and taking her."

"Not exactly a career, is it?" Billy asked.

"Not the one I wanted, anyway. Working for Elena is a career, though. The woman never stays put for long. She's always on the move."

"I know her name, but I can't connect it with anything…" Billy began when he caught sight of Feyhe hugging the archway into the hallway again. He excused himself without finishing his sentence and went to her immediately.

"What is it, Feyhe?" he asked her in a whisper. "I've never seen you like this."

She shook her head and turned away from him, moving down the hallway toward her bedroom. Billy followed her. He caught up with her at her door, took her by the shoulder and turned her back to look at him. There were tears in her eyes.

"Feyhe, talk to me."

"That woman," she said. "I invited her because Frederick asked me to, and she's brought that damn gigolo into my house."

"Roger? The escort?"

"He's a gigolo!" She nearly spat the word out this time. "And my table now has to seat five. It's uneven. It's unpleasant and I only have food for four people. You can't make four game hens feed five people unless you cut them mercilessly and serve the scraps in a dog bowl. I can't believe this!"

Billy had never seen Feyhe this close to rage before. He didn't like it. In the few minutes he'd been in the apartment she had gone from mild anger to light amusement to intense fury. He offered a solution.

"I won't stay, Feyhe. Then you'll be back to four and it will be all right."

"You are not to leave me with that woman and her paid piece of meat. Am I clear, Billy? You are not to leave."

"Feyhe, it's all right with me. I have work to do, other places I can eat. I don't want you to have a heart attack over those hens."

"No! I said, No!" She was adamant and he was worried. "I'll fix it myself."

She charged past him back the way they'd come and disappeared into the kitchen. He could hear her slamming drawers and slapping the flat-side of her Sabatier steel carving knife against the whetstone she kept handy.

about it often when he grew to know his mother's cousin better and himself better as well, he joined it with the thought that had Feyhe had a Kim at that time, things might have been different. But Kim was in her future then. Not in her present.

3

Kim Do-Mun was a robust, smooth-skinned, English-speaking, South Korean college professor who worked summers as a guide in his home city of Gyôngju, the seat of the Silla dynasty, which had endured for nearly a thousand years until the eighth century A.D. The city had fallen into obscurity in the mid-seventh century and that had protected it, in a strange way, until its rediscovery as a historic site after World War II. Gyôngju's vast tombs and treasures were thus protected during the harsh years of occupation by the Chinese, the Mongols, and the Japanese and they had survived, pretty much intact, to the joy of the city's loyal attendants.

Kim do-Mun's family could clock its own history in Gyôngju back to the eleventh century. They had resided in the Gyôngsangbuk-Do province for at least that many generations. He had grown up there, been educated there, and was content to travel around his own region daily, escorting groups of American and British and Australian tourists through the sites of destruction and historical note in the city where he had been born, grown up and lived all of his thirty years. He was content as well with his teaching duties at the Busan National University in the Gyôngsangnam-Do Province, about 100 miles to the south, an occupation that kept him alive the other nine months of the year. He taught Literature of the West with a specialty in Shakespeare. He had written several well-placed and well-thought-of articles on the Bard of

Avon in his homeland and in Japan as well. He was a happy man, a contented man. He was a man with no more ambition than to continue on the course his family had charted for him. He would marry, father sons, publish more, and continue with his simple, straightforward interactions with Westerners. These were the plans, plans that would continue the unbroken thousand-year tradition of complementing his family heritage. Then, he met Feyhe.

The year was 1976. He was thirty. He was engaged to be married within the year; a date had been set for that marriage. Hong Ni-Na, the woman who had been intended for him for many years, was seven years younger than Kim Do-Mun. She also was a teacher at the university, although not as exalted or respected a teacher as Kim. Hong Ni-Na was a lecturer in economics. Unlike her future husband, she had not been granted even an associate professorship. She was a lecturer. It was what suited the structure of the University. Her own field of international finance had been honed to a smaller, more specific area of interest, the acquisition of international funding for local development. Hong Ni-Na was good at what she did, and she knew it. She was fully grounded in her subject and quite lucid when discussing issues that were relevant to the area of development of natural resources in Busan or nearby Masan or the Nam River delta, whether those resources be animal, mineral, or human.

She was also very pretty. Her wide, square-jawed face was punctuated with wide, un-angled eyes of the darkest brown, topped with delicately arched brows. Her lips were full and reddened and exposed a perfect set of teeth when she smiled. Her nose, a trifle flat for the width of her face, was arched slightly forward, flipped like the nose of the American film actor Bob Hope, and attractively exposed. Her perfect black hair shone with a natural oiliness that allowed it to hold the light, sun or moon, natural or artificial, without calling too much attention to it. It framed her perfectly, cut close to the shape of her face. All of this sat on a long and graceful neck above a body that was both pert and demure.

Compared to Kim Do-Mun, she was almost western in appearance, however. He was shorter than his bride-to-be by an inch and much thinner. His brow was high and broad, separating his eyes from his naturally full hairline by a long distance. His eyes were oval and multi-colored, his chin protuberant, and his cheekbones clearly marked by their sharpness and height, leaving deep dimples between their arched loftiness and his central feature, his mouth. It was small, with narrow lips and upwardly curved corners, a natural smile that imitated a smirk. There was a Tibetan appeal to his face, another remarkable throwback to his long ancestry.

Kim and Ni-Na, as they were called, made an attractive couple, and their families expected attractive and intelligent children to grow from this union of two handsome intellectuals. Their expectations were to be met within the year, they thought. But that summer, Feyhe went to Korea. Kim met Feyhe and things changed for all three of them.

Feyhe had asked Billy to accompany her on her trip to Korea. He had declined, citing work and a burgeoning romance that he was afraid to ignore for even a day, let alone a month. He later regretted that decision, for the romance faded and the work disappointed and Feyhe met Kim. Ultimately things changed for Billy as well as for the others.

Feyhe had been commissioned to create a piece for a new sculpture garden that was being cultivated in the Namsan District's National Park, one of six non-contiguous national park areas in Gyôngju, a beautiful mountain area to the south of the city, strewn with royal tombs, pagodas, rock-cut figures, pavilions, and the remains of palaces, temples, and fortresses. Hundreds of paths followed the streams that tumbled down the mountainside. There was also a path which skirted the bower Poseokjeongji. This bower would house Feyhe's work when it was completed. A Feyhe Baumann original sculpture was already, by 1976, a world-class treasure, worthy to live with other world treasures, even those centuries old.

Feyhe was met at the Daegu airport by a car that would take her to Gyôngju. It was a fifty-mile drive through both mountain and plain and, although a railroad line could make the journey, it was felt that an American dignitary who had been invited by the government to come to Gyôngju should not be left to the mercy of public transportation. A guide with a car and an excellent skill with English was required, and Kim Do-Mun was the perfect fit.

He recognized her instantly as she came through the gate. He had no photograph to work with, but this elegant young woman who stood at the entryway was clearly American and definitely an artist, he thought. He approached her without hesitation.

"Kim Do-Mun, Missis Bow-Hyuman," Kim said bowing to the woman. He waited for an acknowledgment before rising again.

"I'm sorry, but I don't speak any Korean," the woman replied. Kim slowly righted himself, a bit insulted at this slap at his English accent.

"I am also sorry, then, for my haste in speaking," he said quietly with a sullen undertone in his voice. An old woman, nearby, laughed out loud and he blushed.

"What did you want?" the young American asked him.

"I am your appointed guide, Kim Do-Mun my name."

"I have an appointed guide? Dear me, aren't I important?"

The older woman laughed again, attracting the attention of them both.

"Are we bothering you, Madam?" the young woman snapped.

"I haven't laughed since we left New York," Feyhe responded to the girl. Then she turned her attention to Kim. "I think I may be the person you are expecting, Kim Do-Mun. I am Feyhe Baumann."

Kim looked from one to the other. Making a hasty decision, he bowed low to the younger woman and turned his attention to Feyhe. "I beg your pardon," he said in a precise, clipped manner. "I was told to look for the beautiful and talented American lady."

Feyhe's smile faded instantly. Kim, who was straightening saw the change in her expression and he returned to his low bow position one more time.

"I must once more excuse myself and beg for your forgiveness," he said. "It was just that the young lady was beautiful so that I assumed her to be my charge. You are so much more beautiful in your maturity. It was merely superficial prettiness that obscured my honest judgement. I beg your pardon."

"It's hard to stay mad after such a pretty apology," Feyhe said, but she was still bristling inside. His attitude about the pretty young thing griped her. The girl had annoyed her on the plane, laughing too loudly, flirting with the steward who served her too many drinks, too many little treats. He had blatantly ignored Feyhe's request for water, preferring instead to sit on the arm of the younger woman's seat, placing his arm around her, caging her in. Feyhe had watched it all with a growing disquiet and she had made a note of his name for her letter to the airline.

Kim straightened up a third time and gave her a smile. His already smiling mouth, with its natural up-swerved corners strengthened into an actual grin and his boyishness caught her imagination. She gave him a smile in return.

"We shall need to retrieve your baggage," he said right away. "We have two hours or more to drive and it would be better to depart in full sun."

"Lead on, Kim Do-Mun," Feyhe said. "I'll follow." And so it began.

It was morning when they met again. Feyhe had been driven in comparative silence from the Daegu city airport to the hotel in Gyôngju where she would stay for the duration of her visit. The Royal-jang Yeogwan Hotel was located in a central area of the city, surrounded by other hotels and places to stay and eat. A short walk from the Noseo-Dong Tombs, it was an ideal spot for a first visit to the city. Prior to breakfast, Feyhe had walked to the park grounds that housed the tombs. They belonged to the 4th and 5th century AD Silla dynasty and had only been discovered and excavated in the period between 1921 and 1946. The three major tombs in this park had produced major finds, and the fact that there was no admission fee made it an ideal spot for the unaccompanied American to start her journey of exploration.

Feyhe made her way through the rubble that still surrounded the last of the three tombs to be discovered, Geumgwanchong, and crossed the road to the site of Bonghwadae. The tomb stood nearly seventy-two feet high. Grass grew on the structure, and Feyhe could clearly make out the imprint of many feet that had trod that grass as people climbed the walls to reach the pinnacle of the building. She set her feet on their own climbing course, but she had scarcely achieved more than four feet in height when the sounds of whistles, official sounding whistles, attracted her attention.

Three men in uniform, whistles in their mouths, came rushing toward her. Behind them, mostly in black pants and white shirt-jackets, swarmed forty or so civilians. They were all babbling and some shouted; she wasn't sure if they shouted at her or about her. She decided the best thing to do would be to climb back down to earth.

As soon as she touched the ground the three park guardians came up to her and shouted what appeared to be insults directly into her face. She shuddered and took a step backward, ending up with her back against the tomb she had just relinquished.

"Please, please, I don't understand," she cried out, her voice almost drowning out those of her assailants. "Does anyone speak English?"

Several people shouted again from within the crowd. The whole bunch of people had surged forward so that she was completely ringed by people who were being held back by the extended arms of the park police. There was nowhere for Feyhe to go, no spot to break through, and the only possible direction she had available to her was up again, back up the side wall of the tomb. She turned her back on the crowd and put a foot on the wall again.

As she hefted herself upward she fully expected an escalation of the shouting and whistling, but instead a hush fell over the crowd, partly in alarm and partly in awe that this foreigner would once again intrude on the sacred space. One of the park guardians whistled and the airy openness of his whistling soon faded into the slight wisp of wind that gently whipped the air around her. She took a second step, then a third.

"Missis Bow-Hyuman," she heard from below. She turned to look at the sea of Korean faces, so alike, so specific. She saw him almost instantly, distinguished by those cheekbones and the small, curved mouth. Without thinking, she waved to him, and Kim called out her name again.

The crowd parted slightly to let him through. He walked slowly and deliberately toward her, extending his right arm, his hand upturned, in her direction. She took two steps back down the side of the tomb and extended her own hand toward Kim Do-Mun. When their fingers touched he spoke again, but she didn't hear him. A numbness, a depressing tingle extended up her arm from the point where he held her hand, directly to her ears and only a faint jingling of bells reached her brain.

She turned to look at the sky and it seemed a bright red, then distinctly turned yellow, then blue, a natural blue finally. She could feel the man's fingers again. There was something happening that she couldn't control, she knew that much, and she suddenly had no desire to control anything. That was odd. That felt wrong. That disturbed her. She pulled her hand free from his grasp. The jingling of bells returned, grew louder, then more strident. Then it broke, and the day's sounds reentered her ears.

"...to your hotel, if you will," Kim was finishing. She nodded and he gently led her forward, through the crowd, past the park guardians and back the way she had come, through the park to the now crowded streets of the city.

Feyhe spread out her sketches on the floor of her hotel room. Around them she arranged photographs she had taken a few days earlier of the space her work would inhabit within the confines of the bower Poseokjeongji. She had been in Gyôngju for almost a week and had accustomed herself to the buses that ran from the inter-city bus terminal out to the mountain park to the south of the city. Poseokjeongji was on the western slope, a one kilometer walk from the Samneung Tombs. It was already inhabited by an impressive granite artwork; shaped like an abalone, it encompassed much of the bower and allowed a small stream to trickle through, although there was not enough water, even in the spring, to truly feed the bower's ponds.

"This is used for banquets," Kim Do-Mun told her on her first visit.

"Yes, I know," Feyhe replied. "It is your government's wish to have a sculpture here that will reflect both the history of the place and the appetites of its frequent inhabitants."

"You know, then, the legend of Poseokjeungjo?" he asked her.

"Not really, no," she said.

Kim smiled and gestured to her, asking her to sit. She found a place on the granite slab that seemed supportive and not too uncomfortable and she settled into it. He stood in front of her, his hands splayed and his palms facing upward. His knees were slightly bent and, seated as she was, their eyes were on the same parallel. He was the ideal storyteller and she the perfect audience.

"King Gyeonegae would come here for the tranquility he found and for the activity he craved," Kim began. "He would bring with him both concubines and courtiers, for the king was never alone, even in contemplation. Each group would sit here in the abalone shell, beside their king, the pond a central point for this gathering, while dancers would perform in the circle formed by this informal court. They would dance the old stories, the tales that lived in the mouths of the storytellers and the minds of those who hear tales. Also they would play games with their sovereign lord. One favorite game was for the king to recite poetry, one line only, and then demand a second line be given in response by a guest in the circle. At the same time, the Lord King would place a goblet of wine in the pond which was fed by the stream from above on the peak of Namsan. The guest must recite the next line of the poetry by the time the wine had reached him. If he could not do it, he was then required to drain the goblet in one single drink, leaving not one drop behind. It is said that if the guest could not recite the perfect line and then could not complete the drink, he would lose something of long-standing personal value."

"And what would the guest lose, Kim Do-Mun?" Feyhe said, smiling.

"A woman would lose her chance to lie with her husband, but would become a cloistered woman with only the Sovereign Lord to visit her in her bed. A man would lose his tongue."

Feyhe's smile slowly drifted off her face.

"This place, Missis Bow-Hyuman, is the only such banquet garden left in the world today."

"Really?"

"Yes, please. We no longer play the Imperial games, but the people may come here and enjoy their food in the tranquility and the beauty of the region."

"I'm delighted to hear that the games are no longer played."

"No longer played, Missis Bow-Hyuman."

Kim Do-Mun showed her the place where her work would eventually be displayed.

Within the eastern wall of the bower there was a wide, natural grotto. It was here, Kim told her, that the punishments would be meted out by the king. It was here that her work would live.

"I don't like the light here," she said. "It seems to be very shallow until you come close and then its deceptive depth reveals itself. Sunlight will never reveal the interior of this grotto."

"Then you must make it live with your work, Missis Bow-Hyuman."

"I'm not sure how to do that. Not yet."

She unleashed her camera from its case and popped off the lens cap. He watched her as she snapped her photos, never saying a word that might distract her. She finished out the roll of film, rewound it, snapped it out of its temporary home and handed it to Kim. Without a word between them, he pocketed the film, took her arm and escorted her back the way they had come.

Since then she had made two return trips without him. She had walked through the bower, coming at it from every possible direction, just to gauge her first reaction to the grotto space. She had brought a measuring tape with her and had carefully measured the grotto gathering every possible dimension including height, width and depth, a circumference of the wall area, diagonals with intrusive rock and without. The one admonition she had received with the commission was not to alter the structure to accommodate her sculpture, but rather to accommodate her own work to the natural space that would house it.

In the evening, in her hotel room, she had sketched her ideas. Some were easily discarded. Dragons and mythical figures were the first to go. Humanity was her best device and humanity was now crying to her for a memorial to the games men play and the men and women who had played them. She was envisioning a full frieze of the legendary king and his court, the poetry competition and the eventual results. Her sketches were taking on a grim, harsher reality than she had supposed possible for such a pretty place. She wished Billy was with her to discuss the possibilities, but he was in New York and she was alone in Korea.

Eventually, she invited Kim Do-Mun and his fiancé to her room to look at her sketches and advise her. Kim had told her about the woman he would marry as they rode the bus back into the city that first afternoon when they returned from Poseokjeongji, and Feyhe was eager to see the woman for herself. She had her sketches ready to exhibit when they arrived. She had herself ready to exhibit as well.

Kim brought Hong Ni-Na to Feyhe's hotel room in time for late afternoon tea. They brought with them all that they would need to prepare and serve the tea in Feyhe's room. Ni-Na wore a simple silk gown, a deep, rich yellow with no particular pattern in it, but simply swirls of a complimentary yellow, perhaps a shade or two darker then the body of the silk. It was sleeveless, high-collared and ankle-length. It clung to her body in places and left the body free and untouched in others, giving her a unique shape. Her dark hair was pulled back into a knot at the base of her skull. It glistened in the room's late sunlight. She was wearing lipstick and rouge, and dark liner had been used to highlight her very oriental eyes. On her feet were soft, silk slippers. Feyhe was instantly captivated by the beauty she saw before her.

"Annyeong, Hong Ni-Na," Feyhe said in her best Korean.

"You speak all-right, Korean, Missis Bow-Hyuman," the girl replied. "And hello to you also."

"My dear, Kim did not do you justice," Feyehe said.

"I blush to hear you," Ni-Na said in response.

"We have brought you tea, Missis Bow-Hyuman," Kim interjected, but Feyhe simply waved the back of her hand at him, almost dismissing him.

"Miss Hong, I am pleased to know you."

"And I you Missis," Ni-Na said. "I would make you tea."

"There's really no need," Feyhe said, but she could see immediately that she had said the wrong thing. A light that had so distinguished Hong Ni-Na's face dissipated instantly, leaving only the paint on the woman's facial surface. "I beg your pardon, Miss Hong, but of course your gift would be most welcome."

As the young woman's smile and her glow returned, Feyhe allowed her own sense of formality to relax back to her more natural mode of expression. "You really are a beauty," she said to Ni-Na. "I am charmed to see you."

"And you are a woman of magnificent perception," Hong Ni-Na responded.

"I have brought you omija cha." She held out her right hand, its fingers clenched into a tight fist. Feyhe stepped forward and Ni-Na opened her hand to reveal the collection of ingredients that she held.

The assortment of five flavors tea included ginseng and citron, ginger and powdered sassafras root. There were pine nuts and the dark green leaves of an Assam tea. Feyhe nodded a tacit approval and Ni-Na bowed back to her, then went to the bathroom with her ingredients and her hotplate, leaving Kim with Feyhe.

"She's lovely, Kim, you're to be congratulated."

"Hong Ni-Na is my heart, Missis Bow-Hyuman," he said.

"That is so poetic, Kim."

"It is not poetry as the king would say it, I am sure, though."

"That legend bothers me, Kim. I'm sure I need not tell you why."

They sat down together on the small couch near the room's picture window. There was a moment of silence through which the sound of water boiling in the bathroom broke their concentration.

"You will enjoy the tea, Missis Bow-Hyuman."

"I know I will, Kim."

"Tell me something about the king, about the person who was this king of poets. I need something to change my thinking."

"During a banquet at Poseokjeongji, the king was attacked by a band of robbers who chose to raid the place as they journeyed from Samneung to Gyeongju. The banquet had gone well and there had been no slaughtering of tongues and no taking of the women. The dancers had danced their finest and the courtiers had been inspired. The concubines had all been satisfied and almost everyone slept, drugged as they were by their wine. It was thus the robbers found the king and his court.

"It is said that the Robber Lord wanted only one thing that night and the only way to achieve his lofty goal was the death of the king, so he drew his knife and slit the throat of King Gyeonegae, killing him instantly and with only momentary pain. This death awakened the king's favorite concubine, the woman Li-Na, and she rushed to his side, using her hair to sweep up the blood that poured from his neck, but she was not able to stop its flowing. She shouted the men awake, but it was too late, for the band of robbers now surrounded the bower. This man who had killed the king then declared himself to be the new sovereign lord, but this woman, Li-Na, would not have it. She forced the robber's hand and, picking up his own knife, she plunged it into the man's heart. 'This is your kingdom,' she shouted at him as he fell in front of her. 'If blood is the succession then your blood is now mixed with my Lord King's blood. It is all yours for this instant and then it returns to the sea, as the stream takes your blood away from this place.'

Her words made no difference to the man, for he was already dead. There was no way for her to live, so she used the robber's knife, which had stolen the life of the king before taking his own, one more time. She plunged it into her own body and stood for a while watching her life force drain from her. Then she too died. It is said that all three of them are buried at Samneung in three of the four tombs that were discovered there."

"You have completed your task, Kim Do-Mun," Feyhe said. "That was some tale."

"It is true."

"I'm sure it is."

"This was more than one thousand years ago, Missis Bow-Hyuman, so no one can say for sure if the girl did this."

"I think, perhaps, she did do it, Kim."

"I, too, believe her capable of this task."

Hong Ni-Na emerged from the bathroom with the tea things, and Feyhe decided not to interrupt the flow of the day with her drawings. She had decided, in fact, not to deal with those drawings at all. They were dead. They were no longer an issue. A new idea had joined the original impulse, and she knew which way she would go with her work. She knew it as certainly as she knew she liked the tea.

4

Feyhe was sketching faces. There were too few that seemed to her to speak of the tortures endured by the concubines during their slaughter at the hands of the marauding robbers who killed King Gyeonegae. She was sitting in the Noseo-Dong park grounds. The tombs she had seen on her first day in Gyeongju were close by, and the people who wandered through the park were all intent on passing close to them as they scurried off to work or to a local store. She had seen literally hundreds of faces in the week she'd been sitting there, and still her mind had not been engaged by any of them.

"I don't know what I'm looking for," she wrote to Billy, back in New York, "but I can't do this piece without a model of some sort. It's so frustrating, Billy, to have an idea, to know what it will look like and yet to not be able to see it."

With her letter she sent five pages of sketches, none of which she intended to use. She wanted Billy to see the people of this region as she saw them, to understand with her the sort of attraction they held for her. She had sketched men and women, children and seniors. She had worked with a greater than usual ease, capturing exact likenesses, but still not one had truly set her imagination on fire.

She found herself constantly thinking about Kim and Ni-Na. She liked their looks, the combination of old and modern in them. She liked the animation she saw in Kim and the placid exterior of his fiancé.

She had not seen either of them for several days and she realized she missed them. She packed up her pencils and her pad of drawing paper and bustled herself across the street toward the hotel. On the way, she noticed how hungry she was. She had been so intent on her work and on her thoughts that she had not paid any attention to her stomach, but now it grumbled and moved its unsupported walls within her. She had to find some food.

Walking with the crowd, she crossed the Daejongno and headed down the city's main street toward the Dukkeobi Bulgogi House restaurant. It was one of the best places in the city for inexpensive pork barbecue. The lunch hour was nearly exhausted, and Feyhe anticipated no wait for a chair at one of the many shared tables. As she approached the restaurant, the neon sign which read, in English "Roast Beef Restaurant" blinked on and off a few times, then went out completely.

The city had been experiencing periodic "rests" from electricity during her stay there, and she was glad that her hotel room was on a floor that allowed her the ease of taking the stairs rather than relying on the old elevator which dominated the center of the lobby. It meant she never got stuck in a small box waiting for someone to haul her out or for the power to resume so that she could advance to another floor. It was healthier to walk the stairs, in any case, and she loved to walk.

The Roast Beef Restaurant light flickered back on for a few seconds and then went out completely. Feyhe stood outside the open door and debated trying for some food or just walking back to the hotel and hoping she had a left-over cracker or two in her room. She opted for the inside of the restaurant.

Dukkeobi Bulgogi House had its reputation in its name. *Bulgogi* meant "fire beef." It was made of strips of meat marinated in soy sauce, sesame oil, garlic, and chili that had been grilled on a hot plate, usually in front of the patron. The resulting food was easily eaten with a variety of dipping sauces from a creamy, blue-veined cheese sauce to a harshly bitter, ginseng inflected, tea-based broth. The restaurant also prided itself on a dish called *Galbi*, made in much the same way but using short ribs instead of sliced beef.

Feyhe found a chair at the first table in from the door and slid into it in the half-light of the room. Her eyes took a moment to adjust to the changed level of light inside. It was a bright day and the room, darkened by the filter-screens on the windows, stood in well-defined contrast to the street, just a few feet away. She could tell from the quiet in the room that she was not alone, but that the place had almost emptied out before the electric "rest" had started. As things came into focus, Feyhe could see that her table was occupied by a young woman and an older woman, clearly together, and a child.

"*Annyeong hasimnikka,*" Feyhe said quietly to the others, and she nodded a short, quick nod as she said it. The formal greeting sat on wooden, unresponsive ears. She breathed a sigh, having recited one of her best phrases in Korean, and looked for a waiter.

He arrived at the table almost instantly. She nodded to him and he nodded in return, taking up his pencil and pad and staring at her.

"*Gimchi, putak hamnida,*" she said immediately, politely ordering the traditional sour cabbage starter. The waiter nodded, but wrote nothing. "*Galbi tchim,*" she continued ordering a barbecued beef rib stew. The waiter wrote the item on his pad. "*Cha,*" she finished her order, adding hot tea to the mix. The waiter nodded and moved away.

"You speak good, Korean," the younger woman at her table said in almost flawless English except for the "comma" pause. Feyhe gave her a smile.

"Thank you very much. I don't speak much of it, I'm afraid."

"Have no fear," the girl said, "for you speak good."

"I don't mean I'm actually frightened," Feyhe continued, "it's just not an easy language for me."

"English not so hard too, for me," the girl responded. "For mother it impossible is."

"It *is* impossible," Feyhe said, gently correcting her. The girl blushed and looked away.

"Oh, I am sorry," Feyhe said hastily. "I always seem to be putting my foot in my mouth here. I didn't mean to offend you, just to offer a helping hint."

"It *is* okay," the girl said, smiling once again. "I thank you."

"And I thank you," Feyhe said. "You have been very generous to offer conversation to a stranger."

There was something in the exchange that attracted the older woman, the girl's mother.

She sat listening, her face almost lit up from within, but the glow dulled by the instant distancing that comes with a complete lack of comprehension. She only knew that her daughter was talking with the foreigner and that the foreigner was being kind.

The waiter brought the gimchi and Feyhe picked up her chopsticks and started to eat. The extremely spicy flat-leafed vegetable scorched its way down her throat and she gasped at the first bite. The young woman spoke again.

"You are in gimchi-hell?" she asked. Feyhe gave her a questioning look. "It IS what we call first bite of gimchi. Too hot. You should take with cha."

"I know, I know. I should have waited for the tea, but I was so hungry I had to eat. It was a foolish thing to do."

The girl laughed and Feyhe laughed with her. Not knowing the joke, the older woman laughed along as did the child.

"This my daughter," the young woman said proudly. "Her father American, like my father American."

"That would explain your excellent English, then," Feyhe said.

"Oh, no, from books for me," the girl replied. "My father I have never met. My daughter father in Newak, Jersey, near to Atlantic Ocean. Far from here. He never see her."

"Well, I am from New York City, which is across the Hudson River from Newark, New Jersey. If you tell me his name, I will write it down and when I go home I will call him for you. I will tell him to come back to Korea and help his wife and child."

"He not come back, Missis, but I thank you."

"Oh, he'll come back if I have to wrap him in a box and mail him back."

"No, no, please. He not come back. He take my baby-girl from me and I never will see her no more."

"That won't happen, I promise you that."

"No, no, please." The girl was the one who was clearly frightened now, and Feyhe realized she had overstepped the natural boundaries one more time. She took an emotional step away.

"It's all right, really it is," she said to the girl. "I won't do anything. I promise you."

The girl was holding her child and something in her face held Feyhe's attention now, something she had not seen before.

"You are very beautiful," she said to the young woman.

"I not."

"No, you are. And you are beautiful, not just for this time, but for all time."

"No, please. I am not."

Feyhe took out her sketch pad and flipped up the cover. She held out the pad in the girl's direction and pointed to the drawings.

"I am an artist and I am looking for a model. Would you be my model?"

The girl looked at the six faces on the page and then she turned up the next page. There were three more drawings there. She studied them carefully.

"I know this man," she said. "Song Bei-Do his name."

"Then I drew him correctly?" Feyhe asked.

"He is here on page."

"May I draw you, also? And your baby?"

The girl looked shy suddenly, her head turned to one side, angled and cocked. Then she turned to look at Feyhe. She nodded and, as if on cue, the room's lights twinkled and returned to life. The waiter brought her stew and her tea and Feyhe nodded back at him, at the girl and her mother, at the baby.

Feyhe was working on a full-face drawing of Mary Yi for the umpteenth time. The young woman and her child, Hana Yi, were both sitting, naked, near enough to the window of Feyhe's hotel room for the sunlight sifting through the bamboo blind to cast discreet shadows across their pale flesh. Feyhe had been trying to achieve some semblance of that light in her drawing, but the day was defeating her.

At the outset of their sessions Mary Yi had been shy, and Feyhe's request for her to pose in the nude had been met with crying and shuffling and dissembling. Mary's modesty had amused Feyhe and also delighted her. The woman's history denied a puritanical attitude toward life, after all she had borne a child out of wedlock to an American soldier. And now she was ashamed of her breasts in front of another woman. Once again the native attitude took longer to set in her mind than Feyhe would have expected of herself.

"It's nothing at all to do," she told Mary when the woman first accompanied her back to her rooms. Mary's mother was holding the baby and making small, clucking noises in the back of her throat as Feyhe tried to persuade the younger woman to pose properly. "This won't hurt and it won't compromise you in any way. This is for my art," she said, but the girl was not giving in to her pleas.

Finally, it occurred to Feyhe that the presence of the grandmother was at the bottom of all this modesty. She suggested to Mary that her mother leave them alone, but the girl resisted the concept.

"No, no," she said to Feyhe, "I cannot be with a westerner without mother."

"You were, I presume, at least once, my dear," Feyhe said to her in a singularly condescending way.

"No, Missis. Mother was with me when I am pregnant making."

Feyhe stood, bemused, searching for the right thing to say. "Well, at least she was in the room with you."

"Was in bed, here," Mary said, holding out her left hand in the vague direction of her own hip.

"Now I really don't understand, Mary. Your mother was with you in bed when the American made love to you and together you made this adorable baby?"

"Yes, was there," Mary said.

"How is that possible?"

"Mother was my arranger," Mary said simply.

"Your mother arranged this meeting of the...body parts?" Feyhe asked the girl. "Your mother is a procuress. Where I come from this is not done."

"Is not often done here, Missis. But mother knows Americans. I am American by my father, but he not marry mother. Mother say to me I should marry American, so she find American man, nice man, to marry me to. She bring him to me. She guide him to me. He love me very much, very nice." Her face darkened as her eyes half-closed remembering the occasion. "But he not for marrying after all that. He already with wife. So mother takes him away from me and I have baby anyhow."

Feyhe smiled wanly at the story. She turned away so that Mary Yi would not catch her smiling at the story, at its simplicity and at its similarity to her own story had she been willing to share it with the girl. Instead she turned her serene expression back in Mary's direction and said, "This is not such an uncommon story, Mary. Many girls have had much the same thing happen to them."

"Not western women, Missis."

"Even western women, Mary. Even urban goddesses from New York City."

She picked up her pencil again. "Let me try this one more time. I know what I want to see, but I'm just not getting it—wait, now, right now, do not move, hold that look, please."

She set to work instantly, sketching the eyes and the mouth first and then connecting them with a nose and the outline of a face. The girl had started to smile and then changed her mind. What Feyhe was seeing was a young girl delighted with new knowledge and unable to properly process what she was learning. With a sure hand she imitated the question in the eyes and the answer on the lips of the face before her. Her art was precise and she managed to catch exactly what she saw and then to transpose it into a flat, two-dimensional variant. She was delighted with the results of her labor and silently congratulated herself on the work.

"I'm done for now, Mary, thank you," she said to her model.

"I may see what you have done?" Mary asked her.

"Yes, of course you may." She held out the sketch and Mary looked at it, studying it without touching it.

"It is me, to be sure," Mary said, but she sounded unsure.

"I am feeling some sadness," Kim said.

"I too, Kim."

"Kim Chong-Han, who is not my relative, in his poetry was said to be 'capable of holding sadness skillfully with wit.' For me, this moment is such a moment. And I do not know if I am capable of such skills."

"Do you know any of his poetry?" she asked him.

"'A Landscape with an Old Well'," he said with a nod, then recited.

A weeping willow stands by an old well, in which snatches of the May sky fell.

—Young lady,
is that the same cuckoo that was singing there last year? You, a quiet lady, smile like a gourd flower.

And you draw up the blue sky flowing over the bucket, draw up the blue legends flowing over the bucket.

The bellow of a bull, again flowing, comes in across the heights, and from the water jar also overflow your blue skies.

"That was very beautiful, Kim," Feyhe said and there were tears in her eyes.

Kim stood where he had been and watched her. He could feel her reaction to the words of the poem in his heart, and his fingers, and in his groin. He had chosen this poem without thinking of its deeper meaning, but only as an illustration of the sadness contained within the words. Now, those words had touched this woman from the West with their sadness and their life. Now, he had touched himself with the same. He saw her, sitting as she was, on her bed, as a woman and not as an American. He went to her and kneeled in front of her. This startled her.

She pulled back slightly and her voice was sharp. "What are you doing? Kim?"

"You are a beautiful woman, Missis Bow-Hyuman."

"I am an old woman, Kim. Get up this instant."

Instead of doing as he was instructed, Kim leaned in to her and kissed her gently on the mouth. He could feel her resistance at first, then it melted away. Then he could feel her hand on his shoulder, her other hand on the back of his head, then the kiss she gave him in return.

She wasn't sure of anything for a while. She lay in bed, alone, trying to get her mind around her actions of the evening before. The early sunrise in Gyeongju brightened her room, even as the sunset the day before had brightened it. Feyhe let her fingers play along the curves of her body, each one memorizing the trail of other fingers, lips, tongue. She blinked her eyes hard and fast, trying to withhold from her sight the image that wanted to be played out there.

Kim had been a sure and certain lover. He had taken her aging limbs and surrounded them with his younger, stronger ones. He had kissed her and stroked her with a passion she didn't associate with the orientals she knew in New York. Her brain was crowded suddenly with movie images, Edward G. Robinson and Nils Asther—two of her favorites— disguised as eastern men of great power with a strange attractiveness to occidental women. They were not Kim.

Kim came back to her suddenly, the memory of his love-making, his sexual prowess, crawling into her as he had done. She could not recall another man whose sexual onslaught had brought her such joy, such intense pleasure. She tried to change the image by shifting her own position, but it was too late. Kim was with her, lying in her arms, kissing the back of her neck. She could feel his long fingers running slowly down her spine, caressing her buttocks, squeezing the muscles at the back of her legs.

She could feel him enter her, move deep inside her. She could touch the memory of his manliness with her own muscles, with her sexual organs. Her breasts stiffened at the memory of his orgasm, her orgasm. She fell back into an uncertain sleep.

In the dream that came to her, she was naked in the glade where her sculpture would reside. Water rushed over the cliff above her and she was shielded from view by the resulting torrent of pale blue moisture. A man walked through the water wall. He was naked too. She turned her head, in maidenly modesty, but he came close to her and took her chin in his left hand, turning her head back toward him. She lowered her eyelids, but he moved her head forward and upward again. She could smell the mustiness of his flesh, wet from the waterfall, hot from his own desire. She could feel his hard sex pressed against her supple cheek.

"Kiss," he said in a dark, husky voice, made so by his desire for her.

"My lord, King," she said in a voice not her own.

Then he was in her mouth, filling her with his passionate need. She stretched her neck up, relaxing her throat and he moved again, completing the joining of the two....

Feyhe woke up. She was sobbing, and she didn't know why. The room was now fully light with the morning sun. She sat up in bed, took a deep breath and caught herself suddenly. She threw her arms around her naked breasts as the dream came back to her and she cried for real.

5

They were sitting in Billy's living room in his Greenwich Village South apartment. His three rooms topped the building, a four-story walk-up just north of Canal Street, just east of 6th Avenue, or The Avenue of the Americas as Feyhe insisted upon calling it. With the windows open, facing west and east, the rumble of traffic could always be heard accompanying any other sounds from within the apartment itself. Its location, just two blocks from the entrance to the Holland Tunnel, made it vulnerable to twenty-four-hour trucks, busses and cars with their backfires, squeals, and honks.

Feyhe had been back from Korea for over a week, but this was their first get-together. Billy had made himself available, but she had put him off, saying that jet-lag was getting her down and keeping her there. She finally agreed to a light supper at his place and, now, here she was.

"This is nice, Billy, this is restful. Thank you," Feyhe said, sipping cognac from a paper-thin crystal snifter. She was leaning back, in her characteristic manner, against the low back of his sleeper couch, her body angled against the corner, her left leg slightly extended and its connected foot dangling somewhere near the middle of the three-seater.

"It's nice to finally see you, Feyhe. You've been avoiding me for some reason," Billy said in as straightforward and non-judgmental manner as he could muster.

"I haven't…I know," she responded, changing horses in mid-stream.

"Why?"

"I really don't want to talk about it, Billy."

"Something to do with the work? Not what you expected?"

"No, no. The work is wonderful. I brought you some sketches and some photos to look at."

She gruffly handed her bag to Billy who took it from her carefully. From it he extracted a stack of drawings which he examined in silence while Feyhe sat quietly nearby. When he'd finished with them he reached into the bag and removed a small packet of photographs, mostly of the grotto. He examined them with equal attention to detail. Then he set those aside and looked at Feyhe.

She was leaning back against the corner of the couch exactly as she had been when he began to look at her work. She was smiling. Her eyes were closed. Her lips were moving, forming words she gave no voice. Billy watched her for a moment, trying to decipher the unspoken, and then broke into her reverie.

"A penny for them," he said softly. She opened one eye and stared at him through it.

"Not for a dime, thank you," she said. Then she laughed. "Maybe for a quarter."

"All right, then. A quarter."

"You're too easy," Feyhe said, a laugh in the words; *the old Feyhe back again*, Billy thought.

"You won't catch me napping again, Billy-Boy."

He grinned. "Don't call me Billy-Boy."

"Why not? Is that what Miriam calls you?"

Billy blushed and she knew she'd gotten that one right. "You still let her push you around, Billy. Why?"

"You're off the subject, Feyhe. I want to know about you."

"This is the subject," she said. "It's just taking a longer way around." He grimaced and the face he made caused her to laugh again.

"I let Miriam call me whatever she wants, as long as she does it to me and not in front of you or anyone else I know."

"She was always like that, you know," Feyhe said. "Even when we were girls she always had her own way."

"She's told me that."

"I'm sure she did. That's one way to stay king, you know. You tell everyone, whenever you can, that you are king. Then it's always true."

"Did you learn that in Korea?"

Feyhe paused before speaking. "No. I learned that in The Bronx." Her face darkened, her eyes closed, her lips parted and for a moment Billy thought she was going to say something else. Instead, she sobbed, then forced a smile, then was fine.

She reached into her blouse, through the gap between the top two buttons and pulled out a piece of paper. Billy watched her do it and wondered why she had done it, and done it just then. She held the paper in her hand and made no reference to it as she continued to speak.

"When I was just a kid, your mother and I were great pals. She was the beauty, the smart one, the girl with all the luck. I was the poor kid from up the block. I was the one who didn't have the advantages of love and security and had a home life that no one envied." She crushed the paper within her fist. Billy watched, fascinated, as he listened to her talk.

"I loved Miriam and I hated her, too. Her parents doted on her. Our Aunts doted on her. All of our cousins doted on her. Even I did. But it made me so angry, sometimes, that she got so much attention and I got so little. Everyone in the family always gave her gifts. It was as though she was created just to get gifts. I didn't even get gifts on my birthday. No, that's not quite right. Miriam always gave me a present on my birthday. It was always something lovely, but I knew it was a castoff, just one of the things she'd been given that she had no use for." She unfolded the paper and began to smooth it out on her thigh as she continued her story.

"Once she gave me a necklace made of small red stones, garnets I think, that looked like baby rubies. I wore it until the clasp broke and I lost it somewhere on the A-train in the rush hour. I was fifteen when Miriam gave me that necklace and I was nineteen or twenty when I lost it. I'd already lost my virginity, Billy. That went early. Miriam's did too, but not like mine."

Billy reached over and touched Feyhe's hand. At impact, she clenched her fist again and crushed the edge of her precious paper in it.

Billy sat back again and let her go on.

"My own father raped me when he was drunk. I don't even think he knew it was me. I think he thought I was my mother, but I don't really know for sure. I only know I hated what he was doing and I cried and I shouted and no one came to help me. Later on, when I stopped crying and stopped bleeding I went to Miriam and to your grandparents, but they wouldn't help me. They sent me home to my mother. I never forgave them for that. I was sixteen years old, frightened, definitely not prepared for anything sexual. I went to them because they were always so loving, but not to me, not then." She paused for a breath. "Not ever again. And I never asked for help again, not from them."

She was silent for a moment, then she sat up and sniffled and smoothed out her paper again. "Kim Do-Mun gave me this note at the airport, Billy. He's the handsome man in those sketches, my tour guide. Would you like to read it?"

"If you want me to, Feyhe."

"Please." She held out the paper and he took it. "Read it aloud. I'd like to hear a man's voice say the words rather than just hear it in my own voice."

Billy quickly ran through it. The handwriting was clean and precise, easy to read and very unrevealing about the pen-holder.

My Dear Missis Bow-Hyuman, it began. "He spelled your name wrong, Feyhe."

"It's how he pronounced it. Just read it, Billy, don't judge it."

"Ok," he said and he began again.

My Dear Missis Bow-Hyuman, Words fail me in English. The weeks of your stay in Gyeongju have been like many miracles for me. Never in this life has someone not Korean brought such joy to this man's heart. You have shown your remarkable talents and your beauty of soul and I am the privileged servant of this beauty. It is perhaps not so easy for us to believe in the thing that is between us. It is what the people in my world call wrong. It is what I believe to be perfection.

"Feyhe, this sounds like a love letter. What is all this?"

She glared at him. "Just read it, Billy!" He gave her a glance, but her face showed nothing.

There is a story in the classic Chinese book of Cheng Shi, Billy read, *who wrote in the 12th century. It is called The Compassionate Man. I will tell you that tale.*

A compassionate man once caught a turtle. He wanted to make it into a soup, but unwilling to be accused of taking life, he boiled a pan of water and, placing a rod over the pan, said to the turtle, if you can get across the pan, I will set you free. The turtle was in no doubt as to the intentions of the man, but he did not want to die. So, summoning up all his will, he accomplished the impossible, crossing the heated water in the pan by traversing the thin rod. Well done, said the man, but please try it again!

It is like this for us, Missis Bow-Hyuman, it is like this for us. I am the compassionate man and do not wish to harm you, yet I hunger for you in my soul and would ask you to try again to release yourself from my grasp. As you depart for your home, and I for mine, there is no separation between us. You must come home to me at some time and I must ask you again to try to set us apart.

I look for that day and pray that we are both able to pass the test that time places in our path. Your ever affectionate, Kim.

Billy held the note in front of his face for a moment, only his eyes visible. He watched Feyhe's face for a reaction and there was none.

"That's quite a letter, Feyhe."

"Do you understand it?"

"I'm sure I do," Billy said with his voice low and measured. "Was he good?"

"That's not a question to be answered," she snapped back at him.

"I'm sorry, Feyhe, but I thought you were sharing—"

"I'm sharing something beautiful and you're making it sordid."

"I'm sorry," Billy shouted as jumped up. "If you didn't want to get into this, you shouldn't have shown me the letter."

"I shouldn't have, no, I shouldn't."

"You don't have to agree so adamantly, you know."

"I don't have to do anything, Billy. I'm an adult, and a much better adult than you." She slammed her hand against her thigh and then shushed herself.

"Oh, this is getting sillier and sillier," he said to his cousin.

"Oh, is it? Really? How profound!" She grabbed her bag and headed for his front door.

"I should never have shown you that letter." She shouted this over her shoulder as she went out into the tiny hallway that was really nothing more than a landing. Billy slowly followed her to and through the doorway. By the time he reached the landing she was halfway down the first flight of old and winding stairs.

"Thanks for coming over, Feyhe. Let's not be strangers, now."

"Fuck you, Billy-Boy!" she shouted up without looking at him.

"May I say, ditto?"

"Go ditto yourself," she called out from even further down the four flights. Her voice carried through the old wood and he was sure his neighbors were all listening to the conversation through their old oak doors.

He heard her thump across the small lobby and then he heard the front door slam shut. There was a hush that rang with his thoughts about his cousin and his foolishness in upsetting her.

"Welcome home, honey," he whispered as he went back inside the apartment and closed the door.

Billy thought he'd wait a week and then call Feyhe and apologize. He didn't have the opportunity, though, because the next morning she was on the phone, bright and bountiful, just as though nothing had happened to upset her the night before.

"Thanks for that lovely evening, Billy-boy," she said before he could catch his breath. He had dashed out of his morning shower to answer the phone and he was standing naked and dripping in the kitchen of his apartment. "I had such a good time. I've missed you."

"And I've missed you, Feyhe," he said. "And thanks for not staying mad at me."

"Mad at you? How could I ever stay mad at you?"

"Well, last night..." Billy began, but he thought better of it and stopped mid-phrase.

"Oh, last night was just nerves. The scrod was delicious." He couldn't tell if she was kidding with him or if she had simply put away the memory of how their evening had ended. "I'd like to see you again tonight, Billy, if you can spare me the time. I have…a situation that I'd like to run past you."

"A situation? What do you mean, Feyhe?"

"Well, there's a man, a young Korean man that I met on this trip and…oh, really, Billy, this isn't a phone chat. I need to sit down and talk with you. I can show you a letter he sent me on the day I left Korea. It says so much about my problem."

Billy hesitated a moment. *This conversation was too weird*, he thought. *It's as though the last half of last night never took place.* He took a slurp of coffee from the cup that had grown tepid while he showered. Then he spoke to her.

"Feyhe, if you want to replay all this, it's fine with me. How's seven-thirty?"

"The time is fine, Billy, but 'replay'? I'm sorry, I don't know what that means."

"The time is fine, Feyhe," he said quickly. "Shall I come to your place?"

"Yes, please." Without a farewell of any sort, she hung up the phone and he stood where he was, water still dripping, coffee cool on his tongue.

"Well, isn't that weird," he said out loud, not a question but a statement. A truck en-route to the tunnel nearby blared its horn and got Billy moving once again.

Clues come in all sorts of shapes and sizes, Billy discovered. They emerge from mists, stick in walls, and tumble out of closets when you least expect them. Sometimes they simply lie there on a table in front of you and wait to be noticed. For Billy, that evening with Feyhe produced clues of all types. It wasn't his fault, he told himself later, that he didn't recognize them for what they were, not until much later.

Feyhe met him at the door of her apartment. He ordinarily entered with his own key, but with the memory of the previous night's altercation still in his head, he had chosen to ring the bell on this occasion. Feyhe called out to him from somewhere inside to just come on in. He tried the knob and found it moveable and unlocked, so he pushed the door open. Feyhe was standing just inside the entry leaning against the archway into the living room. Her arms were crossed. She was smiling at him. He smiled back.

"Why so formal? You never ring the bell," she said, still smiling, still not moving, her arms still protectively linked.

"I don't know," he said, lying and sensing she knew it. "It just seemed like the right thing to do."

"Well get in here and give me a hug." He moved forward and did as he was bidden. "God, it's so good to see you after all this time. I never thought I'd miss a relative the way I missed you while I was away."

The speech was so reminiscent of her words the night before when she had arrived at his place that he stood speechless, not knowing what would be the right thing to say in return.

Finally, he uttered, "well, you know how much I missed you."

"Of course I do." She took a step back into the living room. "And look, in your honor, no guests. Just us tonight."

"Great."

"I wanted a chance to talk with you about my life. A lot has happened in the last six weeks, Billy."

"I know."

"Oh?" She gave him a curious glance that caused him to quickly look over his shoulder, just in case there was someone else standing there he hadn't noticed. But they were alone. "Have a seat. Dinner's not quite ready."

"Okay. What are you making?"

Feyhe smiled at him and he noticed that one of her teeth had a slight chip at the corner. He hadn't paid any attention to that before. "I thought I'd make you scrod. I remember you like it."

"I made scrod last night, Feyhe."

"Well, you like it enough to have it two nights in a row, don't you? I know I couldn't, but you certainly can." She moved off into the kitchen.

This is getting too weird, Billy thought. *Can she have completely forgotten about yesterday?*

"I've laid out some sketches for you to see, Billy, that I did in Korea for my piece. Have a look at them and tell me what you think."

Billy started to respond that he'd already done this but realized that such a statement would not go down well. So he leaned over Feyhe's large, square coffee table and began to reexamine her work. He separated one of the male portraits from the other work and held it up over his head. It was one he hadn't seen before.

"Who's this guy, Feyhe? He's handsome."

Feyhe stuck her head out of the kitchen and looked at the picture he was holding. "Oh, him," she said in an off-hand manner. "That's Kim Do-Mun. He was my government-appointed guide. He's a professor of Western Literature. He's engaged to be married."

"You know a lot about him."

"I spent a lot of time with him, Billy." She giggled. "A lot of time."

"So you got to know him well?"

"Yes," she said, and there was a dead-silent pause, "well."

"What does that mean, Feyhe? Well." She came out of the kitchen and stood behind him, sitting on her couch.

"It means…*well*…you know…*well*."

"He's very nice looking." Bill turned to look at her. He waited for a response, but she said nothing. There was another long, awkward silence.

Then Feyhe sighed, something Billy had never heard her do before. "Is there something you want to tell me about him, Feyhe?"

She took a deep breath before she spoke. "I think I may have done something rather foolish, Billy. I may have given him the wrong idea about me and what I wanted in our friendship."

"I don't understand, Feyhe."

"Billy," she said before she stopped and went totally silent. He stared at her, equally silent, waiting for her to take the next step in the conversation. She turned away from him and moved back into the kitchen. Billy got up and followed her.

"Talk to me, Feyhe. Tell me about it."

"I don't know what to tell you." She seemed so feminine, suddenly, and vulnerable that Billy's heart actually skipped a beat. "He is an extraordinary man."

"You said he was engaged. Did you meet the woman, also?"

"Oh, yes, she's lovely," Feyhe gushed. Then she pulled herself back from that frothier emotion. "That makes it even harder."

"Makes what harder, Feyhe?"

"What I feel, Billy." She picked up something from the kitchen counter and held it out to him. He could see immediately that it was Kim Do-Mun's letter, the same one he had read aloud the night before. He took it from her, glanced at it, refreshing his memory, taking in its tone, then returned it to Feyhe.

"He sounds like a man in love, Feyhe."

"I know." She lowered her eyes. "I just don't know how to deal with that." Billy took a deep breath and then continued.

"Are you in love with him?"

"I don't know."

"Would you like to be in love with him, then?"

She nodded twice, then laughed abruptly. "That damn double nod, Billy. They all do it over there." She slapped herself across the face, a soft slap, almost a mockery of a slap. "I didn't realize how serious it was until now, serious to just nod."

Billy braced himself for the next question. This seemed to be going so much better than their talk the night before that he felt emboldened.

"Did you sleep with him, Feyhe?" He watched her face change, her eyes seemingly filtering light, refracting memories.

She was crying now, tears streaming down her cheeks. "I did. He's the best lover I ever had. That makes everything so much more difficult, don't you think?"

This time Billy nodded twice. Feyhe threw her arms around his shoulders and pulled him close to her. "Oh, Billy, what am I to do?" He held her close and tight, her hot body searing his own. "What am I going to do about this?"

"Don't go back, Feyhe. Just don't go back to Korea. Let the commission go and don't go back, don't look back. Let it go."

She sobbed into his shoulder and held him even tighter. "But I think I love him," she cried out. "I think I love him."

"We all think we love people, Feyhe, but it passes. It goes away. We move on and we love someone else for a while. Let this one go."

She cried a while longer and they both stopped speaking. Then she pulled away from him and he saw at once that her tears were gone. Her face was dry, her eyes were bright, there was a smile on her lips. She turned back to the fish, resting in the iron skillet, cooling while they indulged in their emotional conversation. She turned the heat on under the pan and turned back to give Billy a smile.

"This should be done in a jiff," she said. "Why don't you have a look at those drawings I did in Korea. I want your opinions on the models."

She threw him a smile again, just as if nothing had transpired before this, or had taken place the night before, or the month before that. Confused, Billy returned to the living room and the drawings Feyhe had left for him to peruse.

She was singing as she worked in the kitchen. Singing a song, a tuneless, wordless threnody.

She is actually singing, Billy thought. *I don't get it.*

When they sat down to eat, their conversation rested on Billy's work and his progress with the Ostendorf living room. Billy filled her in on his progress with the room and his prowess in sidestepping all of the man's advances. Feyhe laughed a lot during the rendition of his story and that pleased Billy. When he got to the point of telling her about her sculpture and its place in the room, her face took on a more serious expression. She listened carefully and then she spoke.

"Did I tell you, Billy, that I am going to do a piece on commission for the Koreans?" she asked him.

"Are you feeling all right, Feyhe?" he asked her.

"I'm fine, why?"

"We've talked about little else than your Korean trip and the piece you're going to do, and I've looked at your sketches twice tonight and last night too. Why would you ask me such a stupid question?" The words came tumbling out of his mouth before he could stop them.

"I don't know what you're talking about, Billy." She looked stunned. He instantly regretted his words, his tone, and believed completely that she had no idea why he would say such a thing. His own realizations frightened him.

"Feyhe, I think the jet-lag has really crimped your brain."

"I…excuse me," she said. She bolted from the room and ran down the hallway to her bedroom, slamming the door behind her. He sat where he was and waited for her to return, but he heard nothing that sounded like Feyhe's door, or her footsteps or anything else. He waited for a few minutes, picking at the cooling food in his plate. Then he proceeded down the hall toward her room.

He stood outside her door and listened. He heard nothing. He tapped on the door, waited for response, then tapped again.

"Feyhe," he called out, "are you all right? Do you need anything?" There was no response.

"Feyhe? It's Billy. Are you all right in there?"

This time she responded, but in a faint, shallow voice. "Billy? It's really you?"

"Of course it's me, Feyhe."

"Come in, come in."

He opened the door and walked into her room. There were no lights on, but he could see her form, prone, on her bed with just the light that came in her window and the light that filtered in behind him from the hallway.

"Are you feeling all right?" he asked her.

"I'm just tired, I think. It's nice of you to come and see me. I've just come home from Korea, you know."

Billy sat down on the edge of her bed and took her hand between his own.

"Yes, I know, Feyhe." He took a deep breath. "When you've rested and gotten your strength back I want to hear all about your trip, and the people you met."

She began to cry softly and quietly and he stayed where he was, holding her hand and not speaking. He wanted to ask her more questions, tell her what he already knew, but he resisted the temptation to start this all over again. Feyhe seemed to not realize that he was still there, beside her, holding her hand. He squeezed her hand, but she didn't respond, didn't change the firmness of her grip, didn't alter her position.

She was staring out in front of her, looking toward the place where the ceiling and the wall opposite her bed met. A faint smile gripped her, then left her. She exhaled one long, deep sigh and dropped his hand from hers.

"Feyhe?"

She didn't speak again and they both remained where they were, as they were, silent and lost in their own thoughts, different thoughts that centered on the same thing, although neither knew exactly what was on the other's mind.

Kim.

The name, the face—as Billy now knew him—the letter. Feyhe smiled. Billy frowned. The air between them suffered the difference.

It was as though two strangers stood face to face while a third person, also a stranger, stood between them, an arbiter of struggles not yet revealed.

Kim.

6

Miriam sat opposite her son in the plush, leather banquette that surrounded them. It was a large round table, too large for just two people, but they had chosen a late hour for their lunch and there were few people left to vie for space. This was one of Billy's favorite places, a quiet corner booth at the Four Seasons. They could talk without being easily overheard or observed, its coziness a buffer against the realities of any conversation.

Two days had gone by since Billy's peculiar dinner with Feyhe, two days of wondering and questioning. He had phoned her the following morning and she had seemed to be quite all right.

"It's nice of you to be concerned, Billy," Feyhe said after a short prelude about his worries about her. "I'm all right, really. I suspect I was just overtired. At my age it's not easy to travel those long distances without suffering some consequences."

"You certainly sound all right, Feyhe," he said, his voice nearly a whisper. She laughed at him through the phone lines. It was her old laugh, the chuckle and the throat-catcher.

"You worry an awful lot for a boy your age," she said. "You'll get wrinkles and then end up being one of your own clients." Billy laughed in response.

"Well, as long as you're feeling all right, Feyhe. That's what I was calling about."

"I'm fine. Thanks. Go do something to earn a living." She hung up the phone, a hair too abruptly, Billy thought. He placed a call to his mother.

"We need to talk," he said to Miriam as soon as she answered.

"About…?"

"About your cousin Feyhe. I'm worried about her."

"She's a crazy woman, Billy. I tried to tell you that once, but you never listen to me."

"She's not crazy, just…" he struggled for the right word "…just a little overtired, I think. But I'm still worried."

"So what can I do, sweetie?"

"I don't really know. Have lunch with me and let's talk about it."

"I can't today," Miriam said to her son. "I just can't possibly today."

"All right, then, The Four Seasons, a treat…on me. Tomorrow at 1:30. Will you come?"

"With my son treating, I'd even cancel today."

"No, no. Tomorrow's fine. See you then."

With her Cobb Salad half eaten and his mushroom burger plate only partially consumed, he started on the important part of their lunch chatter. Over drinks and soups they had talked about Miriam and Angus, a possible new car, a vacation trip to Portugal. Now the topic of Feyhe hung between them like netting over a lettuce bed. Neither one could walk too easily on this material, nor reach through the veil to pick a particular leaf.

"Has Feyhe ever exhibited, I don't know, any signs of stress to you?" Billy finally asked Miriam.

"Look, I don't see her that often or talk to her much. You spend more time with her than I ever did, even when we were kids."

"Is that really true?"

"We came from different worlds, right there on the same block." She toyed with a large piece of Boston lettuce. "My father was head of the family and her father was the *meshugenah* asshole who made fun of us all. We didn't spend a lot of time."

"Tell me again the relationship?" he asked.

"My mother's brother was Feyhe's father. So, we were first cousins, but Feyhe and her brother were really poor—even for the depression—so we didn't see them much. And her mother was a whole other kettle of fish."

"Why? I thought your family was so very close all the time."

"Not with them, Billy. There was too much trouble attached to them."

"Tell me about it, please."

Miriam drained her water glass before speaking again. While the last drops were trickling down her throat she held up the empty glass, hoping a waiter would spot her. One did. He came over, refilled the glass and discreetly departed.

"I love it here, Billy. I love it."

"Quit stalling, I want a direct answer," Billy said, an accidental quote from a favorite MGM film song popping into the chat.

"Looks who's Janie Powell, now!" Miriam said and she chortled. Then her face changed, a frown almost darkening it.

"Feyhe and I both loved those old movie musicals. It was one of the things we could always talk about together. The movies cost a nickel in those days, and the Paradise was right around the corner on the Grand Concourse. We were both just kids, Billy, but we'd go. We'd scrounge up our nickels and we'd go. We'd watch little Miss Alice Faye singing her heart out over some guy and we'd both just melt right into one another's arms. For two little girls from The Bronx, those movies were the whole world."

"So you were close to her?"

"I was very close to her for a while. Then…something happened and it all changed. I wasn't so close any more."

"What happened?"

"I don't want to talk about it."

"Hey, I'm paying for this lunch and you're the informer I'm bribing with good food and drink. Give out, Miriam."

She smiled at him and the smile changed again, almost at once, into that thoughtful frown he was growing accustomed to seeing on her face.

"I think we were fifteen, it was probably 1932. It was late. I was in bed. My mother was in the kitchen, where you could usually find her then, and my father was probably reading. I know the radio wasn't on, because I could never fall asleep with the radio on. I don't know if I'd slept yet, but the sound of our doorbell ringing frantically woke me fully up. I jumped out of bed, and looked at your uncle Arnold. We had the same room at the time. He was sound asleep and by now the bell had stopped ringing anyway. I put on my robe and went out into the parlor. My father was standing there in the middle of the room and he was talking to Feyhe. My mother, holding a big kitchen knife as I recall it, was standing in the doorway behind her. This is very good lettuce."

"Never mind the lettuce, go on with the story."

"When did you get to be so impatient? I don't remember."

"Enough stalling. Tell me more."

She nodded, then continued. "Well, Feyhe was crying and crying and her dress was torn and she only had one shoe on one foot. She looked terrible, I remember, and I had missed the first part of whatever she was telling my father. I couldn't see his face, but I could see my mother's. She didn't look any too happy with what she was hearing."

"Which was…?" Billy prompted Miriam during a water break.

"She was making some wild claim, some accusation about her father *bothering* her and it made my mother so furious. Before Feyhe could even finish telling her story, my mother leaped at her with that knife she was holding. Feyhe screamed and my father grabbed my mother's arm and spun her down to the floor and he yelled at Feyhe to go home and leave them alone. Feyhe looked terrible. She looked right at me, Billy, but I don't think she saw me standing there. I was shocked. I was open-mouthed. Nothing could come out of me, not even a whisper."

"What do you mean by 'bothering' her, Miriam?"

"You know, like from sexual things. That was what I thought she meant and I know my mother thought so too, which was why she got so upset."

"So Feyhe came to you all about being molested by her father, and grandpa yelled at her, grandma tried to stab her, and you said nothing. Then she was told to go home and that was that? Nobody did anything? Nobody looked into it?"

"I don't think we did anything at all, no. There's a Jewish saying, *got vet helf'n, ober biz er vet helf'n, zol got helf'n."*

"Which means…what?"

"God will surely help. But until He helps, may God help us."

"I don't get it." Billy took a breath. "Well, maybe I do. About Feyhe, though, how could you do that? You were supposed to love her."

"I was only a child myself, Billy. I don't think I really understood any of it. After all, nothing like that ever happened to little Miss Alice Faye. She was my frame of reference."

"After that, did Feyhe seem different? You know, moody or anything?"

"No, not so much more than before. She was always a little moody. Why? Is she moody again now?"

"A little, yes."

"Well, she's had a long time to grow that way. We were maybe fourteen or fifteen when this all happened and back then fourteen or fifteen was really young, not like now. We had nothing. We knew nothing."

"You kept on seeing her, though, didn't you? At family things and on your own?"

"Not so much. Her parents would come to the family circle meetings and her brother Billy, too. But Feyhe wouldn't come. I don't think she ever came into our apartment ever again after that night. And I was starting to go out with boys then, so we didn't have as much time to be friends anymore."

"I see."

"I went to her wedding. Would you like to know about that?"

Billy nodded and took a forkful of his cold mashed potatoes, tasted them and put the mess back on his plate. Miriam had already started talking again.

"I got an invitation to Feyhe's wedding to this guy I knew a little bit. He was crazy, a radical, a red most likely, but very sexy. I had gone out with him a couple times and then I introduced him to Feyhe, because I thought he'd like her and she'd like him. She was a secret Communist then."

"How could she be a secret Communist and you know about it?"

"We still shared some things, Billy. She still got my clothes that my mother gave to her brother for Feyhe. You know the Jewish saying, *a sheyn ponim kost gelt*, don't you? 'A good appearance costs money.' So I still saw her now and then. This man, his name was Owen Khanzadian, was a very handsome man, Billy. He looked like a cross between Robert Taylor in *Camille* and Robert Montgomery in *Private Lives*. His hair was slick and his lips were lush. He had a beautiful smile that could melt a heart, but his words were all about Communism and sharing the wealth. Well, we didn't have any wealth—don't forget it was the depression—so it sounded fine to us girls. On our first date he took me to a movie. Not at the Paradise though. We went downtown to the city and went to a special movie palace where they showed foreign films and I saw a naked woman for the first time. This was Hedwig Kiesler, you know who she became in Hollywood—Hedy Lamarr. Well, even in school, in my gym classes, you never saw another girl naked."

"It must have been a shock, then."

"A shock? No. Disturbing? A bit. Not so much for me, of course, because I knew what a woman looked like, being one. But I was shocked for him, for Owen, because he was a man and he shouldn't see a woman like that until his wedding night if even then. I made him take me right home, Billy. No supper, no soda, right home. I vowed I wouldn't see him again, but he was such a good looking guy and he was fun when he didn't talk about the political things and about the police state we were living under with Roosevelt just elected again. So we went out a second time. This time he took me to the theatre in Greenwich Village, to a place where all of these gorgeous women sang and danced and turned out to be men in women's things. I was supposed to be shocked again, but I was ready for him this time. I kept my cool and didn't get alarmed or anything, and he laughed and he loved it, but I decided not to go out with him anymore. So I introduced him to Feyhe. I hoped they'd take to one another, and they did. I hoped that so I could still look at him sometimes. He was such a looker."

Miriam and Billy both took a bite of food, both chewed and then discarded the cold meat.

They laughed simultaneously and Miriam went on with her story.

"So I introduced them and he talked about politics and she could match him, which surprised me because I didn't know she had such an interest in the topic, and they started going together and eventually the invitation to the wedding came. It was 1937 and we were twenty. I told her I thought she was too young, but she said that in Russia girls her age already had husbands and children and she was a slacker and not doing her part, so she married Owen."

"Did they have kids?"

"No, Billy, they didn't have kids. Feyhe couldn't have kids. It wasn't part of who and what she was."

"What do you mean?"

Miriam gave him one of those motherly looks that always said "I love you; why are you stupid?" He felt himself blushing from the neck on upwards and wanted to stop the color from drenching his face, so he took a sip of his water, then a gulp of it.

"What I mean, Mister Not-So-Dumb, is that she hurt herself with her father, all those years before and it kept her from ever having kids. Do you get me now?"

"I do, I do," Billy said. "Do you know this for certain or are you just guessing?"

"I know it in here," Miriam said tapping lightly on her chest. "I don't have a doctor's note, though."

"So she married this man, Owen, and then what happened to her?"

"They moved away to New York proper and she worked for a publishing house as an editor and he led some movement or other and she went to meetings and that was their life together. I suppose they were happy. I don't know, because after they moved out of The Bronx I never saw him again and hardly ever saw her."

"Why?"

"They just didn't fit in with us anymore. Suddenly she was too good for us." She waved at the waiter again, pointing at her empty water glass. "Well, I'll tell you something she doesn't know I knew. He wasn't such a good Communist in his private life. *A schlemaz'l falt oyf'n ruk'n un tsebrekht zikh di noz.* That's, for you, 'a born loser falls on his back and breaks his nose.' He had other women and he kept them a lot better off than he ever kept Feyhe. That was why Feyhe divorced him only a few years. And she didn't even keep his name. Not that she ever took it. Can you imagine being called Khanzadian?"

"She never took his name?"

"Oh, no, that was the story I wanted to tell you. At the wedding, which I attended although my parents didn't go, when they took their vows, she wrote her own and that was a first for me, Billy. I was used to the traditional ceremony under a *chuppah* with a lot of stuff in Jewish. They got married in English and when they got to the vows part, he promised to love her and cherish her, which was already a little bit different, but she only promised to love him. Then she promised to never take his name from him. Well I thought that was really strange, odd even. But that was Feyhe. She was always saying things that weren't complete and that you couldn't really take stock in. And since her father's name was sort of French I guess it made some sense to want to keep it, even if she had terrible feelings about the man himself."

"And you lost track of her right then? Right after the wedding?"

"Not completely, because of her brother, you remember? Billy Baumann?"

"He got killed when he was a kid, right?"

"Right, but a kid like Billy doesn't die so easy. Feyhe was almost ten years old when Billy was born, so when he died, she was still in her teens and not married yet to Owen. He doted on her, Billy did. He'd follow her around like a detective with no paying clients. It was like if he stayed really close to her he'd learn something useful. And she loved it. She thought he was terrific the way he kept up with her. With him she was a child. Those were the times I felt closest to my cousin, when we played with Billy. He was an adorable baby boy, a sweet little kid. He loved the whole Jewish thing, which is maybe why I keep falling back on those old sayings of my mother's, thinking about those days and about him."

"I never get them," Billy said.

"Oh, but Billy Baumann understood them when he was only two years old. He loved to hear them, and Feyhe and I would say them to him and he'd laugh and point and sometimes hold his nose and hold his breath. He was a cute little kid. You're named for him, you remember?"

Billy tried not to take his mother's comments as a criticism of his own, labored sense of being Jewish. Instead, after acknowledging her not so new news, he turned the conversation back to Feyhe once more.

"Did she have a favorite expression in this pantheon of Yiddish wisdom?"

"I'm sure she did, Billy," Miriam said, her words a bit clipped and formal in response to his slightly cynical question.

"And do you recall what that might have been?" Billy said, imitating her stiffness. There was a pause in the chatter as she thought about the question.

"Yes, I do." She said nothing more. He waited and she kept him waiting.

"All right, Miriam, are you going to tell me what the expression was? Please."

She nodded. *An aynredenish iz erger vi a krenk.*

"Yes?"

"Really, Billy, with your education…uchh! 'A delusion is worse than a disease.'"

"Okay, Miriam, write it down for me. I'll learn to say it."

His work on the Ostendorf living room was done. It had turned out to be even more spectacular than Billy had envisioned and Frederick Ostendorf was quite pleased. As Billy walked with him around the periphery of the room, the older man seemed to glow with the light and his own sense of pride in the final results. Billy was actually enjoying being in his company for a change. When they completed their walk of the circumference, Ostendorf turned and took both of Billy's hands in his own. He stood looking at Billy while Billy moved his eyes away from the older man's to give the room another full look.

"It's perfection, Billy," Ostendorf breathed in his direction, "and so are you."

"Well, thanks for your nice words about the room, Frederick," Billy replied, pointedly refusing to respond to the second half of his client's statement.

"The words are true," Ostendorf said. More pointedly he said, "All of them."

"You're very kind."

"Certainly kinder than that vicious cousin of yours," the man said. The words stung Billy like a herd of mosquitoes and he finally looked at the man again.

"What do you mean?"

Ostendorf made a sweeping gesture toward the room they had just inspected and, with a flick of his limp wrist, indicated to Billy that they sit. Without his usual hesitation, Billy flopped down on one of the low divans he had used in creating the conversation pit in the center of the room. Ostendorf sat down on a separate low couch and then answered the question.

"I invited her here to see your work and she told me off, Billy. It's not something I'm accustomed to, believe me, especially from an artist whose work I have just incorporated into my design schema for my home."

"I'm sorry, Frederick, but what did she actually say?"

"I don't know if I can repeat those words, Billy. They cut me to the quick."

"No, please. I need to know."

There was something in the sound of Billy's voice that made Ostendorf sit upright before he spoke again. He stared into Billy's face, trying to read statements that weren't printed there.

"Well, the conversation went something like this. I can't guarantee quotation marks. I asked her to come over and see the room. She said, 'thank you, no, and fuck you, too.' I think she said too as in t-o-o, although what she said next made me think that she actually might have said two as in t-w-o. I said to her, 'Feyhe you aren't behaving particularly well today,' and she responded with, 'I can do anything I want and you and Billy can enjoy your little fuck-space without me watching.' So then I knew she'd gotten some idea in her head about the two of us, which is absurd, Billy, isn't it? So I said to her, 'Feyhe you are being foolish and jumping to the wrong conclusions.' And she responded by telling me to rip off my designer clothes and leap through my fuck-view window. I think she said fuck-view and not fuck-you, but Billy, no one talks to me that way. No one."

In as small a voice as he could muster without being inaudible Billy said, "She hasn't been herself lately."

"She hasn't been anyone I'd care to associate with, certainly," Ostendorf said.

"I'm sorry, Frederick. I'll talk to her, reassure her that there's nothing funny going on between us. Sometimes I think she gets jealous when her friends pay attention to me, or to anyone else for that matter. She doesn't handle that very well."

"If she can behave herself, Billy, you are to bring her to the party on Friday night. Promise me, now."

"I'll try."

"She really ought to be here. Her sculpture is a focal point. She needs to know that."

"Frederick, I'll try. That's all I can do."

Feyhe agreed to accompany him to the party. Billy was relieved that she gave him no lip, no attitude about what might have been going on between him and her friend—his client. She was actually sweet about the invitation. She thanked him for reminding her about it. She told him she had been intending to phone Ostendorf and thank him for asking her.

Billy asked her if she also meant to apologize to the man, but Feyhe's only comment on that suggestion was to turn it around and suggest that Billy might need to apologize to her for making such a suggestion in the first place.

He picked her up at the appointed hour. It was a perfect night to inaugurate the room, clear and moonlit with an unlimited ceiling. He knew the views would be perfection, an even match for the room's new look. Feyhe was in an equally perfect mood. She was dressed in a new gown, a wine-colored Chinese silk, floor-length with long sleeves and a high collar. The dress was embroidered with a dragon and phoenix pattern that extended from her left shoulder down to her right knee. She wore long, garnet earrings and a small silver comb in her hair. The comb had a dozen tiny bells that made a most musical sound as she moved.

"You're gorgeous," Billy commented briskly when she opened the apartment door. "Absolutely scrumptious. No one's going to notice my work at all tonight."

Feyhe blushed before she spoke. "You're a naughty little gay boy," she laughed at him. He was immediately pleased at the tone of her voice and the sound of her mocking words. She was in a good mood. He knew that.

"Are you ready for my big moment, then?" he asked her. She nodded, grabbed her purse and a shawl and allowed him to take her arm and escort her to the elevator. On their way down she made a few slightly risqué jokes that got him laughing and as they strolled down Park Avenue toward Ostendorf's building, she kept the raucous tone alive with her pointed comments on the people who passed them by. Billy was loving it all, and he was relieved as well that she was in such good spirits and that they had a hold on her.

Ostendorf greeted them at the elevator door. He gave Feyhe a quick look, then moved forward to kiss her on the cheek. "You will be so pleased, I'm sure, with your extraordinary work and how it is seen," he said to Feyhe. "This boy of ours has done us both up proud."

Feyhe pinched Billy's cheek with her thumb and forefinger, twisting and turning in the manner of a Jewish matron playing with her baby. "He's mummy's little talent, he is," she said in a mocking voice, her lips pursed tightly, the words emerging with the same sense of pain he felt in his cheek.

"Thank you so much." Billy felt his jaws tighten. "Please don't do that ever again."

Feyhe laughed brightly and pushed past her cousin, entering the apartment eagerly, expectantly. With Billy right behind her, keeping apace, she stopped dead in her tracks, gasping. Billy nearly ran her down, but caught himself in time. As he finished his pullback, she turned to face him. There was a look in her eye that smacked of danger, but it changed to delight in an instant. She grabbed Billy by the shoulders and pulled him into her embrace.

"It's incredible, darling. I love it." She kissed him on both cheeks. "Thank you for doing this so beautifully. You make my work glorious." She let him go, turned to the room again, and called out someone's name. Billy wasn't sure who. She moved off in the direction of the long window-wall, leaving Billy alone with Ostendorf, who had caught up with them both.

"She's right, you know," he said to Billy. "It is incredible. It is glorious. And I don't mean the carving. I mean the room, everything you've done with it. I couldn't have envisioned it this way without your eyes seeing it, Billy. I could never have accomplished this without you. Thank you."

Billy was blushing this time. He stammered something vaguely, acknowledging the praise and thanks with thanks of his own. Then, sensing there was something more personal in the offing, he moved off in Feyhe's direction. She was being so bright, so chipper, that he felt the need to stay close to her, just in case something happened to change her cheery mood.

She was chatting with two men he had not seen before. They were well-dressed and about twenty years apart in age, the older being in his mid-forties, Billy assumed. The younger man was wearing an Oleg Cassini suit, a water-marked golden silk with wide lapels that stressed his flat, strong shoulders. His light blue shirt was bisected by an Adrian tie with a fine black pattern of spiderwebs imprisoning human faces in miniature. The older man was dressed in a more conservative black, three-piece Armani suit with an equally conservative tie. His own shoulders sloped and were uneven. He was the better looking of the couple. They stood, their arms around one another, totally engrossed in whatever Feyhe was telling them. The younger man looked up as Billy approached. Feyhe noticed his altered focus and turned to see what had distracted him, saw her cousin and smiled broadly.

"And here he is," she said, gesturing at Billy. "Come and meet these delightful people, darling." Billy joined the group. "Billy, this is

Leonard...I don't recall, and Don...something. Forgive me, but names are not what I do best."

The older man extended his hand to Billy. "Leonard Weissberg," he said taking Billy's hand but not shaking it, "and this is my dearest friend, Donald Freemantle."

"Hello," Billy said.

"Hello, Billy, may I call you Billy?" Don, the younger man, asked.

"Of course."

"We were trying to explain to Feyhe how much her frieze has meant to us, but she won't hear about it. All she wants to discuss is you," Leonard said.

"That's kind of her," Billy replied.

"You three chat a minute," Feyhe said, interrupting the flow of conversation. "I've got to get a drink and talk to Frederick's other friend, the phony Countess." Before he could stop her or even say her name, she had moved off and Billy was left with the male couple.

"So, Feyhe tells us you're a single gent," Leonard continued. "Why?"

"Just haven't found the right...girl yet, that's all."

"The right girl? My dear, really," chortled Don. "The right man is what you should be seeking. You'll have better luck, believe me."

"He should know, Billy. You see his quest led him straight to me."

"Leonard is such a kidder. It took me years to find this one, and I've no intention of letting him go. Now, Frederick was saying that—"

Billy was feeling uncomfortable in the midst of this good-natured chatter, so he excused himself quickly and turned back into the room, seeking Feyhe. She was standing between her statue and the sunken couch, staring out the short window at the view south, down the avenue.

Billy moved up behind her and, before putting his arm around her waist, cleared his throat so she'd know he was standing there.

"You didn't have to do that," she said. "I saw your approach in this reflective glass."

"Thank you for coming with me," he said. "It means a lot to me to have you see the fruits of both our labors."

"I did the easy part, Billy," she said to him. "I introduced you to Frederick and sold him a small piece of my work. You had the vision to transform this sex-pit of his into a showplace for my work. You're the one who makes it all so real."

"Oh, now, you're being a bit too modest, Feyhe."

"Am I? I don't think so. I think the result of your work is what's important here. My little sculpture, which looks so nice from the doorway, is only a meager excuse for what you've been able to accomplish in such a short time."

"Feyhe...?" he said. "I seem to detect a note of...something odd..."

"Do you?" She gave him a strange smile, a half-smile that cracked the veneer of her happy expression. "You shouldn't worry so much about what artists are feeling, not when you have been proven to be such an extraordinary designer, one with a flair for setting art in its place and nature in its place so that you can define an interior with your faggoty taste."

"Feyhe, come sit down, please," Billy now felt his jaws almost clamp shut. "You need to get control of yourself."

"I don't want to sit down, Billy. I want to go home."

"All right, I'll take you home, then."

"I don't want you to 'take me' home. I can get home on my own."

"I think I should take you whether you want me to or not. I'm worried about you."

"Worried!?" she said, her voice louder now. "You faggots worry far too much about us older women. Why is that? Afraid you're seeing yourselves in a few dark years?"

"Feyhe, you're shouting," he hissed at her. Ostendorf came briskly to their sides.

"Is anything wrong, Feyhe?" he asked her quietly. She wheeled on him.

"Wrong, Frederick? You can ask me that? Look at this. It's horrible to have my work in such a ridiculous place, lit this way and seen from this perspective. It's criminal, that's what it is. It's long been my belief that you don't deserve this statue. I didn't conceive of it for you, for this location. I don't like it."

Ostendorf placed his hand on her arm, gently, reassuringly, but she sloughed it off and moved a step or two away from him. Then she turned back to look at Frederick and Billy, still standing where they had been.

"You two make a lovely couple," she said with a sneer. "I hope that makes you both very happy." She started to walk away from them, but a waiter with a tray of drinks was standing too close to her. Before he knew what was happening, she had the tray, complete with empty and still full glasses both on it, in her hands. She turned in their direction and flung the tray at them. Billy ducked, but Ostendorf wasn't quick enough. He took the brunt of the blow directly in his chest.

There was no weight, but there was liquid and he stood dripping as the debris fell to his feet. The moment was just loud and just odd enough to have taken the room's focus and everyone stood silent, waiting for the outcome of Feyhe's abrupt and laughable action.

"Get her out of here. Now." Ostendorf was sounding grim and over-controlled.

"Come on, Feyhe," Billy said as he moved in her direction.

"You are too silly," she said, but no one could tell to whom or about whom she was talking. Billy turned her toward the door and began to walk her in the direction of the foyer, but she jerked her shoulders away from his hands and walked a little bit faster, putting space between them. "I'm going home, Billy. You stay and have a drink. Have some fun." She waggled her fingers at him, but never turned to look at him or at the wasteland behind her.

From the doorway she shouted, still without turning back in his direction, "Loved the room. Thank you so much for the tribute to my work."

With that she was gone.

The following morning he phoned her. The telephone rang a dozen times before he placed it back in its cradle. He wondered if he should just take the subway uptown and confront her at the apartment, but he decided not to, that it was the wrong thing to do. Instead he tried to work.

Work was impossible. All he could think about was Feyhe and her strange and changeable behavior the previous evening. She had started well, had seemingly enjoyed the way he used her work as a focal point, had even enjoyed the two men, Leonard and Don. She had been more than civil to Frederick and loving to Billy himself. Then it had changed, for no apparent reason, changed into something horrible and stupid. Her wrath had been aimed, pointedly, at himself. He was at a loss to understand why. What had he done? What had anyone done to cause her to change her tune so drastically? Nothing at all, he decided, and he felt better for having made such a decision. She was just moody, much moodier than ever before, and he would talk to her about it. She should see someone, maybe take a pill or a rest-cure somewhere. He would speak to her about it.

He sat musing this way for half an hour. A knock on the door of his studio brought him out of it. He wasn't expecting anyone, and he wasn't prepared for people, not in this state of mind. He decided to remain quiet and not answer the door.

"Billy, open up! I know you're in there." It was Feyhe. "Stop playing these games and let me in." He wasn't sure what to do next. "Billy, if you don't let me in I will have to use force." She was being persistent. "You know I have Goliath's hands and the big bad wolf's breath. I can huff and puff and hammer your house down." She meant it and he knew it. He walked to the door, and after a deep breath, threw it open.

"That's better," she said. "Where were you?"

"Sorry," he said, "I was in the bathroom. What are you doing here?"

"I wanted to bring you these, darling," she said and she drew a large bouquet of peonies from behind her back. "I know you love them as much as I do."

They were a stunning mixture of peach and white blossoms, the white ones flecked with a blood-red flaring that was indiscriminately endorsed on some of the petals.

"They're exquisite. Thanks."

"It's an apology, for my bad behavior last night."

"You didn't have to—"

"Yes, darling, I did. I was just not myself. I don't know what came over me. Forgive me? Please?"

"Well, I know my mother would want me to," he said with a half-sarcastic crow in his voice.

"You do know that, don't you?" Then she laughed and he laughed along with her. "Put on something nice. I'm treating you to lunch at Schraffts."

"Schraffts is a long way uptown from here," he said.

"But the counterman is cute," she responded.

"Not my type."

"Not mine either." She shrugged. "So you choose a place."

He took a moment to think about it, and was about to speak when she interrupted him. "Van Gogh was an epileptic, did you know that?"

"No. I didn't."

"Yes, he was."

"That's interesting, Feyhe." He wasn't sure what to say next.

"It affected how he saw things," she continued.

"Okay."

"No one loved him except his brother. And Gaugin."

"Uh huh."

"I'm trying to tell you something." She looked serious.

"What are you trying to say?"

She took a deep breath. "I'm not epileptic." He stared at her, waiting, but that was all she said.

"I'm so glad for you, Feyhe." It was the best retort he could think of.

"Don't you get it? At all?" He shook his head. "Billy, I'm not epileptic but I see Van Gogh's world exactly the same way he saw it. What do you think that means?"

"That you've only seen Arles through Van Gogh's paintings? I don't know."

"Billy, you're an idiot. That man was a genius and I must be a genius too. I see the world the way he saw it. I see the rings and the auras and the colors just the way he painted them. I look at you and I see you, and I see your moods and I see your talents and abilities, all of it reflected in the light around you."

"That's nice, Feyhe."

"I look at everything and everything becomes angels. I know

what the haloes are that all of those medieval painters were so fond of painting. They had the same ability as Van Gogh and me. They could see the auras. They just didn't know what to do about them."

"So, you and Van Gogh and the old masters, Giotto and the like, are all seeing the world the same way. That's cool."

"You're not getting it, Billy. It's proof. It's finally proof that I can do it too. I can be a genius like Vincent and the others. I see what they saw and I can make others see it with my art. I finally know what I'm doing."

"I thought you always did know—"

"No! No, not until now. That's why I wanted to take you to Schrafft's."

"I don't get the connection."

"The counterman. His aura is silver and pink and silver. He glows with a transcendency that no one who can't see it would ever imagine. The Counterman. His name is Franz and he's Alsatian, by the way, and he is pure and sweet, like his ice cream sundaes. It all shows up in the air around him."

"Well, I've never seen it, but I can imagine it, Feyhe."

"You can't. You have to see it for yourself. You have to come with me and see his glow."

"Feyhe, I have work to do, I can't just up and—"

"Come on. Now." She took a deep breath. "Billy, I need you to see what I see, what Vincent sees. Saw. You need to come into the world of the pure genius. You have to if you're going to survive the Ostendorf's of this world."

"I'm doing fine, Feyhe."

"I killed it, by the way." She gave him a smile. "We can all be friends again, because it's dead."

"Excuse me? What? What's dead?"

"This morning? No one called you?"

"What are we talking about?" He looked at her, hoping that something in her face would alert him to what was on her mind. She looked fine, perfectly normal, perfectly ordinary.

"My little display piece. At Frederick's. I killed it this morning. I'll never have to think about it again. It's with its maker."

"You're its maker, Feyhe." He knew his voice was sounding harder and harsher.

"I know that." She opened her shoulder bag and held its mouth ajar as she nodded toward it. He took a step forward and looked down into the gaping hole between her hands. He could see shards and scraps of stone in the bag. Nothing was recognizable or familiar. "That's what I took with me. Just the heart and the groin of the piece. The rest of it is still there, where you and Frederick put it. Its aura is gone, thank goodness. I couldn't see that any longer."

"How—?"

"I used my key. I left it there when I closed the door. I used Frederick's carving knife and I hacked out the heart and the groin. The rest doesn't matter. It's dead now." She closed her bag once again. "These parts are mine. I will cherish them for as long as I live. Let's go to lunch. You must see the counterman's aura."

Reluctantly, Billy let her take his arm and pull him toward the door of his studio.

"It's silver and pink and silver again," she repeated. "I've never seen anything like it."

7

Billy was sitting alone at the counter when the only other customer came into the diner. It was not unusual for him to have the entire place to himself. He only went to the diner after three in the morning and never after dawn. It was a classic, steel-metal structure under the elevated road that ran along the lower section of the West Side Highway. The docks, all commercial dockage now, were across the street. Meat packing plants filled the inland area that surrounded the diner. It was frequented by truckers, the occasional hooker, and the even more-occasional drag queen. He'd found it, late one night, when insomnia had held him in its grasp for several consecutive days. He'd gotten up, dressed and dragged himself through the deserted streets, hoping for some sign of life, some signal that humanity was abroad. That was when he found it.

The diner provided the finest pancakes he had ever eaten. He had reveled in their texture and taste and the maple syrup had been real, not over-processed. He made the diner his personal refuge, telling no one else about it.

Now, he was here, as usual in the wee hours, indulging in his favorite post-midnight pastime, pancakes. One old man had been leaving the place when he got there and the waitress, as old as the faded silk blossom on her uniform, had nodded to Billy in recognition and placed his order before he could. The old man, reeking of Thunderbird wine, had muttered and spluttered for a moment, then staggered out into the deep night. Andrea, the waitress, brought him some coffee and his syrup, started to say something, changed her mind and drifted away, only to appear again when the extra large pancakes materialized on a truly hot plate.

He was sitting quietly, cutting, pouring, chewing, when the door behind him opened and someone else came in. Billy looked up, curious about the new arrival. He saw, reflected in the pie cupboard, a very good looking man, a man with short-cropped blonde hair, wide-set deep green eyes, a dimpled chin, high cheek bones and the broadest set of shoulders he'd seen since Joan Crawford married Pepsi Cola. He gulped without realizing it and swallowed hard a large bit of griddle cake. It choked him momentarily, but he coughed it up, caught it in his teeth and swallowed it again. Angry at himself, he looked sheepishly down at his plate, ignoring the newcomer.

"Gonna be okay?" the man behind him said.

"Yeah, fine, thanks," Billy replied with an almost hostile tone in his voice.

"Cool."

The interloper took the stool next to Billy. The counter was long and hosted at least a dozen others, but the man sat next to him. Billy couldn't believe his luck.

"You're out late," he said to the new man.

"Yeah."

"This is late for me, too," Billy said, not knowing what else to say.

"Yeah?"

Andrea came over and poured the man some coffee, smiled and licked her over-lipsticked lower lip.

"The usual, Joey?" she asked him.

The man nodded. "Cool, baby." She moved away.

"You must be a regular here, too," Billy said.

"Yeah."

Billy took a breath before speaking again. It was clear that this encounter was not going swimmingly. "So, what's your 'usual'?"

"Three eggs, over easy, ham steak. No potatoes, no toast."

"Okay." He took a long breath. "Ah. Pancakes for me."

"Yeah. I see."

"I'm sorry. Clearly you didn't come in here for conversation." Billy averted his eyes and went back to work on his breakfast.

"It's okay. I just don't usually talk much."

"Okay. That's fine."

"No. I mean, I'd like to talk. I just don't ... usually have much to say."

"It's okay. Really. My name is Billy." He held out his hand.

"Joe Ryan." The man took Billy's and gave it a firm, strong, single shake.

"Live around here, Joe?"

"No. I just got out of work. You?"

"Yeah, I live about a half mile ... that way, I think." Billy gestured vaguely in the direction of the eventual rising sun. "I come over here a lot when I can't sleep. Which seems to be a lot lately."

"Insomnia, huh?"

"Sort of. Family stuff."

"Oh. You married, then?"

"Me?" Billy laughed. "Not really, no."

"Yeah, me too," Joe agreed. "Who's got time for that when there's work to do?"

"I've got a cousin who's a handful. She doesn't have anyone else but me, so she gets a lot of my attention."

"And I've got a kid who takes up my spare time." Joe waved his empty cup at Andrea who sauntered over, the half-full pot steaming in her hand.

"A kid? You were married then."

"Yeah. About six years. It didn't work out. But we had a kid. So, now I take care of the kid."

"Boy? Girl?"

"A girl. Her name is Cynthia. But we call her Sandy."

"Not Cindy?"

"No, Sandy."

The two men ate in silence for a while. A steam whistle blew in the distance, and Billy wondered if it was on land or on the Hudson River somewhere, or even across the expanse of water in New Jersey.

"That's a scow, probably with upper Manhattan rubbish, heading out to the Jersey shore," Joe Ryan said.

"How did you know I was wondering?" Billy asked him. "And how do you know what it is?"

"I saw it in your face," came the reply. "And I work around here. You get to know the different whistles."

"I see."

"She's five," Joe said.

"I'm sorry…?"

"My kid. Sandy. She's five years old."

"Oh, I'm sorry," Billy said quickly. "I wasn't thinking, or paying attention, or something."

"No, it's okay. I just wanted to tell you that."

"Does she live with you?"

"No. That wouldn't be right, would it? I work at night. There's nobody who'd be at home with her. She lives with my mother in Brooklyn."

"Where's…where's your wife, Joe?"

"She's not my wife. Not now. She left me about two years ago. She said she couldn't stand being married to me. And she left Sandy. Said she didn't want any reminders of me cluttering her life. She left me flat."

"I guess so," Billy said.

"I don't know where she is now, but she left me and went to Chicago for a while, then moved on to St. Louis. I don't know why."

"Why couldn't she stand being married to you? Doesn't sound possible," Billy said before he could stop himself. Joe just smiled at him and Billy felt compelled to return the smile. Joe's green eyes flashed in the glare of the diner's steel reflected lights.

"She told me she hated my work, mostly, that it made me unfit to be a husband. She said I was too busy being *a* man to be her man. She said I wasn't human, that I couldn't love, that I could only lust."

"Wow!" It was all Billy could think of to say.

"She was probably right."

"So she saw you as a lusty beast, or something."

Joe laughed. "Yeah."

"Well, you seem nice to me." Billy said in an even voice.

"Thanks…Billy, isn't it?" Billy nodded. "So. Are you a bit lusty yourself, Billy?"

Billy gulped again, nearly downing another large piece of pancake that he had just placed in his mouth. He cleared his throat again. "No. I wouldn't exactly say that, no."

Andrea came by and poured more coffee in both their cups. They resumed eating and finished up together. Andrea slapped their checks down in front of them and moved away in the direction of the cash register which sat on the other counter, the one beyond the slight separation that gave the staff their access to the galley.

Billy reached for his check and found Joe's hand on top of his own.

"Let me get that for you, Billy. You lent me your ear. Let me buy you your breakfast."

"There's no need, Joe. Thanks. I can handle it."

"I'm sure. But I'd like to."

"No, thanks."

"Please. You were kind to me. I'd like to do this."

Billy's mother had taught him, long ago, that to refuse such an offer three times was impolite, so he demurred and allowed Joe to pick up his tab.

"Thanks. It's very nice of you," the man said.

Billy nodded, smiled. His hand, where Joe's fingers had held it down against the counter, tingled with a sensation he didn't recognize. It was warmth coated with moisture, tempered with a heat that was not just the body's normal essence. He felt himself blushing and tried to think about something else. Joe came back to where Billy was still sitting.

"You on your way home?" the man asked him. Billy nodded. "Come on. I'll walk part way with you." Billy nodded again and slid off the stool.

Standing there, next to Joe Ryan, Billy realized for the first time how much taller the other man was. Billy stood just over five feet nine inches, but he now had to look up at a fairly severe angle in order to see

Joe's face.

"I didn't realize how tall—"

"Six five and a half," Joe said, before Billy could finish. "It's all in the legs, though. I have a short torso."

"D'you have big feet?" Billy asked before he could stop himself.

"Size thirteen, triple D."

"I'm not going to ask any more questions," Billy said, wishing he'd only thought this last. The two of them stepped outside and down the four concrete steps to the sidewalk. They started to walk, but at the corner Billy decided this was not a comfortable situation.

"Look, I'm all the way over on the far side of Canal Street. You don't want to come over that way, I'm sure. Thanks for the breakfast. Goodbye."

Joe looked a little taken aback. "Hey, don't you like me?"

"Sure."

"So why the quick brush off?"

"It's just…it's a long walk and you should probably go…home or something."

"I'm in no hurry."

They stood there for a moment, the ball in Billy's court. "Okay," he said, finally. "If you want to take the walk, let's walk."

He turned the corner and headed up the dark street, Joe coming up quickly behind him and moving beside him. "You're a quick walker, Billy," he said.

"I guess I am."

"These streets aren't safe for a guy like you."

"I do okay. I've been living down here for years. No one bothers me."

"That's dumb luck, that is."

"Really. I know where I am and how to get around. I do all right."

They crossed Reade Street. A street-cleaning truck barreled down on them as it turned the corner. Joe reached for Billy's elbow and helped him onto the curb. Billy pulled his arm away and put some space between them.

"Why did you do that?" he said to Joe.

"I didn't mean to offend you. I just wanted to hurry you along, that's all."

"Well, I didn't need your help." He could hear the anger coming into his voice. He didn't care. He was feeling uncomfortable in this man's company.

"Sorry." They set off again. Billy was trying to find an excuse to part from Joe, but nothing real enough was coming to him.

"Look," he said, "I think this is far enough. You've probably come a long way from your car or whatever you drive and I'm almost home and it's very late…"

"D'you live alone?" Joe asked him.

"What?" Billy was clearly rattled. "What business is it of yours?"

"Well, you know about me. I just thought—"

"What! What did you just think?"

"I just thought…well, you're an attractive guy and out late—"

"Yeah? So are you. So what?" He heard his voice rising.

"So, I thought maybe you were out cruising for…you know."

"No, I don't know." Billy's face was flushed and he glared back at the man.

"I thought maybe you were looking to hookup for sex."

"I was hooking up with a large stack of cakes."

"Look, Billy, I'm sorry. I didn't mean to upset you."

"Yeah? Well, you did."

They were passing through the warehouse district and were only a few blocks from Billy's apartment. He wanted to shake the guy, but he didn't want to run. He knew he was a slow jogger, at best, and Joe Ryan had really long legs and large feet. He'd be no match for what this guy could achieve sprinting. There were fires burning in two large metal cans, commercial-hauling jobs, and an old street-dweller sitting on a crate near them. As Billy and Joe passed him he muttered something under his breath and Billy could smell the liquor that fueled the man, if not the fires.

"God, I hate that stench," he whispered, not thinking that Joe could hear him.

"So do I."

"I dream, sometimes, that I'll end up like that, out here on the streets, rotgut liquor keeping me warm and alive."

"That couldn't happen to you. I know it," Joe said with an unforced, yet unnatural sincerity.

"How do you know that? You don't know me."

"I know you," he said. He reached over and placed his hand on Billy's shoulder. They stopped walking. Billy turned to look at Joe, look up at Joe, the taller man's face clouded in the dim light shed by a single light bulb illuminating the transom over a doorway into the next building.

"I can't see you clearly," Billy said.

Joe noticed Billy's voice was now low and soft. "I can see you just fine." Then he took a step forward in Billy's direction and moved Billy back against the doorway. They were both in shadow now. Without breaking the movement, Joe bent down and kissed Billy, first on the cheek then on the lips. It happened so swiftly, so smoothly, that it seemed to have been both orchestrated and choreographed. Billy's response was immediate. He flung one arm around Joe's neck and held him as close as he possibly could.

Billy's bed was accommodating, but not large. A three-quarter size, it allowed him to sleep comfortably in the center of its wider than single space, but with two people in it there was a need for bundling. The small room that the bed filled had one large casement window that faced east. Morning sun had a habit of shining through it, casting a hot, fat line of light across the bed, striking Billy from just above the knees to just above the ankles.

The heat it threw on the two men that morning served only to surprise Joe and nothing more. He was on his knees, the backs of his legs exposed to the sun as it shifted its baking rays across the bed. Billy's legs were not affected, his ankles hooked, as they were, around Joe's neck.

Their lovemaking had begun on the stairs and had not ended, five hours later. Nothing about the two of them, about the way they blended romantically and sexually, came as a surprise to Joe, he said often and loudly. Everything about it stunned Billy. He hadn't thought it possible to find this sort of symbiosis with a stranger.

Every gesture of Joe's brought an answering sound from deep within Billy. Every word the stranger spoke sparked a physical reaction in the bed's owner. By nine o'clock that morning, they were fast asleep, Billy cradled in Joe's arms, their knees bent, their heads cocked to one side on the same pillow. Their even breaths came at the same rate and for the first time in his life Billy slept as though he were safe in his own bed, in his own home, in his own life.

They awoke around noon. Billy's telephone was ringing in the other room and he struggled out of Joe's grasp to answer it.

"Hello?" he said, needing to clear his throat.

"Are you all right?" It was his mother.

"Yes," Billy whispered. "Why?"

"Why are you whispering?"

"I'm not."

"You are, Billy. Are you alone?"

"Um…no, I'm not. I'll call you back. Bye." He hung up.

He looked over his shoulder. Joe was lying on his side, his head cradled on his open hand. He was smiling, his green eyes gleaming.

"Sorry she woke you," Billy said looking over his naked shoulder. "My mother."

"You look good naked," Joe said, ignoring the apology.

"So do you," Billy said.

It was the way Joe smiled at this that made Billy blush. The smile said more than just "okay, that was nice." It implied a deeper appreciation and that was something Billy wasn't accustomed to receiving.

"I work out a lot," Joe said simply. "It's part of my daily life. I just get up and get to the gym."

"My workout consists of lifting the coffee cup all the way to the dry toast," Billy said.

"Even so, you've got pretty definition. You should join me at the gym."

"No. I don't think so."

"Why not, Billy?"

"I might be…I don't know…a little too gay to pull it off."

Joe moved over, the sheet that had been draped across his lower body shifting enough to reveal the modest, half-erection that Billy inspired. He patted the bed, indicating that Billy should sit or lie down, Billy wasn't sure which. Instead, he stayed where he was.

"You're not *that* gay, kiddo," Joe said. "It doesn't come screaming off of you."

"That's not what my cousin thinks." He sat down on the edge of the bed.

"That same cousin you told me about? She doesn't sound all that reliable when it comes to personal judgements."

"She does all right," Billy said, the picture of Feyhe in a state of anxiety crossing his mind. He frowned without realizing it.

"Don't frown, Billy," Joe said, smoothing his hand across the furrows on Billy's brow. "You don't want to look like that your whole life, do you?"

Billy gave him an uncertain look.

"Frowning is bad for the face. Forces the eyes, the mouth downward, pulls the lines of the brow into deep crevices. You do that enough times and it never changes back. It ages a person. Makes you look much older than you are."

"Thanks for the advice."

Billy was realizing that he wanted Joe to go, to leave his apartment, to let him get back to his own life. He also understood that he didn't know how to do that. He moved back into the doorway of the room.

"We really should be getting ourselves up and out, Joe. I have work to do. And your daughter probably needs to know that you're all right."

"She's in school. I never see her in the morning." He smiled again, not moving, his erection now full and strong. "Come back to bed for just a few minutes more. Please."

Billy resisted all the way to the pillows.

It was nearly two o'clock when they finally got up, showered and dressed. Billy made coffee and offered some to Joe who refused it.

"I've got to get going. Can I see you again, kiddo?" He smiled broadly and the warmth behind it made Billy blush again.

"I don't know. Really. I don't. I'd like to, but I don't know."

Joe looked upset, but his voice sounded fine, controlled and normal. Still, there was something in his eyes that assured Billy that he wasn't happy with this response.

"I don't usually ask to see someone again unless I think there's a possibility of something more than just sex, Billy. Believe me. I'm not looking for three a.m. quickies."

"Quickies? After ten hours?" He shrugged once, smiled, continued. "I understand, Joe. I do. I just know how I am and I don't want to give you any false encouragement. That's all."

"Okay, so you're not a champion in the relationships department. Neither am I, when you come right down to it."

"Let me think about this, okay?"

"Sure. Here's the deal. I won't take your phone number or give you mine. Every night this week, when I get off work, I'll be at the diner. If I see you there, great. If not, that's fine too."

"Joe, I'd really like to…" Billy started, then he took a breath and changed directions. "That will work for me. It's a deal." He extended his hand to shake on the agreement. Joe took his hand, pulled him close and into an embrace, leaned down to kiss him and then held him close for almost a minute. Then he stepped back, turned away and headed for the door.

Billy remained where he was, his heart racing, his penis straining in his pants. He wasn't used to this sort of behavior. He wasn't sure what to do next. He wanted to shout to Joe, tell him to stop where he was, not to leave, not to trust the agreement. He wanted to leap onto Joe's back, hold him around the shoulders and dig his teeth into the taller man's neck, kiss him, give him a hickey, brand him as his own. He stayed standing where he was and watched Joe open the door.

"See ya," he shouted but Joe never replied.

—✦✕✦—

Three nights later Billy took the long walk to the diner. He had been thinking about Joe almost every waking minute since the man walked out of his door. He had two important new projects to design, but the pencil in his hand distracted him from its use. The lights over his desk shone too brightly on the paper and the paper itself developed a texture not unlike the taut, warm skin of the man Billy was thinking about. Colors reminded him of Joe Ryan. The blues and greens he worked with were the color of Joe's eyes, the yellows and the reds and the browns were as complex as the mixed hues of his hair. Tans and beiges seemed to be the exact same colors as Joe's skin and the green he selected for one couch and chairs was the green of the tall man's shirt.

The counter was empty when Billy entered the diner. He sat down, smiled at the waitress and nodded without saying anything. She called in his usual order. He was tempted to ask her if she had seen Joe in the past several days, but he restrained himself. Instead, when Andrea brought him his pancakes and syrup he started up an innocuous conversation.

"Empty tonight, Andrea," he started. "Been like this all week?"

"Nah. You know how it goes. One guy here, one guy there. The beat cop."

"You always work this particular shift?"

"Yeah. I like it. You never work too hard, the pay's the same as days and the tips are usually a little bit better. Customers, 'specially guys, feel sorry for me, working these hours. They tip good." She gave him a charming smile through her over-reddened lips.

"Is that a hint?" he asked her, returning the smile.

"Nah. You're okay. You're regular." She took a breath, then smiled a broader smile. "Oh, hi, hon. Let me get that order in." She turned away. Billy sat still, hesitating about moving his fork full of soggy pancake toward his mouth. He waited.

Joe sat down next to him, his strong, firm, muscled left leg brushing Billy's right leg as he sat. He didn't speak. He looked straight ahead, ignoring Billy visibly while pressing his knee up against Billy's own knee.

"Hello," Billy said quietly. He didn't look over at Joe.

"Oh, hi there," Joe said.

"I've seen you here before," Billy said a little bit louder, for Andrea's benefit, if not for his own. "Just a few days ago, the last time."

"Oh, yeah, sure. How are you?" His knee was slipping up and down Billy's leg and Billy was feeling the result between his legs of this not-so-subtle stimulation.

"Fine, thanks. How are you doing?"

"I'm okay."

"And how's Sandy?" Billy asked.

Joe turned to look at him. "You remembered about her name."

"I remembered everything," Billy said, still not looking directly at Joe, but only at his dim reflection in the pie cabinet.

"Yeah. Me, too." He moved his leg away from Billy. Billy waited a moment, then moved his leg over into the vicinity of Joe's stool, connected with his leg and hooked his foot around Joe's. Joe gave a slight sigh and Billy was sure that his action had gotten the same sort of reaction out of Joe that Joe had produced in him.

"I was hoping to see you down here," Joe said a little bit breathlessly.

"I was, too."

"So…here we are."

Andrea brought over Joe's eggs-over-easy and poured him some strong coffee. "Jeez, Joey, three nights in a row you're in such a hurry you don't even change out of your uniform before you come in. You know you keep out some of my regulars when you do that." Andrea flashed her lipstick-highlighted smile once again.

"Can't be helped, Andrea," Joe responded. "Can't be helped."

Billy turned to look at Joe, confused by the light banter between him and the waitress. He blinked twice before he spoke.

"You're a cop?" he said.

"You're perceptive," Joe replied.

"I don't get it," Billy said.

"I'm a cop. That's it."

"Am I arrested?"

"Do you want to be?"

"No."

"Then, you're not."

They returned to their plates and ate in silence until they were both finished. Billy picked up his check and went to pay Andrea. He heard

Joe right behind him. Andrea rang Billy out in the cash register, handed him his change and winked at him.

"Don't forget about the tip, honey," she said.

"No, I won't." He shook his head to clear it. He walked back to his stool and left some money on the counter near his plate. He looked at Joe's place and saw that he had already left his tip. He heard the cash register ring again and then he heard Joe and Andrea laughing. He turned to look at them.

She was standing on tiptoe, giving Joe a kiss on the cheek and he was bending into it.

Then she reached up and, with her thumb, removed a touch of her lipstick that had lingered after the kiss was through.

Billy moved to the diner's entry and found that Joe was there at the same moment. They both called out a good night to Andrea who acknowledged them and together they walked out into the night.

A few feet away from the diner's door, and in the shadow of the building itself, Billy turned to Joe.

"You're a goddamn cop and you didn't tell me," he said, nearly whispering it but not doing it right. It came out as a raspy, angry sound from the middle of his throat.

"What was I supposed to do, Billy? Handcuff you in bed?"

"No. Just be a little bit honest about who you are. That would have been nice."

"Would you have invited me home? I don't think so. Would you have slept with me? I doubt it."

"You're right, Joe. I wouldn't have done that. I wouldn't have put myself in that position."

"Then really how could you expect me to be that honest with you? I was honest about everything else I said to you. Everything."

"But you're a cop!" Billy said again, louder this time.

"And you're a fag. Right. Those two things never go together, do they?"

"Were you out to entrap me? Was that it?"

"Did I do that? Did I take advantage of you and then arrest you?"

"No. But maybe you reported me and my name and address are

now in some goddamn police blotter somewhere, waiting for the big day when you or someone else on the force needs to make an arrest to keep up appearances."

"Do you really think I'd do something like that?"

"I don't know. Jesus, you're a cop!"

"I'm the same man you made love with four days ago. Get over this."

"I came here to find you, because I can't stop thinking about you, Joe. Now I'll probably dream about you for the rest of my life, whenever the nightmares set in."

"Oh, that's nice, Billy. That's really nice."

"So, what are you? What rank? What's your job?"

"I'm about to make Lieutenant and leave the streets behind me."

"You're a vice cop?"

"I have been. Prostitution is big down here, you know."

"Yeah, I know." Billy smiled at a strange concept that him suddenly. "Would you have arrested me if I asked for money for the sex we had?"

"That is my job," he replied.

"But would you have done that to me?"

Joe didn't respond at first. "No. I wouldn't."

"Why not?"

"I think I would have tried to reform you, first."

"Why?"

"Billy, I…" Joe stopped mid-thought.

"What? What were going to say?"

Joe took Billy by the upper arm his hand firmly, but without undue pressure, ensuring that Billy moved the way he wanted him to move. They walked to the corner.

"Go home, Billy. I can't do this with you. I can't play this cat-and-mouse game of 'what if?' with you. I can't."

"I don't want to go home. I want to know what you would do."

"What I would do, right now, is kiss you until you're too weak to resist me."

"You're in uniform."

"I don't care." He shoved Billy gently against the wall of the building and stepped forward to kiss him. Billy never hesitated, but threw his arms around Joe's neck, pulling him forward and down. Their bodies melded into one another and they kissed until Billy was, actually, too weak to resist Joe's advances.

"I want to make love to you all night and all day," Billy said when their lips finally disengaged.

"Me, too."

"And then, I don't care if you do arrest me."

"I won't." Joe grinned a broad, open-mouthed grin. "But I might handcuff you for the fun of it."

"Okay," Billy said.

The city's night lights rusted into dawn. The early light woke Billy and Joe from an almost non-existent sleep. They lay there, naked, each of them running fingertips over the other one's torso, waist and hips. They stared into each other's eyes and could see the smiles on their own lips reflected in the colorful early sunlight.

"We need to discuss some things," Billy said.

"Yes, indeed, we do," Joe replied. "Yes, we do."

8

"Hi-Ho, Hi-ho, It's to Gyeongju I go," She sang over the phone to Billy.

"Already?"

"Yes, dear one, it's time."

They hadn't seen one another for a while. Billy was nervous about introducing Feyhe and Joe. He had thought about her reactions to his new friend and decided that none of them was ready for the confrontation that would inevitably follow. Billy and Feyhe had actually discussed his love life one night about four months after her first trip to Korea. They had been sitting in her living room, her bare feet tucked up, as usual, under her, a martini in one hand, her inevitable cigarette in the other.

She had stopped misbehaving, as he thought of her strange ways. She had become her old self once again and he was happier to be with her, most of the time. Except, of course, for times like this one when she took on the dual roles of friend and surrogate parent.

"You need a special friend, Billy," she started. "You need someone to hold onto in the wee, small hours of the morning."

"I do all right, Feyhe. I like being alone."

"That's a sin, liking being alone. We're not made to be alone, you know."

"You are."

She took a long drag on her cigarette, letting the smoke fill her lungs and then releasing it slowly, talking through the escaping smoke.

"I'm not like you, Billy. I've been married. I've had lovers. Alone isn't really alone any longer for me. It's an old friend, a state of being that I cherish for myself."

"Well, it's like that for me too, Feyhe."

"You're just a boy. You need to exist, not just for yourself, but for someone else."

"That's a silly, feminine, romantic notion, Cousin."

"Don't ever call me that," Feyhe said, glowering at him through the diminishing haze of the smoke.

"Call you what? Feminine?"

"No. Cousin. Either I'm your friend and colleague or I'm some nutty old relative. I'd rather be the former, thank you."

"Why not both?" He asked the question and waited, somewhat impatiently, for an answer.

She stared at him without speaking.

"Why not?" he asked again.

"I simply cannot do the honors, Billy. If I'm a relative, I'm torn in my duties to you and to your mother. If I'm your friend, then I'm *your* friend."

"I see."

"So, as a friend, your friend, I tell you, find yourself a man!" She chuckled, took a sip of her drink and a puff on her cigarette. "And don't wait, youngster. You're starting to lose your hair, you know."

Now another two months had passed and Billy had found a man, after all. He and Joe had been spending more and more time together, and he was finding it hard to spend time apart from the policeman who had become his secret lover. He had met Joe's mother and his daughter, spent a day with them both at the Central Park Zoo, had lunch, fed the seals. It had been an easy time for him, with no strain, no fuss. Joe had been pleased to see his family respond so easily to his friend and was delighted with the ways in which Billy had ingratiated himself to the women in his life.

He had pressed Billy about meeting Feyhe, and Billy had found a number of excuses to prevent such a meeting. But now, with the news of her imminent departure to Korea, it seemed like the right thing to do. He was less concerned about her behavior. She had calmed down, had not been so excitable, so exhaustingly inconsistent. She had clearly gotten over her fatigue and over the strain of her odd sexual escapade in Gyeongju. He thought he'd ask her to dinner and introduce her to Joe at the same time.

"Dinner? Here? Thursday?" he said to her on the phone.

"Very nice, Billy, an invitation from the heart, obviously. So sweetly and sincerely stated." There was an edge to her voice which bothered him.

"I'm sorry, Feyhe, let me start again. Darling, would you please come to my place for dinner on Thursday? It would please me so much to have you here, in my humble dwelling for a simple repast."

"Don't get snotty with me, kiddo," she said, that edge still evident, but then she laughed. "Seven-thirty sound about right?"

"That would work for me," he said. They left one another with assurances that the evening would be special. He sat still for a moment, the sound of Feyhe's voice still in his ear. There had been something there, something unsettling, but it was fading even as he thought about it, tried to pin it down. Billy waited a full minute before he picked up the phone again and made two more calls.

"Beef Wellington. Garlic Mashed Potatoes. New Peas. Caesar Salad. Cherries Jubilee." Billy announced the menu to his guests from the door to his kitchen. No one spoke. "Don't all speak at once, please."

"It sounds delicious, dear," Miriam said sweetly. No one else chimed in, so Billy took a giant step forward. "You didn't say, May I? darling." Miriam added.

"Was I that obvious?" he asked.

"Aren't you always?" Feyhe said coldly.

She had not been pleased to find other people at Billy's apartment when she arrived. She had given Miriam a cold greeting when she spotted her cousin across the living room. Miriam had been effusive. She rarely saw Feyhe any longer, now that her cousin and her son had become such close friends. She was genuinely delighted to be in the same room with Feyhe, but Feyhe was not as gleeful as Miriam.

Feyhe was even less pleased when Billy introduced her to Joe Ryan. To Billy's surprise, after that conversation the cousins had had about "a man," Feyhe was harshly critical of Billy's choice of a companion. She had been visibly appraising the man, taking in his height and physical stature, his looks, his clothing, with a highly cynical expression. She sat across the room from him, using Billy's work stool as her personal perch for the evening. She held the martini glass that Billy had given her between her thumb and her forefinger, the rest of her hand clenched in a mini-fist. She kept her eyes trained on Joe, as if she expected him to pounce on her if given half a chance at surprise.

Conversation among the guests had been strained and nearly non-existent.

"I understand you're working on a large project for the Korean government," Joe had said, properly coached by Billy the night before.

"Yes." Feyhe's reply was clipped and dry.

"She's a wonderful sculptor, a real artist," Miriam added.

"Um hum," Feyhe said, barely responding at all.

"Billy said that this was based on an ancient historical legend about a Korean Prince and a massacre of his entire court," Joe went on.

"Yes," came her response.

"I'd love to see your sketches," he said.

"Did you bring any with you, Feyhe?" Miriam asked.

"No," she said. "Where's your husband?"

"Oh, Angus has Canasta on Thursdays. He never misses it."

"I didn't know any men played Canasta, Mrs. Duncan," Joe blurted out, not meaning to be cruel, but not finding himself able to say anything else. "I mean, I don't know any men who play Canasta."

"Neither does she," Feyhe said gesturing to Miriam. Then she laughed.

"I didn't mean anything by that," Joe said, stung by Feyhe's peculiar vehemence.

"Pity," Feyhe said. "I almost liked you then."

Billy, listening to all of this from his kitchen, was regretting the invitations. He'd been looking for a sense of security, people who might make one another a bit more comfortable through the awkward moments. Instead he had produced a room full of discord and an almost Universal Pictures-like horror film in the making.

"I'll be right out," he called from the kitchen. No one asked him to hurry, or not to hurry.

No one responded at all.

The three guests sat stony faced and silent as he announced the menu, and Miriam's light banter about his movements did nothing to lighten the night. Billy passed a tray of canapes, took a seat on the window sill and cleared his throat.

"I suppose you're all wondering why you're here," he said. "I wanted to have a little dinner party for Feyhe. She's heading back to Korea in a few days, and I thought it would be nice if you," and he gestured toward Miriam, "had a little time with her. I also wanted you both to meet Joe."

Both women turned to look at Joe, sitting on the right-hand side of the couch. Miriam was at its opposite extreme.

"Joe and I, well, we've been seeing a lot of one another lately. I'd have to call him my dearest friend, right now."

"Being a bit coy, aren't we?" Feyhe said with a slide in her voice.

"No. I don't think so."

"Are you two fucking?" Feyhe said, her right eyebrow rising as high on her face as an eyebrow might. Miriam swallowed something, coughed and turned away.

In the quiet that followed Joe spoke. "Nightly," he said. Miriam coughed, choked, coughed again. Feyhe laughed.

"We're trying out a relationship," Billy said. "I'd better check on the beef." He got up and went quickly back into the kitchen leaving the room in total silence. He could hear the quiet, the uneasiness he'd left behind. He could hear the steady, measured breathing that he knew was Joe. He could hear the metallic clink of Feyhe's teeth as she sucked in breath and let it out again. He couldn't detect a sound from his mother.

"If you three would like to talk, feel free," he shouted out in their direction. "Just pretend I'm not here."

"I don't understand this, Billy," Miriam called back. "What are we supposed to do now?" Billy sighed and was about to speak when he heard Joe chiming in.

"I think Billy would just like us all to get to know one another a little bit."

"That would be nice, I suppose," Miriam said.

"Billy has spent some time with my mother and my daughter," Joe said, "and they all got—"

"Your daughter?" Billy heard Feyhe say with a particularly familiar snicker in her voice.

"Yes. I have a child. Her mother and I are divorced and the girl lives with me."

"I suppose your wife left you because you're a fag?" Feyhe said.

"Oh, my," Miriam muttered just loud enough to be heard.

"Actually, no." Joe remained calm and Billy was impressed. "She just wasn't a very happy person. She didn't like my work or my devotion to it. She thought I should devote myself to her, I guess. And she hated being a mother, too."

"I can't imagine that," Miriam said.

"I can." Feyhe's voice had softened a bit but even at a distance Billy could hear the slight edge that remained.

"What is your work, Joe?" Miriam asked.

"I'm in law enforcement," Joe replied.

"Oh, an attorney! How nice."

"No, no. Don't let me give the wrong impression. I'm a cop."

There was a short burst of complete silence which was broken almost immediately by Feyhe's hysterical laughter.

"Don't tell me," she shouted through her hysteria, "that you're on the vice squad. That would really get me going." She laughed a bit more.

"I am in vice," Joe finally said as Feyhe's laughter subsided. She burst out again and everyone waited for her to stop.

Then Feyhe called out, "Billy, congratulations. I didn't think it could be done, but you've gone me one better. A vice cop, for God's sake."

"Dinner's ready," Billy said, coming back into the doorway. He surveyed the room, taking in everyone. Miriam had been blushing and her face was still a bright crimson. Joe looked uncomfortable and Feyhe seemed to be the only one in a party mood. Suddenly. "Come and get it," Billy said, placing the Wellington in the center of the table.

"Now that's what I should have said," Feyhe announced as she hopped off the stool and headed for the table.

With the exception of Feyhe's insistence upon smoking while she ate, much to Miriam's annoyance, the rest of the evening went smoothly. Occasionally Feyhe would burst into laughter when she looked over at Joe Ryan. This discomfited Billy enough to cause him to rise from the table and leave the room on one pretext or another, usually looking for a dish to bring to the table or clearing Feyhe's ashtray.

Joe seemed to take it all in stride with an ease that delighted Billy. Miriam was clearly uncomfortable with the entire situation and she ate quietly, bird-like, not saying much, not looking at anyone. Feyhe was herself, smoking, laughing, making jokes. Billy was finally able to relax into the evening and, after coffee, they all moved back into the living room and settled back into their former places. Billy sat between Miriam and Joe, a little bit closer to Joe than to his mother.

"I'll be gone for three months this time, Billy," Feyhe said. "I won't come back until the installation is complete and the opening of the grotto has taken place."

"You'll write and tell me how its going, I hope," he said to her.

"I will if I can," she said, refusing to commit.

"You will, period," Billy said a bit too loudly. Joe pressed an impatient hand against his leg. "Please," Billy added.

"Three months is a long time, Feyhe," Miriam commented.

"There's a lot to do, Miriam. Each panel has to be completed in the studio and then the installation has to take place with time spent making sure that the match-up works. Once the whole piece is fitted together and I'm satisfied that it looks the way I intended, there's still final work to be done on the figures. Then, when I finish all of that, I have to supervise the lighting of the work and the flow of the water. I think we may have to divert some of the brook around the central female figure."

"A sculptor's work is never done," Billy said. Feyhe shot him a quick, harsh glance. "That's sexist psychobabble, Billy," she snapped.

He visibly bristled. "I didn't mean it to be that."

"Well, it was."

"Doesn't sound like you're going to have too much time for fun," Joe added to the conversation.

"Fun? Officer Ryan, fun has nothing to do with this trip."

"He's not Officer Ryan, Feyhe," Billy quickly responded, trying to keep the chatter playful. "He's Lieutenant Ryan, please."

Feyhe's eyes played over Joe's outstretched form, his long legs crossed at the ankles, his right arm hanging over the edge of the couch's thickly upholstered arm.

"Lieutenant," she said appreciatively. "All right, then, I'm impressed." He gave her a quick, small salute and flashed his best smile at her.

"As a matter of fact, Lieutenant Ryan, I am attending the wedding of friends while I'm there. That will be my chief source of fun."

"Who's getting married, Feyhe?" Billy asked.

"Kim."

"Oh, of course. I'd forgotten that he's engaged. You did tell me that."

Miriam gave her son an odd look, then settled back into her corner of the couch. "Who's this Kim?" she asked.

"He was my guide the first time," Feyhe said. "The government appointed him to chaperone me. He did a lovely job." She smiled strangely and Billy knew why.

"And he's invited you to his wedding?" Miriam asked.

"I met his fiancé, Miriam, a beautiful and intelligent young woman. She made me tea in my hotel room. They both invited me."

"Ni Na is her name," Billy added. Miriam nodded as though she already knew that, but it was actually new information for her.

"I have to bring them a gift, Billy. I don't know what it will be yet."

Billy bit his tongue. He wanted to suggest something lewd but knew he couldn't with his mother sitting there, and probably not even in front of Joe.

"I thought about framing some of my sketches of Kim as a present. What do you think about that?" Feyhe asked him.

"They are handsome drawings, Feyhe."

"I'd redo them, of course, ink on good vellum and make a composite. I think he'd like that. I think Ni Na would also."

"I'm sure."

"Yes, that's what I might do..." she said, almost to herself. Then she chuckled.

The evening wound down from that point and Miriam was the first to leave. She clearly felt a bit awkward with Joe, shaking his hand, moving to kiss him, changing her mind in mid-movement. She hastily bid Feyhe a good night and patted Billy on the cheek. That left the three of them. Billy expected Feyhe to say something trenchant and, like the good artist she was, she didn't disappoint him.

"Good night, you two," she said. "I'd ask you to escort me home, Lieutenant Ryan, but I suspect that would take too much time for your satisfaction. So I'll just mosey on home by myself."

"Good night, Feyhe," Billy said, kissing her on the hand she offered him. "We'll talk tomorrow."

"Will we?" she said coyly.

"Will we." A flat statement.

She turned and moved out the door. Billy and Joe walked to the doorway to watch her descend the first flight of stairs.

"Stop watching me, you two," she called out to them. "I'm neither helpless nor nosy. Just get to the fucking."

With that she was gone, a trail of gray smoke wafting upward, the signal that she had lit up one for the road.

Inside his apartment Billy let himself hang for a moment, limply over the back of the couch.

"Thank God that's over with," he said. Joe laughed. "Are you laughing at me?"

"I am. That was so strange."

"It was my own fault. I should have warned them both about you before they got here. I wasn't sure how to do that."

"You mean I was a total surprise?"

"I do."

"Well, that explains a lot, Billy. Now I don't feel quite so bad about myself. I thought I was just screwing up somehow."

"No, Joe, it was me screwing it up."

"Well, we'll do better next time, won't we?"

"Yes, sir."

"And now, the question of questions." He looked very serious, and Billy, in reaction, felt his brow squeezing into that look that Joe disliked. "Dishes or sex?"

"What's wrong with dishes, and then sex?" he asked the policeman.

Feyhe called the next morning. Billy was in the shower and, hesitantly but with a certain sense of self-assurance, Joe answered the phone.

"Billy Does Interiors," he said in as characterless a voice as possible.

"I think he should change that to Billy Does the Department," Feyhe said with a chuckle. "Billy doesn't," Joe said. "Good morning, Feyhe."

"Where is he?"

"In the shower. If you hold on, I'll tell him you're on the line.'

"No. Don't. It's you I want to talk to anyway." She sounded definitive, strong and not unfriendly. Joe relaxed a little, but kept his guard up, deciding automatically that he would not say much, would not reveal much, no matter how persuasive the woman might be.

"What about?" he asked simply.

"You. I want to know about you."

"Why? What would make a difference for you?"

"I don't know. That's why I think we should talk."

Billy called out through the slightly open door to his rustic, early American bathroom, "Who's on the phone, Joe?"

Joe put his hand over the mouthpiece of the receiver as though he was protecting the person at the other end of the connection. "It's for me, Billy. It's private. Shut the door, please."

Billy did as he was asked, and Joe went back to the conversation.

"Well, you're good at keeping mum about things, anyway. That's a good sign," Feyhe said.

"It's part of what I do," Joe replied.

"I want you to take me to lunch today. Can you arrange that?"

"I'm sure I can. When and where?"

"One o'clock, sharp, please. And let's meet at the Brasserie. Do you know where that is?"

"On East 53rd?" Silence.

"I do."

"You are full of surprises, Lieutenant. I'll make the reservation in your name and meet you there." She hung up the phone and after a brief pause during which Joe whistled a long, strained single note, so did he.

Billy came out of the bathroom, still damp but drying, a moment later. "So who was that and how did they get this number?"

"I left it for my mother, in case she needed me, you know, for Sandy."

"So what's the problem?"

"No problem. Just a question. Money for a school project." He hated lying to Billy, knew he could do it far too easily. "Nothing to concern yourself about."

"I should get dressed, Joe, and so should you. Work calls."

"Not here," Joe said, not really listening to Billy.

"Excuse me?"

"Oh, nothing. Sorry. I was thinking about last night."

"All of it? Or just the part where we thrilled one another?"

"All of it. Your mother was a bit overcome by me, I think."

"She'll get over it. She gets over most things."

"And your cousin was a different world, entirely."

"I know. She always is. She'll get used to you, too, you'll see."

"I hope it happens soon."

"Hey, she's going overseas again for three months. By the time she gets back we should know where we stand, I hope." He brought Joe a cup of coffee and after Joe had it in his grasp, clinked it with his own cup. They both drank deeply.

"I needed that. Thanks." Joe said, giving Billy a broad open smile.
"The coffee?"

"The reassurance, Billy." He paused a moment. "And the coffee, too, of course."

Feyhe was already waiting on the tiny balcony entry to The Brasserie when Joe arrived. He quickly checked his watch. He was five minutes early. He smiled at her and gave her a quick, half-wave. She smiled back, then frowned at him.

"I'm not late, am I?" he asked her.

"No. You're just about on time." She signaled the headwaiter, pointing at Joe and then at a particular table, just inside the archway, up three steps from the main dining room. The maitre d' nodded slightly, gestured them in and led them to the very table Feyhe had indicated.

When they were seated, the massive menus in their hands, Joe spoke.

"That was well done, Feyhe," he said. "He knew exactly what you wanted."

"He did," she agreed. "He knows his place and his job and how to do it."

"What are you saying?"

"You know what I'm saying, Lieutenant Ryan." She picked up her menu and he couldn't see her face.

They studied their menus in silence. It didn't take either of them very long to make a selection from the vast choices. The restaurant was known for certain foods. Both Joe and Feyhe had been there before, so their choices were obvious ones.

Feyhe ordered the onion soup and the lox platter. Joe asked for the triple cheese omelet and the roast beef hash. When they were done with their waiter, they turned their attention back to one another.

"I don't know if I like you yet," Feyhe said quietly. "I want to like you. I know that would be important to Billy if he really, really wants this relationship to succeed."

"I think he does. It was hard for him to commit to it at all, you know," Joe said.

"I can believe that. We've talked often enough about his bizarre desire for the single life."

"That's not what he wants, Feyhe."

"I never thought it was." She sipped some water from the large tumbler the waiter had left for her, then she held the glass up in front of her face while she spoke. Again Joe had no sight-line with her eyes. "He's very young in a lot of ways. I was never that young. Do you believe that?"

"I do."

"He hasn't seen a lot of happiness in his life," Feyhe continued as she put down her glass. "You've met the mother. The father is a stick with a sense of humor, but not much of an emotional base. He likes his son, but love doesn't really enter his equation."

"I thought Miriam was a pleasant woman." Joe looked directly into Fayhe's eyes as he spoke. There was something there, but he couldn't quite grasp it.

"Billy took you both by surprise, I'm afraid, presenting me the way he did."

"That's proof of what I'm saying, Lieutenant. He has never seen the gracious side of a relationship so he has no way of knowing how to make it happen."

"Call me Joe, please." He gave her a cozy smile, not the big grin he had given Billy.

She did not respond to the smile or the suggestion.

"You may not believe me, but Billy is my friend," she said. "I will stand by him in his choices, no matter my feelings about them. I won't stand by, however, and see him abused in any way. He is not to be taken advantage of. That is not why he was created."

"I wouldn't—"

"Billy is an artist, Lieutenant. Artists are sensitive creatures. I am an artist. I know." Her voice was getting louder and higher-pitched; there was a fire behind her eyes now and they shimmered with an interior light. "We are changeable, cat-like beings, with emotional swings that we cannot account for, nor should we be made to do so. You may find yourself on the downside of an emotional pass one day with Billy. What will you do? How will you defend yourself and still defend him? You may enjoy his elations, but can you suffer his depressions? These are things you need to consider. You have a child. How will she react to his part in your life and to your part in his?"

"I've thought about a lot of this, Feyhe," Joe said calmly and quietly. "I think I'm capable of understanding a problem and dealing with it accordingly."

Feyhe picked up her water, downed a large gulp of it and returned the glass precisely to its water-marked spot on the table cloth.

"Why did your wife leave you? Devotion to your work, you said?"

"That's right." He felt himself tightening as the conversation took itself into his own life, rather than hers or Billy's.

"I don't believe you." Her voice darkened and so did the glow in her eyes. "I don't think you're being honest about it."

"It's what I know," he said.

"I think you're deluding yourself, Lieutenant."

"Please call me Joe," he said again, a bit more brusquely this time.

"I think you're not facing the truth about your marriage or your choice of a mate. I worry that one wrong choice, made too hastily perhaps, might be echoed in your second choice, in Billy."

"I don't act in haste, Feyhe," Joe said, indignation arriving in his tone.

"Don't you? You keep asking me to address you by your first name, as though we were friends already. We're not friends yet, Lieutenant Ryan. We may never be friends. When we are I will call you Joe."

"When do you think that might happen?"

"I have no idea."

The waiter brought Feyhe her soup and a small salad for Joe. They ate their starters in silence. Joe finished first and spent the time between swallowing his last tomato vinaigrette covered lettuce leaf and Feyhe's final spoonful of soup examining her, judging her, sizing her up as he would a suspect in a case he was investigating. He knew he had a face that did "impassive" well. He could observe without being obvious about it. He employed all of his talents in the short time allotted him and, by the time she put her spoon down and dabbed at her lips with her napkin, he thought he had assembled a pretty accurate picture of the woman.

The fire in her eyes had been unmistakable. The fervor and the speed of her speech had borne out what he already suspected. And then, the sudden quiet, the darkness, the implied threats, keyed into his prognosis of the situation.

"Thank you for your patience, Lieutenant," she said.

"Not at all, Ma'am," he replied, bringing the slightly more clinical and formal style of addressing her into their chat.

She caught him in the act and addressed it herself. "Of what do you suspect me, Lieutenant?"

"Ma'am?"

"Exactly. You've been calling me Feyhe, as though you had a right to do so, ever since you met me. Now it's Ma'am. You've changed your tune, it would appear."

"I'm just placing myself at the same reserved distance that you seem to consider appropriate. The intimacies that your cousin assumed would be ours are not, so I am respecting that."

"You're a very funny man, Lieutenant."

"I want you to understand something, Ma'am. When I met your nephew I had no intention of seducing him, entrapping him, or anything else. Unfortunately he proved to be a highly engaging human being. I found myself drawn toward him, undeniably drawn, by some force of nature I do not claim to comprehend. I don't think he does either. And, before you say a word on this subject, I don't believe you do."

"All right." She gave him a half-smile, then turned her face away as if alarmed by her own, highly visible, reaction.

"We spent the night together and the morning too. Nothing about him was identifiable as the one thing that attracted me irresistibly. I made an offer and he turned it down. That could have been the end of it. That might have been the end of it, except that he came looking for me. He wanted to see me."

"Did you want to see him as well?"

"It was all I wanted, Ma'am. I waited for him for three nights and for three nights he managed to not come after me. I wanted to call him up, tell him not to come, tell him about myself, everything about myself, but I had said I would not pursue him and I didn't. I made that promise, Ma'am, and being a man of my word, I honored that promise. I didn't pursue him."

"What was it you wanted to tell him, Lieutenant Ryan?"

"I wanted to tell him who, and what, I was…am. I had told him about my daughter and my broken marriage. I had told him about my feelings, but I hadn't told him what I am. I wanted him to know it."

"Why was that so important? That one thing."

"It makes a big difference, Ma'am, in how people see you. Once people know what I do for a living, they see me as someone different from the person they thought they knew. It was the most important secret I kept from Billy."

"And how did he react when you told him?"

"I never told him. I showed him."

She stared at him for a moment, her eyes widening with an understanding that she thought she had discovered. "You arrested him?"

He started to reply, but instead broke into laughter. "No, no, no. Of course not. I just wore my uniform when he came to find me. I wore it on purpose. I wanted him to see for himself." He laughed again.

Feyhe smiled again, but this time she didn't turn from him.

"And was he as amused as you seem to be, Lieutenant?"

"No, No." He tried to contain his merriment, and it was hard to do. Through the gurgles that escaped his throat he related Billy's reaction to the news.

"I see. He reacted the way I would have, I'm afraid. He and I are so very much alike, in so many ways, Lieutenant."

"You are alike, Ma'am," Joe said, no laughter in his words this time. He was seeing, actually, how much alike the two cousins could be. They were both analytical rather then emotional, both creative minds that thought in leaps. "Perhaps that was why I felt comfortable using your first name right away."

"And perhaps, Joe, it was why I was not as comfortable as you seem to have been."

"The truth is, Ma'am, Billy is as drawn to you as he is to me. I don't like that. I want him to be drawn to me more. I'll always have a problem with this. But I promise you I'll deal with it. I'll never interfere with something that works as well as your friendship." He gave her his most confident smile.

"I'll never make him choose between us, Joe," Feyhe said. "I won't have to. I have plans."

"And do they include any more of the drugs you take?" he asked her.

"I don't know what you mean, Lieutenant." She shot him a look that started grim, then turned airier. "Let's just say, plans, and leave it at that for now."

The waiter brought their main courses and they set in to eating them. Joe had been aware of Feyhe's gentle, if temporary, alteration into the use of his first name, and he never enlightened her, although, by the end of the meal, he had dropped the "ma'am" and reverted to her name again. They had both laughed through their coffee, sharing tales of small horrors they had witnessed in the city.

As they finished their meal and prepared to split the check, Feyhe addressed him one more time on the question of Billy's divided loyalty.

"What if, Joe, the boy decided to devote himself to me, what then?"

"And why would he do that?"

"Who knows. Kindred souls or something. Theoretically, what if he did?"

"I'd deal with it, I suppose, as it happened."

"Not the answer I want."

"Well, you never answered my last question, Feyhe, so why should I answer yours."

From her unsure gaze he knew that she didn't recall a question left unanswered. He smiled, feeling he had the upper hand.

"Do your plans include any more of the drugs you take?" he asked her again.

"I don't know what you mean?"

"You're probably not taking them now. You're in one of the high places on the chart, I'm sure. You seem to be so much in control of everything around you."

"Lieutenant—"

"Let me finish. And don't be afraid. I'm not going to discuss this with anyone, least of all Billy, especially if he's not aware of it."

"I don't—"

"Yes, you do, Feyhe. Lithium, I suppose?"

"Lithium." She faltered, averted her eyes.

"What...eight or ten milligrams?"

"I'm not about to answer such inane and insulting questions."

She rose from the table and knocked over her chair which collided with one a few feet behind her. A waiter quickly retrieved it, almost as though he'd been waiting for such an incident to occur.

Joe stood up and tossed his napkin down on his empty plate.

"I won't let you hurt him," they both said, almost at the same time. Joe broke into an instantaneous smile, unable to stop himself. Feyhe, after a slight hesitation, did the same.

"I'm glad we understand one another," she said.

"So am I." He took her hand and led her around the table toward the restaurant's doorway.

At the entry, before the revolving door, he stopped her for a moment. "Thanks for the call. I'm glad we did this."

She looked him over, standing there in front of her, confident, strong, manly. "I'm glad we did it also," she said. "And I won't forget... any of it."

"Have a safe trip," he added. "Come back to us well and happy and with all in control." He smiled, thought about giving her quick kiss, then changed his mind.

"Lieutenant Joey, you're a treasure."

She turned from him, entered the revolving door, and before he could meander through it, she was gone, down the street and around the corner.

The competition had ended in a dead heat.

9

Feyhe stood up, alone, in front of the long, oak table behind which six men sat. None of them looked at her, addressing her through an interpreter and referring, both physically and vocally, only to him. She, on the other hand, spoke directly to her questioners.

"Why do you address this legend in this way?" came the next question.

"I believe, gentlemen, that it was this woman, the concubine, who saved the day. For me she is the central figure in the panel, the central figure in the story. When the king, her lover, her lord and master, was killed so violently she had few options. One of them was the seduction and slaying of her lover's killer. She avenged his death with that of his murderer, then in remorse for having betrayed her king with her body, she destroyed herself as a final act of loyalty." Feyhe spoke her formal speech with care, allowing the interpreter to break in with a gesture as he translated each section to perfection for his listeners.

The board had convened to investigate the American woman's work for their government. She had been in Gyeongju for only a few days when the letter had reached her, conveyed by a representative from the American Consul. She had read the piece and panicked.

Dear Mrs. Baumann, you must appear on Thursday before the Cultural Commission of Gyeongju to defend the work you would install at Poseokjeongji. It is our understanding that under the terms of our agreement none of the historic places shall be altered beyond their current recognition, it read. *It has come to light that your plan will alter the stream which has not fed the bower for many long years. There is also the granite bower of concern. Please be prepared to answer many questions and demonstrate the understanding of our intent.*

It had been signed by Park Li-Wang, Commissioner of Culture for Gyôngsangbuk-do. Feyhe telephoned the University and left an urgent message for Kim Do-Mun. He phoned her within minutes.

"Kim, it's so good to hear your voice," she started. "I need your advice at once. Can we meet?"

"It is difficult," he said quietly. "Many things are changing in Korea now. I am not to work as a guide for the future."

"I don't need a guide, Kim, I need a friend and an advisor."

"I shall always be your friend, Feyhe," he said in a more reassuring manner.

She read him the letter from Park Li-Wang and listened to him draw in his breath in a long, single half-gasp.

"Is it bad, do you think?" she asked him.

"It is bad." He was silent; she waited in equal silence. "There is a new fear of influence from America, from the United Nations. It is believed that we are too dependent upon your country for our present and our future. Our President, General Park Chung-Hee, is very much on the watch for trouble from within the government. Much has changed since you were here."

"What should I do, Kim?" He could hear the angst in her voice, and being unaccustomed to it, was unsure how to speak to it.

"You shall wait, Feyhe," he said. "Then you shall go to this gathering and tell them plainly and honestly what you intend. That is all you can do."

"I need a friend, Kim," she said. "I need a friend to be there with me to make sure, for me, that my words are given their proper weight and meaning."

"I can send someone, if you like," Kim said.

"No! I want you there with me. I know you and I trust you."

"It cannot be me. I am sorry, Feyhe."

"It must be. There is no one else."

"It cannot be me. There are many reasons for this."

"Give me one, just one good one then." Her voice cracked as she spoke and she heard herself in panic. She smoothed her hair with the back of her free hand and calmed herself again.

"I am for the government, Feyhe. My work is at their disposal. If they would question you, then it is an official act of this government I serve. I cannot serve for you and for my government at the same time."

"I don't ask you to serve for me, whatever that means in your language. I ask for you to be there as my friend, to make sure that my words are translated properly. That's all."

"I cannot. I would wish to, but I cannot."

"You're afraid, Kim Do-Mun. That's what I'm hearing in your voice. It is fear."

"It is not fear. I have no fear from my government. I only fear for you."

"What am I to do? Tell me that, please."

"I will send Ni-Na to you. She will stay with you and help you at this hearing."

"Her English isn't good enough, Kim. I am a subtle woman. I need a translator who comprehends the artistic subtleties."

"There is no such one, Feyhe, in this district. Depend upon Ni-Na. She will act in your favor."

"Kim, I want you." She was more demanding, more insistent, but Kim held back, protected himself from her, grateful that this was a telephone conversation.

"I will send Ni-Na," This came across as clipped and final. "You will wait for Ni-Na, Feyhe. She will come to you tonight." He hung up, leaving her feeling more alone than she had for a long, long time.

Feyhe sat by the window of her hotel room watching the day pass away. The light that had enthralled her on her first trip seemed to be completely altered now, different, colder, unwelcoming. It had changed, just as the official attitude toward her had changed during the six months she had been away.

She glanced around the room filled with crates and boxes containing sections of stone that she had carved in New York and then shipped to Korea. Each one held a portion of the frieze, the large sculpture that she had labored over for hours, days, months. Each one symbolized a tear, a sob, an act of love, each one felt by Feyhe as she worked. Now the boxes and crates appeared gross, over-large, out-of-scale with their surroundings, with her own life.

She had depended upon the loyalty of Kim, her friend, her one-night lover, her exotic paramour. She had expected him to fall into her arms, grateful to see her again, but he had remained distant on the phone, supportive but distant. She wanted to see him, to hold him, touch him, kiss him. She wanted him to possess her again, as he had over and over in her dreams during the first months that followed her return to New York. She had let the fantasies go, she thought, let them leave her long ago. Now she knew that the absence of fantasy was a mere delusion. She had never stopped wanting him. He had stopped wanting her, however. That was obvious.

She waited. Night approached from the south of the city and she understood, suddenly, the coldness of the day's waning light. Her memory of the days before was in a season that had passed. It was another time, so another light would make its shadows felt on the spaces she recalled. Everything would change, she saw that at once. As Kim had changed, as the cultural commission had changed, as the light had changed, so she would change also.

Feyhe rose from her chair, her limbs stiff with so much sitting. She staggered into the bathroom and turned on the cold water tap. She stood there, ignoring her drawn and wan face in the mirror and listened to the flowing of the water. Then she splashed some on her face. The cold shock of it brought her upright, caught her up short and brought her home again. She would be all right, she thought, if she could remember this water and how it felt. It was how she wanted people to feel when they came to the grotto to see her work. She wanted them to reach into the stream and to splash the water on the statue of the concubine, on the face of Mary Yi who had been her inspiration for the statue, on their own faces as well to feel what the concubine had felt.

She went back into the salon of her room. She touched the boxes, the crates and the sense of what lived within the six walls of each gave her renewed strength. This was good work, important work. Her concepts would be accepted and appreciated and loved. It would all work out for the best, she knew that. This was who she was: the work. This was who she had always been. Always.

It was September, 1936 and Feyhe stood at the back of the large meeting hall just off the Grand Concourse in The Bronx. She was eighteen and she had a dream. In her dream she was with a man and he was bigger than she was and stronger than she was and still she dominated him. He looked to her for decisions. He came to her for money. He depended on her for everything. But he was bigger than she was and stronger than she was and when they made love he was always in control. That was her dream. She was eighteen and she was looking for the man in her dream.

This hall, sometimes a wedding hall, sometimes a meeting place, was being used for a Socialist Party gathering. Feyhe knew that before she went in. She was not a Socialist, but she knew a girl who was and that friend had invited her to attend the meeting. There was a man speaking there that her friend thought she would like to hear, perhaps meet. Feyhe had agreed to come to the meeting.

She stood just inside the door for a minute or more, looking through the smoke and the dimness, searching for Patricia Miller, her girlfriend. There were more people than she had expected, people smoking and talking loudly, laughing more than she thought Socialists laughed. It all seemed quite ordinary and not at all threatening. There were more men than women present, but most of the women in the room had gathered on one side, huddled together, ignoring the men. Feyhe started to move in their direction.

She hadn't gone more than ten feet when a hand suddenly grabbed her elbow, turning her around. She found herself facing a tall, blonde man with a nose too wide and a mouth slightly vicious, turned down on one side, up on the other.

"What are you doing?" she said, keeping her voice low, though wanting to shout.

"You look lost, dearie," the man said, a snide tone evident in his speech.

"I'm not. I'm meeting someone here."

"I'll help you find him, then."

"It's not a him. It's a her."

"Oooh. You a Lez?" He chuckled and she felt herself blush a little.

"Let go of my arm or you'll find out exactly what I am," she snarled at him. He dropped her arm immediately. "And as for being a Lez, whatever that is, I'm probably not."

"If you're 'probably' not," the man said in that same snide way, "then you probably are, sister." He gave her an off-hand, dismissive wave of his hand and he moved quickly off into the crowd. Feyhe felt a bit shaken, thought of leaving, then resolved not to let one crass man make her do something she had no intention of doing. She turned around and continued on to where the other women were talking.

Patricia was not among them, but there was another familiar face. Feyhe gave her a smile and her cousin Peachie returned it at once. "What are you doing here?" she asked Feyhe in a much sweeter way than her assailant had a moment before.

"I'm meeting Pat Miller," Feyhe responded and she noticed three of the other women turn and give one another a knowing look. She spoke a bit hesitantly, "Have you seen her, Peachie?"

"Not yet," Peachie replied, equally carefully and with a slight hush. "She'll be along, soon, I'm sure.'

"She wanted me to hear some guy speak tonight, she said," Feyhe confided. Then she turned to include the other women, "I'm not a Socialist myself. I just came to hear this man speak."

"We're not Socialists either, honey," said a tall tow-headed woman Feyhe guessed to be about twenty-five. "We're just here because our men are here." Then she laughed. "You got a man here, honey?"

Feyhe shook her head rapidly. Her hair, held back in a bun, jiggled from the force of her movement.

"Let's get you something to drink, dear," Peachie said. "Excuse us girls. Come on Feyhe." She led Feyhe away from the women.

"They're a bunch of pinko-stinkos," Peachie confided as soon as they were out of earshot. "Don't you pay them any mind."

"What are you doing here?" Feyhe wanted to know.

"That's nobody's business, Feyhe. I won't tell that you were here, if you don't tell on me. Okey-dokey?

"Okey-dokey."

They wandered over to the coffee-bar and Peachie poured them each a cup, added some warm milk and handed one to Feyhe.

"If my sisters knew I was here, they'd have my head," she said to Feyhe as she sipped the warm brew.

"Banana would, certainly," Feyhe agreed. "And my father would probably kill me."

They both drained their cups before speaking again. Feyhe kept looking for Patricia Miller, but the girl was not in sight.

"I'll tell you why I came, Feyhe, if you promise not to tell." Feyhe nodded her assent and Peachie continued. "I came because the man I'm seeing is a member, a card-carrying member, mind. I don't approve of it, myself, but he's such a dear. I want him to like me, Feyhe."

"I'm sure he does," she responded. "Which one is he?"

"Oh, he's over there, near the dais. He's the one with the red hair and the tiny, little moustache. It's so darling!"

Feyhe glanced over to the speaker's table and easily found the red-headed man Peachie was talking about. He was attractive, she thought, and there was something oddly familiar about him, too. She turned back to her cousin.

"What's his name? I think I know him." Peachie gave her an odd look.

"I doubt it, Feyhe. He's an intellectual."

"You mean girls don't interest him?"

"No. He's brainy, is all. He likes girls all right. He likes girls just fine."

"So, what's his name already?"

"Owen. Owen Khanzadian. Isn't that romantic?" Peachie was

practically squealing as she said his name. Feyhe smiled at her, a soft, warm, no-hint-of-what's-to-come sort of smile.

"Owen. Sure. I do know him."

Peachie looked troubled, but her voice was steady and sure. "You know him, do you? How would that be?"

"He dated Miriam once or twice, that's all. She introduced us once."

"Miriam? He went out with Cousin Miriam?"

"They went to the movies. Saw naked women. She wasn't impressed."

"Miriam. That *kurveh*."

"Miriam's all right," Feyhe said, defending her cousin whom she had no desire to defend.

"She's a loose girl, Feyhe. Mark my words, her children will make her sorry for the day she was ever born. That's retribution, Peachie-style."

Feyhe laughed. "You're funny, honey." When she finished chuckling and looked up she saw the red-haired man approaching them. Peachie saw him also and she stepped away from Feyhe, greeting Owen on the run.

"Owen, here's someone who thinks she knows you." He held out his hand to Feyhe as he approached her. She extended her hand also. Peachie was hanging on his arm.

"Of course," he said, clearly wracking his brain to discover a way to not make a fool of himself. "How've you been?"

"How've you been—who?" Peachie chortled.

"How've you been—who?" he repeated and then he laughed. Feyhe found herself liking the laugh and the man who laughed it.

"Feyhe," she whispered in a loud stage-whisper.

"Oh, sure, that's right. You're Miriam's cousin, aren't you?"

"And mine, too," Peachie added. "I didn't know you dated my cousin Miriam."

"I've probably dated all of your cousins, sweetie-lamb," he said to Peachie. "Yours as well, I guess," he added, turning to Feyhe.

"Not all of them. More than half of them are boys," Feyhe said looking up into his eyes, not taking her own away from his for a second.

"Well, you got me there, kiddo," Owen replied. "Although there are one or two boys I wouldn't mind..."

"Oh, you!" Peachie said, slapping Owen on the shoulder. "Isn't he a card, Feyhe?"

"Yeah, the Knave of Hearts," Feyhe said.

"You're the card," Owen said. "The Queen of Same."

Feyhe gave him her best smile, then spoke. "I'm not familiar with that particular suit."

Peachie broke the small silence. "Oh, isn't she the smart one, Owen. Feyhe, you're such a smartie!"

"D'you want to join us up at the head table, Feyhe? It's about time for the show to get started."

"No, thanks. I'll just hang out in the back somewhere. I may have to leave before it's over."

"Okay, suit yourself. They say he's a great speaker, though." Owen was giving her that smile again.

"I'll still stay back here, thanks."

"See ya later, honey," Peachie said, taking Owen's arm again and leading him away. Feyhe waggled her fingers at them, realizing even as she did so that they wouldn't see her do it. Their backs were toward her as they headed for the front of the hall. Then, without warning, they stopped. Owen leaned down and said something to Peachie who shrugged and kept on walking toward the table. He turned around and came back to where Feyhe was still standing.

"Can I call you?" he asked before he actually reached her side.

"Why?"

"I'd like to talk with you sometime. I think you are bright and I'd like to know you."

"You didn't seem interested when Miriam introduced us."

"You didn't seem interesting."

"Oh, thanks." She felt herself blushing again.

"You're pretty with a little color in your face."

"I'm not." But she was glad he had said it anyway.

"So, can I call you?"

"No. Sorry."

"Because of Peachie?" He looked a bit crestfallen.

"No. Because we don't have a phone." She said the words, paused for a breath and then laughed. He laughed with her.

"Can I meet you somewhere, sometime, then?"

"Sure. Take me to a movie with a naked lady."

"I will. How about Tuesday?"

Feyhe agreed to meet him downtown on Tuesday. They set a place and a time, shook hands and smiled at one another one more time. Then he moved quickly away from her and took his place at the head table. Feyhe leaned up against the wall and let her shoulders support her weight. Her back was arched and her right leg was cocked, bent at the knee, her foot slowly ascending and descending the wall behind her.

Two men spoke briefly from the podium and Feyhe was just about bored enough to entertain the thought of leaving when Patricia Miller bustled in through the street-side door. She spotted Feyhe at once and rushed over to her.

"I'm sorry. I'm sorry I'm late. My mother started to lecture me about stuff and, well, you know how that all goes."

"It's okay. I spoke to some people and had some coffee. My cousin is here, too."

"Did he speak yet?"

"Gad, I hope not. The two men so far have been dull, dull, dull."

"Oh. It's okay. This is him now." She poked Feyhe in the arm and they both turned to look at the podium. Standing there, his smile so familiar, was Owen Khanzadian.

"You mean, him?" Feyhe asked. Patricia just nodded, standing rapt, her mouth open slightly. Feyhe turned to listen to Owen preach.

He had already begun and, through her short chat with her friend, she had missed his opening gambit. She picked it up midsentence and listened intently.

"...so, if there were no God, it would be necessary to invent Him. This is not a new conclusion. The inexorable "ye must be born again, and born different" recurs in every generation. Ours is no different from our grandfather's generation in this concept. But this has always been silenced by the same question: what kind of person is this God of yours to be? Unfortunately, you do not know what sort of man you are, or what sort of idol you want.

"As for the method, well, what can be said except that where there is a will, there is a way. The assassin, Czolgosz, made President McKinley a hero by assassinating him. The United States of America made Czolgosz a hero by the same process. It is the deed that teaches, not the name we give it. Murder and Capital Punishment are not opposites that cancel one another out, but the same thing, breeding their kind. When a man wants to murder a tiger, he calls it sport; when the tiger wants to murder him he calls it ferocity—meanness. Where is the distinction but in the minds of men. It is not necessary to replace a guillotined criminal; it is necessary to replace a guillotined social system.

"The golden rule, you all know the golden rule. Well, the golden rule, really, is that there are no golden rules. Do not do unto others as you would that they should unto you. Their tastes may not be the same as yours. Never resist temptation: test, to prove, all things: do not love thy neighbor as thyself.

"Nothing can be unconditional, consequently nothing can be free. Liberty equates to responsibility. That is why most men dread it. We choke ourselves to job, family, religion, keep freedom apart from ourselves. These things hold us to the earth, keep us from freedom. A woman should not be kept from her job because she is bearing a child. She should work, as the Chinese women do, until the moment of birth, then return to the field, to their factory, their store, the child in tow. A man must not be saddled with the burdens of another. That is not liberty. That is not freedom.

"We hear much about revolution, but the true revolution is in the heart and the mind of each of us. We all pay the costs of our liberty and we must be allowed to use that liberty as we see fit.

"'Beware of a man whose God is in the skies—he bears a burden.' 'In heaven an angel is nobody in particular.'

"'Moderation is never applauded for its own sake.' 'Home is the girl's prison and the woman's workhouse.'

"We are told that when Jehovah created the world he saw that it was good. Well, what would he say now?

"Revolution, as we know, it is not enough any longer. Men have raised up arms and fought off the oppression of other only to oppress those who follow them. Now is the time for revolution. It is our only hope. We must replace this image of man we worship and follow with a new image, a superman. We must aspire to the next step up the ladder and the next, and the next. This is the dream of our movement, the attainment of true greatness and true equality and true liberty for all. We seek a world where the cost of something is equal to its value and the purchase price no greater than an individual assessment of it. If you begin by sacrificing yourself to those you love, you will end by hating those to whom you have sacrificed yourself. An end to the folly of our youth. A beginning to the true beginning of a new order. Thank you all."

Feyhe listened to much of this with her eyes closed. She would open them to watch his face, then close them again to shut out the visual image. His strength and self-assurance, along with the sound of his voice caressing the words was truly wonderful. When she opened her eyes again, finally, the sound of applause seemed wrong, intrusive and deadly. She looked across the crowded room at Owen and found him looking at her, only at her. She started to blush again, then turned away, murmured a hasty "g'nite" to Patricia, and left the hall.

He met her on Tuesday at the appointed hour at the appointed place. She was waiting, not so very patiently, when he arrived twenty minutes late.

"I know. I'm sorry," he said before she could utter a single syllable. "It was the subway, not me."

"That's fine," she said. "It's not a prob."

"A vernacular cutie," he said and he smiled, expecting her to return the gesture. She didn't. "So, what's really wrong?"

"You're not going to like me much, Mr. Khanzadian," she said.

"Why? What's up? Did you bring your mother along?" he asked, still joking, still being light about things.

"No. I brought this." She reached into her purse and pulled out a thin, slender and tall pamphlet. She held it up so that he could see its title and author. Her eyes followed the angle of the pamphlet's cover, so that as he looked at it, he could see her thoughts playing out behind her eyes.

"Well, aren't you the clever girl?" he said. "Not one in five hundred would have known it."

"Certainly not in The Bronx, Mr. Khanzadian."

He took the booklet from her, flipped it open at random, pointed into it with his forefinger and showed her the place. "Go ahead, read it aloud," he said.

"When a man wants to murder a tiger, he calls it sport; when the tiger wants to murder him he calls it ferocity—meanness. Where is the distinction but in the minds of men. It is not necessary to replace a guillotined criminal; it is necessary to replace a guillotined social system."

"Yeah," he said softly, "I should have rewritten that one, but when you've got George Bernard Shaw writing your speeches for you, its hard to make any substantive changes. The guy writes good."

"Too good, obviously," Feyhe agreed. "You barely bothered to even paraphrase him."

"The Revolutionist's Handbook would be classic if you could buy it outright," Owen said.

"You're a phony," she answered him, "but a dynamic one."

"The best kind." He gave her his good smile and she countered with her own.

"I'd love my father to meet you," she said. "One phony deserves another."

"And you're the genuine article?"

"The cream of the crop, actually."

"Are you always this secure?"

"Get to know me. You'll find out."

The cream of the crop, always secure, Feyhe thought, remembering this ancient scene. *Get to know me. You'll find out.* The memory of her meeting Owen tickled her and she couldn't help smiling. For the first time since she'd received the commissioner's letter summoning her to a hearing on her work, she felt all right about things. She had always been the cream of the crop, always secure. Nothing could touch her, nothing could hurt her or stop her. This wouldn't stop her either.

———◆ ✕ ◆———

Ni-Na arrived at 6:30. Feyhe had achieved enough self-assurance to nap and she was surprised at the tapping on her door. She had actually forgotten that Kim was sending his fiancé to meet with her. When she opened her door, finally, and saw the young woman there it took her a moment before she realized who she was.

"Missis Bow-Hyuman, how good it is to see you once more," Ni-Na said from outside the doorway.

"Ni-Na, how well you look," Feyhe said, observing the formalities Kim had taught her. "Will you grace my rooms by entering now, please." She bowed to Ni-Na who bowed in return and then moved forward one step. The formality was not complete, however. "Please come in and join me in these humble surroundings," Feyhe said and Ni-Na, bowing one more time, entered Feyhe's suite. When she saw the large number of boxes and crates, she uttered a low, long whistle.

"Yes, it is a lot, isn't it?" Feyhe said, dropping the rigid speech.

"Is all of this for the grotto?" Ni-Na asked her. Feyhe nodded and Ni-Na whistled again. "You have been working hard."

"I have, indeed. That's why I am so upset about all of this nonsense. I hope you can help me here."

"I will do what is possible."

"Your English has improved a lot, Ni-Na."

"Yes, thank you. Each night Kim and I speak in only English and we read from American novels. It is a great help to know the collected works of the illustrious authors, Mark Twain, Ira Levin, Norman Mailer, and Stephen King."

"No Shaw?" Feyhe asked without thinking, then adding, "never mind."

"May I see your letter, please?" Ni-Na asked. Feyhe got it for her, then sat down while Ni-Na studied it. Finally, she looked up at Feyhe.

"This letter contains many secrets, Missis Bow-Hyuman. We have two days in which to decipher all that it contains and prepare our rebuttal. They will question you on many issues. Among them shall be politics."

"Why politics? I'm not here on a political mission. This is art."

"In Korea today all there is would be politics. For our President these would be difficult times. Allow me to explain history."

Feyhe nodded, relaxed deep in her chair and wished for a martini or a cigarette. Neither was possible here with Ni-Na, who neither smoked nor drank. Custom would not allow it.

"In 1961," Ni-Na began as if by rote, "elections in Korea were corrupt and false, no—fraudulent I think. The students rose up and protested and many of the working force also. It was bad publicity for the regime of President Syngman Rhee, who was both corrupt and weak. Korea needed a strong leader to inspire the people. Finally, President Rhee resigned and a new government was formed under the military leadership of Park Chung-Hee. It was a dictatorship with the military to hold the people in check. Still, the people of Korea were not accustomed to such a way of life at that time, so they forced once again a change and Park Chung-Hee resigned his commission as General and stood in 1963 for election as a Democratic Republican party chairman. He has been elected again and again, although in 1971 it was difficult for him. It was clear that one more free election could not take place for General Park Chung-Hee, so in 1972 he made martial law again and destroyed his political opponents. While many good things have happened in these last years under his administration of the law, it is now harder to live free and to express one's self. Last year, shortly before you arrived in Korea, there was an attempt on his life which did not succeed, but it killed his wife. It is known that since that time he is more than suspicious of any outsider in Korea."

"Why should all of this affect me and my art, Ni-Na?" Feyhe looked as perplexed as she sounded. "I have nothing to do with all of this."

"You are making art of our history, Missis Bow-Hyuman. You are altering the images of our lineage. It must be in accordance with the regulations of the Park regime."

"This man who wrote to me is named Park Li-Wang," Feyhe said. "Is that of importance?"

"I think it may be so. Park Li-Wang is a cousin of the President. You must be very careful how you address him when you speak."

"What do you mean?"

"I believe that each word you say will be reported to President Park.

I believe that in the balance is the report and the opinion of this court on your feelings for the Korean people and for our history. You must not say anything that will give them strength in an argument that you are only a capitalist democrat American who wishes self-aggrandizement."

"Well, I'm not a capitalist and I'm not a registered democrat. I'm safe there, anyway," Feyhe said, laughing. Ni-Na did not join in the laughter.

"Where this summoning is specific you must take note. '*Demonstrate the understanding of our intent*' reads this last part. You must show them clearly that you believe what they believe about the nature of this place and show them that your work will not violate the beliefs of the government."

"Ni-Na, I do not know the beliefs of this government. If I don't know them and I violate them, it is not out of any sort of intent to harm or diminish the truths they hold dear."

"It is not enough. They will want much more than this."

"It's all I have to give."

"You must make concessions, I fear."

"I cannot. Art cannot conform to politics."

"In Korea, it must."

"In my heart, I cannot."

They had come to an impasse and both women knew it. They sat and stared at one another. Then Feyhe stood up and nodded to Ni-Na. The younger woman also rose to her feet and nodded in return.

"I just want someone I trust to listen to my statements and make sure that they are translated correctly to this board. I trust you, Ni-Na. Can you do this for me?"

"I can try."

"What does that mean, exactly?"

"I will get the permissions necessary to accompany you as your translator. It is known hereabout that I am a Political Science teacher and it may prove difficult to have me speak in this courtroom."

"Then what good would it do me to have you there?"

"It may prove of no use whatsoever. Of course, it may be that I can do exactly what you ask of me. That would be good. Again, my credentials are impeccable."

"As are my own, Ni-Na." They nodded again. "I want to thank you for doing this, and so close to your wedding day. I appreciate this so very much."

"I am glad to be of service, Missis Bow-Hyuman."

"I think you should call me Feyhe from now on."

Ni-Na's face broke into a wide, open grin. The joy of the invitation to a closer relationship heartened Feyhe. She stepped forward and embraced the girl who threw her arms around the woman's waist. Feyhe was a foot taller than Ni-Na, so the Korean woman's head rested neatly on her own breast. After a few minutes, they parted.

"I will petition the court in the morning and then we shall meet again to discuss your statement."

"I appreciate this very much, Ni-Na. Very much, indeed."

Feyhe had completed her statement to the board, had listened to their interpreter translate her words into the formal Korean, had seen Ni-Na nod to her, approving the accuracy of the translation. She was satisfied that she had said and done what could be said. She remained standing, two of her sections balanced against the legs of the table behind her.

"May I say one thing more?" she asked the room. There was a babble as six heads conferred. Consent was given and she continued.

"I was asked to come to Korea by your government and to create a piece of art, in my own style, that would be appropriate for this place. I lived here for four months and I studied and listened and I meditated. I spoke to many people, both the government officials and to those who work in shops or tend the parks. This story is of such importance to all, to everyone I met specifically, that it has always felt right to me that I should create such a work. It is designed to live within the grotto where the incident occurred. There is no other place for it. If it is decided that your government cannot place my work where it should be, I would rather see it destroyed than seek another place for it. I am a westerner and a woman and entitled to have and express my feelings and desires on this subject. Thank you for hearing me out."

She turned, prepared to return to the table. A voice, in perfect English, spoke to her from the oak desk she had been addressing.

"You would destroy what is Korean property if it is not dealt with in a manner to which you subscribe? Is this, my understanding of your statement, accurate?"

Feyhe turned again to look at the man who spoke to her. It was Park Li-Wang, the commissioner himself. Her first instinct was to challenge him, cry out that his English showed he had understood her every word perfectly. Ni-Na caught her eye and the frightened look on her face helped Feyhe catch herself in time.

"I would destroy my work rather than see it abused, or wrongly displayed, yes."

"This is Korean property, the property of my government, and you would willfully destroy it?"

"No, Mr. Park. Your English is clearly not as perfect as you would have me believe. I would not destroy Korean property, only my own."

"What is your property here? The stone is ours. Your work is a commission and the commission is completed. You have been compensated for this work. And the stone on which you worked has always been ours. You have no property here."

"The work is mine, sir. It will always be mine."

"This work is here in Korea, is property of Korea. You have no control of this work. This work is on our property, our stone, our legend, our images. Nothing in this is any longer yours."

Feyhe raged. She was unable to control her rage. She shrieked as she had never shrieked before. "Nothing in this is yours, Mr. Park. All of it is mine. The stone is mine, a gift from your country. The idea is mine, based on legends that the whole world has access to. The images are mine, created by me from the faces and the hearts of the people I met last year, people I loved. All of this is mine. The design and placement that had been approved are mine. Nothing—I repeat—*nothing* in all of this except the grotto itself is yours. Everything is mine. I am the artist and this is the art."

The room was so utterly silent that a pin dropping would have been heard in the hallway outside. No one breathed except Feyhe, and the intake of breath was so sour that it caused her to cough, softly at first, then uncontrollably. Commissioner Park sat down slowly. He muttered something Feyhe didn't understand. Then he shouted something she didn't understand. Two military officers in uniform appeared. They moved swiftly to either side of Feyhe, taking up their positions without looking at her. She stared at Park.

"Does this mean something? Am I under arrest?"

Park eyed her carefully, cautious, remembering her outburst. "You are not under arrest. The artwork in this court is under arrest. It shall remain here when you leave. Before you leave, men will be in the rooms you occupy to remove the balance of the artwork and bring it here."

"Those are my rooms. You have no right to enter there—"

"We have the right. This is not your country, I remind you. You have made threatening words against the property of this state and we must protect what is ours."

"It's *not* yours," Feyhe said, her voice whining against her will. She caught a glimpse of Ni-Na whose head was bowed, whether in sorrow or in fear Feyhe could not tell.

"This is the property of the state, I remind you. What is done with it is no longer of any interest to you. It is also the judgement of this court that you shall vacate your rooms no later than two days from today and that you shall leave Korea no later than twenty-four hours from that time."

"You're giving me three days to get out of town?" Feyhe nearly snarled at him as she said the words.

"This is the judgement of this court. You shall remain here, under guard, until all of the property has been retrieved and brought here. You shall identify the pieces and remove only such items as are personal to you. All else shall remain here. When this procedure has been completed you shall be escorted to your rooms and then you will have seventy-two hours in which to extricate yourself from Korea."

"I am supposed to attend a wedding here in two weeks, Mr. Park."

"I suggest you say goodbye to any such notion. In two weeks time you shall not be able to appear in Korea ever again."

"This is not fair!" she bellowed.

"This is democracy in Korea," he shouted back at her. "What is fair is what is best for the Korean people, not for stubborn American women who demand their own way in things over which they have no control."

He waved a very dismissive hand in her direction. The two soldiers took her by the arms and escorted her to a seat at the back of the room. They deposited her both unceremoniously and a bit harshly, then took up their former positions on either side of her. Park and the other members of the commission were filing out of the room.

"May I at least speak to my friend who accompanied me here today?" Feyhe called out to them. Park turned around and looked at her.

"You may speak for three minutes only. Goodbye Madame."

Feyhe looked over at Ni-Na, who looked up, finally, at Feyhe. The girl stood up and came quickly to Feyhe's place in the room.

"I'm sorry, Ni-Na. I lost my temper."

"Not much lost. I believe it was instantly found by the commissioner, Feyhe."

"I believe you're right." She laughed. "Now what do I do?"

"I think what happens next is that you pack and go home to America."

"I don't want to leave like this. I don't want to leave my work and I don't want to leave without attending your wedding. I don't want any of this."

"I do not want this for you either, Feyhe. But this man is powerful and he has made an official declaration of his intent to expel you from Korea. There is nothing to be done."

"I'll go to the American Consul."

"They can do nothing. I know this for a fact."

"I'll appeal to President Park. I'll go over his cousin's head."

"Feyhe, I think this will not do. I think that what we have seen here is because of President Park. I think he has asked for this in advance."

"Ni-Na, why?"

"It is what I spoke about to you before. It is history."

"I see," Feyhe said simply. She reached to take Ni-Na's hand, but the

Korean woman stepped away from her.

"I'm sorry. That was inappropriate."

"You are now dangerous, Feyhe. I cannot risk more."

"Are you compromised already, perhaps? You and Kim Do-Mun? Just for knowing me?"

"I do not think so, but I do not know."

"I don't want to lose you both. You are precious to me. You have been my friends."

"We were to ask you for this favor, Feyhe, to be the Godmother to our unborn child when the time comes."

"What do you mean?"

Ni-Na lowered her eyes, then her entire head. She turned away to avoid Feyhe's gaze. "I am pregnant with Kim Do-Mun's child. When we wed I shall be nearly three months gone. I am so ashamed for my actions."

"Does anyone else know this, Ni-Na?"

She shook her head. "No. We have not told the parents or anyone else at all."

Feyhe reached out and patted her gently on the shoulder. Ni-Na pretended not to notice, but Feyhe could feel the difference in the young woman. Her tensions were lessening, her shoulder more relaxed.

"We shall make plans, Ni-Na. Don't worry. Something good will come of this."

The door to the room burst open and men began entering, shoving the cartons, and boxes, and crates that had so recently been cluttering Feyhe's rooms. The men paid no attention to the delicacy of the contents, but roughly moved the pieces about, bringing them into the room as though time was the only important or relevant item involved in their arrival and deposit.

Feyhe began to weep, but caught herself before the tears had truly exploded out of her. "There's a time for that, Girlie," she said to herself, but Ni-Na heard her words and assumed they were meant for her.

"You are a good God-Mother, Feyhe. Even in adversity, you are a good mother."

Feyhe smiled, in spite of herself. Then she laughed.

10

Billy threw his paperwork at the wall. Joe, reading in the next room, heard the sound the half-ream of paper made as it struck the desk on its re-entry pattern. He thought about saying something, then checked the impulse. Billy stormed out of his office and through the living room of their new apartment. He went on, without a word, into the kitchen and slammed the door. Joe listened carefully for any words or noises and, hearing nothing, went back to his book.

It had been like this for several weeks. Ever since leaving his SoHo apartment, Billy had been testy. The decision to live together openly had been a big one for both men and, being vulnerable, Joe had been especially nervous about it. He had expected Billy to stand by the choice they made, to take it in stride. He was, after all, the one with the least to lose in terms of reputation and work opportunity. Joe was the one taking the greater risk. Still, it had turned out to be Billy who had the hardest time making the transition.

The apartment, on West 79th Street between Broadway and West End Avenue, was large, a three bedroom, two bathroom rental with relatively unobstructed westward views across the Hudson to the Palisades of New Jersey and a north view as well that was almost as pleasant. They were on the nineteenth floor with roof garden privileges and they had a balcony that could easily accommodate six people for dinner. One of the bedrooms, the corner one with views in both directions, had been taken over as Billy's studio. The place was seemingly ideal for them. It was close enough to Joe's mother's apartment, since she had left Queens and found a place on West 81st Street, to allow him more access to his daughter. It was a bus-ride across Central Park directly to Feyhe's apartment on East 82nd Street. The living room was large and the dining room was also. The kitchen boasted new appliances. The bathrooms had oversized tubs and enclosed showers with six shower heads. Their neighbors were musicians, singers, actors, a famous playwright, two world-class journalists, a financier and a gay-rights activist with an upper-class background and middle-class appreciation. But Billy was feeling out of place.

"I love the location and the rooms," he said one night at dinner. Joe nodded, but said nothing. "I don't know what's wrong. I'm having trouble getting used to it."

Joe swallowed a mouthful of lasagna and said, "It's a period of adjustment, that's all. You'll be fine with it in a few days." Billy nodded and they went on eating in silence.

They had made an agreement that Joe would never wear a police uniform in the hallway.

His new job rarely required him to don a uniform but, even so, the thought of him tramping through the halls dressed as one of New York's Finest made Billy nervous. Joe said he understood but, in reality, he had no idea why Billy was being so careful about this one particular part of their lives.

Joe, on the other hand, was perfectly happy with the change in their status. He had said to Billy, not long after they began spending all of their nights and their free time together, that he longed for a stable home that they would share. For him the period of adjustment had been an almost seamless one. He had known, almost from the beginning, how their lives, lived together, could be: strong, contented, supportive. There were no surprises that he anticipated. From the first night he had felt that he knew Billy and knew how Billy would react to anything and everything. He had been wrong, to be sure, but he was still secure in his knowledge of the man he had come to love and to share his life with on a full-time basis.

It was just taking Billy a little bit longer to come to terms with the public aspects of his private life. They had talked about it more than once, but the conversation was always the same one, time and again.

"What's wrong, Billy?" That was always the first thing Joe said. "You're treating me as though I was something hateful or distasteful. What did I do?"

"Nothing," came the usual response from Billy. "I just...I don't know...this isn't what...I don't know."

"Can you give me a better hint, please, honey?"

"You're the detective. You figure it out."

"Even a detective can't work with nothing."

"I'm nothing? Is that what you really think of me?"

"No. You know it isn't what I think of you."

"What do you think of me, Joe? Do you think I'm stupid? Or lazy? Or what?"

This was the point in the argument where Joe had to hold himself back from really saying what was on his mind. His thoughts often ran to *I think you need a stick up your ass, you bratty little kid. The world isn't just about you.*

What he usually said was something along the lines of "I think you're terrific, intelligent, talented and hard-working. I also think you just need some time to get used to this big change in your life."

That was when Billy would fall apart.

"God, I love you, Joe. You're so patient with me. I don't get it."

"I love you too, honey. I know you'll work through this stuff and we'll be fine."

That was the usual course of their problem in understanding one another. Joe was confident, as he said he was, that the difficulty would be short-lived. Billy said he felt the same way but he secretly nurtured the concept that things would never be all right in this new place. He blamed the apartment and the furniture. He accused the view of being too enthralling for him to be able to work. He cited the nineteen story elevator ride as too disconcerting for him to think once he arrived on their floor. He looked at every external and then, inevitably, he blamed Joe.

He agreed with Joe that it was childish of him to make such an assumption. They had picked out the apartment together, made all of their decisions together. Billy had designed the living room and dining room, and Joe had gone along with every single one of his choices. Their bedroom had been decorated by the two of them, together, agreement reached on each selection—bed, fabrics, wall colors, lamps, furnishings, window-treatments. It had all gone so smoothly and yet it had all gone wrong when they actually moved in.

On this particular afternoon, after Billy stomped by the couch where Joe sat reading, the cop decided that this uncomfortable situation had gone on for one day too long. He put down his book, got off the couch and walked to the kitchen door. Without a word of warning, he pushed the door open, fast and hard. He hoped Billy wasn't standing too close to it and his hope was realized. Billy was at the far end of the room, sitting on the windowsill, gazing out into the airspace that gave a view of the kitchen windows of three other apartments on their floor.

"Billy, enough!" Joe said. "I can't keep living like this."

"*You* can't?" Billy replied. "What about *me*?"

"What about you? I've been trying to get a handle on that for some time."

"I'm not happy, Joe."

"Well, who is, honey?"

"I don't know." He had a sullen look on his face that darkened his eyes and tugged his mouth into a high-arched frown.

"I won't live with that answer any more, Billy. 'I don't know' doesn't cut it."

"I know." He gave Joe a half-smile before his face regained its dour expression. "I just keep trying to feel right about this, but I can't."

"About what? The move? About us? What?"

"I think it's a little of all of that, Joe."

Joe went to where Billy was sitting and put his arms around the younger man's shoulders.

He held him close but not too tight. He leaned forward and kissed Billy on the top of his head. "We'd better talk about it, then. We've made commitments and if we already can't keep them, then we're heading for big trouble."

"Joe, I love you. You know I love you, that's not it. It's the being together that makes me a bit crazy."

"Why, Billy? I don't get it."

"It was exciting at first, Joe, being part of a couple, seeing friends with someone in tow. And I liked that it was you and not some Park Avenue big shot with cash and an attitude. You're very real and I love that."

Joe smiled and nodded, blushed at the neckline and snorted once.

"But since we moved here, nothing feels the same to me anymore. I'm bothered by something I can't get my fingers around."

"Try, Billy. Try hard for me—no, not for me—for us."

"My work isn't going well, Joe. That's a big part of it. I don't know if I'm distracted with you in the apartment or caught up in the sights and sounds of the city up here. It was never quiet down in SoHo. I had all that traffic going to and from the Holland Tunnel. I think I miss that din for one thing."

"I'll make you a sound tape. We'll put it on a cassette and you can have it running all day long if you like."

Billy laughed for the first time in days.

"And, Joe, I think I have a problem with the apartment itself."

"What do you mean?"

"I mean, the apartment is ours, right? We bought it together and designed it together and put it together, together. Do you hear what I'm saying?" Billy had gotten more and more intense during this short monologue.

"I guess so."

"I think most of my problem is centered there," Billy said. "I think it's all this sharing that we do. It's not right for me."

"Explain, please," Joe asked him, making no question out of no statement.

"I want you to understand this. Really I do. Everything here, everything you see, or touch, was a joint decision, our choices, our concepts."

"Okay."

"Don't you see? Isn't it plain enough yet?" He looked at Joe, waited, then went on. "I'm a designer. Wherever I live and work, the end result has to be mine. Without that I'm nothing."

"You hate my taste? Is that it?"

"No! No, Joe, that's not it." He turned to look out the window, his back to Joe. The cop could see the tension in the designer's shoulders and back. He reached out his hand and gently rubbed the palm of his hand over Billy's shoulder blades.

"Joe, my biggest problem is that I don't own my environment. It's what I do for my clients, Joe. I build them an environment that becomes their own once I leave it. That's why I'm successful. That's why people want me to create something for them."

"And you think I don't want you to provide a home for me? Is that it?"

"Not a home, a place."

"I'm still not clear, I guess. What's the difference, Billy?"

"Let's say I went on a stake-out with you, Joe. Let's say I got the drop on some guy you were after. Let's say that once I did that, I handed the mug over to you to be your collar. You'd be glad you got the crook, but you'd never be comfortable with the fact that I did what you should have done. That's what this is like for me. You did what I should have done, and done for you and for us."

"I'm catching on, honey."

"It's not that I don't like everything we've got here. I do. It's just that the choices, the decisions weren't mine."

"It's ego, Billy. I hurt your ego by sharing too much."

"It's ego. I admit it."

"Does talking about it help, Billy?" He waited impatiently for his answer.

"No," Billy said finally. "It doesn't help one bit."

Joe put his arms around Billy again and squeezed in next to him on the windowsill. He looked into Billy's eyes and tried not to break into too broad a grin when spoke again.

"Send it all back, then," he finally said. "Do whatever you want. I'll love it. I always love the rooms you design."

Billy leaned forward over his own bent knees and kissed Joe lightly on the lips. "I don't want to, Joe. I just want to feel like I own it."

"Well, how do you do that without redoing it all?"

"Well, I'm not sure, but I think you just gave it to me to do and I like what we've done, and that could be it."

"If anyone asks me, honey, I'll tell them it's all yours."

"And I'll tell them I did it the way I knew you'd like it."

They kissed again, then sat back against the large window frames, staring at one another. "You put me through hell for this?" Joe finally said, smiling.

"I did."

"And you're not going to say you're sorry?"

"I'm not."

"You are a bratty little kid," Joe said to him. And Billy agreed.

It was neither the beginning nor the end of their stormy times together. It was a newfound rhythm, however, that established a way through whatever troubles might assail them later on. In the next few months of their relationship they got through Angus Duncan's fury at his son's "arrangement" with a law officer, handled the outrage of a failed loan application they filed together for needed repair work on the apartment, and neatly sidestepped the tragedy of Joe Ryan's ex-wife's death and its emotional bath.

Coming home in a limousine from her funeral, which no one seemed to be overwhelmed with or depressed by, they discussed Joe's future with his daughter.

"Maybe she should come to live with us," Billy offered, but Joe just shook his head in silence. "Why not? She knows me. She knows, more or less, who we are to each other."

"No." Joe was definitive when he said these one word sentences.

"Don't say 'no' like that. This is too important. It needs some thought."

"I've thought about it, honey. It's not going to happen."

"She likes me, Joe, and she trusts me. So does your mom."

"It's not you, Billy. It's me."

"What? I don't get it. You don't want Sandy thinking of you as... *what*?"

Joe had grabbed Billy's arm and was holding it tightly between his thumb and forefinger.

The pain surged upward into Billy's shoulder.

"I don't give a rat's ass about that. You know that, Billy. I just don't want her living her life with two guys. It's not healthy for a little kid."

"Let go of me," Billy said as though he had not heard Joe's last statement.

"Not until you acknowledge that you understand the reality of this."

"Let go of my arm, Joe."

"Agree with me, please."

"Let go." He wrenched his arm free of Joe's angry grasp. "That hurt, you bastard."

"I'm sorry. I didn't mean to hurt you."

"It's like revenge or something, when you do that. What did I do? I mean, what did I really do to deserve that?"

Joe gulped, turned away to stare out through the car window.

"Joe, don't do this. Don't shut me out of the process. I'm part of it, no matter what you may believe."

"I know you are. That makes it harder."

"Well, talk to me then. Let me be your inner ear and your inner voice for a while."

Joe turned back to look at Billy. His face was granite. Billy gave him an encouraging grin, and finally Joe smiled back at him.

"Yes, Sandy knows about our feelings for one another. Yes, she likes to be with you. I still feel it's better for her to stay with my mom than to live with us right now. We've still got a lot of shit, just ours, to get through. We're not stable yet. At least I don't think we are. I don't want to offer her a home that may fall apart, like the last one."

"You think I'd leave you?"

"No."

"Then you think you'd leave me, is that it?"

"No. Of course not."

"So, where's the unstable part?"

"It's…it's in the little things, Billy. You go back and forth in your feelings about things and it can be really confusing for me and I'm an adult who deals in clues. You drop clues all over the place and I can't find my way back to you sometimes."

Billy watched Joe's face for a moment, hoping for a clue of his own as to how to address this. Then he spoke. "You're the bizarre one, Joe. You're deeper than a well in the Rockies. No matter how far down I send my bucket, I never get back more than few drops of water."

They rode in silence for a while, watching the city's streets unreel before them.

"We'll be home soon, Joe. What do we do when we get home? Go to our separate corners and wait for the bell?"

"This isn't a fight, Billy. This is dealing with life."

"Believe me, that's a fight," Billy said resolutely.

Ten minutes later they entered the apartment, the chill that had sprung up between them still in evidence. From across the vestibule they both saw the blinking light on the answering machine. Neither one raced to get it, their usual habit on such an occasion. Ultimately, Billy pushed the play button and waited while the tape rewound itself.

"Billy, it's Feyhe. I have momentous news. Absolutely staggering news, actually. Call me. Or tell Joe to call me. Or someone call me. This is big." Her voice went up in volume and tone on the final sentence. A click and a beep followed. Billy looked over to Joe who was hanging his jacket up in the hall closet.

"Did you hear that, Joe?"

"Just call her, Billy, and get it over with, okay?" He walked out of the hallway and into the kitchen. Billy stood where he was and heard Joe at the refrigerator, heard its door close, heard the clicking of the metal tab as Joe popped the top of his beer. Billy went into the living room, sat down on the long, brown leather couch and picked up the receiver of the phone on the coffee table. He dialed his cousin.

"Feyhe, it's Billy, what's up with—?"

"He's here, Billy." The excitement in her voice was unmistakable.

"He? Who?"

"Kim. My friend Kim from Korea."

"Kim from Korea, hmmm. Isn't that like Fanny from Frisco, or Rosie from Riverdale or those three chorus girls from *No, No, Nanette*?"

"Don't be so flippant, Billy. Do you know how hard it was to get him out of that country of his and over here safely?"

"No." Billy sobered his tone. "No, of course I don't Feyhe."

"Well, remind me to show you the paperwork someday."

"So, you got him out of Korea and he's here. That's terrific."

"And where have you two been? I've called you three or four times."

"A funeral. The ex-wife."

"Ah, well, good riddance to bad rubbish, as my mother used to say."

"Did she say that often, Feyhe?"

"Often enough. She said it when I left Owen." Neither of them spoke for a moment.

Feyhe's bad marriage was usually a verboten subject. "Come and meet Kim. I want you to know him. I want you to like him. He's a special man in my life."

Billy took a breath before speaking again. "Isn't he still married, Feyhe?"

"Of course he's married. What does that have to do with this?"

"I don't know, I guess."

"Well, come for dinner and meet him. Come tonight. It's special. My cousin Sidney and his wife, the lovely Lenore, are joining us too. Bring Joe."

"I'll try, Feyhe."

"Good. You'll come. See you at seven." She hung up and eventually so did Billy.

Feyhe's cousin Sidney and his wife, Lenore, clearly disliked Billy. Even Joe could spot that without trying. The instant they entered Feyhe's living room Joe saw the two of them freeze into a phony pose of friendliness.

"Billy, how nice. And what a surprise," Sidney Ginsberg said, not rising or holding out his hand for a handshake.

"Hello, Sidney, how are you?" Billy said, a much friendlier note sounding in his voice.

Sidney didn't respond and Billy turned his attention to "the lovely Lenore."

"Lenore, you're looking lovely," he said, and they could all hear Feyhe smirk in the kitchen. "How are you tonight?"

"Hello, Billy," she said coldly. "Aren't you ever going to grow into William?"

"Never," Billy confided loudly. "I'll be Billy until long after you and Sidney have passed on and lie cold your graves."

"This must be Joseph?" she said, curiously.

"Joe," he said, extending his hand. Lenore didn't take it. Neither did Sidney. A silence fell over the quartet, a silence broken by Feyhe entering from the kitchen.

"Don't hate me for this," Feyhe said as she moved to the coffee table with a tray of canapes, "but you four are boring as bat shit."

"Thank you, Feyhe," Sidney said as huffily as possible. "I find it hard to hate you at all."

"Sidney, you're a prince," she said with a slight chuckle in her voice. "Like Prince Spaghetti, actually."

"What is that supposed to signify, Feyhe?" Lenore was on the crack instantly.

"Oh, Lenore, lighten up," Feyhe snapped.

"Where's your young gentleman, Feyhe?" Joe asked, attempting to change the subject. "If you mean Kim, he'll be here in a minute or two." She paused. "I sent him out just before Sidney and Lenore arrived."

"Sent him out? Is he staying here...with you?" Lenore asked the question.

"Of course he is. Where else do you think he'd be. Does everyone have a drink? Have what you need?"

There was a general murmur as Feyhe moved back into the kitchen. Joe turned to Sidney, gave him a smile and spoke.

"So what do you do, Sidney? In business of some sort?"

"Yes. I sell ladies hats. Why?"

"Just the idle curiosity of the newcomer. Billy doesn't talk about you two."

"Billy doesn't know us. We're not related to him," Lenore responded.

"We're Feyhe's cousins on her mother's side," Sidney said. "At least I am."

"And I am," Lenore added. "Marriage counts, even in this peculiar family."

"Quoth the raven, lovely Lenore," Billy muttered under his breath. Joe barely heard him, but he smiled at the words he thought he had heard.

"Working much these days, Billy? Or is the city supporting you now that you're an official partner of one of New York's finest?" Sidney sounded snide.

"I am not a declared partner of anyone, Sidney," Billy said quickly before Joe could get in on this chat. "I have a very profitable business and I am sharing my home with a good friend. That's all you know."

"Oh, but I could surmise a lot more, Billy boy," Sidney added.

"If that's what you need to fantasize about when you're screwing the lovely Lenore, then enjoy yourself, Sid." Billy hated this man and it was showing now.

"Billy, that's a terrible thing to say about Sidney. You're implying he's queer!" Lenore sounded truly upset.

"Well, Lenore, you do have your one requisite kid and no more. Maybe Sidney is a little off-balance sexually."

"Billy, calm down," Joe offered, but no one really heard him.

"This is Kim," Feyhe called out from the entryway. No one had heard the door open and close. No one had paid any attention to the presence of a newcomer in their midst. The shouting that had been about to erupt faded into the cocktail glasses that they all held. The foursome turned to look at Feyhe and the young man beside her.

He was wearing a dark suit and thin, black tie with no design on it. His dark hair had been slicked back and his face shone with the scrubbing that had been done not an hour before. He stood nearly a foot shorter than Feyhe and he looked no more than nineteen years old.

Someone gasped. Not even the gasper was sure who had made the sound.

"Well," Feyhe said, "don't all say hello at once."

Billy took the initiative and moved forward, his right arm outstretched to greet the man.

Kim took his hand, firmly and warmly.

"You are Billy, I suppose," he said. "It is a pleasure to meet you."

Billy nodded, then introduced the others. Joe joined him, but Sidney and Lenore stayed where they had been.

"Kim is my guest until he can find a place for himself and his family," Feyhe said without anyone asking. "He is a most welcome guest, I should add."

"Are you planning to stay, then?" Sidney called out from across the room.

"It is my intention, yes, sir." Kim spoke slowly and with great self-assurance. Billy found himself impressed with the Korean's manner, addressing a stranger who spoke an attack.

"How long for?" Sidney asked.

"For as long as I am able, Mr. Sidney," the Korean replied.

"I mean how long here, in Feyhe's house," Sidney said.

"Kim has privileges, Sidney," Feyhe responded. "He can stay for as long as he likes."

"What sort of privileges, Feyhe, are you referring to?" Lenore asked over-brightly.

"Oh, boy," Billy muttered under his breath. Joe gave him a shot in the ribs.

"Kim is my friend, Lenore, and I've invited him to stay for as long as he needs a place. That's all."

"We're just concerned, Feyhe, about someone taking advantage of you."

Feyhe gave her cousin Sidney a sharp look, then let it soften before she responded. "No one is taking advantage of anyone, I assure you."

"What Sidney means, Feyhe—" Lenore began, but Feyhe cut her off.

"I know very well what Sidney means. I've known what Sidney means for a long, long time."

"And what does that mean, Feyhe?" Sidney demanded. Billy tugged Joe's sleeve and the two of them began to move away, but Feyhe stopped them dead in their tracks.

"Don't even think about it, you two," she said, pointing a long, bony finger at them. Joe stopped first, then Billy. She turned to face Sidney again. "I've known you since we were three years old, Sidney. You've always been out for one thing and only one thing. Yourself. You don't care about me, or about Kim, my friend. You're just worried that something might happen to something of mine that you might stand to inherit some day."

"Feyhe, how dare you!" Lenore roared, a veritable lioness protecting her cub sort of roar. "I dare only when I know I'm right," Feyhe roared back, then she instantly broke into a gale of laughter. Lenore stood stunned. Her face slowly fell, her mouth twitching all the way. Sidney just stood where he was, his face and body betraying nothing, no reaction, no sense of even being alive. "Tell them, Billy. Tell them how I am."

"She's a devil, all right," Billy said. He had moved forward a bit, but Joe was hauling him back. "She's the one and only stand-for-no-nonsense lady."

"Thanks, Billy," Feyhe said, her laughter subsiding. She put her hand on Kim's shoulder and brought him forward a bit, so that he was almost half way between her and her cousins. "I ought to tell you something, right now, that I was going to reserve for later. I ought to, but perhaps I won't. Perhaps I won't ever tell you, actually."

"Tell us what, Feyhe? Tell us what?" Sidney threw the challenge back at her.

"Tell you about Kim. And me." She smiled and put her hands on her hips. Billy nudged Joe who leaned down and let Billy whisper in his ear.

"About their sex, I hope," Billy whispered. Joe blushed and Billy shoved him lightly, allowing Joe to stand up and move off a foot or so.

"Billy, come here," Feyhe snapped. "I want you with me when I tell Sidney."

"Why, Feyhe?"

"Why? Because you're my favorite cousin. You're my favorite *friend*. You're the only relative I've ever known who hasn't judged me. That's why."

Feeling just a bit guilty about the last bit of praise, Billy moved slowly to her side. She was sandwiched in between him and the Korean. She put one arm around each of them. Joe moved back into the room so he could see their faces.

"Sidney. Lenore. These are my two babies. Billy I love because he never lets himself think about what I do or who I am or who I'm with. He just accepts it. Kim I love because he is a vastly superior person, vastly superior to you and your friends and our relatives and just about anyone else I've ever known. I love and respect these two men. When they've needed my help I have given it, given it gladly. I would do it for them any time, because I know they would do it for me."

"Well, really, Feyhe—" Sidney began to bluster, but Feyhe stopped him before he could get any further.

"Sidney, you are my closest relative, really. I've always wanted to love you, and I do adore your daughter, which is as close as I can come to loving you. You are always welcome and I particularly wanted you to meet Kim because what I've done affects you." She turned to the room, leaving Billy and Kim alone, parted by the space she had abandoned between them. "I am making a new will and these two men are my special beneficiaries. Sidney, you need to know that, because I have named you my executor."

"Feyhe, what the hell is this all about?" Billy demanded.

"You heard me. I was clear. You and Kim are my designated beneficiaries. If anything happens to me you both will split whatever my fortune may be.'

"I don't understand—"

"And you don't have to, Billy. It's my choice. It's my will. Sidney will be paid from the estate to handle whatever there is. All of you will benefit."

"And Mr. Kim?" Lenore asked. "What part does he play in your life, Feyhe?"

"Not that it's any business of yours, Lenore, but he's my son. Legally.

I've adopted him." There was a hush in the room that left no room for much else. "Now let's eat. Dinner's ready."

"Feyhe, I don't—" Billy started, but she pressed a finger against his lips, silencing him.

"Later, dear boy. Later."

11

Later came much later. Several days went by before Feyhe answered any of Billy's telephone calls. He was beginning to worry, beginning to think he should rush across town and see if she was all right, if she had been murdered in her bed by the Korean, or by her hateful cousin Sidney.

Sidney had called him at home, three mornings after the dinner party and berated Billy for supporting Feyhe in her choice. His anger had been overwhelming, causing Billy to vomit up phrases that wouldn't ordinarily cross his lips.

"You greedy, little son of a bitch," Sidney had started, not pausing for a hello or to ascertain that he had dialed the right number. "You and that queer cop just want her money and you see this as a way to get it, don't you?"

"Who is this?" Billy demanded, knowing all along who it had to be, just from the tone of the attack.

"You fucking well know who this is, you cock-sucker," Sidney shouted. "Sidney."

"Are you at your desk, Sidney?" Billy asked, still in control of his temper, still on the borderline of shock.

"What the—?"

"Is your secretary listening in on your conversation and are we being taped?" Billy asked.

"Look…look, this is not a joke, Billy-boy," Sidney went on, undeterred. "That crazy old coot has adopted this gook. Legally adopted him and made him her fucking heir."

"Sidney, I don't think we—"

"You don't think at all, faggot," he shouted a decibel louder.

"Stop calling me names, Sidney," Billy shouted back suddenly.

"I'll call you anything I want, schmuck. You are one fucking idiot to think I don't see through all this shit."

"What the hell are you talking—let me say ranting—about?"

Billy held the receiver about an inch from his ear, able to hear every word that Sidney uttered without really trying.

"You and Feyhe, two crazy *gonnifs*, two lousy hucksters, two brainless shitheads. You think Lenore and I couldn't read between the lines and see what you've been cooking up in your swishy little kitchens?"

"Sidney, you bastard, what the fuck are you accusing me of?" Billy demanded.

"Manipulation, queer-boy. You and that miserable old bitch found a way to cut me out of the fucking will."

"I did no such thing, you asshole."

"Don't you call me an asshole, pervert," Sidney snarled. "If anyone's taking it up the ass it's gonna be you and not me."

"Oh, really," Billy shouted back through the phone lines. "I think you've just been fucked, and royally, and by a woman. You didn't even have the pleasure of knowing you satisfied another person. You just stood there and took it and, like usual, never gave anything back."

"Don't you be playing those games with me, Billy."

"You're the idiot, Sid. You're the asshole. You're the fucked and not the fuckee. You're the one getting the shaft in the worst way. Think about that when you call me those bigoted little crap names." He slammed the phone down, angry at himself for letting himself get angry and angrier at Sidney for bringing him to it.

He called Feyhe, but there was no answer.

When Joe came home he told the story of the phone call. Joe roared and Billy was taken aback.

"You think this is funny?" he asked Joe.

"I think it's hilarious," Joe said. "You and that mean-tempered old man spewing expletives across the East River. I love it."

"He called me names, Joe. He accused me of manipulating Feyhe into this thing for my own greedy reasons."

"And did you?" Joe asked, a half-smile wrinkling his cheeks.

"What! You know I'd never—"

"You listen to the tone in my voice, Billy," Joe said. "You just listen to the sarcasm."

"I know." He felt himself calming slightly. "I know you're joking with me, but if you'd heard that stuff—"

"I know. People like your cousin's cousin are shallow and mean and stupid. We just suffer them, that's all."

"I'm going to have to face them at some point, you know."

"What's the problem, Billy? You know you didn't do anything to justify his foolish accusations. You know that."

"I know. It's just...it's just hard to stand accused, is all." They hugged one another and kissed and then went out to dinner.

The subject of Sandy came up again the following morning at breakfast. It had been plaguing Billy, Joe's resistance to the topic, and he tried to make it as palatable as possible.

"I was thinking," he started, "about Sandy and your mom. We should include them more in the things we do, Joe."

"Such as?"

"Well, we're planning on that series of dance tickets to the Joffrey and the A.B.T. and City Ballet. Why don't we make it a matinee series and buy tickets for them too?"

"My mother isn't your mother, Billy. She hates ballet."

"And Sandy?"

"Oh, she'd go, she'd love to go," Joe said, a bit sullenly. "I just don't think that going with both of us is the best thing for her right now."

"Oh? Why is that?" Billy tried to sound nonchalant, but knew that an edge had crept into the *that* in his question.

"It's not you, Billy, and it's not us. Not really. It's just that a kid her age gets asked a lot of questions and I don't want her feeling forced to lie about things. Not to her friends at school, or to her teachers."

"What would she have to lie about, Joe?" Billy's eyes had hardened a bit, almost into a squint. "What?"

"She'd probably say that she went with me. That's all."

"That wouldn't be a lie."

"It wouldn't be the whole truth, though, Billy. That would hurt her."

"She could say you and a friend, couldn't she?"

"She could…but…no, she couldn't."

"She doesn't think of me as a friend, then?" Billy asked.

"No. She doesn't." Joe looked very uncomfortable saying this. Billy decided to press for more details, hoping he wouldn't regret the decision.

"How does she think of me, Joe? What has she said to you about me?"

Joe got up from the table and took his plate, fork and spoon to the sink. He placed them carefully before he turned around and looked at Billy from this discreet distance.

"She asked me…" Joe paused in mid-sentence, then went on slowly. "She asked me if you were supposed to be her next mother. What should she call you? How should she mention you?"

Silence captured the kitchen the way an army encircles a fortress.

In a very quiet voice Billy spoke finally. "I thought she was a brighter kid," he said. "I thought she was smarter than that."

"I think she meant it in a good way, Billy. I think she was thinking of us as her parents. I think—"

"I think that's enough, thanks," Billy said. "I think that's enough."

Billy sat where he was, his eyes downcast, his chest heavier than he'd ever noticed before. Joe stayed where he was at the sink. He was drumming absent-mindedly on the porcelain, the rhythmic thrum digging its clipped nails into Billy's thoughts, cracking holes into them, keeping them unformed.

"I have to call Feyhe, again," he said to Joe. "Excuse me."

He quickly rose and left the room, leaving Joe alone at the sink, his fingers still stealthily drumming. When he went into the living room, a few minutes later, Billy was sitting on the large leather couch. He had captured the exact center of this piece of furniture and was just sitting there, staring straight ahead. Joe walked around and into his direct sightline.

"I have to go to work, Billy. I have to leave soon," he said.

"I have work of my own," Billy replied.

"I love you, you know," Joe said.

"I know. I love you also."

"I'd like it to work out, Billy, but it's hard. She's nine."

"Sometimes," Billy responded, "I feel that I'm about nine, too."

"Did you get Feyhe?" Joe asked. Billy shook his head and stayed where he was. Joe watched him for a whole minute before he left the room.

Two days later, Billy went to Feyhe's apartment. It was late afternoon and he hoped he'd find her there, alone and working on a new project. He hoped that he wouldn't find Kim there. He prayed he wouldn't have to confront Sidney. He rang her bell five or six times before getting out his key. He opened the door, stepped inside and called out her name, over and over, expecting to hear her shout a "hello" from her bedroom or her studio. The echo of his own voice was all that came back to greet him.

He moved into the living room, but there was no sign of any life there at all. Then he checked the dining room. Their little dinner party had been cleaned up and the room was spotless. He moved down the hallway, checking each door, room or closet, for any clues as to Feyhe's whereabouts. Everything seemed to be in place, not touched, not moved. Everything felt right about the place, except for the place itself.

There was an acrid smell that seemed to fill the hallway, a smell of death. Billy put his hand over his mouth and nose as he approached the bedroom at the far end of the hallway. The door was open and he moved through the opening and into the room. The smell was coming from here—he knew it, from something in this room. He looked around, expecting the worst, but saw nothing unusual, nothing out of place. It was almost too perfect, too clean and neat to be Feyhe's room. That was the real problem. The room was too neat.

Billy reached for the closet door and pulled it open. Nothing moved or shifted inside, and after a moment of hesitation Billy reached into the clothes hanging there and shifted them back and forth. He wasn't sure what he expected, but the result was a little more nothing. He closed the closet door.

He walked around to the far side of the bed, still hesitant, still guarding his nostrils and taste buds. He looked warily at the floor and saw...nothing. Still there was the smell, the awful smell. He considered kneeling down and checking under the bed, but couldn't bring himself to do it. He hesitated again, trying to decide what to do.

Then, he saw it.

There was something caught in the window. He moved closer, realized what he'd found, and stepped back, away from it. He choked back the growing angst that threatened his throat, the clear, ugly taste of digestive acids turning his brain and nostrils sour. The window was secured, but there in one corner was the bloody corpse of a rat. This was just a New York City rat, dead, killed by a heavy oak window frame, slammed into place.

Billy left the room, wandered back through the apartment and left it behind him. He was six blocks away before he thought about the door and whether or not he'd locked it when he left. He wasn't sure.

Joe was ironing when Billy returned to their apartment. Billy always found sights such as these to be amusing. Coming upon the large, virile Irish cop, wearing only his underwear and socks, standing behind an ironing board with its flat-topped workspace clearly at arm's length from Joe's shoulders, blue cloth draped over it in all directions, clearly had its humorous side. It also provided a practical springboard for conversation.

"What did you need, Joe?" Billy sang out as he entered the living room.

"Pants."

"You must have at least three other pair in the closet," Billy said.

"I like these. They fit me."

"They all fit you, Joe. You haven't gained a pound, or moved one around, since I've known you."

"These are my favorite, then," Joe said softly.

"They're all identical."

"They're not, Billy. They're different."

"Okay," Billy said. He smiled at Joe, took a deep breath and then said, "but if I mixed them up in your closet, could you really tell them apart?"

"Of course I could," Joe said without thinking about it, taking the bait that Billy had dropped in his path. "I'm a detective."

"That's quite a skill you've got there, detective, telling one pair of pants from another." He laughed. After a moment, Joe laughed with him.

"And I can tell the difference between the men wearing them, too," Joe added through his giggles.

"You'd better," Billy said, a mock threat in the affectionate tone he couldn't help using.

Billy passed through the living room, leaving Joe to finish his chore. He checked his answering machine, hoping for a blink indicating a message, hoping the voice on the tape would be Feyhe's voice. There was no message, no blink. He picked up the pile of envelopes that Joe had left on his desk, the day's mail, hoping for a note or a postcard from his cousin. As with the phone message, there were no notes or letters.

He sat down at his desk and turned on the overhead light that illumined both his desk and his drafting board. The rooms he had been working on were there before him. They were incomplete. They were a problem. Somewhere, he thought, he had missed something in the conversations he'd had with the apartment's owners. They wanted him to create something that would complete them, but Billy wasn't sure about the parts he was meant to connect. Ryan and Grey Kendall had been introduced to him weeks earlier by Frederick Ostendorf.

They were a young couple, comparatively, and wealthy without a doubt. Grey had been the debutante of the year, in her year, and when she married Ryan it had made headlines in *Women's Wear Daily* and *The Wall Street Journal*. The trouble Billy had sizing them up was not who they were or might be, it was who they weren't.

For one thing they weren't very different from one another. When he first met them he had been taken to a cocktail event, a fundraiser for the Museum of Modern Art, and they were among the five society sponsors of the event. Ostendorf pointed them out from the Museum Garden's entrance. They were standing near the Paris Metro Entry which dominated the northeast section of the garden. They both had their backs turned to where Billy and his host were standing. From behind they were virtually indistinguishable. They both had shoulder length blonde hair. They were both slender and tall with gathered waistlines and long legs. They were wearing matching tuxedos and they were both holding cocktails in their right hands.

"Ryan? Grey!" Ostendorf called out to them. They both turned equally slowly, exposing their faces at the same time. They were a choreographed, Jerome Robbins ballet of a couple, Billy thought, as their faces emerged from the far sides of their bodies. "Ryan, Grey, darlings, how are you?" Ostendorf gushed. He pulled Billy forward another step. "This is Billy Duncan. You know, I told you—"

"Billy Duncan, how nice," Grey said, her voice as soft as a ripple on a country stream in mid-spring.

"How very, very nice, indeed. Welcome," Ryan added in a voice equally soft and delicate.

"It's a pleasure," Billy said graciously, all the while wondering which of them was whom.

"Fred showed us the room you designed for him a while back," Grey said. He could tell, now, that this was Grey because he could smell her perfume, deliciously feminine and appealing. "It's such a charming concept."

"Especially for a room I make love in," Ostendorf added quickly. "Billy was aware of that when he created it."

"It helps to know a bit about your client's needs and ... things,"

Billy said awkwardly, not really sure where he had been headed when he spoke.

"Ryan and I think that's lovely, Billy," Grey said. "We seldom get to know the tradespeople we employ." Billy winced inwardly at the sound of those words.

"That's why we asked Fred to bring you along," Ryan added. "We thought a chance to meet would help us decide if you're the man for the job."

Billy's eyes widened a fraction. "What job is that?"

"Freddy didn't tell you?" Ryan asked.

"Oh, you poor dear," Grey said, "you must have been so confused, being asked to attend a party like this one."

"Not at all, Grey, dear," Ostendorf injected. "Billy is seen in all the best places."

"Even after the work is done?" she said. "My, my." Grey was clearly sizing him up. "Billy is Feyhe's cousin, Grey," Ostendorf said, nearly whispered actually.

"Feyhe…? Oh, not really!" Grey was nonplussed. "But he's so nice looking and so gentle."

"Feyhe has her moments, too," Ostendorf said quickly. "Now behave yourself, or I won't let him design for you."

"Not even for ready money," Billy added, quoting Oscar Wilde. Grey laughed a startled laugh.

"You've read Wilde?" Ryan asked him.

"I've performed Wilde," Billy said, then immediately regretted his answer, realizing from the expressions on Ryan and Grey's faces that they had misunderstood him. "I played Dorian Gray once in college and also played Lane, the butler, in *Earnest*," he added.

"Of course you did," Ryan said.

"How nice for you, too," Grey said.

"Where was that?" Ryan asked.

"An Ivy League school?" Grey asked.

"Or one of those fancy trade schools here in town?" Ryan pursued.

"Or not—" Grey added.

"Princeton," Billy said.

"You went to Princeton?" Ostendorf asked, the question double-edged.

"Twice," Billy said, an air of amusement in his voice, and he immediately changed the topic. "What is this job I should have been told about?"

The Kendalls looked at each other, vying for the opportunity to explain. Then Ryan took the lead.

"We purchased an apartment recently, quite far from here actually, on Little West 12th Street. It's an old SRO living space and we want it turned into something extraordinary, like us. The thing is we hate the current layout and we want it altered. We also have a neighbor who occupies the top two floors. We cannot disturb him for reasons I'll explain at a later date if we decide to hire you. Currently the triplex is conceived around a central circular stair that we hate. It has ten rooms we abhor and a garden that's in deplorable condition. We want it all redone.

"Fred thought we should have one designer redo the whole place, but I wasn't sure about that," Grey added. "Then he showed us your room."

"Well, hardly my room. It's Frederick's room. I just recreated it in my own image, or something." He was feeling uncomfortable with this couple and it was showing in his syntax. He knew he had misspoken but didn't correct himself.

"You're charming, you know, absolutely charming," Ryan said exuberantly. "When can you come over and see the place?"

"I could... is tomorrow too soon?" Billy blushed mid-sentence. He was trying not to sound eager, but the idea of designing an entire house and garden intrigued him.

"Noon." Grey handed him a calling card with the address on it. Then, without a word, she and Ryan turned, simultaneously, back the way they had been standing when Billy and Ostendorf had first approached them.

"I would have to guess that the *audience* is concluded?" Billy said quietly to Ostendorf. The older man nodded solemnly and they moved off toward the dais at the far end of the garden.

Now, weeks later, he stared at the drawings he had made and wondered how he could have gotten himself into such a mess. He had met the Kendalls the following day at noon, toured the building and proposed an overhaul of the entire space, converting three stories of brownstone building into seven levels of living. He had suggested the ramping and stepping of areas and the arrangement of colors growing from hot below to cool above and he had even dared to suggest the placement of rooms in the new spaces. All of this had been met, surprisingly, with an eager handshake and an offered contract.

The latter had been forthcoming and was now an accomplished fact. The only problem was that the deadline for final design approval was moving closer but the ideas weren't keeping pace with that due date. Billy picked up a pencil and moved from his desk to the higher angled drawing board. He looked carefully at the workmanship, studied the placement of angles and planes, gauged the height of windows and tossed his pencil back onto the desk. The only thing on his mind was Feyhe and that apartment of hers, with its stink and with its queer emptiness.

He debated calling Sidney, but the idea repulsed him. He opted for a phone call to Kim. This was difficult as Billy wasn't at all sure where Kim lived. He was afraid to learn that Kim and Feyhe might be shacking up together at her place. He decided that the one person who might know how to reach Kim was, actually, Sidney. So he called Sidney.

"So now you need a favor, you call me," the man said in as ungracious a manner as possible. "So, now that you and Feyhe aren't speaking who do you call for a little help? Sidney."

"I don't need any help, Sidney," Billy said, then he corrected himself. "Well, I do, actually. Feyhe hasn't been around for a while, a week maybe, I'm not really sure."

"Well, she's not living with me, Billy," Sidney said abruptly.

"I didn't think she was, Sidney. By any chance do you know where she is, or how to reach her?" Billy waited through the silence on the other end of the line.

"Yeah," he finally said. "Yeah, Billy, I do."

"Can you tell me or is it a secret?"

"I can tell you. What's it worth?"

"Excuse me?"

"What's it worth to you to know where Feyhe is? That's my question to you."

"Sidney, this isn't a game. I'm concerned about her."

"That's cute, Billy-Boy."

"And that's offensive, Sid."

"You think that's offensive, try this!" He slammed down his receiver, leaving Billy with nothing more than a slight reverberant earache. He debated calling Sidney back, then changed his mind. He had confirmation that Feyhe was somewhere, was probably all right and in touch with people. That was all he needed, he decided. He went back to work on the Kendall's house.

Two weeks after the dinner party, eight days after Billy discovered the rat in the windowsill at Feyhe's apartment, she phoned him.

"I hear you were worried about me?" she said lightly. "No need, sweetie."

"Where are you?" Billy demanded.

"I'm here. In my apartment. Airing the place," she said.

"You had a rat in your window."

"I know. I should have dumped it out after I killed it, but it was still squirming a little bit and I had a plane to catch." She sounded fine to Billy, like the Feyhe of old.

"Where did you go?"

"Kim and I went to San Francisco, darling," Feyhe said. "Didn't I tell you that? I thought I did."

"No, you didn't," Billy said, sounding annoyed. He pulled in his reins.

"How was the Gay capital of the western world?"

"Gay, gay gay," she laughed. "We had such a good time."

"Oh?"

"Yes, especially once Ni-Na arrived."

"Ni-Na? The wife?" Billy was confused and it showed in his voice.

"Yes. I told you we were going to bring her out. Well, she and the baby are here. We all spent a lovely week in San Francisco and then we all came back here."

"You have them all living with you now?"

"Yes. For the moment. They'll find a place of their own soon enough."

"And there's a baby?"

"There's a beautiful bouncing baby boy. They want me to be the godmother."

"Can you do that? For a Korean baby?"

"It's all right. This is America. No laws are being broken."

"What's this one called?"

"His name, Billy, so you know what to call *him*," she emphasized the "him" for Billy's sake, "is Mitchell."

"Mitchell? That doesn't sound very Korean."

"Smarty. It's not Korean. They named him for my father. To honor me and my ancestors, in gratitude for my help in getting them over here."

Billy thought about that statement before he responded. He was thrilled to hear from Feyhe, yet troubled by the conversation.

"I hope they don't regret it later, the move, not the name. I hope they don't blame you in the end."

"What?" She sounded perplexed, not angry.

"Well, if they hadn't met you they wouldn't need to be here, would they? If you hadn't involved them in your battle over your artwork they wouldn't have had the need to leave their homeland."

"They would have left anyway, Idiot. That regime was stifling them."

"He's a philosopher, Feyhe. She's an economist. They would have been fine."

"You think you know so much, Billy, when you really only know half of what you think you know."

"Feyhe, I only—"

"You only want to make trouble for me suddenly. I don't understand it at all, Billy."

"Feyhe, please listen to me—"

"No. I'm sorry, but I can't. You and Frederick and those awful Kendalls deserve one another. Leave me alone from now on. If I need something from you I'll let you know, all right?"

"No, it isn't all right, Feyhe—"

"Good-bye Billy. My best to Joe." She hung up the phone.

It was their last conversation for nearly a year, but Billy was so busy during that time, that he hardly missed her at all.

12

Ryan and Grey Kendall and their house-obessed Billy, each in equal measure. The house itself was a double-width brownstone on Little West 12th Street in the far western reaches of Greenwich Village. Built in 1814, it was a five-story brick residence with a dark, high-walled garden. It had last been redone in the early 1950s and the internal space, boxes within boxes, low-electrical wattage, facilitating toilets, reflected its owner's sense of use in that era, low-income rental studios. The Kendalls had purchased it and slowly, over a period of two years, emptied it of tenants, all except for the man on the top two floors. They, themselves, had not taken up active occupation of the building. It didn't suit them.

Ryan was born to money, but he had developed a sympathetic nature in his youth that had never left him. He was an avid reader, a romantic in his tastes in literature, music and art. He worked, if one could call it work, at a small business that he had inherited along with everything else from his father. The business consisted of brokering relationships. Ryan put people together to construct whatever they could create in the absence of a vacuum. Sometimes it was a shopping mall with a concept: kinetic art, for example, or actual second-shops, retailing at wholesale prices. Sometimes it was a larger, more artistic idea that grew out of Ryan's meddling with people: theatres, dance companies, small museums. It didn't seem to matter which way his talents took him,

Ryan's taste and his sensible head kept things on track and resulted in successful ventures.

Grey had also been born into a world of privilege and wealth. Her childhood had been spent packing and moving, for her family never settled in one place for long. The only daughter in a family dominated by boys, she had grown aggressive at an early age, just a precaution against being lost in the shuffle. Her parents hated the idea of settling down. They liked to be in a constant state of flux. Her education had been totally home-schooled until her final two years of prep school. She had been surrounded by tutors, brothers, parents and grandparents, cozened, pampered and spoiled. The transition into the later teen years and a stationary schooling had been difficult, almost impossible, really, until she met Ryan.

They had taken to one another instantly and had rarely been apart since the day they met. Their tastes were similar even if their understanding of those tastes was not. They liked the same places, things, and people—the three categories they agreed existed in life. For them there was nothing else. They married at twenty-two, bought their first home the same year, and moved constantly.

Now, in their mid thirties, they had found this extraordinary building in the west village and decided to settle down into it, create the perfect cocoon for their middle years.

Billy was their choice for the home's design. Though not an architect, they knew he could give them the sort of place they craved. For the Kendalls, appetite was everything and Billy was another morsel, a tasty piece of humanity, to quench their joint palate. Billy was willing.

Billy presented them with his first drawings on schedule, late on a Thursday afternoon.

This, in spite of his problems with Feyhe and his difficulties at home with Joe, was no surprise to him. He had always been a slave to his work and his deadlines and, he believed, worked best under the determined pressure of such a schedule. He met them at their current temporary home, an apartment on East 58th Street. They stood in the library of the seven room condominium, Billy's plans and drawings spread out on the large library table.

The oak top, three inches thick, a large, graceful oval shape, was supported by a single table pedestal in its center. Also made of oak, it was nearly three feet across and was itself supported by four sturdy oak legs. Strong enough to support all three people leaning hard against it, the tabletop allowed Billy to show off his work.

"As you can see...here," he said, "the gradual flare of the inner walkway allows you to move without pause from one level to another. There's no need for conventional stairs in this house. That's the depth, of course."

"Of course," Grey said.

"It's an unusually deep space, you see," Billy continued. "From the front wall to the rear it's nearly eighty-two feet on the current first floor and only diminishes at the top to seventy-six feet." He smiled, expecting a smile in return, but received only a sigh from Grey and nothing from Ryan.

"As for the width of the building," Billy said immediately, "we're almost as lucky. The front of the building measures internally to an exhausting thirty eight feet, while the back wall flares a bit to a full forty feet. This prevents the structure from taking on a pyramid-like appearance."

"What do we have to do," Ryan asked, "to make it all work out?"

Billy turned his attention more squarely to the man. "We have to gut the interior completely. We have to just rip out everything, top to bottom and start from scratch."

"Is that really possible?" Grey asked. "Won't the whole thing come tumbling down somehow?"

"No, not at all." Billy went on to explain the physical dynamics of the structure. The walls, he had found on examining the original plans, were brick veneered, inside and outside, over a sturdy internal structure consisting of interlocking metal and wood beams, both horizontal and vertical. The linking of the floor beams grew similarly from struts applied to the uprights within the three-foot thick outer walls. These could be cut, leaving enough protruding to act as the basis for new beam work that would supply the needed strength to maintain the interior floors and stairs and ramps that Billy had plotted.

"It would take about three weeks to do the clearing out of the current interior work, including the electricity and plumbing," Billy told them, "and then we could begin to consider the actual work of creating this house for you."

"How long would it take?" Grey asked the question sharply.

"A year, I think, maybe thirteen months depending on the materials we decide to go with," Billy replied.

"A year is doable," Ryan offered, "if we consider the alternative."

"Which is?" Billy asked.

"Which is not doing it at all. We've talked about just selling it, or maybe tearing it down and selling the land."

"But it's a wonderful place, or could be," Billy said, protesting a bit more than he had intended.

"It's still an alternative," Grey said coolly.

"I suppose so," Billy said.

"But we do like your plans, Billy," Ryan offered, placing his hand firmly on Billy's shoulder and leaning in a bit too close, Billy thought.

"Yes. They rather match our own," Grey added, putting her hand on Billy's other shoulder. The two of them now leaned in ever so slightly on Billy, pinning his arms at his side.

"I'm glad to hear that," Billy said, his voice a bit small and closed in.

With his free hand, Ryan took Billy's chin and turned his face to look closely at Ryan's own face. Billy was uncomfortable with this closeness and hoped that it showed. Ryan, however, was undeterred by what he saw there, if indeed he saw anything at all.

"We like you, Billy, and we like your ideas. Grey and I are both looking forward to this association."

"It will make your reputation, you know," Grey said.

"I didn't think it needed to be made, actually," Billy said.

"A reputation always needs to be made, or enhanced," she said smiling.

"I suppose."

Billy edged his way backward, releasing himself from the three hands of the couple he was climbing into professional bed with for this project.

"I can leave these with you to look over at your leisure," he said. "I have copies of everything." The Kendalls didn't respond. "If you have any ideas or suggestions, you can just mark them right on these plans and when I pick them up from you next week, we can talk about your needs..." He hesitated, then went on. "...or your special ideas about the building itself." He sighed too loudly.

"We'll do that, Billy." Grey was more effusive than usual. "Can we offer you a drink?"

Billy declined, thanked his hosts and beat a hasty departure. He hailed a cab as he hurried from the apartment house and, once he was snuggled up inside, his body hard against a corner of the back seat, he breathed a sigh of relief and found himself breaking into tears.

"You all right back there, Mac?" the cabbie called out to him.

"Yes, yes, I'll be fine." He wiped away the tears. "Take me to West End and 78th, please."

Joe was waiting for him at home, he knew, and he didn't want to keep him waiting too long. Thursdays were special for Joe, and Billy liked to be a part of those evenings when Joe's family dined together, his mother and his daughter, Billy and Joe, all together for a few hours. It was time he cherished, time for Joe that he never begrudged his partner.

The city bustled by the windows of the cab as the driver poked his way through the heady and intense traffic on the cross street. Billy, keeping his eye on what surrounded him in the center of the city, couldn't keep his mind from wandering back to Ryan and Grey. He could still feel the tightness of their hands on his shoulders, the feeling of their bodies pressed into his hips, his thighs, his arms. He liked them but they unsettled him. They never made a move that was even remotely seductive, but he couldn't escape the sense of attraction he felt whenever he was with them. What he couldn't make plain was whether that attraction was his own for them, or theirs for him. He just wasn't sure.

He loved the cold, calculating sounds that Grey made when she spoke to him. He found himself wondering how she spoke to Ryan when they were alone, whether he had ever suffered her insolent verbal ways.

Likewise, he adored the warmth and genuine interest that Ryan always seemed to show him. He thought about Ryan's gentle fingers and sensuous lower lip and long, flared eye-lashes.

I'm a little bit in love with these people, Billy thought. He closed his eyes and their faces swam before him, moving through gelatinous waters in a fluctuating vortex. Sometimes their mouths were closed in this vision, sometimes their lips parted and moved, forming words that he could not hear. *At least I know that, and understand that*, he thought, *that being in love with two people. I know it. I'm safe from it.*

The cab emerged from the side streets and turned onto Amsterdam Avenue, heading uptown. The buildings here were a mixed bag of old, gothic design and more modern, low-income high-rises. Then came Lincoln Center and the starkly expensive buildings that had sprung up around it, including the Martin Luther King Jr. High School for the Performing Arts, a school dedicated to the talented underprivileged of New York City, it's monolith sculpture rusting away in the foreground of the school's courtyard. The cab took a few more turns, ending up on what would become West End Avenue. Before long, Billy was stepping out of the yellow cab and breathing in the noisy air that siphoned through the internal courtyard of his own apartment complex. He was home. Joe was waiting. He was safe again.

"I didn't think you were going to make it in time," Joe said as Billy came into the bedroom. Joe was already dressed for the evening in a grey turtle-neck, matching trousers, and a blue blazer.

"Traffic," Billy said apologetically. "I took a cab and I began to wonder if I'd ever even make it across town." He pulled out a shirt and a pair of black, dress jeans, tossed them onto the bed and kicked off his shoes.

"So? How did it go? Did they like it?"

"Joe, they liked it. I don't really know much more about it than that. They were responsive to every idea, and I left the drawings with them so they could think about it."

"But they liked it?"

"Yeah. They did."

"I'm proud of you, Billy. I'm really proud of you."

Billy blushed and pulled off his tee-shirt, tossing it on the floor randomly. He picked up the clean shirt he had taken from the closet and swept himself into it, rather grandly.

"You do that so well. I love it." Joe was beaming.

"So, what's the plan for tonight?" Billy asked him, still dressing. He was stepping out of his wool pants, and then he tossed them, as he had the tee-shirt, somewhere in the room, somewhere on the floor.

"We're picking them up on the corner of Broadway and 79th in about ten minutes, going to the Burger Joint for dinner and then on to the Natural History museum for a special show of South American dance music in the Andes exhibit at the Museum."

"A full evening of fun," Billy said.

"I think so," Joe said quietly.

"And you'll dance with your mom, and with Sandy," Billy said, "and I'll watch from the sidelines and have so much fun just sitting there."

"Billy," Joe said, a cautionary note in his voice.

"I know. I'll behave." He pulled on the jeans and zipped them up as he walked to the dressing table to look at himself in the mirror. "Hmm, not bad for someone who was actually working half an hour ago and caught in traffic until five minutes ago."

"Not bad for anyone," Joe said. He reached out and gathered Billy into his arms, held him close in an embrace that filled Billy with the heretofore un-gathered sadness he'd been avoiding all day. He choked back a sob that threatened to break out. He hoped Joe hadn't noticed. "What's wrong?" Joe asked him instantly.

"Nothing. I think nothing."

"Work's going well. We're doing okay," Joe said. "What is it?"

"Nothing," he repeated. "Just a long, hard day and the frustration about the Kendalls. They don't exactly react, they … they do … whatever it is they do."

"Sure?" Joe was staring into Billy's eyes. He reached out and took Billy's chin in his hand, his thumb and forefinger bracing Billy's cheeks. Billy pulled away from his lover's grip.

"Why did you do that?" Joe asked him.

"No reason."

"No reason. Nothing. These aren't the answers I like, Billy," Joe said.

"Those are the answers. Take it or leave it." Billy turned away from Joe, picked up a comb and ran it twice through his hair. "Let's go. They'll be waiting for us, wondering what I've done now to delay us. Let's just go."

Without waiting for Joe, Billy hurried out of the bedroom.

He ate lunch with Ryan Kendall almost every day for two weeks. Over their light meals, broth, salad, tea, and bonbons they discussed the house and its layout, the placement of rooms and the privacy issues that each room or suite seemed to dictate. The most intriguing concept, Billy realized, was the separation of the master bedroom suite into two completely different pairs of rooms, connected by a large bathroom and closet arrangement. Ryan and Grey had both been adamant about this and had even given Billy a layout concept page with furniture, windows and artwork already indicated.

"You want it exactly like this, then?" he had asked them both.

"Not exactly like that, darling," Grey had cooed at him from behind her martini glass. "You do it like that, but in your own fashion."

"Exactly," Ryan had said, agreeing with his wife. "You understand, of course."

"I don't, exactly," Billy had said, daring to fail in an instant, "but there's nothing I can't comprehend eventually."

"How like you," Ryan had said softly. And Grey echoed his sentiments exactly.

The word *exactly* seemed to have been invented expressly for these two to utter. Billy heard the three syllables exclaimed, shouted, whispered, hooted, honked and simply stated in every conversation he had with the two of them. It came up less often when he was alone with Ryan. They were alone this afternoon, lunching on the usual complement of non-fattening foods. Except for the bonbons.

"Do you realize where the bonbon originated, Billy?" Ryan asked him, holding one between his upper and lower front teeth. In spite of the inserted ice cream ball, the words emerged crisp and distinct.

"No. I've no idea," Billy replied, also holding a chocolate covered vanilla ice cream ball between his teeth. They both laughed.

"The Story of the Bon Bon—the Good Good or the Sweet Sweet. In the fifteenth century, Billy, the lords of France were inventing, or stealing, the best of the world's music, literature, art, religion and food," Ryan said. "The Beau Monde, under the leadership of the Beau Lion were creating the Bon Mot and pretending to the Bon Ton but, in reality, it was all *Bon gré mal gré.* No one knew what anyone else was doing. In the royal courts there were spies everywhere and, as William Shakespeare would define it later on, the Bonaroba were in control of the heads of houses. It was to please one of these well-dressed ladies of the night that Monsieur Henri de Bon Coeur invented this little dessert. The idea was that it would sweeten her kiss without messing up her dress, or her fingers which would be put to use to sweeten others things for him."

"Sweet story, Ryan," Billy said. "True?"

"Who knows." He laughed aloud. "Who cares, really? Do you think this sweetens my kiss, Billy?"

"I wouldn't know."

"Come and try one then, and tell me what you think." He placed another bonbon in his mouth and smiled at Billy. The awkwardness of the moment was made even more so by Billy's inability to move closer to Ryan without leaning over the table. There was no easy way around the pedimented impediment. He stood up and leaned forward, expecting Ryan to do the same, but Kendall stayed in his chair, still smiling, still holding the cold sweet between his lips. Billy reached as far as he could, then gave up and sat back down.

"You disappoint me, Billy," Ryan said, swallowing his ice cream treat. "But most people do eventually."

"You didn't really expect me to kiss you, Ryan."

"Didn't I?" He looked beyond Billy, toward the door to the room. "I don't know that I did or didn't. Hello, darling."

Billy knew at once that Grey had come into the room. "So he didn't kiss you, Ry, didn't take the bait."

"No."

"All professional, was he?"

"Not all, no."

"Listen you two, if you want to discuss my social and sexual politics I can go elsewhere," Billy said.

"No need, sweetie," Grey said. "I'm just on my way out, metaphorically speaking. I'll be back around eleven, Ry. Get him into bed and I'll treat for dinner. Bye, loves." She was gone.

There was a silence between the two men that Billy finally broke. "What was that about?"

"Oh. We have a little wager."

"You and your wife? A bet about me?"

"Yes, dear heart, a wager over your soul and your body."

"I don't understand."

Ryan looked at Billy and sighed. In that sound was everything Billy needed to know. There was a longing and a strength of purpose. There was a sexual need and a psychological ploy. Billy blushed, as he often had in the past, but this time his body temperature volleyed upward all the way to his knees.

"That's a lovely color, Billy," Ryan said. "I'd kill to see more of it."

"You'll have to, I think," Billy said. "I'm not really available."

"Oh, morality, is it?" Ryan snorted. "You have a boyfriend and so you don't fool around. Not even with married men?"

"I never sleep with a client," Billy said simply.

"Well, all right, you're fired, then." He chuckled. "Now what are you willing to do to get back on the payroll?"

"Ryan, this is getting very inappropriate," Billy said. "Let's get back to work."

"You don't really think this is just playtime, do you?"

Billy hesitated before he answered. Something in Ryan's tone told him that this final question was not a part of any sort of game. This was real.

"No, Ryan, I don't," Billy said. "I think that this topic is much more serious than either one of us wants to admit right now. Therefore, I'd like to table this discussion." He stared into Ryan's eyes as he said these words. Neither one of them batted so much as an eyelash. Ryan broke the lock that held their eyes in synchronicity.

"On the table would be fine with me," he said to Billy. "I like a hard surface under my back."

Billy couldn't help himself; laughter burst out of him with orgasmic fervor. In a moment, Ryan was laughing just as hard.

Kim Ni-Na gave birth to a baby boy in the late summer of that year. Billy received a card from Feyhe alerting him to the new arrival, named Jimmy. When he phoned her to offer congratulations and to inquire about where to send a gift he got Feyhe's answering machine. He left a message and waited for a response, but she didn't call him back. He left a second message and a third one, but Feyhe never responded. Billy gave it up. Instead he called his mother for whatever news she might have on the subject.

"So, you heard the latest from Feyhe?" Miriam said to him immediately. "She's a grandma now, she said."

"I guess she meant it, then, about the adoption," Billy said to her.

"I guess she did. You sound disappointed, Billy."

"No, of course not. I hope she's happy, that's all."

"She looked happy when I saw her, so I would guess she is happy." She paused for a breath and began to chew something. Billy could distinctly hear the sounds of mastication through the earpiece of his telephone. "You don't see her anymore?"

"No. I haven't seen her in a while now. We argued."

"What about?"

"I wish I knew. I really don't know, you know."

"Do you want me to say something to Feyhe when I see her?" Miriam asked.

"You see her? Often?" He tried not to sound too eager.

"Not what you'd call often, but I see her. You know she stopped."

Billy took the pause this time and in that moment he clearly heard his mother chewing again. "Stopped what? Smoking?"

185

"We should both live long enough to see that!" Miriam exclaimed. "No. She stopped with the statues. No more, she said. Not one more piece would she create, she told me."

"Why? Did she say why?"

"You sound upset, Billy. What is it? What's wrong?"

"It's Feyhe. If she stopped sculpting than something is very, very wrong with her. She won't answer my calls, and she stopped carving. What's going on with her?"

"You are upset, kiddo. Listen, she's fine. She's just got a new preoccupation, that's all."

"No. No, there's something else. There has to be."

"Billy, calm yourself, she's just Feyhe. You don't know her like I do. This is who she is. She does things. She stops doing them. It doesn't matter to her."

"But she's an artist, Miriam. An important artist. She can't just stop. It's not reasonable."

"Was it so reasonable of the Koreans to destroy all of her work like that? Was it so reasonable of that man to put her piece in his sex chamber? Was it so—?"

"Wait a minute, Miriam. That man, that piece of hers. She destroyed it. She got into his place and she destroyed the work, herself and no one else."

"That's not how she describes it."

"What did she tell you?"

"Well," she audibly chewed again. Billy pulled the phone away from his ear, but he could still her chewing. Then her voice came back and overrode the other, more irritating sound. "She said he went crazy and got something ugly and scummy all over her statue and when she asked for it back he broke it."

"That's not true. I was there."

"Billy, Feyhe doesn't tell lies (chew, chew)."

"She told you one about that statue, Miriam."

"Feyhe doesn't tell lies (chew). I know this about her. I didn't know it when we were girls (chew), but I do know this now."

"She didn't tell you the truth. That story is a total fabrication."

"Feyhe doesn't lie, Billy (chew)."

"Miriam, what the hell are you chewing. It's making me nuts!"

"What are you talking about? Billy, what's going on with you?"

He hung up the phone and when it rang a moment later, he just let it ring.

At dinner he asked Joe if Feyhe had been in touch with him at all. He shook his head, leaving Billy helpless, without a comeback. Over coffee he told Joe about his conversation with his mother. Joe was, once again, marginally interested in the tale.

"What's with you now?" Billy asked him as he walked into the living room where Joe was already seated, a book open on his lap.

"I'm fine. I'm just bored with all of this nonsense," Joe replied. "I'd like to see us get back to being a team, a pair, a couple."

"And we're not?"

"No, Billy, we're not. We both go to work and then we both go out to deal with our different families or our associates or something. We spend very little time together and most of that is spent over meals and they seem to involve you telling me about your mother, or Feyhe or the clients. I probably only talk about my daughter. It's frustrating, Billy, that we never seem to have time to do things together, explore each other's minds on anything other than the mundane, humdrum, day-to-day of our own individual existences."

Billy sat down on the chair opposite Joe. The room's light, artificial at this hour, but enhanced by the final stages of sunlight over the Hudson River and the New Jersey shoreline, threw long shadows over his shoulder in Joe's direction. Billy watched his own shadow, noting how it leaped over the coffee table, its head lying distinctly in Joe's lap. Joe, noting it also, slowly brought his knees together, enclosing the shadow-head between his thighs. As expected, the shadow would not be contained by Joe's muscular legs.

"That's what I mean, Billy," he said, gesturing toward his groin. "You and your shadow are one and the same in my life. I try to hold you both, but neither one is really there."

"You mean sex?" Billy said.

"No. I mean togetherness. Even this conversation is sort of

ephemeral. It's going to dissipate in a minute or two, just like your shadow is going to fade into the basic hues of the room as soon as the sun moves onward a bit."

"Joe, I don't neglect you. I never do that."

"No. You don't. You cook for me and you do the laundry. You make the occasional weekend plan for us both. You go with me to see my mom and my kid."

"I keep telling you I want her to come and live with us. It's time, Joe."

"It's not, Billy. It's really not."

"This is old ground, Joe, and we've covered it a lot."

"It's not the same. I think I finally put my finger on the problem and it's not the gay thing." Billy looked surprised, but Joe hardly noticed. He went on with his revelations. "The real problem is us. We live different lives and we don't connect in them, only outside of them. As we grow more and more intensely involved with career and with our family situations, we have less and less time to find a relationship that's actually ours. We're sharing space and living alone."

"It's not true, Joe." Billy shouted the words out, but he felt the reality of them crashing all around him.

"It is, Billy." He gave his lover a half-smile. "We're not really suited for one another."

"Ryan Kendall wants me for his lover," Billy blurted out suddenly. "Maybe I should go with that."

"Maybe you should, at that," Joe said quietly. Billy was off his chair instantly and kneeling in front of the cop.

"Don't make me do this, Joe. Don't throw me away. Don't throw me out of your life, too."

"What do you mean my life, too?"

"Everyone I care about discards me," Billy said pathetically. "Everyone. I can't bear to think that you would, too. Like my Dad. Feyhe. It would kill me." He looked away from Joe, his eyes cast down onto the floor.

"You're a lot stronger than you know, Billy." He placed his hands on Billy's shoulders.

Billy looked up at him.

"And you can't stand to be the one to say what it is you're obviously thinking," Billy countered, a new bitterness in his heart showing up in his voice. "I can be as melodramatic as you want. I can be sweet. I can be a holy terror. I can be anything you want, Joe."

"I don't know what I want, Billy. I only know I don't want what I have right now."

"Don't do this. Please don't do this."

Joe stood up, his book closed around the index finger of his right hand. He moved off in the direction of their bedroom. Without looking back at Billy, he said, "Don't sleep in here tonight, will you? I think I need to sleep alone for a while." He entered the room and shut the door, leaving Billy, still kneeling, on the floor. He stayed there for a while. He expected to cry, but he didn't. He waited for a sign, for a call from the other room; it never came.

He reached for the phone, his first thought to call Feyhe. He picked up the receiver, dialed, waited and then, when he heard the distinct sound of someone picking up the phone on the other end of the connection, he said, "Grey wins."

There was a low-voiced chuckle, followed by a whispered response, but whose voice he heard he really couldn't tell.

"Ryan," he whispered. "Is that you?"

"You'll never be sure," came the response, and Billy knew he wouldn't.

J. PETER BERGMAN

13

When she read the announcement in the Times Feyhe reached for the phone. Her hand hadn't reached the dial, however, when she realized that she would have to say something nice to Billy. She had been eating lunch, fighting her way through the mass of dull news that permeated the thin pages of the newspaper, thinner than she liked, much thinner than she remembered them being when she was younger. The news seemed equally thin to her. Stories of no consequence detailed in language with no style. She hadn't been expecting the shock of seeing Miriam's name in bold letters on the page when she turned to the obituaries. She hadn't expected that at all.

Usually when she got to the death notices she would spot a name, or even two, that rang a bell somewhere in the depths of her memory. It could be a former colleague or friend, a faded film star or a politician she had taken note of in his day. Once in a while there would be a person who had actually meant something more to her, but not too often, for there were few enough of those people left. Miriam had come as a shock. She was sure she'd read it wrong, so she put the tongue and cheddar cheese sandwich down, picked up the newspaper with both hands and read the notice again.

Miriam Greenberg Duncan, 68 the entry began. Feyhe calculated the years between her cousin's birth and now and the age was almost right. She let her eyes drop to the bottom of the paragraph to see who survived this particular Miriam Greenberg Duncan and she found the names she knew would be there: husband Angus, son Bill. She slowly allowed her gaze to fall on the text between the name and the survivors. She read the information, absorbing it the way a sponge would take in the thick nectar of a guillotined peach. The words slowly crept into her consciousness, making no real sense, yet saying everything she needed to know and to understand.

Miriam had suffered a massive coronary and been taken to Astoria General Hospital where she arrived already dead. The cause of the heart trouble was unknown and the dead woman showed no signs of suffering any violence whatsoever. The death, ruled accidental and heart failure, was assumed natural.

Below the obituary was a notice concerning funeral arrangements. Feyhe couldn't read the words, wouldn't read them. She put the paper down and returned to her sandwich. She reached for the phone once again, this time picking it up and holding it, hearing the dial tone, trying to find the numbers she wanted. She dialed a few, then returned the handset to its cradle. She thought about the word cradle, examined it for hidden meanings, found none, cried.

"This has got to stop," she whispered. "This has got to stop right now."

Her tears kept coming. She pushed herself away from the table and got up, went into the living room and plunged down onto the sofa. She lay there for a while, not sure of her next move, but being prone on the deep cushions softened the emotional blow of Miriam's death for her. She stopped crying.

One more time she picked up the phone and dialed numbers, a complete set of numbers. She heard the ringing on the other end of the line and she waited, counting off the rings, saying some of the numbers aloud, saying others only in her mind. When the rings equaled the number of minutes she had cried, twenty, she hung up the phone. She realized that the information she needed would already be in her grasp, in the obituary notice, in the kitchen. She went back, picked up the paper and, without tears to block her vision, read what she needed to read.

The funeral parlor was on the west side of Manhattan, in the mid-seventies. She had been there many times in her life, mostly for the funeral services of old friends. Most of her family were buried out of a less-expensive chapel in the Rego Park section of Queens, not in this posh upper west side mansion. Miriam's funeral, she surmised, was in Billy's hands. That was the only explanation for this change of venue from the cheaper version. When she came out of the elevator on the third floor, she could hear the crowd at the end of the hall. Without hesitation she sauntered down to the reception room, her eyes on the alert for cousins, for Angus and, especially, for Billy.

It had been nearly a year since they had spoken. During that time she had wanted to sit with him, hold his hand, confide in him. She wanted to see him with Joe, see his work, experience what he was learning. Her stubborn nature had prevented even the slightest, most casual connection. Her stubborn nature had kept them unnatural enemies. She regretted her stubborn nature. Especially on this occasion, she regretted everything.

Angus spotted her first, before she saw him. He came up to her and embraced her. She stiffened slightly at his touch, tried not to, tried to soften, couldn't. He held her in a tight arm lock, her own arms at her sides, his head on her shoulder.

"Thank you for coming, Feyhe," he said through his tears. "She would be so pleased."

"I'll miss her too, Angus," Feyhe said softly. "She had no reason to be my friend, but she was, right up to the end."

"She loved you," the bereft widower said simply.

"I know she did," Feyhe answered him. "I know."

She glanced around the room, hoping that Angus would let her go, and soon. As thoughts communicate in strident times, he instantly moved back a step, releasing Feyhe as he did so. He saw her eyes darting around, taking in the people behind him. He smiled.

"He's here," Angus said. "You'll find him."

"Who?"

"You know," Angus said and he actually smiled. "Come, let me show you."

He took her by the hand and led her through the crowd. Several of her cousins acknowledged her presence and she acknowledged theirs as she and Angus slowly crossed the large room. She gauged that there were at least a hundred people here for Miriam's funeral. A hundred people for a woman no one had ever heard about. A hundred. Feyhe was impressed. Angus changed direction suddenly, without a word, and Feyhe was dragged, seemingly against her will in a new direction. She wasn't paying attention to where she was being led, but kept looking around her at the sea of familiar and unfamiliar faces. They came to a stop.

"Look who came?" Angus was saying. Feyhe turned to look at Billy, her first sight of him in so long. It wasn't Billy, however, whose eyes met hers, but another important man from her past. It was Owen, her husband. Her former husband. The ex.

"Feyhe? Look at you," Owen said. "I don't believe it. You're young again."

He looked the same as he had when she left him Feyhe decided at once. Nothing about him had changed. He was still young, still handsome, still trim. He still wore the same clothes, the same expression on his face. His hair was still loose and fell across his brow the way it had the last time, and the times before the last time.

"You're still young," she said to him. "No 'again' about it. You haven't aged a day."

"You're being kind," he said. "I'm not used to that."

"Of course you're not," she said. "You were too busy to notice that I was often kind, kinder than you deserved." She moved a step closer to him. "What are you doing here?"

"I saw the notice in the Times and I had to come. I knew Miriam before I knew you, remember."

"I remember."

"And I've actually known Angus for a while now," he added. "It's a business thing."

"You have a business? That's new."

"A lot's new, Feyhe. I'd love to tell you about it."

The sweetness in his voice, the cordiality of it all repulsed her suddenly. She took back the step forward she'd made and took another one in addition. From this new distance he didn't look quite so wonderful. "Another time, perhaps," she said. "I have to find my cousins. This is a funeral, not a dancehall."

"I'll call you," he said to her back as she moved away.

"Try to," she said without turning in his direction, "and see what it gets you."

She moved through the room, packed now with even more people, as though she was a raisin pushing out through thick gruel. She kept her eyes trained on the faces around her. She spotted Peachie talking to two men and she moved in their direction, finally coming upon them. She knew, before she reached them, that neither of the men was Billy.

"Peach...help me, please," she said, extending her hand through a narrow passageway comprised of male shoulders covered in dark wool. Peachie took her hand and held it firmly as Feyhe edged her way between the human obstacles. Finally free and in Peachie's corner, she turned to look at her cousin's companions.

"Ozzie?" she asked. "Is that really you?"

He returned her gaze with an air of innocence that confused her. Then he smiled as though recognition had been difficult, then worthwhile.

"Feyhela, mein Feyhela. I don't believe my eyes," Ozzie sang at her. "Look at you, never a beauty, yet a classic."

"How have you been, Ozzie? Where have you been?"

"I've been healthy for a man who's sick and I've been around for a man who never left home."

"Still the same Ozzie," Feyhe said to her cousin. "You are still the same old joker who can't answer a simple question with a straightforward response."

"Feyhela, the world's fairest princess," he said, "and you remember Morris?"

"Of course I do. Of course." She was being definitive, sounding strong. Her eyes darted quickly at the men behind Ozzie. She couldn't see Billy anywhere. She turned to the other man and looked at him, trying to recognize him, finding it impossible.

"And this is Morris?" she asked both men.

"It is," Peachie said over Feyhe's shoulder. "Be nice, now."

"Morris, it's Feyhe. Do you remember me?" The man looked at her, stared at her really, but his own face showed little. He was bald and round-faced, with no neck, no facial hair. His ears were pinned back and there was a spot of drool on his lips. "Morris?" she said again.

"He's fine, really, Feyhe," said someone else near her. "He can't be expected to remember someone he hasn't seen in more than forty years."

She turned toward the voice, the voice she knew so well. Owen was standing there, somehow near her again, no longer on the opposite side of the room.

"How would you know that?" she asked him, a bit snippy in spite of herself.

"He's one of the people in my care," Owen responded. "I told you there was a lot to tell."

She looked at him, a mixture of hatred and awe in her face; he saw the mix and he laughed. She felt herself blush, turned away, saw Peachie staring at her and turned back to Owen. He was offering her his hand, an open palm, a handshake hand. She spat in his hand and moved quickly in another direction.

Just then the doors to the chapel were opened and a strange, tall man, thin and with thin hair, announced that the funeral services would begin shortly. He urged everyone to take a seat. Feyhe pushed past several other people and entered the chapel. Billy was already there. She spotted him instantly, standing near the front of the chapel, near Miriam's closed casket. Joe was with him. She sidled past a few more people who were finding seats in the middle rows, and hurried down the now empty aisle in Billy's direction. He looked up, just as she rounded the corner, coming toward him. He smiled. He couldn't help himself.

As she approached him, he opened his arms to receive her. She fell into them and they hugged. Joe put his hands on each of them simultaneously, softly, the connection completed, the circle of energy connected once again.

"Thanks for coming, Feyhe," Billy said softly in her ear. "It means so much."

"I didn't know…" she began, then changed her course. "…it never would have occurred to me that this would be the catalyst."

"I know that." Billy was soft and non-judgmental.

"I loved her in my way, Billy. You know I did."

"I know you kept up the conversation between you."

"She told you?" He nodded.

"She told you everything?"

"You lied to her about us. I know that."

"I lied...?" she said quietly, unsure of herself.

"It's all right, Feyhe. I corrected her impressions of us."

"What are you talking about?" Her words and her body language spoke reams.

"It's all right, Feyhe. I understand." He smiled at her. "You'd better take a seat. They want to start." He turned away from her, but Joe stayed next to her, taking her back up the aisle.

"Give him some time, Feyhe, please," Joe said. "He's very upset today."

"He's not the only one," she said.

"Just give him time." Joe was gone. Feyhe was standing near the rear of the room. Suddenly it was all too much for her. She turned back toward the reception room, fled in its direction and kept on going until she was approaching Central Park.

There was a bench in the park where Feyhe liked to sit. She had never mentioned this to anyone and no one she knew ever expected to find her, an old lady with a bag of bread crumbs, sitting on a bench feeding the pigeons. Still, she liked it. There was a satisfaction she achieved in this that didn't come often or lightly.

She sat there for a while, her mind swimming with images that threatened to connect into a memory. She fought them, pushed them aside, rid herself of the impulse to dream of the past. That never did her any good, she knew, and she only wanted to feel good again. That was all she really wanted. She reached into her paper bag and pulled out the not-quite-dry piece of white bread. She wanted it to crumble, but as she moved it in her hands it began to take on other shapes instead. There were long, cylindrical shapes and funny round ones. The crusts held their firmer stiffness and the bread attached to them, as clay to a ligature, assumed the firmness, length and breadth of their staff. In a quiet rage, Feyhe pulled the lengthy cylinder apart and tossed large pieces of it to the ground in front of her. Birds immediately flocked to retrieve the lumps of bread.

She watched them eat, listened to their effervescent chirping. She laughed a few times, each one shorter than the one that preceded it. She began to cry, to remember, to dream awake.

She and Owen always spent Sunday morning in bed together. There was no reason not to do so, she knew, but somehow she always felt a bit too nervous about what they might be missing. She was never comfortable with doing nothing. On this particular day she was especially uneasy.

"Stop fidgeting, Feyhe," he said to her, had said to her more times already than he could count.

"I can't help it. I'm too edgy to just lie here like this."

"What do you want, then?"

"I'm not sure," she said to him. "I don't really know."

They had explored this subject recently, her indecision, her lack of her previous self-assurance, the quality he had most admired in her when they first met. Their dialogue on the topic, not a true conversation she would later swear in court, had been brittle, educated, surface. Now, here it was again in a different format.

"I like you naked," he said to her, starting to lean over her.

"I'm not naked," she replied. "I'm wearing my shift."

"You could be naked for me," he said.

"No. I couldn't," she answered him.

She shoved him harder than she had intended to and he collapsed out of bed, hitting the floor hard enough and suddenly enough to inspire a shout. She took the moment to throw back the covers and flounce out on her own side and hurry out into the bathroom. He was cursing at her and she was laughing behind the locked door of the small john in the hallway across from their bedroom that they shared with the faggots who inhabited the other half of their apartment.

Feyhe liked the two young men, almost more because Owen didn't like them. They were witty and charming and baked goodies in their spare time and liked to dance and were up on the newest song hits from Broadway. Lew Alberti, the younger of the two men, was a model and a dancer who had once been a protégée of Ted Shawn. He was a blonde Italian, with naturally-died blonde hair and very dark green eyes. At the age of twenty-eight he was working round the clock, his face and his lithe figure gracing the covers of magazines constantly.

His partner, a young editor for a major book publishing firm, was almost as pleasant, but stiffer, more rigid in his habits and his manner. She liked him, though, as he talked with an intelligent comprehension of the world around them. His name was Frederick Ostendorf and no one called him Fred, or Freddy. It was always Frederick. He was tall and dark and had a large, elongated jaw that could be attractive when he wasn't being too serious. He and Lew were a most attractive combination and Feyhe was glad when they came to answer her advertisement for house-mates.

She and Owen had been living in impoverishment for a while. The 1930s were truly taking their toll, especially on the young Socialists who worked more at their creed than for their personal need. Owen was high on the list of the impoverished and Feyhe, in spite of her job with Alfred A. Knopf, publishers, was lumped in alongside her husband. When she posted the notice about the available space in their two-bedroom apartment on the upper east side of Manhattan, she anticipated little. She knew that the rent they were asking was high and she didn't really think there would be any takers.

Frederick came into her office at the publishing firm, holding her notice in his manicured fingers.

"This is yours?" he asked her with a slightly superior manner.

"It is. What are you doing with it?" She looked at his face and knew immediately that he was tossing it away, probably reprimanding her for putting it up in the first place.

"I've removed it from the eyes of those hideous Philistines out there in the typing pool and the editorial staff."

"Why, Frederick? I really need to find someone."

"You don't have a need to do so, Feyhe," he said in the same annoying way. "You have found someone."

"Oh? Who?"

"Lewis and I will take the room," he said.

"And who is Lewis and Hi?" she responded without thinking.

"I am *I* and Lewis is Lewis."

"Oh, you..." Feyhe said, a bit too loudly, a bit to sharply.

"Won't that suit you?" he asked her.

"Oh, sure. I know you can afford it."

"Money is an object," he said, "but not one that stands in my way."

She gestured toward the chair across the desk from her own. He sat and they carefully worked out the terms of the lease. He and Lewis could have the room and share the living quarters for a mere $100 a month, she told him, but they would have to share the bathroom, the only one in the apartment on East 85th Street. He countered with an $80 offer, considering that they would indeed have to share the loo. She bargained to a $95 dollar level based on their lack of personal items for kitchen use and their reliance on whatever Feyhe already had on hand. He countered at $90 and she accepted. The total rent on the apartment was $87.35 a month, so she was still coming out ahead by a few dollars and she thought that Frederick Ostendorf and his friend might not be too difficult to live with.

She hadn't counted on Owen's reaction. He hated the whole idea of sharing the place and he resented her assertion that he couldn't pay his part of the lolly. Still, she had prevailed as usual and the two men had become a part of their lives.

They had all lived together for a year and a month and during that time her relationship with Frederick had strengthened and her marriage to Owen had started to come undone.

"I should never have married a handsome man," she told young Ostendorf. "I should have known better."

"He is adorable," Frederick said.

"He's a skunk. He runs around with every chippy who comes along. He spends every dime he has on the movies. He brings nothing into the marriage, nothing at all."

"He makes you look good when you hang on his arm at those meetings of yours, doesn't he?"

"That's not a real benefit, Frederick."

"It would work for me, darling," he said, snickering.

"A cucumber would work for you," she said haughtily.

"Bitch!"

"Cunt!" And they laughed and hugged. It was an established routine for them already. It was a comfort zone that neither had expected at the start of this arrangement.

Now, on this ill-fated Sunday, locked in the bathroom, Feyhe thought about these two very different men. She saw the reality of the locks she had placed on her heart and her mind, locked in with the sexual relationship she enjoyed with Owen and the intellectual one she had found with her house-fag. She wanted the first relationship to be the easy winner in a competition between them, but she couldn't bend her own rules to make that happen. Owen was giving her less and less and taking more advantage of her good nature and her well-paid editorial position. He was sneaking his hand-written pamphlets into her bag and sending them off to the publisher in her finished manuscripts. Her first realization of that had come, thankfully, from Frederick who had taken the book to his desk to thumb through after reading Feyhe's notes on the text and its values.

When he found the pamphlet, not so discreetly placed, open between two pages of otherwise risible words, he had been automatically self-righteous about it and taken it back to Feyhe at once.

"Yours?" he asked, tossing it onto her desk. She glanced at it for only a moment, then shook her head in response. "Get rid of it anyway," Ostendorf said to her, "and tell Owen that if he does that again, you're fired."

She went home mad, and a mad Feyhe was not a pretty sight. As she yelled at Owen and berated him for his stupid, thoughtless actions, she repeatedly struck him with the pamphlet, an ineffectual beating until she caught his cheek with the edge of the paper and left a bleeding scar through the stubbly beard that graced that side of his face.

He slapped her, a reaction he later said he regretted, later cried he regretted to be exact, but really only said in words and not in thought. Feyhe recognized the missing element in the apology and she noted it for future use.

He tried several more times to sneak his philosophical missives into her work, but she usually caught them before handing the manuscripts over to others at the publishing house. Each time she tried to talk Owen out of following these impulses in the future, but each time he merely shook his head and voiced an apology and then tried one more time.

On the Saturday night preceding Feyhe's precipitous Sunday morning flight to the bathroom, she and Owen had been out with friends. They had gone to Chinatown for dinner and were sitting in Lum's Restaurant on Crosby Street at the fringe of Chinatown when a large party came in and noisily made their way to the long banquet table on the opposite side of the room. Feyhe tried to ignore them, but they were too loud, too boisterous and she had started the night with a headache.

"Can you do something to shut them up?" she asked Owen. He shook his head, his usual response to a request for something active.

"Then I will," she said and before anyone at their table could stop her she was up and walking in their direction. She was preparing an opening comment in her head, silently, as she moved among the tables, but before she could speak, a woman at the loud table, wearing a yellow dress and a lot of cheap jewelry, spoke up.

"Well, will you look what the cat drug in," she shouted to her compatriots, "it's Owen Khanzadian's wifey." The woman laughed and the sound was raucous and unpleasant.

"You know me?" Feyhe asked. "I don't seem to—"

The other woman jumped in before Feyhe even finished speaking. "I know you. I know Owen, too."

"And you are...?"

"You better believe I am, toots," the woman shouted. "And that's some stud you got yourself, there."

She felt his hand on her shoulder, knew that Owen was standing there behind her, knew that he wanted her to move away, to come back to their table. She wouldn't turn to look at him. She couldn't take her eyes off the woman.

"You're his mistress?" she asked the girl.

"Not on your tintype, Lady," came the reply. "He's okay for an hour or two, but put up with him for more than the sex...I don't think so."

Feyhe turned away, the woman's outrageous comments and her equally outrageous laughter still ringing in her ears. Owen's hand slipped off her shoulder and she didn't stop to say good night to their friends. She grabbed her coat and her bag and kept on going.

She never stopped moving until she was safe at home in the apartment. She undressed before she put on the light, washed herself over and over and over again until her skin burned from the over-exposure to the cheap soap Owen always bought. She had put on her night things and settled in beneath the counterpane before Owen even reached the apartment.

She heard him coming in, heard him moving about, and heard him breathe her name once or twice as he stood in the doorway. She debated speaking to him, changed her mind, then did it after all.

"How could you...?" she said, but she got no further in her question.

"I didn't do much, really," he responded.

"I know!" she spat back at him. "She made that all too clear!"

"What are you upset about, Feyhe? That I cheated or that I didn't do it enough?"

"You're a disgrace to me, Owen. How could you let her mock me like that?" She felt the tears in her eyes holding on tenaciously to their source.

All night long she listened to Owen's claims that there was nothing to what the woman had said, that it wasn't true. She had stayed in bed with him, as had been their custom, but finally, the sound of that laughter had been too overpowering. When he tried to touch her, she had done what she had to do and now she was sitting in the bathroom, locked in, wishing there was a way out.

There was one, she knew, and she meant to take it. Divorce.

The thought, made real, made her cry finally. Emotions swam in many directions, touching on many places in her memory. Her father's face loomed darkly in the forefront and she found herself sinking into a melancholy like none she had ever known before. She drifted in the limbo-land of unswept emotional detritus, her brain and her heart reaching for one another and causing a distress in her chest, lungs, throat, and nose that was palpable.

She hardly heard him calling to her through the door. She didn't recognize his voice, or her name, or anything being said. She drifted in this nothingness state for a long while, not caring if she even emerged from it.

"Feyhe," Frederick aspirated through the keyhole. "Is it that old melancholia again? Feyhe!"

A phrase blossomed in front of her: *wrong guy!* and hung there looking pretty, then out of place, then pretty again. The two words blended into one: *wrongie*, then into a new word: *raunky*, then into another: *drawnkey* before falling away into its odd components: *raw 'n' keen*. Feyhe said the last out loud, several times, trying to understand it.

Again a voice called to her from outside the door. "He's gone." She tried to smile, but her mouth would only turn downward into a frown. She stood up and looked at her face in the mirror, tried to force the corners of her mouth upward but not even her fingers could make that work. The frown remained. And with it, the word *melancholia*. She opened the medicine cabinet and took down the pills her doctor had given her months earlier. "For Melancholia," he had said. "When things get bad, take a pill," she heard her mother reciting in the dim past.

The label on the bottle said simply: Lithium. Take as necessary." She would do just that, she thought, just that.

Feyhe remembered all this as she sat there on her favorite bench in Central Park, so many years later, and the tears she felt swarming like May Flies in heat burned the memory into her conscious mind. She cried until she couldn't cry any longer.

14

Kim Do-Mun of Gyôngju Province, Korea, now Dominic Kim of Paterson, New Jersey, sat alone in the dining room at Feyhe's apartment. He read his newspaper slowly, absorbing each word like a sponge in ice-cold water draws in its liquid sustenance, encouraging thoughts to join older ones in his brain. He needed to understand the words on the page so that when Feyhe came home he could speak to the matter with care and precision. He liked Feyhe's dining room. It was a warm, nearly concealed space, opening out severely from its doorway which nearly hugged one corner of the room. The table and chairs were teak, carved latticework backed and rattan-cover seated. The sideboard matched the table with its claw-feet corners stretching out across the Asian carpet toward similar feet on the pedestal based uprights at either end of the shelf-like eating surface.

Kim, for so he would always be known in this apartment, enjoyed the Asian elegance of this room. It gave him comfort and provided him solace when he missed his old life in his old home. He loved his wife and his two small sons, but he definitely was a stranger in a strange land.

He returned to his reading, scanning the help-wanted advertisements, seeking a way to use his knowledge, his education, his upbringing in this place he had come to out of desperation. In the seven years since he had arrived in New York, his wife and newborn son in tow, he had worked in restaurants, in a Korean-owned grocery on Amsterdam Avenue, in a laundry, and now in a notions store in New Jersey. There was no satisfaction in this. There was nothing to hold on to, to grasp, to feel pride in when he came home at night. There was nothing to tell his parents and his sisters and his brother when they contacted him. There was nothing at all to keep the man a man in his own eyes. He was chattel now. He was little else but a dray pulling someone else's plow, plowing someone else's furrow. He was not the man he had known himself to be in Gyôngju. He had not the future prospects he had once enjoyed. Where in former days there had been the expected call from the Capitol to come and speak to the President, or to address the council, here there was only the occasional opportunity to visit the amusement park or to find a museum. There was no place, no way, in which he could shine.

Ni-Na worked in a grocery store, wearing a Japanese Kimono and fashioning sushi behind a see-through glass counter. She had to pretend to be something other than Korean and this hurt her, wounded her deeply, every day. Even so, it had to be done, that or working in the laundry; they needed the money and Kim was not able to earn enough to support their family on his own.

Their two sons—Mitchell now called Danny, the oldest boy, and the two-year-old, Jimmy—were easy children by and large. Danny had a temper and it would flare now and then, but Jimmy was the possessor of a sweet disposition, an attitude that made him his parents' delight. One gurgled utterance from the baby would produce streams of white-water swift laughter from the adults and even a hearty, if choked, chortle from his big brother. Jimmy was the winner in personality, but Danny was a sharp-minded and evil-tongued little boy.

Kim admired his older son for the way he had learned, early on, to protect himself from other children. It was as if he had been born with fists instead of fingers, for all too often his hands would be drawn up into massively tiny balls that could hit and hurt at the slightest provocation. Kim loved the youthful manliness of his son. He enjoyed the attempted fights that his son would jump into with almost anyone who got in his way. When Danny wanted something there was no obstacle too large. When Danny didn't want to perform an assigned task, his fists would destroy something precious; this child would rather court punishment than risk boredom or go against his own instincts.

Kim loved all his family, often with a blind eye and stilled gut. He would not allow himself to see danger signs in Danny, or anything wrong with either son actually. He turned his anxiety, instead, on his wife, Ni-Na. He was often sharp with her, addressing her the way he had heard his grandfather deal with his grandmother. No one thing she did ever truly pleased Kim.

No effort on her behalf to see to his comfort or his pleasure was ever complete enough, or good enough, or rich enough. That, indeed, was the crux of the matter: rich enough. They were not rich enough, so nothing could satisfy enough.

Some days Kim blamed himself for what had befallen them. Other days he blamed Feyhe. This rich woman had completely destroyed his life, forcing him to live someone else's dream of the present. She had disemboweled him and left him, half the man he once was and nowhere near the man he might have become, to suffer in this foreign wasteland.

He glanced over the ads again, trying to find something for a man of supreme education and high cultural background. There was a need, he read, for plumbers and mechanics and accountants. There was a crying call for nurses. There was nothing for him in this newspaper. There was no opportunity in this "land of opportunity."

When he looked up this time, Feyhe was standing in the doorway of the dining room watching him. She gave him a smile, her teeth showing, he hated that. He returned the smile. "Anything, today?" she asked him, not greeting him but getting on with business.

"Nothing. There is nothing in this country of yours for me."

"There is everything here," Feyhe said. "You just have to look for it until you find it, that piece of everything that is yours."

"Your philosophy reeks of American capitalism," he said.

"It sure does," she agreed, and she stepped backward into the hallway and headed down the corridor to her bedroom. Kim sat where he was, wondering if he was to follow her down that long, sickening passageway one more time. He sighed heavily, folded the paper in half, then in half again and stood up. He could see himself in the mirror that bordered the top of the credenza at the far end of the room. He looked young in it. He looked strong and he looked handsome. He started on the journey to Feyhe Hell.

She was already out of her dress and stockings and was standing near the window in her slip. She smiled at him as he came into the room and he smiled back, or at least hoped he smiled back. He knew in a moment that he hadn't quite managed it.

"You're so somber today, Kim," she said. "What's wrong?"

"I am not in love with your land," he replied. "I try to feel something better for it, but I am not able."

"You will be. You will be," she reassured him. "It's just a matter of time."

She reached behind her body and bent slightly, then bent her knees, her feet coming up quickly, first one, then the other one. She stood up and held out her yellow panties, with ruffles at the leg holes. She laughed.

"I'm naked under this slip, Kim," she said.

He regarded her for a moment, then slowly closed his large eyelids, held them shut for a moment before opening them again.

"Not for too long, Feyhe," he said sweetly, as sweetly as he had ever said anything to her. "You will be wearing me shortly."

When the sun had moved from the windowsill into the alley beyond, Feyhe sat up and fluffed the pillows behind her head, standing the front one on its end rather than its side. Kim still lay there, completely naked, still strong and young and vital. His penis was still hard and she could easily run her hand along it and feel the firmness and the youth in it, if she chose to do so. She decided against it. Instead she reached for a cigarette, lit it and inhaled deeply, holding the smoke in her lungs for as long as she could before slowly letting it loose again.

"Now I will have to shower, Feyhe," Kim said softly. "Ni-Na will surely detect the smoke on my skin if I do otherwise."

"Surely she knows, Kim."

"Most certainly she does not, Feyhe." He was adamant about it. "Ni-Na would never forgive us, should she know. This would deprive me of my life, Feyhe. Not one word should you say, not one indiscreet look shall you pass to me in her presence. Not one."

"You're such an assertive bastard, Kim," Feyhe said, stubbing out her smoke.

"Why must I make you promise me, Feyhe, each time that this is the last time and that nothing shall be said?"

"I don't really know, Kim," she responded, "since you obviously always come back for more."

"This time, this is really the last time."

"You're addicted to me, Kim, and I am addicted to you. It's like any other addiction. It's impossible to cut off completely."

"Feyhe, a woman may take many lovers in her time, but a true man only one."

"That's not even good eastern philosophy!" She laughed.

"It is of my own creation."

"It stinks!"

He pulled himself off the bed and stood addressing her, still naked, still aroused, erect.

She moved forward as he spoke, his voice so quiet she could barely hear him from just a few feet away.

"Feyhe, I am a father and a husband and provider of all that is necessary for my family. For me to come here and to be with you like this, in this way, is not as easy for me as you would like to suppose. You have been a good friend to me and to my family and we have always been appreciative, but this is not..."

Her mouth had reached his erection and she was exhaling hot, moist air in his direction.

He shivered but went on speaking.

"...seemly for two such friends as us. My family is indebted to you for all your kindness and consideration. There is not a way to tell you, to show you, to make you..."

She had enveloped him with her mouth and was moving forward to take him inside her throat. He gasped at the sensation, relaxed and reached for the back of her head, his fingers entwining in her short-cropped hair. He held her close and let her take him at her own speed. They were dressed and presentable when the doorbell rang. Kim went to answer its call and found Billy on the other side of the entryway. He bowed slightly and stepped back to let him into the vestibule.

"Is Feyhe here?" Billy asked loudly, ignoring Kim as completely as he could.

"Where else would she be, you idiot," she shouted from the living room couch. "Get in here."

Billy walked briskly into the living room and Kim followed him, at a much slower pace.

Billy watched him re-enter the room.

"Been having a game of whist?" Billy said with a smirk. Neither of his questionees answered him. "Oh? Not yet?"

"Kim is just about to leave actually, Billy. Go get yourself a drink. I'll be right with you." He could hear them talking in the hallway and he knew how that dialogue would go.

Feyhe would tell him she loved him and that the money was just a token of her undying affection for him and his family. Kim would demur and say that nothing he did for her was for money. She would remark on his understanding and gentle nature, but tell him that she knew he was in need and that his earnings couldn't handle all the necessities and she would press the money on him.

He would hand it back to her, say he was insulted, that his friendship could not be purchased. She would apologize for offending his oriental sensibilities and remind him that he was here because of her foolishness and this was only part of a debt long owed. He would accept the payment, kiss her with thanks and there would be a door slam. Then Feyhe would appear. Billy had heard it all before.

"Come and sit down," she said to him as she came back into the living room. "Kim is so stubborn about accepting a little gift of cash. I wish he'd grow up and learn to take what is offered."

"Payment due on completion of services," Billy said with a smirk.

"Don't lecture me, you slut-puppy," she said.

"I'm a decorator, Feyhe, a professional."

"Is that what they call it now, when a man takes money for doing other people's bedrooms?"

"Designing them."

"Designing in them, you mean."

"You're terrible!"

"Obviously, Billy, you're not. You look well."

"I am."

"Connecticut agrees with you, then."

"Oddly enough, it does. I like being out of the city, away from the noise and the dust and the masses of people."

"And what do you have masses of this time of year? Daffodils?"

"Feyhe, for someone who has just had sex with an alien, you're being outright judgmental. Stop it."

"It's been four years since you left that nice policeman and moved away with those awful people, that hippy commune for the nouveau riche, that marriage-menage you live in. I never will understand it."

"I don't sleep with them, Feyhe. They manage my career and I share a wing in their home."

"You mean you don't sleep with *her*. That's what you mean." Billy blushed.

"Well, what if that is what I mean? What of it?"

"You're mother would be horrified."

"She's dead, Feyhe. Remember her funeral? You almost came to it."

"Don't remind me. That was a very bad day."

There was a silent moment in which they both relived the lowest moments of their friendship, Miriam's funeral. They both let it pass at the same time.

"I was horrible to your father, you, everyone."

"You weren't prepared, that's all."

"No. I was just bad."

Billy sipped his drink, offered the glass to Feyhe who tried it, made a face and handed it right back.

"What do you call that ... thing?" she asked him.

"Bourbon," he replied.

"Well, it's ghastly."

"Owen told me it was all you would drink at one time."

"Owen eats shit," she said. "On a stick." She smirked. "With sprinkles."

"You know, if Joan Crawford was still alive you two could duke it out and I think you'd be the hands-down winner."

"You are a dear and you do make me laugh…and then, of course, I pee a little."

He gave her a hard look, trying to see behind the word and the false jollity. "That's still a problem, is it? Did you ask the doctor about it. You said you would last week."

"I know I said that, but you know how I feel about sharing intimate knowledge with a doctor, Billy. I'd rather face that damned Korean tribunal again. I would."

Billy was alone for the night, not something that happened often to him these days. Ever since taking up residence in the Kendall's town house he had been constantly in the company of people, most of whom he liked. Ryan and Grey had a slew of close acquaintances, one or two friends and a virtual repertory troupe of lovers, all of whom Billy met within weeks of becoming the third wheel on their social cycle.

He had a book he'd been planning to read. He'd even started it once before, but had been distracted by the round of parties that always seemed to be happening. He picked it up shortly after returning home from Feyhe's apartment, thumbed it as though he wasn't sure the pages wouldn't stick together, then tossed it onto the easy chair he liked to use. It was overstuffed, leather-bound, womb-like in its enveloping of his body. It made him feel loved, he realized, then quickly forgot before the thought could depress him.

He poured himself a drink, a not infrequent activity these days, and kicked off his shoes, one of them falling just short of the massive plants in their Arabica jars around the floor-to-ceiling arched picture windows he had designed and installed in this room. Their pitch gave him a view of the buildings beyond and the sky above. The glass, shaded and coated, gave him a more discreet space, not visible from outside. It was a room to romp naked in when he felt like it. This was not one of those times, however.

He plumped the pillows and his own rump as he snuggled into the chair with his book and his drink. Two sips and three pages later he was asleep.

The telephone startled him, woke him suddenly. He had no idea how long he'd been slumbering there in his favorite chair before being so rudely brought back to consciousness. He was still clutching the glass of bourbon and he nearly tossed it into his own lap as he twitched awake. He deposited it on the nearby lamp table as he reached for the phone which, conveniently, lay on the floor not far from his feet.

"Yeah, hello?" he said without much grace. There was a silence on the other end of the line that bothered him for a moment. Then he realized that he hadn't pushed the button to activate the line. He rectified his mistake and started over.

"Hello?"

"Billy? Hi, it's me."

Those four words seemed to hit his eardrum and reverberate there into a gentle obscurity.

He knew the voice, knew the words. He didn't know what to say. "Well...hi...how are you?"

"I'm doing well. I am. Doing well."

"What can I do for you, Joe?" Billy said, wished he hadn't, then was glad he'd gotten the words out cleanly.

"Well, nothing much, really, at least it's not for me."

"Are you okay? You sound so frazzled." He knew the concern in his voice would show through to Joe. The detective in the man would spot anything false and anything true about his responses.

"Yeah, I know. I'm in the middle of something over here and I thought you could help. If you want to, that is."

"If I can," Billy said softly as though someone might be overhearing them, "I will, you know that."

"Yeah. Right."

"So, tell me what's up, Joe."

"Billy, I'm coming out."

"Oh, please don't, Joe. I'm really not dressed or anything, and Ryan and Grey are due back in a few minutes and—"

"No. You're not hearing me. I'm coming out. Here at the station.

I'm letting them know I'm gay."

"Wow! Joe. What'll they do to you?"

"Cashier me if they can. But I won't let them do it."

"Why are you doing this? Why, Joe?"

"It has to be done."

"But why you and why now? You've always been so careful before this. We were such a big secret."

"I know. I think that was the problem...with us, I mean."

"No. No, Joe, really, it wasn't..." Billy's voice trailed off as he thought about what he was saying, what they both were saying. He wasn't sure if he was right, or if Joe had a valid point. He had not thought of Joe in a long time.

"I can't take you back, Joe, if that—"

"That's not it, Billy. Believe me, that's not why I called."

"Then...?"

"I just need your support. I need the words I'm having a problem with. I need some of your style, I guess."

"How are you planning to do it? A letter?"

"No. I want to do it in person. Any other way is a coward's way, a stereotype's way. I won't be the stereotype Gay, Billy."

"You aren't. Don't worry."

"I would be if I let a letter talk for me. I have to face those guys I work with and say it out loud. Otherwise it won't be real, won't work for me."

"Yeah. I see that."

"I just need the right words, the style. You're good at style and words."

"When—?" he began to ask, but Joe cut him off.

"I'm just around the corner. Can you meet me now?"

"Well, Ryan and Grey—"

"Yeah, I know. But this won't take long. I drafted some stuff. I just want you to read it over and tell me where I go wrong with it. Please, Billy."

There was something in the way he said the word please and said his name right alongside it that made Billy cringe just a little. He heard himself agree to the meeting and he hung up the phone. He looked around for his shoes, only saw one of them and decided against them. In his socks he paddled downstairs to the front door.

Joe was already there when he got there. He pulled open the door and let his former lover inside.

"You didn't waste any time," he said.

"I told you I was right around the corner."

"Yeah, you did. Come on in." He held open the door and stepped back to let Joe go by him, then closed the heavy oak door, leaving the chilly street outside where it belonged. Joe stood taking in the vista before him as the house stretched up and away from them into distances not discernible from outside the building.

"This is really something, Billy."

"Thanks."

"No, I mean it. I remember you drawing the plans for this, but I've never seen it before, not like this, not for real."

"It turned out."

"It's fabulous!" Billy looked at the cop. That was a word he'd never heard the man utter before.

"Don't use 'fabulous' Joe. That's too gay."

"Okay. How's about terrific? Sensational? Pretty damn impressive?"

"Yeah, yeah, fine. Whatever."

He was leading Joe out into the garden behind the kitchen. Joe followed at a respectable distance and Billy was sure the man was keeping an eye on his hips. He could almost feel the gaze burning into him. He wheeled around and stood facing Joe as he caught up to his host.

"Can I offer you something? Or are you on duty?"

"No. I could have a beer, if you have one?"

"Domestic or imported?"

"Whatever. I'll leave it to you."

Billy opened the Genair and removed a Späten, wiped the mist off of the glass and popped the tin lid off, handing the bottle to Joe.

"No glass?" the cop asked him.

"I'm sorry. I didn't think you'd want one."

"I don't. I was just surprised you didn't offer me one."

"Okay. You've pretty much defined us. Do you have those notes you wanted me to look at?"

He held out his hand, expecting something in return. Joe reached into his jacket and removed a single piece of paper, folded in half and then in half again. He delivered it into Billy's keeping, then looked behind him for a place to sit down. There were a half-dozen deck chairs, some with cushions, some without. Joe chose one with a deep plush cushion and sat back in it.

Billy took the paper over to the retaining wall and fountain. He sat down on the highly polished black marble wall and began to read.

> *Every once in a while a man has to stand up for what he believes in. This is my time to do just that, guys. I've been living a lie for far too long and I have too much respect for you and for myself to keep it going any longer. What I'm telling you is no secret to people I love. My mom and my kid, my ex-wife, and my former lover all know that I am gay. They've all been good about keeping it under wraps, not telling a lot of other folks. I appreciate that, but it doesn't make things any easier for me. That's because of you. You're the people I spend most of my time with. You're the people I respect and, yes, I'll use the word, love. But by lying to you, I am not showing that love or that respect.*
>
> *I want you to know that for me nothing changes now except that I don't have to pretend anymore to think that a woman is more attractive because she has big knockers or a trim ankle. I don't think she's more attractive, because I don't rate women that way. I think in terms of honesty and pleasantness and decency. I'm not interested in keeping up the pretending when it comes to women.*
>
> *I'm also not interested in bringing my personal life here. Understand that I'm not about to screw around in the station or on the job. I never have and I never would. There is no reason why any of you should be concerned about that with me. You know me. You've known me a long time.*
>
> *I just want to keep your respect and I want to do it honestly. That's all I want. I don't want to lie about myself and I don't want*

to lose your respect. This has been hard for me, believe me. I like doing the work I do and I know I do it well.

Billy looked up from the paper and found Joe ignoring him, pointedly looking away from him, studying the textures of the marble and rock that formed the backdrop for the pond wall.

"This is good, Joe," he said. "It's direct. It sounds like you. It doesn't need my help." He held the paper out to Joe, who reached up and took it from him.

"Thanks," he said, then he folded it back up and put it back in his inside jacket pocket.

"You didn't need my help."

"I did, Billy. I did."

"Not with that, you didn't."

"No." Joe stopped after the one word retort. Neither of them moved or spoke. Then Billy took the plunge.

"So what do you want?" he asked. "Why did you come over here?"

"It's real, Billy. Understand that. This speech is real. I'm making it tomorrow."

"Okay." Billy crossed his arms over his chest. He was standing with his feet matching the breadth of his shoulders and he thought to himself, "I must look like Mr. Clean in a Brooks Brothers outfit. More hair, though."

"I need to do that, Billy. It's been too long in coming."

"And then what, Joe? What do you expect to happen next?" He thought, *then you'll want me back, won't you? You'll expect things to be like they were.*

"And then I can go about my life, Billy, live it in the open the way I never could before."

"It can't be like it was, Joe—" Billy started, but Joe jumped in and stopped him mid-sentence.

"I can introduce my lover to my friends, if I want to, I can bring Alan to the station without having to book him."

"Him…Alan?" Billy said, a bit softer than he meant to, a bit more reflective than he should.

"Alan Vallarta. You don't know him."

"How…" Billy wasn't sure where to go with the question, but he turned it quickly. "How long has this been going on, Joe?"

"A few months, I guess. November."

Billy added the months up quickly, in his head. "Five months. That's a lot of time."

"You'd like him, I think. He's smart."

"You like him. That's the important part." Billy could feel the tears pushing up past his larynx, yearning to rush freely from him. He held them back behind the margin of his emotions.

"I do. I like him a lot."

"Who..? How did you meet?"

"That's not important, Billy."

"No, really, I'd like to…were you introduced or…did you pursue…?" His mind was racing over their own relationship, its earliest moments running past his inner eyes like an old movie on a wide-screen. He thought of the diner, of Andrea, the waitress, of his pancakes.

"Billy, I'll bring him around sometime, or we could meet somewhere."

"No, really, that's not necessary."

"I'd like you to meet. I would."

"I appreciate the thought, Joe, but…"

"I mean, he knows Feyhe, so he should know you too."

"He knows…how would he know Feyhe?"

"Well, she introduced us. She never said anything?"

"I didn't even know she still knew you. She's never said anything."

"Oh, sure, we get together for lunch every once in a while."

"Joe, she never mentions you. She tells me so much, but she never told me this."

"Maybe she thought you'd be hurt."

"Or maybe she just likes to have something that could hurt. Maybe that's it."

"Billy, behave yourself."

"You better go, Joe. You should just go, okay?"

He moved out of the garden, leaving Joe behind, advanced toward the door and stood there waiting for his former lover to catch up to him. Joe did, in almost record time.

They stood in the vestibule, their chests so close they could feel one another breathing.

Joe looked down on Billy's upturned face and he tried to smile, but Billy's sour expression made it difficult.

Joe tilted his head and lowered his voice. "A kiss goodbye?"

"No," Billy said. "Just goodbye."

He opened the door and without another word, Joe stepped through it, out into the night.

Billy shut the door after him.

15

Owen Khanzadian peered out the window at the activity in the street below. The noise had distracted him from his work, had claimed his attention when that was required elsewhere.

"It's nothing," he said out loud. "Try not to hear it, okay?"

"But I hear it already," his charge seemed to be saying without the words being spoken. His eyes were distracted forward, although his head was tipped high as always. His lips moved, forming no words, his tongue tortured itself into postures that permitted nothing but a spitting, a gurgle, no more. His shoulder undulated and his hands, loose at the ends of a pair of dangling arms, made funny shapes and formed odd symbols.

"They're moving away now," Owen told the patient. "Everything's fine. No one was hurt."

Owen tried to decipher the hands, the lips, the eyes and came away with less than he'd hoped. This was his work, this was his life, trying to make sense out of the physical expressions of the utterless.

"Okay. Let's try something new today," he said to the patient. "Let's try something new." He reached into the folder that lay on his desk and withdrew five thin pieces of cardboard. They were face down and the backs were blank, not even a pencilled comment making an appearance. "Look at me, now," he said. "Look at me and watch what I'm doing. See what I'm doing. Respond if you can, okay?"

He turned over the top piece of board and held it up in front his patient's face. He watched the man's eyes and mouth, hoping for a visible, recordable reaction to what was on the board. There was nothing forthcoming.

"What do you see? Can you understand what you see there?" The patient eyed him for a moment then returned his gaze to the picture. Owen watched him closely, hoping for some recognition in the man's face. There was no reaction. He slowly lowered the cardboard back to his desk and deftly reached for the second piece. He held it up, moving it slowly into position, right before the eyes of the patient. He watched the man's response as his eyes followed the progress of the picture.

"Try again, okay? What do you see? Do you see anything there you recognize?" A response, when it came, came slowly to these patients, Owen knew, but he was surprised when nothing seemed to happen. "Do you see someone you know?"

The man seemed to move forward, but his arms were still jerking from the excitement generated from below in the street and Owen couldn't tell what was prompting the reaction. "Is there anybody you know in this picture?" There was no reaction at all to his question. He put down the second cardboard and reached for a third.

His patter remained the same for this one and the two that followed it. Each time he encouraged the patient to try to exhibit any sense of recognition and each time he failed. Finally, he put away his cardboard tools and sat down again at the desk, facing the man who sat emotion-free, though not motionless, before him. He pulled out a pad and made a few notes for himself. Then he pushed the buzzer for his assistant. She was in the office in an instant.

"Yes, Mr. Khanzadian?" she said, asking the question that brought an answer she was already sure she knew.

"Ask his brother to come in, please. We're done for today."

She nodded and backed out into the outer office. A moment later, before he could even fold up his notes, the door opened again and Ozzie entered quickly, going to his brother Morris immediately.

"So? Anything?" he asked Owen. Owen shook his head.

"We had an incident out in the street, Ozzie, and I think it distracted him too much. We'll try again on Thursday. If you like I'll keep the pictures here."

"I don't know why we keep trying, really I don't," Ozzie said. "Morris has been like this since boyhood and we're not kids no more."

"You just never know, Ozzie. You just never know what might happen, okay?"

"Yeah, sure, okay," the man replied. "You're a good fellow, Owen. Who knew back then? Who knew?"

"I didn't even know, Ozzie. Not even me."

"So, thanks for trying." He extended his hand to Owen who took it, gave it a squeeze and returned it. "Come on Morris, you little *pishkie*. Let's go home."

Morris didn't move. He stayed at the desk, sitting in the chair, staring at Owen, twitching just a bit, responding to something no one could grasp.

"Morris, come on," Ozzie said again. "We'll get some ice cream on the way, you'd like that, no?" Morris stood up instantly, turned and grabbed his brother by the shoulder. "Again, thank you Owen. You're a prince." The two brothers moved more rapidly, more as one, than anyone would have anticipated. Owen's assistant, still at the door, closed it behind the men, leaving Own alone in his office. He moved back to the window and, again, looked through it at the street below.

"Okay," he thought out loud, "so you clean it up and you move on. That's what we all do, I guess, clean it up, move on. It's like a Lewis Carroll world out there. Clean cup, move down, more tea, no tea." He sighed, turned around and sat down.

As if on cue, his telephone rang. He picked it up before the second ring.

"Hello?" There was silence—no response. "Hello, again?"

"Hello, Owen." The voice was familiar. He could almost place it.

"Hello?" he said a third time. "This is—"

"This is Feyhe."

Without meaning to, he exhaled into the mouthpiece.

"Thanks. I needed that," she said. "I like a man who expresses his emotions so sweetly." Then she laughed. It was a sound he hadn't heard in thirty years.

"Feyhe, how are you?"

"I'm doing well. How are you?"

"Fine. Feyhe, can I call you back. I have a waiting room full of people."

"So, you're successful then. Good."

He smiled in spite of himself. He felt sure she was doing the same thing.

"I've been meaning to phone you," she continued. "I wanted to invite you to dinner."

"I…I'd love to," he said.

"I hear the hesitation. It won't be just the two of us. Nothing like that."

"Okay," he said.

"Thursday?"

"Friday would be better for me."

"Friday, then," she said. "I'll call your secretary with the address. Bye."

She was gone. He held onto the receiver for a while, then put it down. He buzzed his assistant, ready to alert her to the phone call. He felt himself exhaling again, just as he had on the phone.

Feyhe's apartment was all a-glitter and a-glow with candles everywhere, surfaces polished to a high sheen. People, well-dressed and demi-glamorous, dotted the living room alternating with attractive pots, trays and free-standing dishes of cold and hot hors d'oeuvres. Owen was hoping, when he got there, to be able to recognize some of the people, but he wasn't having much luck. He knew Billy Duncan, of course, but Billy had been avidly engaged in conversation with a handsome couple who seemed to move with him when he moved, to stand guard around him when he stood still. There had been something impenetrable about the trio and Owen had waved, smiled and moved on.

There was an oriental man, well dressed in a Brooks Brothers three-piece dark wool suit and a woman with him in a silk kimono covered in dragon and phoenix designs in royal blue, gold, and an autumnal shade of maroon that he couldn't name. Feyhe was nowhere to be seen, but Owen knew instinctively that this was not unusual. There were two people who seemed to know him; they nodded at him as he came into the living room and one of them, the man, winked almost too broadly.

A few others had given him a quick glance as he stood in the doorway and then returned to their conversational companions. The winking man extricated himself, ultimately, from his friend and came over to him, his hand extended for a handshake even before he was within reaching distance. Owen stepped forward to shorten the awkward distance between the thought and the gesture.

"Khanzadian, nice to see you," Frederick Ostendorf said instantly, and loudly Owen thought.

"Thanks. A pleasure to see you, too," he responded, feeling awkward at not recognizing the man.

"It's been years," Ostendorf said. "How many, would you say?"

He shrugged. "Got me!" he said.

"Do you even know who I am?"

"You know...I don't." Owen felt himself blush.

"Frederick Ostendorf. Publishing." He smiled a grinnish sort of smile, broad, cheek to cheek, his lips never parting.

"Oh, my God! Freddie!" Owen dropped the man's hand and took one more step toward him, throwing his right arm around Ostendorf's shoulder and pulling him into a bear-like embrace.

"Dear Owen, always such an animal!" Ostendorf loosened himself from the grasp of his old acquaintance.

"You look like someone else, though," Owen said. "I don't know who. I just don't know who, okay?"

"Some people think I resemble Prince Rainier, you know the husband of Grace Kelly, but I don't see it myself."

"No, no. Let me think. Xavier Cugat, perhaps."

"Cugie? Well, that's a chunkier, clunkier version of the prince."

"Yes, of course, you're right, Freddie. A prince it is."

"You, on the other hand, look exactly like yourself. You've put on no weight, aged no years, lost not one hair, and your handsome exterior is still just as exacting to behold as it was when Feyhe first worked for me."

"You've never lost that verbal flair, Freddie, have you?"

"Never, charming man." He threw a true smile at Owen with that statement. "But of course you know everyone here, don't you?"

Owen looked directly into Ostendorf's flashing eyes as he spoke.

"Not one soul, except you—and you were a surprise." He smiled in return. "So, with you as the first new person to return, I just might know everyone here. But I don't think so."

Ostendorf turned, took Owen by the arm and led him forward into the room.

"Everyone, this is Owen Khanzadian, the guest of honor." He turned to face Owen and began to applaud. Within seconds the entire room had burst into a fanfare of clapping. Owen blushed for real this time. "And Owen, dear, you know all of these delicious people, I am sure."

One by one, they formed a line and came over to meet the confused Khanzadian. As they stepped up and shook his hand, he heard their murmured names and the things they said and none of it registered in the permanent memory banks of his brain. It was all too quick, too confusing, too silly for words. And still there was no Feyhe.

When Billy approached him to give his version of the greeting, Owen took him aside and asked the question: where was Feyhe?

"Oh, you haven't heard, I guess," Billy said instantly. "She's in the hospital. It happened this morning. Her bladder has been bad, you know. She pees all the time. That's why no one is sitting down in this room. In spite of the aerosols you can still smell the urine if you get too close to the fabrics on the chairs and the couches."

"What happened to her, Billy?"

"Details are slow in coming, Owen, but it seems she had a sort of dam-burst thing happen when she got out of bed today. She wasn't able to contain her water, and then she began to bleed. At least she had the presence of mind to call her doctor. He sent an ambulance over and they whisked her off to Lenox Hill Hospital. She called me from there and asked me to play host if she couldn't make it back in time."

"What's the diagnosis?"

"I don't know. She didn't say."

"I should get over there."

"Why? She gave this dinner party for you. You should stay."

"But she might be seriously ill."

"Feyhe has always been seriously ill, Owen, at least for as long as I've known her. And you haven't been around, haven't been the attentive and caring husband, so why bother now? She'll call. I know she will."

"It doesn't feel right, Billy."

"It will. Just a word of caution, Owen. Don't let Frederick get too close for too long. He's a quick one with a pinch."

Feyhe phoned at ten o'clock. Billy answered the call, said very little and hung up quickly. Ni-Na had just served a marvelous soup from a complex contraption that cooked its ingredients simultaneously in separated compartments and then allowed them to mix together quickly just before being served. The acclaim for the dish, the fourth course in the meal, had been universal, even Frederick Ostendorf shouting praise. When he returned to the table, Billy gave them all a smooth smile and Owen asked the question that was on every mind.

"Is she all right?" Billy let the smile fade slowly before he answered.

"No, she's not." The statement was simple and not revealing.

"And...?" Owen prompted.

"And she asked me to not say much more than that. I'll tell you this, though, she's not coming home for a while."

"What is it, hon?" Ryan asked him.

"It's a bad thing, and the meal is what we must put our minds to," Billy said. "The food and the company is what concerned Feyhe, so it's what we should let ourselves enjoy."

"Nice touch, kid," Owen said, but there was a harsh quality to his voice.

"I do so adore your sense of taste, Billy," Ostendorf added.

"Eat up," Billy said. "And no leftovers for the absent hostess!" He picked up his wine and hoisted the glass high. "To Feyhe!" The others echoed his action and his sentiment. And so the evening proceeded.

Owen and Billy were the only ones left after the cleanup had been completed. Kim and Ni-Na had just gone home, back to Paterson,

New Jersey where they now lived with their two young sons. Owen was drying dishes and getting them onto the shelves in the kitchen cabinets. Billy was policing the dining room, searching out crumbs and stains. Neither one was speaking much.

Billy had turned on the tape deck and put on a reel-to-reel tape that he'd found on Feyhe's bookshelves. It was a compilation of music, classical and popular and they'd already run through Beethoven's "Für Elise," the overture to Bernstein's operetta *Candide*, three bluesy songs sung by Peggy Lee and a Bach solo cello sonata. For now the music had turned to a less mellow, less sombre tone with the return of Bernstein's "Wrong Note Rag." Billy thought it was the recording with Rosalind Russell and Edie Adams, but he couldn't hear it clearly from the dining room. Still he thought he knew it well enough to be sure.

"Cute piece," Owen called out from the kitchen. "I don't know it."

Billy told him what it was and who was singing.

"Really?" Owen said, the skepticism in his voice unmistakable. "I didn't know she ever sang, or at least made recordings."

"It's an original cast recording," Billy shouted back. "from *Wonderful Town*." There was no response to this information.

"Bernstein with Comden and Green," he continued shouting. "A musical version of *My Sister Eileen*." There was still no response from Owen.

"It was a pretty big hit. I think this is the Broadway version. Russell did it again for television and that recording came out too, with Jacqueline McKeever instead of Adams." He waited for Owen to say something, perhaps to admire his deep knowledge of the Broadway lexicon. He heard nothing. "McKeever was the female star in *Oh, Captain!* the musical that Tony Randall starred in. You know, based on the Alec Guinness movie, *The Captain's Paradise*?" He waited, but Owen still had nothing to say. Billy was getting a bit annoyed. He didn't usually have trouble impressing straight people with his encyclopedic recitals. He walked out of the dining room and into the hallway.

From his vantage point at the corner of the enclosed dining room, he could see into the kitchen and what he saw was startling. Owen, his back to Billy, was in a deep and involving embrace from a woman, clearly Feyhe, who held him very tight in her arms. She was "sucking face" for real, holding onto Owen's lips with her own until it seemed he would have to force himself free in order to breathe again.

Billy, riveted by the picture of the two of them, stayed quiet and stayed put. He held his own breath, instantly frightened by the passion he saw before him. Passion in his vision was nothing new. He saw it often between Ryan and Grey Kendall. That was part of their menage system, the witnessing of passion, one for another in any number of rooms in their house, in any number of postures. But this was a different sort of passion. For Owen it flared and relented, then flared again, then relented. For Feyhe it was constant, hot and overwhelming.

Finally, unable to watch any longer, he noisily cleared his throat. Before they could fully part, Billy said, "Well, I suppose I should be getting on home, now."

"No, stay there," Feyhe said. As she took a step back, Billy saw that under her coat she was wearing a hospital gown. Her legs were bare and she wore slippers instead of shoes. Her hair was uncombed and she had on no makeup at all, not even her usual shot of lipstick, the undercoat that enlarged her lips, giving them a fullness that nature had denied them. From her wrist there dangled a plastic bangle, with her name and room number and another set of numbers.

"What have you done?" Billy asked her. "Have you just walked out of the hospital, Feyhe? Just got up and walked out?"

"They hid my clothes." Her statement was a simple one.

"They didn't hide your clothes, Feyhe."

"They did."

"No, they didn't. You weren't wearing any clothes when they took you to the hospital.

You were naked, Feyhe, wrapped in warm sheets by the paramedics."

"They hid my things."

"You didn't have any things. I brought your bag with your keys and some money. Remember that?"

"They took my things away from me."

"Okay, Feyhe, they took your things away," Billy said to her gently. "They'll give them back to you, though, when you leave."

"I left," she said.

To Billy's surprise and a bit to his growing sense of fury, Owen had said nothing, and still said nothing. He looked at the other man and saw nothing in his eyes, nothing on his face, no betrayal of feelings, no ideas.

"Why don't you sit down, Feyhe?" Billy asked her. "You must be very tired."

"I want to kiss him again," she said, turning her head to look at Owen.

"No," Billy said. "No."

"I want to kiss him again."

"Not right now, Feyhe. Come and sit, please."

He held out his hands to her and she came to them, took them in her own hands and followed him as he backed into the living room. He led her to the couch, helped her to sit and to settle into the pillows she liked to use to support herself. Then he moved away from her, back to the kitchen, back to Owen.

"Why don't you say something?" he asked Feyhe's ex-husband.

"I don't know what to say," he answered immediately. "I've never seen her like this."

"What do we do?"

"You're doing fine, Billy. You have a natural aptitude for this."

"I don't. Don't say that!" Billy looked even angrier than he sounded. His face flushed and his ears burned. His eyes were tearing up and burning as well.

"Keep her calm, just like you were doing. I'm going down to her bedroom and call for an ambulance. She has to be under the proper care. She has to."

He was gone in an instant. Billy, before he knew what to expect, found himself heading back to Feyhe.

"Was there a party?" she asked him.

"There was. It was a good party. You would have been proud of it."

"Was there a party?"

"Yes. A party."

"Was there a party?" she asked a third time.

"I don't remember, actually," he said. "Maybe there was."

"Ask the man," Feyhe said.

"I beg your pardon?"

"Ask the man was there a party," she said. "I think he knows."

"Feyhe, can you hear me?" he asked her. She nodded. "Then let me tell you about the party." He named off the guests and she nodded after each name. He told her about the soup and the other dishes they had all enjoyed. Again, she nodded at each detail.

Owen came back into the room. He looked at Feyhe and began to cry. Before he got too far into the emotional play that was being performed in his heart, he dried the tears and spoke to Billy.

"They're on the way," he said. "They didn't know she was missing."

"What's going on?" Billy whispered. "She was so lucid on the phone."

Owen pulled Billy away from Feyhe, out of her hearing. She was sitting quietly, staring forward, seemingly unaware of their existence, but Owen didn't want to speak where she could overhear them.

"They had her on an IV medication for her infections, liberally laced with painkillers—" he said, but Billy interrupted him.

"Oh, my God, she can't take painkillers. She's on medication. They don't mix."

"Yes, they realized that, but not until she was sedated and stuporous, Billy. They took her off the stuff, changed the mix and tried to restore her, but she fell asleep. They thought she was safe and secure, asleep like that, but when they went to check on her, she was gone."

"I'll sue them!" Billy shouted, then clasped his hands over his own mouth.

"You can't. Calm down or they'll sedate you when they get here."

Billy gave him an odd look. Owen went on.

"Her bladder problem isn't the problem, Billy. It's her mind. She has something, and I've suspected it for years, called manic-depression. That means she swings, her moods swing, from elated to suicidal. It can happen in an hour, a minute, or it can take months for the cycle to complete itself. There are drugs, but it's hard to manage, because when someone with this illness is in the manic sweep they feel so good they forget to take their medicine, or refuse to take it, and they plunge back into the depression. That can be dangerous too, because they refuse to take their pills."

"I've seen this," Billy said.

"What do you do?" Owen asked him. "How do you handle it?"

"I make her take her medicine, Owen. I make her take it."

"How? You don't live here with her? How do you compel her to do what you tell her to do?"

"I just do. I talk her into it and it works."

"Apparently not all the time."

"A-apparently not," Billy stammered, having started to shout it, but then pulling himself way back. "Why aren't they here yet?"

"Maybe they didn't have an ambulance available," Owen said.

"What'll we do?"

"Talk to her. Keep her company. Keep her calm." Billy nodded and they both went back into the living room.

Feyhe was still sitting where they'd left her. She was sitting there, slightly hunched forward, her hands clasping the purse she had carried with her from the hospital. Her coat hung open and her lower lip was hanging loosely from her cheeks. She looked helpless. That was the word, Billy thought, helpless. No way to help.

"Feyhe," he said. "Can I get you anything?"

"I'm all right," she said.

"Can I get you anything? Do you want something to drink?"

"A martini—straight up and don't hold back on the olives. Lots of olives."

"Anything else?"

"A martini—straight up and don't hold back on the olives. Lots of olives."

Owen shook his head, clearly signifying the negative.

"Owen will make it for you, Feyhe," Billy said, shrugging his shoulders in Owen's direction.

"Owen the bartender? Owen the bar-fly?" She sniggered. "Owen the bar-boy? Owen the Barbell? Owen the bellhop? Owen the hop-hog." The questions, odd as they were, had slowly become statements.

"Owen the busy bunny," Billy added.

Feyhe giggled.

"I like you Billy," she said. "I always like you. Sometimes I hate you, but only when I like you."

"You're drunk, Feyhe," Billy said lightly.

"No, no, no. You can't drink, Feyhe," she said. Then she laughed again, a bigger laugh, a heartier laugh. The door buzzer rang. Billy was moving away from Feyhe, heading for it, when Owen rounded the corner from the kitchen and intercepted the call.

"Come up," he said into the intercom and he buzzed the door. He and Billy exchanged a quick look, then he headed back into the kitchen and Billy returned to the living room.

"Company's coming," she said loudly. "Got to dust."

"The room is fine, Feyhe."

"Got to dust," she said. She tried to stand up again, but her legs wouldn't support her.

Billy grabbed her arm and helped her into a standing position. As he did so, she let go her bladder and began to pee on the carpet, the couch, and on Billy's shoes. He stayed put, stayed where he was, holding on to her until she stopped. It didn't take long, only a few seconds actually, although it had seemed an eternity to him.

Feyhe was swaying slightly, humming something vaguely familiar but not the music emanating from the stereo system. The changes that had gone unnoticed by Billy were an unreachable list. Just now the music had moved to a recording of Maria Callas singing the "Caro Nome" from Verdi's opera *Rigoletto*. Feyhe was singing along, but not even remotely singing the same thing. He wracked his brain, trying to put away the recording and hear his cousin clearly, but he couldn't make it happen.

"What are you singing, Feyhe?" he asked her.

"Don't Put Your Daughter on the Sage, Mr. Worthing's Man," she said.

"You must mean 'Don't Put Your Daughter on the Stage, Mrs. Worthington'," Billy said.

"Don't tell me. What I mean. Is my cousin well?" she said.

"Which cousin, Feyhe?"

"Little cousin Billy?" she said loosely.

"Billy's good," Billy said.

"Yay! He's such a stupid kid," she said. "I love him."

"We know that," Billy said, his cheeks stinging again from another blush.

The doorbell sounded and Owen was there to answer it in an instant. A moment later two EMT workers were standing in the room.

"She it?" one of them said.

"Yeah, she's it," Owen confided. "Now, no violence, no danger. She's nothing too important right now. Just to be detained. She's already checked in—"

"Yeah, we know. We got the work orders, remember."

"Well," Owen said, then paused, "should we come along?"

"Nah. No need. Paperwork is done already. You can see her tomorrow." The man laughed a loud and hearty laugh. "Of course she may not see you, or remember you. They got to work hard to maintain this kind of level." He and his pal took custody of Feyhe, removing Billy's hands and body from the picture.

"Say 'bye-bye' now, granny," the first EMT man said. The other hadn't spoken at all, although he looked much more simpatico, Billy thought.

"She's not a granny," he said.

"Well, she is for me, sonny-boy," the hospital worker said. "Say 'bye-bye'!!"

With a certain ease and grace, the two men maneuvered Feyhe out of the apartment and into the hallway. Owen shut the door behind them.

"How often is she like that?" Owen asked.

"I don't know!" Billy blurted out. "I've never seen her like that. I don't even know from your description which state that was? Maniacal or Depressioned."

"Manic or depressed," Owen corrected him. "It doesn't matter because people with this just don't have control over their emotions."

"But I want to know. Was she suicidal? Or over the top?"

"I'm not the expert, Billy, but I think she was heading into a downward spiral. I think she was on the depressed end of the spectrum."

"Well, my God…well…what do you do?"

"Hope for the best, Billy. Keep a weather eye on the situation and hope for the best."

They went back to their clean-up chores without another word.

In Lenox Hill hospital, in a room with softened walls, in a bed not too close to the window, not too close to the dresser, Feyhe lay quietly, staring at her ceiling. Her mind was full of thoughts made solid. She could see a few of them, feel the rest. On her wrists, now, were cloth strips that had been wound around her, snugly, several times and then attached to the two removable gates on either side of her bed. Similar restraints had been applied to her ankles. A fifth cloth had been wound six times around her head, across her forehead. It was secured to the bed screen with a series of knots. She was immobile.

She was still humming, but now the tune had altered into something so nondescript that even she didn't have a name for it. She stared upward and watched the show being played out over her bed. It was better than a Marx Brothers comedy, just as funny and satirical, but with less plot. In this show, or movie, Billy was sitting cross-legged on a large stool, but the stool was moving and coming out of its corner. Billy bounced up and down and was chortling with each bump the footstool took. Then he pulled out his hookah and took a long drag on his opium cigarette. The water gurgled and so did Billy. Feyhe laughed. Then she slept.

Her sleep didn't last long. She woke with a start, tried to move and couldn't. She tried to look at her arms and then at her legs, but her head wouldn't move. Totally immobilized, Feyhe suddenly screamed. It was a curious sound, softer than she expected and then she understood that she couldn't hear herself either. She screamed again. She screamed, expecting someone to come and release her from some strange bondage she couldn't decipher.

But no one came.

16

Billy awoke to the sound of soft rippling music abetted by the gurgle of the fountain. Fingers, how many he wasn't certain, played delicately with the hair on his forearms and his thighs. He forced his eyelids to part and peeked through the slits they engorged to see who was playing so softly and sweetly with his limbs. It was, he happily noted, Grey and not Ryan. He smiled at her and she stuck out her tongue in response.

"Do I have to get up?" he all but whispered.

"No," she said. "I'll take care of everything." Her face disappeared from view as she moved down along his body, finally taking his morning-hard organ into her mouth. He lay back and simply let her do what she did so well. As soon as he had climaxed, she lay back down on the pillows near him and her fingers began their soft caresses once again.

"Where's Ryan?" Billy asked her.

"Out somewhere," she said. "Who knows?"

"You're something, you two," Billy said. "I was so lucky to meet you."

"Luck had nothing to do with it, sweetie. We wanted to meet you and that was that." Billy lifted his head up to look at her. "What does that mean?"

"Frederick had told us about you and we were intrigued. We asked to meet you and he arranged it for us."

"What did he tell you?" Billy was curious and slightly fearful at the same time.

"He told us you were…talented," she said. "He told us you were attractive, too. He also told us how good you were in bed, darling."

"How amazingly intuitive Frederick must be, then," Billy snapped. "I never had anything to do with him, outside of designing that room."

"Of course, Billy," she cooed at him. "Whatever you say."

"It's the t-truth," he said.

"Well, then, I believe you, sweetie. No need to go all huffy about it."

"I think there is a need, Grey. I really do."

"But it all worked out, so why the fuss? You made us a wonderful home and you make us a delicious companion. It's all for the best."

"But it's based on a lie," Billy said. "I don't like to be lied about."

"You like to be lied upon, though," she said, a slight tic coming into her voice and her cheek.

"I want to talk to Ryan and you about this. I think we have some air to clear."

"Well, later on we can do just that," she said. "Right now, I'd like a little pleasuring, please."

Billy turned sharply away from her and, rising from the bed, pulled the quilt up around his midriff. He stood there for a moment, his back turned to her, his eyes following the falling water that cascaded down the wall of this room and into the pool two floors below. He could hear her breathing, could feel her approaching him. He turned to face her. She was already too close for comfort.

"No," he said. "Not now."

She took a step back and sat down on the edge of the bed. "All right, darling. We'll talk about it…later…when Ryan comes home."

They didn't have long to wait. Ryan showed up half an hour later, looking somewhat odd, Billy thought.

"Are you all right?" he asked the man, and Ryan just nodded slowly, indicating that all was well, but Billy wasn't convinced. "You don't seem like yourself."

"I'm fine," Ryan replied.

"Well, we have an issue to discuss, you and Grey and me," Billy said.

"Something came up this morning and I'm not comfortable with it."

Ryan nodded again, then called out to Grey. She was in the room with them instantly. "It would seem that we've been misled," she said without even a hello or a where were you? in her voice.

"I'll tell you later," he said. "What's up?" he said to Billy.

"Apparently we seduced a baby, not a Don Juan," she said quickly before Billy could respond.

"I beg your pardon?" Ryan responded.

"I hear that Ostendorf was bragging about my sexual prowess when discussing me with you," Billy said. "It's a subject on which he knew, and knows, nothing."

"Oh, I wouldn't say that, Billy," Ryan said. "He seems to have been pretty accurate about your varied talents."

"Yes, there is that," Grey agreed.

"I don't know what he said, but I know he had no first-hand knowledge about any skills except the designing ones."

"And he got those right also," Grey said. Ryan nodded an instant agreement.

"And what's the difference, really, Billy? You're happy here with us and we're happy here with you. Isn't that all that matters, really?"

"No," Billy said. "I don't like you thinking that I'm some slut who sleeps around with all of his clients."

"Oh, we don't think that, not at all," Ryan said. "If we did think that was the case we wouldn't have you here with us, not for five minutes."

"No, we looked for loyalty and we found it in you, darling," Grey cooed into his ear.

"You took me from someone who loved me," Billy said.

"That cop, you mean?" Grey asked. "If he loved you as he said he did, we couldn't have taken you from him. But you were easy."

"That's not fair, Grey," her husband said instantly. "Billy took time, he wasn't easy."

"I forgot," she said. "You did the work and I was just an innocent stand-by."

"Never innocent, dear heart," he said back to her.

"When you two are finished," Billy interjected, "with your asinine love-making, I'd like to finish this conversation."

"Of course, Billy, what can we say," Ryan said. "We loved your work, and when we met you, we loved you also. You were unhappy, dissatisfied with your life with Officer Joseph, miserable in your upper west side existence. We loved you and we wanted you to be happy. We invited you to live with us during the work and after it was complete, to live with us forever. We love you."

"I...see..." Billy started to say something that wouldn't pass his lips.

"We know this is an unusual situation, darling," Grey added. "We understand that you never dreamed of a marriage with a couple like us. We realize how hard it was for you to make the decision to come away with us into the life. We appreciate your feelings and we know you feel hurt and misunderstood. That nasty Frederick planted a seed and watered it with innuendo. We took the bait, and curiously enough, that stupid Cupid Ostendorf shot his phony arrows into the right hearts, all three of them."

Her cooing was making Billy uncomfortable again and, as she droned on, he moved involuntarily a step or two away from her. She noticed his movement and subtly followed him, keeping the same distance between as there had been at the beginning of her speech. As they shuffled, Ryan came into her full view.

"And where were you all night, my dearest?" she hissed at him. "Why were you anywhere other than here where there are people who adore you?"

"I am sorry, both of you," he said with a cat in cream smile. "I met a charming fellow last evening at the AA meeting and after a quick bite together I went back to his place and saw his etchings, as they say."

"How vile of you, Ryan," Grey said. "How absolutely vile. You know that Billy would never do any such thing and you know that I never would. How do you dare to violate our trust that way?"

He stared back at his wife, a haughty expression in the arch of his shoulders and neck. "My dear, I am the man in this menage and I take what privilege I may."

"Excuse me, Ryan," Billy said imperatively. "You're not the only man."

"Really? Hmmm. I see. Baby wants the same rights as Daddy?"

"Stop it, Ryan."

"Baby angry with Daddums?"

"I said stop it."

"So you did," Ryan admitted. "And twice now." He gave Billy a chuck on the chin, then turned and did the same to Grey. He walked into the salon and went right to the bar. He opened a cupboard door and removed a bottle of fine single malt scotch. From below the bar he took a double shot glass. As he poured out the amber liquor he looked up at them, still standing where they had been.

"Anyone else care for a drink?" There was no response. "No? Fine. I'll drink alone."

"A.A. darling," Grey called out to him.

"Fuck them! I need a drink now." He threw the scotch into his mouth, cocked his head back and swallowed the double-shot in a single gulp. "I need another."

"Well, dear, he's your daddums now, not mine," Grey said to Billy as she headed for the stairs. "I'll be in my room if anyone cares." She was gone. Billy was still standing in the hallway.

"What am I supposed to do, Ryan?"

"I don't know. You might think I don't care, Billy, but I do, actually."

"I didn't like being lied about," he said. "It makes me uneasy to think that you came to me believing that I was a tramp, a slut who slept around for the work."

"If it makes you feel any better about yourself, dear boy, I never thought that about you."

"Thank you."

"In fact, I thought you a very reluctant little tramp, when I couldn't get you into bed right off the bat."

"Excuse me?" Billy could feel his blood beginning to boil. He had broken out in a cold sweat and his eyes were clouding over.

"Oh, yes, but I knew how good you were at your job and so I thought I'd just press on and see if you took the bait. You little Jewish boys can't resist WASP money when it's tossed on the ground in front of you. I knew that."

"This is getting very offensive, Ryan."

"You know I have another job for you, if you're willing to continue under the same terms. We've bought a house in The Berkshires. You're just the man for the interior."

"I see. You're still buying me, aren't you?"

"I do like you Billy. I like you very much. So does Grey and that means a good deal to me. If she's happy then I have some freedom to explore when I need to do so. You make her happy. That makes me happy. When I'm happy I like people."

"I don't think I care to hear much more of this, Ryan."

"Don't you? Oh well, too bad."

"I'm going up to my room."

"My room, actually. You just have the use of it for now."

"Oh, that's the way, is it? Think I'm helpless? Think again."

Billy walked to the stairs, hoping that he wasn't moving too quickly, praying that his exit was making an impact. He wanted Ryan to want him, wanted him to stop him and tell him that it was all a joke, that he hadn't meant the cruel things he said. He expected to hear Ryan call him back, apologize, coax him into his arms. He kept moving out, then up, then across again. He listened for Ryan's voice, but all he heard was a hoarse coughing from below and nothing at all from above.

He opened the top drawer of his dresser and started to take out all of his things, one at a time, slowly, deliberately, resolutely.

"Two nights, that's all," Feyhe said to him. "After that I need the room."

"Okay, thanks." Billy threw open his suitcase. His rumpled clothes seemed to stare accusingly at him. "I'll find a place quickly, I know."

"I warned you about them, Billy. I told you they were no good."

"You did, Feyhe, thanks."

"I tried to keep you out of that snake pit, Billy," she continued, nagging at him.

"And you know snake pits, Feyhe, don't you?"

"Talk like that and your two nights could turn into one, Billy."

"All right, Feyhe, I take it back." He felt bad, felt sadder than he had since Miriam's death. He turned to face her. "I really do apologize. I shouldn't have said that."

"You shouldn't have. It hurt me."

"I don't want to hurt you, Feyhe. Believe that, please."

"I do." She hugged him close to her and he could smell that faint combination of dried urine and old lipstick. He pulled his head back, moved his nose away from her skin. "Now unpack what you need and leave the rest. I want you to help me prepare dinner."

"Okay. So, what's for dinner?

"Nothing you like," she said. "So I'll need all the help you can give me."

She was out of the spare room in a flash and Billy had the place to himself. He hadn't been in this room in a while and it was clear that Feyhe hadn't been in there either. Formerly her studio, now a place to store things she couldn't use and couldn't part with, it was musty and dusty. He fully anticipated staying here for a week or more and cleaning it up, making it habitable. As he looked at all of the pieces, some only half finished, he marveled at her talent and ability to sculpt and draw. Some of the pieces were so lifelike that Billy felt he was not alone in the room.

He shuffled through some piles of sketch pads and a few small, experimental busts, trying to uncover the window which looked out over the street and the rooftop of the building next door. Light was drifting in through the five and six-foot-high piles of old experiments in art and old books. It was a good and easy chore for him, one that would bring him some satisfaction. He wondered if Feyhe would appreciate his organizing and cataloguing everything in the room, giving her a comprehensive overview of her possessions. He made a mental note to talk to her about it, thinking it might buy him some extra time in the apartment while he searched for a new place to live.

Finally he reached the window. He reached up to loosen the latch-locks and then, with a hard jerk, he pulled the window open, letting in the city's rancid air and ancient dust molecules, letting out the smell of old charcoal, old marble dust, old clay. The breeze felt good and the air, smelling of car exhaust and day-old garbage, was a relief. He had the image of Grey that morning in his head and the breeze wafted it away from him, out of his brain's clear sightlines. He was beginning to think that things were taking a positive turn, that things would be all right.

As he turned back to face the room and its task of order, Feyhe's words came back to him: "Two nights, that's all. After that I need the room." *What for?* Billy wondered. *What for?*

The morning of the second day, Billy got his answer. It came from an unexpected source and gave him more of a jolt than a surprise. He was sipping his second cup of coffee, fully expecting Feyhe to show up in the kitchen, listening for her steps in the hallway when the doorbell rang, not once or twice, but with a rapid, constant, insistent rattle that nearly caused him to shake his mug and spill his drink. He moved swiftly to the front door of the apartment and pushed the buzzer without bothering to ask who was at the downstairs door, a mistake he had never made before. He cursed himself for the idiot he was becoming with all this change in his life and waited where he was for the doorbell to sound. He didn't have long to wait. The whirring of the elevator shook the apartment door slightly. Billy felt the tremors, understood their meaning. He unlatched the door and opened it, stood in the opening and waited for the sliding door panel to move and then for the outer door of the elevator to open into the hallway. It did just that and vomited forth its two inhabitants.

A boy, about ten years old, lurched into the hallway, dragging behind him a full-grown man. Billy recognized the adult instantly—Kim. The boy, he realized, must be the older son.

"Kim," Billy said with all the sarcasm he could muster at 9:30, "what a surprise on a Thursday morning."

"Hello, Billy Duncan," the Korean said to him. "It is early in the day, I know, and I am disturbing your tranquility, I see. My apologies."

The boy gave Kim a hard yank, nearly jerking him to his knees there at the entry to the apartment.

"Grandma," the child said shrilly, ordering the two men to respond to his single-word sentence.

"We have come to see Feyhe," Kim added instantly. "She is here?"

"I haven't seen or heard her yet this morning," Billy said, still not letting the two Koreans into the apartment. "Is she expecting you both?"

"Yes, Billy Duncan, she is." Kim smiled as he said these words, then let his mouth turn into its more normal pouty frown.

"Grandma," the boy said again, this time louder. His soprano voice echoed against the marble inlay of the hallway and off the marble tile floor.

"You'd better come in, then," Billy said, "before the neighbors start to complain about the noise."

The boy pulled his father hard again, and Billy realized for the first time that in his other hand Kim held a large suitcase and that there was a knapsack slung over his far shoulder.

The telephone was jangling as the three of them came into the apartment. Billy ducked into the kitchen to grab the receiver and he was jolted once again by the hard reverberation that occurred as the door slammed shut behind Kim and son. Billy rubbed his free ear with the heel of his hand as he put the receiver up to his other ear.

"Yes, hello?" he said. There was no voiced reply, but there was a lot of coughing. "Who is it, please?"

After a breath, an actual breath in his ear, she spoke. "Are they there yet?" Feyhe asked. "Don't say my name."

Billy smiled at Kim who was watching him from the doorway. "Where are you?" he asked his cousin.

"I'm at Grand Central Station. Don't ask."

"How long have you been there?"

"Since about five this morning. I couldn't sleep so I got up and took a walk. This is where I ended up."

Billy smiled again, then spoke carefully to Feyhe. "Will I see you anytime soon?"

"I don't know," she whispered. "Are they there yet?"

"Yes," Billy said.

"Keep them occupied a while, will you?"

"I do have to go to work and I'm supposed to move today."

"No, no," she said quickly. "Everything is off. I'm changing everything, Billy. You have to stay for a while, a long, long while. I can't have him there."

"Who are you talking about?"

Kim moved out of the doorway and went in pursuit of his son.

"Danny Kim," Feyhe said. "He's been a problem for his father and I promised to take care of him for a while, but I'm not up to it, Billy. I'm just not up to it."

"When you say problem—" he began but she stopped him.

"He's tried to kill his baby brother, twice."

"Is this not a job for someone with more experience?" Billy asked, still cautious about his word choices.

"Billy, Kim asked me to help and I said I would, but I don't know if I can."

"It certainly won't be easy," Billy replied. Kim stuck his head in the other door and waved to Billy who smiled back, waved and turned away.

"Feyhe?" Kim hissed at him.

Billy put his hand over the mouthpiece and turned back to look at Kim when he spoke. "I don't really know what's going on, Kim. Hold on, just a minute, this is business." He turned his back on the Korean again.

"Look, I don't think I can handle this alone," he said to Feyhe. "I think we should meet and try to find a solution for you."

"Fifteen minutes, Billy, at the deli on 76th and Madison, okay?" she said.

"Fine. I'll be there. I'll be the one with the plastered-on smile." He hung up the phone and went to find Kim and son.

They were already ensconced in the dining room. Danny Kim had a book open on the table and he was absorbed in the contents. His father stood watching him. As Billy entered the room, Kim took a step closer to his son, but didn't turn to look at Billy at all.

"Kim, I have to go out. A new client wants me to look at some swatches. Feyhe is out, somewhere—I couldn't really say where right now—but she should be home soon. I don't know if you want to wait or come back later."

"We wait," Kim said. "Danny has a book. I have checkbook to balance."

Billy nodded at him, went back to the room he'd been sleeping in and got dressed.

Ten minutes later he was alone in a booth at the deli, waiting for his cousin to show up. He had ordered coffee and eggs and a bagel toasted with a *schmear*, and he was thumbing his way through the New York Post, a copy that had been left behind by the previous occupant of the same booth. The articles were over-written and overwrought and the accompanying photos made Billy laugh out loud. The pompous seriousness of small issues always amused him when little else could. He kept looking up, checking the door, checking his wristwatch. He noticed that time was passing him by. He had been there for twenty minutes, then thirty and still Feyhe had not come in.

He wondered if she had walked uptown from the station. That might take her a half hour instead of the fifteen minutes she had dictated as probable. He asked for a refill on the coffee and turned the pages to the comics. He tried to chuckle at them as he read his way down the page, but nothing came across as funny. He gave that a thought, wondering if it was the comics themselves or the tenor of the day, his second eviction in three days. It was clear to him that he was being deposed by Danny Kim. What wasn't clear was the circumstance surrounding the changing of the guard.

He checked his watch again. Forty minutes had passed since he sat down. He looked up at the door, expecting to see her, hands shielding eyes from both sides, peering in the window, checking to see if he was still there. Instead he saw Kim coming through the door. He was alone. He spotted Billy immediately and moved through the narrow room to his booth. Without waiting for an invitation, he sat down opposite Billy.

"Billy Duncan, hello," Kim said to him. "Feyhe will not come to meet you."

"I beg your pardon."

"Feyhe has come home to take up duties with Danny, my oldest son."

"She's supposed to meet me here," Billy said, then regretted it, remembering his white lie to Kim earlier.

"She has come home instead." He bowed his head slightly to show his humility in regard to both Feyhe and to Billy. "She has offered to care for Danny Kim and to take him into her home with her."

"Kim, I don't understand—"

In an unconventional way, Kim interrupted him. "My son has many problem," Kim said. "More than two doctors say he must not stay with Ni-Na and me and our younger son, Laun-Nu. Danny wants to be his brother and be the more loved son, but he is difficult for us."

Billy nodded as if he understood the crisis.

Kim continued speaking. "Two times he has almost strangled Laun-Nu and left him for dead," Kim said. "We do not want state of New Jersey to take him, so we ask Feyhe, his godmother, to be guardian and to protect him from himself and to protect us from him. This she has said she will do. Danny, today, is come to live with Feyhe. I am most grateful."

"She's not prepared to care for him," Billy said. "She can hardly take care of herself."

"It will be good for her to have other person to care about and to look after," Kim said.

"She will now focus on herself to be there for Danny Kim."

"I don't think so," Billy said. "It will be too much for her."

"He is loving grandson and godson for her," Kim responded. "He think more of her than of my wife or me."

"Why is that, do you think?" Billy asked him. "Is it because she is indulgent with him? Is it because she gives him candy and buys him presents all of the time? Could that have something to do with it? Is it her irresponsible attitude about life that appeals to him? I don't think this is a good idea."

"We have not asked you your opinion," Kim said.

"You should have," Billy said abruptly. "I know more about her, than—"

"You have not known her at all," Kim said to him. "I have been the closest to Feyhe in these years. I have held her in my arms to comfort her. You have only come to her for your own help."

"I'm not getting into this senseless sort of spat with you," Billy said.

"I have to move out so your bratty little son who just needs a good spanking or two can move in. I need to go back to the apartment now and get my things."

"In my car," Kim said.

"I beg your pardon?"

"Your things are all in my car," Kim said. "Feyhe has packed them for you and I have brought them here. I will take you where you go."

"I don't know where to go." He slammed his hand against the back wall of the booth, causing a picture on the wall to rattle its metal frame against the fading paper that enshrouded the room.

"You will go to Khanzadian," Kim said. "Feyhe has arranged this."

"I'm sorry, did you say I'm going to rent a room from Owen?"

"Is what Feyhe said. 'Take him to Owen Khanzadian's apartment.' So this is what I am prepared to arrange, your transportation."

"This is preposterous."

"I am ready to take you now," Kim said. "Bill is already paid. Come Billy Duncan." He extended his hand to Billy, who without really thinking about it, took the hand and was helped out of the booth, off the bench and into a standing position.

"I am not going to stay with Owen," Billy said.

"Why not?" Owen asked him from inside his large vestibule. "I've got the space, kiddo."

"Because this is an imposition, on you, and on me," Billy said.

"I don't mind." Owen chuckled but didn't smile. "I've got four bedrooms and I only use two of them, one to sleep in and one to work in. That leaves two more."

"One to sleep in and one to work in for me also?" Billy asked him.

"Why not?" He extended his arm backward, inviting Billy in. "Is that everything?"

"No," he said. "Most of my things are still at the Kendalls."

"I'm not surprised that didn't work out," Owen said. "Was it a difficult parting for you, Billy?"

Billy shrugged, then broke into a grin. "Surprisingly, no. It hurt a lot at the moment of realization, but it didn't take me long to see how foolish I'd been with them, from the start of it."

"You're growing up," Owen said. "We all do, but it takes a while sometimes."

"Like you, you mean?"

"What has Feyhe told you about me?"

"Not enough, apparently." They were still standing in the foyer, Billy still holding the front door open with his foot. "I suppose I should come in and we can talk about this."

Owen smiled at him. "That would be a good idea, Billy. We should talk."

He took Billy's suitcase and his hat out of Billy's hand and led him forward into the living room. Billy followed, less reluctantly than he expected.

17

Dawn is not an easy time for the depressed, Billy noted. The cold, isolated gray light that seeped through his window at 5:40 the next morning barely served to announce the beginning of newness. He stretched, yawned and turned over, hoping to sleep again, but he knew that there was little chance of that. He was awake and he was in a strange place and he was unhappy about his situation.

He was Billy Duncan, the boy genius, the designing whiz, the man of the hour. He was Billy Duncan, the man in the back room of another man's apartment, of no man's life, of no conceivable future. He was Billy, the cousin, the son. He was Billy the ex-lover, the ex-houseboy. He didn't know who he was or how he would face the world when there was enough light outside for the world to see him by.

He lay where he was and cried, except his body produced no sobs, no shakes, no sighs, no tears. Even so, he cried and he hurt and he wanted to die.

The night before he had sat up with Owen, talking about life and its emptiness and its cruelties. Owen, as he had known him to be, proved a good listener, an excellent sounding-board for Billy's effortless rendition of the dark sonata of his misspent youth. Owen had been openly sympathetic but not overly mendacious in that sympathy. Billy was not so far gone that he couldn't relate to honesty, even when it was couched in pat phrases.

"You have to take charge of your destiny," Owen had said to him more than once during their session. Billy considered their conversation a session and was sure there would be a bill at some point in the near future. "No one else can tell you what to do or how to do it, Billy. You're a man, not a child. No one will want you, not personally or professionally, if they perceive you as an infantile person. You have to make your future by coming into your present."

"You're preaching to the converted, Owen," Billy had replied. "You don't have to convince me."

Owen hugged Billy, several times actually, during their evening's talk. That physical contact had given Billy some pleasure, but it had also set his teeth on edge. This was the man who had betrayed Feyhe, had cheated on Feyhe, had left her. He was the one failure in her life, at least the only failure she talked about with any real passion. Now, she had given Billy to him.

Was he, Billy wondered, to be counted another Feyheliar? He laughed at the word, the juxtaposition he had affixed. Owen asked him why he had laughed and Billy had told him. Owen, however, didn't laugh.

"What exactly did she tell you about our break-up?" he asked Billy.

Billy told him the story of the Chinese restaurant and the woman who scoffed at Feyhe.

He told him about Feyhe's anger over the pamphlets that he had slipped into her work, that Ostendorf's anger about such behavior had infuriated Feyhe. He told Owen everything he could recall from Feyhe's fragmentary story-telling. Owen listened silently, occasionally nodding or shaking his head to indicate his sense of the reality of each detail.

"Feyhe, as is her way, only told you pieces," Owen said. "There was a whole lot more going on."

"Was there?"

"Oh, yes. Those pamphlets, those commie tracts that I sent to Freddie Ostendorf were a joke and he knew it. I was already moving away from the whole party thing. I had been disillusioned, as had so many of my friends, by the restrictive morality of the party. It wasn't for me any longer."

"Then why send those things to Ostendorf?"

"Well, Feyhe was a bit in love with him, back then at least. He was very handsome and urbane and witty and she doted on those things. I liked to upset that applecart whenever I could, show her his dark side, his anger, hostility. She didn't know, then, that he was as queer as a three-dollar bill."

"But you did?" Billy asked.

"I did."

"How?"

"Well," Owen paused, not for effect, but to put his thoughts into a clear pathway, "at that time, unbeknownst to Feyhe, Freddie was having an affair with a married man—with me." He stopped to let this information sink in to Billy's brain. "We had been getting together for almost a year at that point. It was a slow start, for me at least, because I was a novice, I had never been with another man."

"He went after you?" Billy said.

"Not exactly, Billy. Not precisely. He never pursued me, but he had made it pretty clear to me shortly after Feyhe introduced us that he found me very attractive and would be interested in…bringing me along, as it were. I was intrigued, I guess."

"Why? You were such a 'stud' according to Feyhe. You had women eating out of your hand, including my mother and my cousin, Peachie."

Owen laughed, in spite of himself. Billy watched his nose crinkle as his low-pitched chuckles emerged. He enjoyed the look, but before he could consider that, Owen had become serious again.

"I always had a bisexual streak, Billy. I had never pursued it before Freddie, though."

"Did Feyhe know that when you two got married?"

"Yeah. We talked about it a few times, but she was pretty secure about me. She knew I occasionally screwed around with a girl or two, but she always forgave me that because her own sexuality was limited. She was good in bed, but she wasn't as curious about 'things' as some other women were. I think she was actually relieved that we kept things fairly 'normal.' Feyhe wasn't the sort to expand too many horizons."

"That's changed," Billy said.

"Yes, I know that. But the divorce. You wanted to know about that. Well, I think I remember the Chinese Restaurant thing and that did happen and Feyhe was pretty hurt by it. Still, we went home and made love and it was all right. And yes, she was upset over the pamphlets to Freddie and I did promise they'd stop and they did. It was when she found out that he and I had been playing house on an occasional basis that the shit hit the fan. It wasn't the bisexuality bit, not really. It was the specific man I chose to play around with, the man she had a crush on, that really did us in. That was a blow to the ego that she couldn't handle."

"Did you see it that way, then?"

"You know, I did. It was what changed things for me, sent me in a new direction professionally. I began to understand that the human mind and heart were really the same thing and they both needed to be cherished and sustained."

"So Feyhe divorced you. In spite of the growth, she left you and took off on her own."

"In a way, yes."

"What do you mean?"

"Well, she left publishing. I mean, she left Ostendorf's publishing house and went to work with an agent as her assistant. In those days that was a key-word for 'lover' and they lived and worked together for about five years. But it couldn't last. Feyhe is not a lesbian, and she couldn't keep making that work, no matter how hard she tried. Also, the woman took up with a Swiss import whose career she was handling. Feyhe was hurt by that, too, I imagine. Then she found her art, her sculpting and everything was different for her after that. I was pleased for her, very pleased in fact. I loved her and I wanted her to be happy. I had taken my first master's degree in social work by then. I was seeing her, and myself, with a new and better understanding."

"How did the divorce hit her? Was she upset?"

"No. It was her idea, you see. Once Feyhe gets an idea it becomes a reality and there's nothing else."

Billy smiled instantly, recognizing the description of his cousin as apt.

"She got a lawyer, got the papers, set a court date, did everything right on schedule, Billy. It was as though we were a book to edit and publish with a rigid schedule to be maintained. She followed the outline she had drawn up for the dissolution of our marriage. She followed it right up to the end. There was no emotion in it. There was clarity. There were no foul-ups, just that inevitable schedule. Then, suddenly, something happened to her, something neither of us understood at that time. She suddenly changed her mind."

"Excuse me? What does that mean?"

"She never signed the papers, Billy. She never finished what she had begun. We've never been legally divorced."

"You're still her husband?"

"I am."

"Didn't you want your freedom from her? Couldn't you have pursued it yourself?"

"No, to both those things. She's the only woman I ever loved."

"But you never saw her again until a short while ago. Why?"

"That was what she wanted. Those were her terms. I could only live by them."

"That's wimpy!"

"I was pursuing my own interests. I had no need for another marriage. There was a protection, somewhat, in knowing that I was legally bound to Feyhe. It worked for me."

"I don't get it," Billy said, the depression that he'd been holding off suddenly taking a giant step up the ladder into his psyche.

"Security is a strange thing, Billy. It's hard to explain. But at least you now know all the facts in the case."

Billy nodded, thanked Owen for the use of the room and went to bed where he lay wide awake for several hours before he finally fell asleep and dreamt of falling rocks and crumbling buildings, of Joe and Ryan, of Feyhe and Owen, of himself and no one.

On the third night after Danny Kim moved into the spare bedroom, Feyhe was awakened by a strange sound and an even stranger sense of danger. Her bedroom, darkened by the shades that prevented any light from spilling into the room from the street below or the moon above, was illuminated by a shaft of light pouring in through her open door. Standing in the doorway, backlit and only vaguely recognizable was ten-year-old Danny. He was standing, legs apart, arms held away from his sides, staring at her, just barely caught in the bordered edge of the light. She shook herself awake and looked at the boy before she spoke, trying to appraise his mind-set.

Then she heard the sound again, and realized it was emanating from Danny.

It was a low, grumbling sound, not a stomach rumble, not a growl, but a disturbed sound, a musing of misery coming not from an open mouth, but from a pit in the earth, a concealed place.

"Danny, what is it? Are you all right?" she whispered.

The boy didn't answer, didn't move, but the sound persisted. Feyhe tried again to force a response from the child.

"Danny, can I help you? What do you want, Danny?" She tried not to sound too urgent, too eager, too concerned. "Danny?"

"I miss my Mama," the boy cried.

"Of course you do," Feyhe said, sighing in relief, more for the sound of the answer than for the answer itself. "And I know she misses you too."

"No. Not her," he shouted. "She hates me."

"Danny, she loves you. She does."

He was still standing in the doorway. He had not changed his position at all. Feyhe slipped out from under her covers, totally forgetting that, as usual, she had slept in the nude. "Danny, come here to me," she said softly.

"No," he said indignantly. "No, I won't."

"Feyhe loves you and won't hurt you," she said sweetly.

"I'm alone," Danny said suddenly, changing from one dark mood to another. "I don't like to be alone. At home I sleep in the same room as Mama."

"Well, here you are a big boy and the man of the house," Feyhe said, "and you get your very own room."

"But I'm alone," he repeated. "I hate to be alone."

Feyhe's emotional responses were fighting with her strictly mental ones. She wanted to embrace the child, comfort him, but she also wanted him to be more confident, more self-sufficient. The mother she had never been was in conflict with the regimented disciplinarian that she had become.

"It's late, Danny. Go back to bed and we'll talk about this in the morning," she said. The boy stood his ground. Feyhe stood up and moved toward him.

"You're naked," Danny said to her when she was closer to him than to her bed. It was the first moment since awaking that she realized how inappropriate it was for her to be dealing with another human being.

"I'm sorry," she said, turning away from him and moving swiftly back to her bed, to the relative darkness that it offered on the opposite edge of the light that streamed in from the hallway. She tucked her feet under the counterpane and drew the blanket up to cover her pelvis.

"Mama sleeps naked," Danny said, revealing a secret that Feyhe had never known.

"Does your daddy sleep naked too?" she asked the boy without stopping to think.

"No. Daddy wears a suit," he said.

"You mean pajamas, surely," Feyhe corrected.

"He buttons up to the neck," Danny said. "He has a high collar and a belt."

"Well, it does sound like a suit," Feyhe agreed.

"Daddy sleeps in Laun-Nu's room and I sleep with Mama."

"In the same room with your mother," Feyhe said, correcting the boy again.

"With Mama," Danny said, correcting her in return. "I sleep in the bed with her and she holds me and I don't cry."

"Well, here, Danny Kim, you will sleep in your own bed, in your own room."

"I am alone," he said one more time. "I don't like to be alone."

The sweetness in his high, treble voice on which he floated his sadness gave her a chill and she pulled the covers up a little bit higher, concealing her breasts. She felt the shivers in her spine and she was frightened by them, then comfortable with them, then frightened again.

"You were all right alone for two nights, Danny."

"No, Granny Feyhe, I was not. I was alone and I was scared and the noises from the street made me tremble."

"You said nothing about them."

"I was scared."

"You slept through the night."

"I was scared. I was too scared to move."

"Why are you not scared tonight?"

"I am scared. I am alone."

"You are safe here, Danny. Nothing can hurt you."

"I am alone."

She heard the sound of his voice alter from the child's to the man's. She couldn't fathom the change, the odd alteration of tones from son to father. She wanted the sound of him to be his own and not his father's, but she had made the change in him happen, she knew, and she didn't know how to make the reverse occur.

"You are not alone," she said. "I am here."

Danny moved through the stream of light and was instantly larger, more adult, more the man Feyhe had known so well for so long. He stood by the side of her bed and looked at her, a softness she was not accustomed to playing in his eyes, eyes that she could not see clearly but knew so well she imagined their brightness.

"I am alone," said the boy, this time the boy again, in the boy's voice.

Feyhe pulled back the covers and lay there, naked, in front of him. She smiled at him and a tear formed in the inner corner of her left eye. It accumulated there, fluids marring vision, alkaline creating a dull pain that softened slightly when she smiled again.

"For tonight, and only tonight, you can sleep with me, here in my bed. Only for tonight, mind."

Danny moved into the bed and Feyhe covered him with the sheet and the blanket. He lay in her arms, his head nestled on her diaphragm, his short black hair favoring her breasts with tingles as he breathed and moved slightly, his warm exhalations moistening her flesh. He slept almost instantly, cuddling her. She slept not at all. There was something not right about this, she knew, but he was a child and only a child, and a child in her care. She had to care for him, give him the love that he needed to grow and to be a man that other men would respect. She had to provide for him all of those things his own mother, and his father too, could not give the boy. She would educate him and she would discipline him. She would be the perfect grandmother, the ideal mentor.

She was thinking these things, these noble and true things, these altruistic things. She was letting her mind see him in the years to come, watching him mature into the man his father had once been in Korea, only he would be that man here in New York, and he would be successful and loving and kind, and he would make her proud. He would make her feel so wonderful and so proud. He would make her feel that she had done more than any mother had ever done for her son. He would...

His body, pressed against hers under the covers, had altered. His head was higher than it had been. His cheek now rested on her bosom, his hips now pressed against her own. His penis had grown hard, had lengthened, was moving. Feyhe moved her legs, trying to alter the pressure of one body against another, but her movement only caused movement in him. He entered her vagina and, without meaning to, her reaction only brought him further inside her.

He sighed and murmured something she couldn't hear. Her heart was pounding so hard that it drowned out all other sounds in the room, outside the room. She opened her eyes and saw that the hall light was still on, its broad shaft of illumination still entering her room, just as the man in her arms was entering her own body, part way, not all the way, part way. She reached for the light and took the sexual organ of her bed-partner as deeply into herself as she could. They both sighed at the same time. The boy began to move inside her and she let the tear in her eye fall on the pillow beneath her head.

Billy sat on the edge of his bed. His arms crossed one another as his hands gripped his sides. He could feel, between his fingers, the beginnings of the blubber that he would one day equate with his biological forebears. There were tears shining on his cheeks, his forced smile holding them on the slight planes that the grin presented to his face. The early morning light that peered through the exposed panels of window behind the too-small window shades in the room fell in awkward patterns on either side of his feet and legs. His own body, still in the relative darkness of the departing night, hung in that semi-still limbo provided by man-made safety nets such as the window shade and the diary.

His thoughts raced faster than he meant them to do. He stretched for them, inside his head, but he could only fasten on a few of the slowest concepts—his loneliness, his aging process, his misery at being unloved and unlovable. Surrounding these were the thoughts he wanted to find, wanted to hold fast, wanted to know better—his communication skills, his youthful energy and enthusiasm, his sweetness and willingness to give in a relationship. These fled from him, from the hands he mentally extended to catch them, as though being held would destroy them utterly. The tears stayed on the tops of his cheeks and gathered into ponds behind the floodgates of his face.

The patterns of light widened slightly. His eyes tightened their focus onto the streams of white, then yellow, then white again light. His right hand slipped away from his body, aided only by need and not by Billy, the real Billy. It took his right arm with it and together they slipped into the tip-end of the light stream. He watched as his fingers lit up, the nails shining in the newborn sunlight. He laughed at the sight of it, his laughter appealing, yet frightening.

His left hand, still gripping the fat layer on his side, squeezed his body and tickled him. There was brittle laughter again and one pond of gathered saline fluid slipped off the flattened portion of his face onto the curved cheek and fell away onto his bare-flesh leg. The splash attracted his attention away from his hands and Billy stared at his leg. He couldn't see the water, already oozing away from him and onto the bed sheet.

His mouth formed two words and he tried to say them, first together, then one after the other. They emerged as a single utterance and made no sense to Billy at all: "Whom makes..." he slurped from between his dry lips, the tightened skin over-riding the *m*'s, bringing them together into one slurred sound. In frustration he lifted his left foot and put it back down on the floor again, a little bit harder than he had earlier.

I need a pill, he thought. *What pill? What?* He couldn't find the answer to the question, but only the question providing no answer.

The morning light broadened once again as the sun came up over Central Park to the east and into the West Side apartments whose windows were fortunate enough to find the sunup vista. He looked up at the window and began to cry, finally, for real. With the tears came the sobs and these were followed by the shrieks and whoops he had not experienced before in his adult life.

He fell backward onto the bed and once again held himself tightly with both his hands, both his arms. His feet flew upward, his knees bent, his muscles constricted, hard and taut. He rolled over onto his side and into a ball, a fetal ball of absolute submission.

He didn't even feel the second set of arms that came around him. He didn't hear the consoling words whispered, then spoken, then shouted, words that included his name and the phrase, "it will be all right" and the sentence "you're not alone." He was not able to smell the morning breath of the man who spoke those words. He had no sense of the cloth of Owen's pajamas, the strength and confidence of his large hands, the gritty essence of his beard as it pressed against Billy's own bare cheek.

The only thing Billy knew for sure was that morning had come and this was not like other mornings. This was a morning that had no end, would bring no afternoon, no sunset, no evening, no night. He only knew it was morning and he had to face it, like it or not.

"You're not alone," Owen said again and again. "It will be all right, Billy. It will be all right."

After the sunlight filled the room, Billy collapsed into sleep and let his body go limp. Owen let him sleep, but he stood in the doorway and watched the younger man for a long time before he went back to his own room to dress.

18

"So, what now, Doc?"

"Doctor, please."

"Okay, what now, Doctor, please."

"Let's not get too smart-mouthed. Let's keep it civil."

"Sure. Why not?"

"Now, what would you like to know? Be specific."

Feyhe eyed him suspiciously. She didn't like him and he knew it. She could see that in his face. She could sense it in the way he placed his hands on the desk, his fingers splayed and arched.

"I've been here two weeks, Doctor. I've been away from my baby for two weeks. He needs me."

"He's not your baby, Feyhe."

"Not a baby any longer, a young man," she snapped back at him. She reached for her cigarette which had lain long enough in the ashtray to accumulate nearly three quarters of an inch of unsmoked, gray stubble. She was smoking constantly now, or at least lighting cigarettes all the time. Sometimes she smoked them down to the filter tip, sometimes she just held them annoyingly near other people's faces.

"He's a responsibility you shouldn't take on any longer," the psychiatrist was saying, but Feyhe wasn't listening. She was losing her mind in an internal reverie designed to block out the useful, the practical, the everyday.

"You need to concentrate your energy on yourself. You need to remember your daily instructions and to take your medicine and to check in with this office and with your medical doctors regularly. The boy will grow up and be taken care of by others."

That was the only part of his speech she heard, the final sentence, *the sentence of isolation* Feyhe thought. She took a long drag on the cigarette and puffed out her chest to hold the effervescent smoke in her lungs for a while. She slowly let loose her breath and the thin trail of recirculated smoke drifted across the expanse between them, wafting under the nose of the elderly psychiatric specialist.

"Feyhe, you're not listening to me," he said to her. "You're off in a dream somewhere again. Come back to me and pay attention."

"You're an idiot, don't you know that?" she said in a sweet voice. "No one cares what you say or what you think. No one pays any attention at all."

"A lot of my patients pay meticulous care to my words."

"A lot of your patients are in your care for a very long time, too." Feyhe chuckled after she spoke, caught the chuckle in the middle of an exhaled breath and choked on the smoke that, confused, changed direction and was swallowed back into her lungs.

"Feyhe, you've been in my care now for six years. You make no progress. You fight reality."

"Would you rather I fought fantasies? What good would that do?"

"I want you to fight yourself and to win the battle."

"I don't get you."

"Who are you, Feyhe? Who and what are you?"

"You ask me that too often, Doctor Doofus. You know the answer. It's always the same."

"I want to hear it now. Tell me."

"No!" She pouted like a child, then altered her mouth and her arms and her posture. She sat up straight in her chair, her arms loosely draped on the chair's arms. She smiled. "You tell me."

"I don't know who you are," he said. "I know who I'd like you to be, but not who you are."

"Who would you like me to be, then?" she asked him.

"The woman who marched into my office six years ago and announced that she was cured, that would be a nice start."

"But that was a lie," she protested.

"I know it, but it was a nice beginning. It was strong and affirmative. It was a positive look, even in the fear that prompted it, at the future. I don't see that anymore."

She shifted a bit in her seat. Her cigarette had gone out and she reached for another one, knocking it out of the pack on his desk with a single tap on the bottom. She caught the flying missile and held it tentatively at first, then firmly.

"Light me?" she said.

He did it. She took a long, slow pull on the new tobacco stick and let her head loll back as though she had imbibed a strong narcotic and was letting it transport her out of the realm of reality.

"That's a very effective posture," he said to her. "Very seductive. Very feminine."

She laughed, her head still thrown back over the top of her chair. Then, without a moment's hesitation, she sat up straight again and the humor in her face drained away. She looked old, and he reacted to the change with a startled glance. She noticed it right away.

"Am I ugly like this?" she asked him quietly. Then she shouted out the question. "Am I ugly like this?"

He nodded to her. She burst into tears.

"Feyhe, if you would take your medication on schedule this would not be such a problem. If you could be trusted to take the pills, to check in with me, to visit your doctor on a regular basis, you would be just fine. You could have the boy back in your home with you. So much would be different. You wouldn't be here, kept in a room, kept quiet, kept sedated. It would all be different, better, the way you want things to be."

"What's wrong with me?" She nearly cried as she said it.

"You know. You already know the answer."

"Tell me again. I don't remember the words."

"You are manic-depressive. You have extremes when it comes to your emotions. Sometimes you are suicidal because you are unable to see even one hour ahead in your life. Sometimes you are so giddy that it pains you even to laugh. You live in the extremes. Your medications would allow you to live in the middle, like a normal person should. To live in the middle."

"I'm an artist, doctor. We have no middles. It's always an extreme for us."

"What is your art? Where is your art? Three months ago you went to an art class and three months ago you left it without doing anything. You never went back. What is your art?"

"I'm a loving mother, a mentor."

"You're not a mother."

"I'm loving, though."

"You're smothering."

"I'm a mentor. I make it possible for others to be creative."

"Who are your protegees? What are their accomplishments?"

"I'm something. Aren't I something?"

"You're a woman who needs to gain control of her emotions to become something."

"I must be something. Now. Right now. Tell me what I am now."

"Feyhe," he said gently, more gently than he had said anything for minutes, "you are a wonderful person who needs help and needs to help herself. Put down the cigarette."

She flared up, rose from her chair and leaned over his desk. "Don't tell me not to smoke. I know I can smoke. I know how much I can smoke. I know I can smoke whenever and wherever I want. Don't ever tell me not smoke." She threw herself back into her chair.

"We're done for today, Feyhe," the doctor said, ringing a bell on the side of his desk. His office door opened and two orderlies entered. Both were burly men in their early thirties. They took up positions on either side of Feyhe, still in the chair. She looked at them, one at a time, then looked back at the doctor.

"I'm going back to my room now, doctor. You'll find me there later. Bring your prick." She stood up and let herself be escorted out of his office. Without much emotion, he noted a few things in her file before summoning his next patient in from the waiting room.

Billy was resting comfortably in the chair near the door to the deck in his and Owen's apartment. He had a book on his lap that he'd started to read more than once and failed to connect with in spite of his several efforts. He could hear Owen in the kitchen, slapping a pot onto the cast iron leggings of the old stove. He waited for a moment, the resounding ring of iron against iron receding into the dimness of the curtains on the archway between the two rooms.

"What's for dinner?" he called out. "It sounds heavy."

"You'll like it," his partner responded. "Chicken Provençal. It takes the cast iron skillet to make it right."

"Thank you, Gourmet from Hell," Billy shouted.

Owen came into the room and looked at Billy, dressed only in his undershorts, for a moment before responding.

"You're a lovely sight," he said. "What if someone came in and found you like that?"

"So what?" Billy said. "Who cares?"

"You're not that pretty anymore," Owen said to him. "You have to take a little more care with your appearance."

"I repeat…who cares."

"You're taking me for granted," Owen said, squeezing in next to Billy in the overstuffed arm chair. They made a snug pair, nestled in the large, auburn velour arms. "And I'm a bit overdressed for this, I think. Too many layers of cloth."

"Or a touch too much chicken fat in the diet," Billy said and he snickered. Owen gave him a chaste peck on the cheek. Then he bared his teeth and snarled.

"Move an inch, can't you? I'm stuck here," Owen said.

"Knowing you, an inch will never do. I better give over a mile."

"Flatterer!" He had indeed developed an immediate erection at the touch of Billy's skin. He knew it, and he knew that Billy was aware of it also. "Come on, move kiddo. I've got to get back to that pan or we'll lose the chicken, the shallots, and the kitchen when the whole thing goes up in flames." He squeezed himself upward and over the chair's arm, to stand in front of Billy.

"You're a sweetheart to do all this," Billy said to him. "I really don't need it."

"Yeah, you do," Owen replied. "But you better get dressed before Angus shows up. He shouldn't see you like that."

"He's my father, Owen. He's seen me in less."

"Not since you learned to develop one of those…boners of yours." Owen laughed at his joke and turned away, heading back into the kitchen.

Billy had been living with him for six years. They had been uneasy years for both of them, first developing a friendship, then a love relationship, then a lover's and companion's commitment. Owen had been bothered by much of it, but he found himself inextricably drawn to the younger man in spite of his efforts to keep away, maintain a distance. There was the obvious difference in their ages as well as Billy's tendency to the same sort of morbidity and mood swings his ex-wife suffered. Billy was nowhere near Feyhe, as far as Owen could tell, when it came to those variations and to the behavior problems that accompanied them. He was grateful for that. Very grateful, in fact. Both men were so close to Feyhe and to her care, and Owen believed that seeing first-hand how difficult Feyhe could be helped Billy to maintain some composure and control.

"I have to laugh when I think about you and your father taking baths together when you were a little kid," Owen shouted down the hall at Billy. "It's too sweet an image and too sick at the same time."

"Well, we were very clean about it all," Billy shouted back. "The yellow sweater or the brown?"

"Brown, please." Owen couldn't control the smile that lit his face. He had chosen the brown one as a gift for Billy a week earlier. He loved the brown sweater, a soft, wear-against-the-skin cashmere with a deep V-neck that gave Billy extra height in his appearance. He loved the offer from Billy to wear it, to acknowledge him in this simple way.

Billy came down the hallway and Owen could watch him walk without leaving his place at the stove. *Billy walks like a panther*, Owen thought, *with each step a pace and each pace a thrust.* He smiled again.

"What are you smiling about?" Billy asked. He moved into the kitchen and gave Owen a kiss on his mouth. Owen pulled back at first, hesitated, then responded. "Why do you always do that? Pull away?"

"I'm not used to it, I guess," Owen said. "This is all still new to me."

"Don't say I seduced you, Owen. It's not true."

"I know it's not. That doesn't mean I'm used to it though."

"All right, truce. No more surprise kisses. I'll ask first." He touched Owen's lips with his forefinger. "Remember, no surprises."

"Billy, this wasn't supposed to happen. You were supposed to stay here for a few weeks at most until you got started again, gained back your composure."

"I know."

"I'm still not sure about…us…about all of this. I'm supposed to be the one who gets these things, professionally, but I don't understand it at all. I'm a confirmed heterosexual. Oh, there were one or two men in my day who were a turn-on, but they were feminine, in every other way, and you're not. You're a man like any other man. This shouldn't have happened to me."

"I know all that," Billy responded. "You've told me that stuff before. My theory tonight is the same as the one I had last week, and the time before that and every other time too. You fell in love with me, for me, for who I am. What I am wasn't a part of that. It didn't matter because it doesn't matter. End of theory."

By the testy age of sixteen Danny Kim had developed a method for getting what he wanted, whenever he wanted it. He had a bank account of expressions—facial, body, verbal—to draw upon that could assure him success. He knew how to use the equipment he'd been given, and he used it often.

With Feyhe's illness flaring up, he had been sent to live with a family of Koreans who had known his mother, first in Gyong-Ju and then in Paterson, New Jersey. They had twin daughters a year older than Danny and a son nearly five years his junior. At first he had resented his awkward position in this family group, but then he realized how he could make it worth his while.

Within days of taking up residency with the Wusans, Danny had wormed his way into bed with both the twins and had managed to sexually abuse the boy into obeying his every order. "I am the Lord here," he said to all three siblings and for their own, personal reasons, they acquiesced.

His first target had been Linda Wusan, slightly prettier than her sister Donna, slightly more full-figured. The second night in their home in Newark he had called Linda into his room and asked for a favor which she was willing to do for him.

"I feel awful," he had moaned quietly in her direction. "I need medicine, but the doctor says I shouldn't have any. Can you bring me something, please? I feel so terrible."

"Where do you hurt, Danny?" Linda asked him.

"My legs and my groin," he had told her.

"Is it much pain?" she asked.

"More pain than you can imagine. No girl can feel such pain. Only men."

"Only men, little one?"

"I am not so little," he said defensively. "Here, see for yourself." He whipped back the coverlet on his bed and revealed his lower body, naked, with his penis erect.

"See the pain for yourself, Linda Wusan," he said as he took her hand and placed it on his erection. She hesitated for a moment, then gripped it tentatively.

"It throbs," she said.

"That is the pain."

"How do you alleviate this pain?"

"There are three ways," Danny said. "There are pills to make it go away, or you can make it stop hurting yourself. You can massage it until it releases the fluid that causes the pain. Also, I can bury it within your body and the warmth there will cause the pain to lessen. The choice is yours."

They had ultimately explored two of his three options. A few days later he had brought Donna Wusan into his circle of pain alleviation. Both girls were fascinated by his need and had, indeed, developed their own. Before two weeks had passed, they had become a bedded threesome.

Milton Wusan, at eleven, was a less willing target for Danny's obsession. Still, he was nearly powerless in the grip of Danny's needs. With the twins safely tucked into his growing sexual menage, Danny expanded his horizon with a simple conversation one afternoon. He had come upon Milton, alone, studying geometry in his room. He came in quietly, sat down on the boy's bed and waited for some sort of acknowledgment. Ultimately, observing Danny's patience, Milton thrust his chin up and spoke to him.

"What do you want?"

"What do you think I want?" Danny replied.

"I don't know. I ask because I don't know."

"I want you to love me as a brother should," Danny said.

"You are not my brother."

"I am."

"You are not."

"I can prove you are," Danny said seductively.

"How?"

"Come here." The command sounded less authoritative than it might, more inviting, less threatening.

"Why should I?"

"Because I want you to. Come here." This time the sound in his voice was more adult.

"I didn't want you to come here. I don't like you. I don't want you here."

"Come over here. Now." There was no mistaking the sense of directive, the domination of will over will. Milton faltered for a moment and Danny knew he had the boy where he wanted him. "I want you to sit here, next to me, now." He pointed at the bed, a position between where he sat and the headboard.

"I...I don't want to." There was a hint of whimper in the response.

"I am your elder and I tell you to do this. You will do it, you will obey and you will not question. Do you understand me?"

The boy nodded in response. At the first hint of "elder" he had cringed and changed his formerly bold posture. He moved slowly across the room and sat where he had been told to sit.

"Now then," Danny said, "you will not treat me as an enemy any longer. Do you understand?" The boy nodded.

"You will not disobey me and you will not run to your sisters or your parents to oppose me. Am I clear?"

"Yes, Danny," he murmured.

"I will never hurt you, because you are a good boy. I will only hurt you if you are bad. Is that all right?"

Milton nodded silently again. "I don't want to be bad," he whispered to Danny. "I only want to be left alone."

"To be left alone is always bad," Danny told him. "It is good to be with another whom you can serve. I am such a one."

He put his hand around the boy's mouth and pushed his lips into a circle. Milton flinched at the touch and Danny gripped him harder. Then he put his face close to Milton's and spit into the boy's slightly open mouth.

"That is my taste," Danny said. "You will crave it always. In your sleep you will taste it and you will not cry."

"You scare me," Milton whined.

"You will be frightened of me," Danny said. "You will crave me. You will do my bidding and you will love me."

"I don't like you, Danny."

"You will love me," Danny said firmly. "You will do my bidding and you will love me."

"No—"

"I am the one who says *no* and not you. Say *yes*. Say it whenever I tell you something or you will be the bad boy who is hurt. Do you understand?"

Milton hesitated a moment, then nodded his head slightly.

"I do not hear you. Say *yes*. Say it now."

"Yes."

"You are a good boy, Milton. Here is a reward for you." He pulled his hand away from Milton's face and leaned forward to kiss the younger boy. Milton pulled back, not meaning to, but merely reacting naturally. Danny instantly slapped the boy's face hard, then grabbed it with his other hand and, once again, distorted the face to form an open 'o' of Milton's mouth. There were tears in the boy's eyes, threatening to explode out of them, glowing there in the room's artificial light.

Danny once again spit into Milton's mouth. He pinched the boy's lips closed and leaned forward to whisper to him, his eyes never leaving Milton eyes.

"I will slap you every time you disobey me, do you understand?"

Milton nodded.

"Stand up before me," Danny said. Milton obeyed. "Kneel down before me," Danny said. Milton obeyed. "Open my pants for me," Danny said. Milton obeyed. "Taste me," Danny said. Milton looked at him, not comprehending.

Danny pulled on his erect penis and looked down at it. Milton followed his gaze. "This is the source of my taste," Danny said. "You crave my taste. Taste me."

After a moment, the boy did as he was told.

19

Feyhe leaned back in her chair and took a long, long drag on her cigarette. Owen and Billy watched her, her behavior so very masculine and assertive. Even her face, now flecked with chin hairs and a darkening, slight moustache, had altered into a manliness that neither of them recognized.

"Feyhe, do you have to smoke at the dinner table?" Owen asked her.

"I do, faggot," she said. Then she laughed. "No one can tell me what to do or not to do. Remember that."

"Then there'd be no point in telling you not to call me names," Owen added.

"Not anymore, no," she said and she laughed again.

"Names won't hurt me, Feyhe," Billy said. "I've been called them all and they don't hurt me any longer."

"Billy grows up and finally changes his name to Wilhelmina," Feyhe said a bit too loud.

"You are being offensive, Feyhe," Owen said, jumping into the conversation again. "And your smoking is almost as offensive as your language. You make our food taste like shit."

"I'm sorry," Feyhe said with a seeming instant change of mood, "but it is shit."

"Feyhe! Owen cooked this."

"What did he use, an old patient?"

"Feyhe!"

"Look, if I'm not wanted here, if I can't be myself, I'm not staying."
She stood up, thrusting her still lit cigarette into the roast on the platter
in the center of the table. "You two are horrible to me. I'm the only
woman in the room and you don't respect me. Faggots!"

"Medication…" Owen hissed at Billy and he disappeared into the
kitchen, leaving Billy to manage to Feyhe.

"Feyhe, are you taking your medication?" Billy asked her, but her
rant had continued and she paid no attention to his question.

"…and you and my husband are sleeping together and making little
unborn babies and that's disgusting." She threw herself down onto the
leather couch and pulled her knees up close to her chest, clutching them
with both her arms, her hands holding onto their respective opposite
forearms.

"Feyhe, hold on. Owen is—"

"Owen is a faggot. That explains what went wrong with us. I should
have known it. Faggots. All around us. Faggots."

Billy suddenly realized that her cigarette wasn't in her hand. He
panicked, then remembered that she had stubbed it out on what would
have been their leftovers under other circumstances. An acrid odor
brought him out of his momentary reverie. Feyhe had peed on the
couch.

"Owen, she's pissing," he called out. Owen emerged from the
kitchen with a syringe and a cloth. "I'll hold her." Billy reached for
Feyhe and wrapped his arms around her upper arms and shoulders,
pushing her back down on the sofa. Owen came forward quickly.

"This won't hurt, Feyhe, so be calm," he said as he pulled up the
hemline of her dress, exposing her thighs. "Pew…this is the worst yet."

"Don't you touch me, you pervert. You fuck my little cousin. You
miserable pervert." She kicked out her leg and Owen caught it in his
available right hand, gripping her just above the ankle.

"Thank you, Feyhe. Hold it right there, please." He jabbed the
needle into her thigh and pushed the plunger steadily downward until
the chamber was empty. Then he lowered her foot and leg and watched
as it and the woman it was attached to eased into a softer, more reliable

state of mind and body. "Give her a minute, Billy. She'll be all right."

Billy moved away from the couch and stood looking at Feyhe. Owen had seen him like this several times when Feyhe had gone haywire. He was almost catatonic, moving automatically, not rationally. He was familiar with Billy's staring eyes seeing something more in Feyhe than Owen himself could ever see. He joined Billy on the other side of the room and put his arm around the younger man's shoulders.

"You're not Feyhe, Billy. You will never be her." Billy nodded silently.

"I promise you. You will not be like her. This is a madness that can be controlled, if she would only cooperate. She doesn't have to be like this, you know that. And you have to remember that this is her, and not you. You are fine. Billy, you are all right."

Billy nodded again, then turned his back on Owen and the image of Feyhe, nearly asleep, on the couch.

"She ruined dinner," he said half-heartedly. "Even the leftovers are crap now."

"We'll replace the roast tomorrow. I promise."

"Why does she have to be like this? She was so wonderful once."

"I don't know. It's an imbalance in the brain, a chemical thing. It's not her at all."

"I know that, but why? Why?"

"I don't know. I don't think there's an answer. I don't know if there ever will be one that completely answers the question."

"Owen, I love her and I miss her terribly."

"She's here and she'll be with us again."

"I'm not so sure." He was crying. They could both see he was crying and that the tears were meant to be there on his face, on his hands. "We have to clean up the couch again."

"Yes," Owen agreed. "Good thing we went for leather." He laughed and despite his tears, so did Billy.

"I'm not like her, am I?" he asked Owen.

"No. Emphatically 'No.' And you never will be." He gave Billy a kiss.

"That's sweet," Feyhe said still lying down on the couch. "Which one of you peed on me? Silly perverts." She laughed and instantly fell into a short sleep, snoring, smiling.

Owen walked back over to the couch and stood looking at his former wife. After a moment, still in silence, Billy joined him. He placed his left arm around Owen's trim waist and held him firmly but gently. Without an utterance of any kind, Owen threw his right arm around Billy's back and shoulders, tweaking his upper arm with a strong, firm grasp. They stood there, together, hip to hip, side to side watching the sleeping Feyhe.

"She's not a bad person," Owen said in a half-whisper.

"I know that. I do."

"And she loves you dearly, Billy."

"I love her too."

"And I love her as well. I always have and I always will."

"It's just that we share blood, Owen. I see so much of myself in her—her spirit and her lust for things. I compare myself to her, talent for talent and I always come up a little bit short. She's been such an accomplisher."

Owen held him a bit tighter, trying to be more comforting, becoming less so through the force of his grip.

"You're hurting me, Owen," Billy said finally.

"I'm sorry." He pulled away from Billy, releasing him entirely. "I didn't mean to—"

"You don't have to let me go," Billy said, "just don't hold me so very tight."

"I'll try," Owen admitted. "It's hard for me not to hold you tight, though. I'm so afraid you'll—"

"What? Turn into my cousin?"

"No!" Owen was emphatic. "I'm afraid you'll realize how much more you could achieve without me. I'm afraid you'll look at me and realize how absolutely ridiculous we are and leave me."

"You've kept me sane. You've kept me whole and alive."

"That's not a perfect relationship, Billy."

"It's what I needed and it's what I want."

"You're going to have to learn to live without me someday. I'm thirty years older than you."

"Thirty six years older," Billy said, then regretted saying.

"And I won't last forever."

Billy turned to look at Owen and found that his lover would not meet him, eye to eye. He reached for Owen's face and turned it towards his own. Owen looked older than he had only minutes before, looked fragile, looked ill.

"Are you all right?" Billy asked him.

"Yes, I'm fine. I'm fine. Don't worry." He stepped forward to hug Billy.

"This conversation has been too bizarre."

"I love you, kiddo. That's all that really matters."

"I love you too, Owen. And you're not really old."

Owen took a deep breath, hugged Billy again and moved out of the joint embrace. He turned away and walked to the door to the kitchen. Standing there, backlit by the kitchen's brighter lights, his trim body and his full head of hair gave the impression of a young man, strong, sturdy, upright. Billy looked admiringly at him and a faint smile spread into a broad grin on his face at the vision he saw standing there. Then Owen pulled up his shirt, tucking its tails under his armpits and he stepped back into the kitchen, allowing the back light to become front light.

His seventy-two-year-old breasts sagged in a half moon across his flabby upper stomach. His sparse gray hair flecked itself across the pink and wrinkled skin. The double flaps of fat that covered his gut left deep shadows where only a slight crevice had once made an enticing fold across his midriff. There was a scar across the upper left side of his chest, witness to the by-pass surgery he had undergone five years earlier. He tapped a spot near the large scar and mouthed the word "pace-maker" as he did it. Then he let the shirt drop back down to cover this view of his aging body.

He threw back his head and Billy could see all of the furrows that criss-crossed his neck, light and dark patches of skin, liver spots and broadening freckles. As he brought his face forward once again, obscuring the neck, Billy could clearly see the two chins reforming in front of him.

Billy turned away, turned his back on Owen and the sleeping Feyhe. He heard Owen turn away also and heard him walk through the opposite door at the other end of the kitchen. He heard his footsteps going down the hallway and he heard the bedroom door close. Billy stayed where he was, the two people he felt closest to now obscured behind him—one sleeping and one mourning, and he wept one more time.

"I'm moving to San Francisco and Danny is coming with me," Feyhe shouted into the telephone and Billy had to hold his receiver away from his ear to keep from being deafened. "I've found the most darling little apartment and my friend, Dugana, has already started to furnish it for me."

"What are you talking about?" Billy demanded.

"Aren't you listening? I'm taking Danny to California and we're going to live in San Francisco."

"You can't take Danny out of New York. The court told you that."

"He's my legal grandson and he lives with me and I can do whatever I want with him."

"No, Feyhe, you can't. When the judge allowed him to come back to you he made it very clear that you have some limitations. You can't even take him to Disney World for a vacation. He's not allowed to leave New York without the court's permission."

"You can be so stuffy, so old-maidish, Billy," she snapped. "Why don't you grow up and get a life?"

"Feyhe, please listen to me. You're going to be in big trouble if you do this."

"Well, it's too late. I've already taken the place, put down the deposit, paid the first and last months' rent and told Dugana to buy, buy, buy."

"Get your money back!"

"If you won't come to the airport to see us off, that's just too bad, Billy."

"Feyhe, I won't—when are you leaving?"

"The plane takes off in one hour."

"Is Danny there with you?"

"He is."

"Feyhe, don't do this. Please. I'm begging you."

"Come visit us." She hung up.

Billy stood holding the receiver, listening to the crackle of dead air. The sound was a relief to him and seemed to make as much sense as the conversation that had just abruptly ended.

Finally he placed the instrument back in its cradle and sat down on the window sill, his back instantly heated by the sun. There was a chill that pervaded his body, however, and the sun did little to warm him up. He was cold. He felt cold. He relished the chill. Then he laughed quietly, catching an errant sob that pushed its way through and he returned to the telephone. He dialed and was instantly connected to Owen's personal line.

"Khanzadian," came the usual response.

"Owen, it's me. Feyhe's at the airport with Danny and they're going to San Francisco to live. How do we stop them?"

"Oh my God. Which airport, Billy?"

The short pause told Owen that Billy hadn't gotten that information.

"Never mind. We'll call all three of them and get security to stop her. She's a kidnapper. They'll do it for me. Can you phone out to Newark? I'll call LaGuardia and Kennedy. Just tell them you're from my office and give them this number if they ask. Can you do that, Billy?"

He nodded, not thinking, expecting Owen to hear him, and hung up. He ran into the kitchen to fetch the telephone directory, found it, opened it, located the numbers for Newark International Airport and dialed from the kitchen phone. The number connected and the ringing began. After seven rings a woman answered the phone.

"Newark International. Hold please." He was on hold. There was the usual Muzak—mindless music, string-heavy, brass and percussion free, tunes from the latest Andrew Lloyd Webber sensation with the grit and rock removed from the arrangement. He listened, afraid to let the receiver move even an inch from his ear, sure that such an action would prove disastrous, that the operator would return, say one word, hear no reply and disconnect him. He held on. He held on.

"Newark International, how may we help you?"

"Security please."

"In reference to what, Sir?"

"I have to locate a potential passenger. It's an emergency."

"May I ask the nature of the emergency, Sir?"

"Can I please talk to security? There isn't a lot of time."

"Is this a bomb threat?"

"No. Don't be stupid!"

"I beg your pardon, Sir?"

"I'm sorry. I'm just very worried about a relative of mine. My cousin. I need to talk to someone who can do something."

"What is the nature of the problem, Sir?" The woman was becoming indignant and Billy was matching her in intensity.

"That is not your concern. I must speak to your Security Officer."

"I must be able to alert him as to the nature of the problem."

"We are wasting valuable time, here. Please put me through."

"When I know what you're calling about, Sir, I will do my best to get you to the right person."

"It's...a kidnapping," Billy blurted out. There was a stunned lull.

"Your cousin has been kidnapped?"

"No! Oh, this is insane. My cousin is kidnapping a little boy."

"Is this a joke, Sir?"

"Let me speak to someone in charge. Now!"

"Hold, please." She put him back on hold and the silence was maddening, even more maddening than the conversation had been. Billy paced while waiting. The wait was interminable.

"Sir, I'm sorry to keep you on hold, but there is no answer on the Security Officer's line. I'll have to page him. Hold on." She snapped him into the ether once again. Billy screamed a wordless, guttural incantation to an earless God.

"Hold on, please, Sir. I'm going to connect you now. You'll be speaking with Mr. Frank O'Donnell."

"Is he the security officer?" Billy shouted.

"No, Sir. I'm sorry. He's not. Hold please."

Before Billy could respond he was on hold, then he was hearing a new voice, a male voice.

"Frank O'Donnell. How can I help you?"

"What is your job there?" Billy demanded without even giving his name.

"Sorry?"

"I'm trying to reach security. What is your job? Are you security?"

"No, Sir. This is the help desk. How can I help you?"

"There is a woman, leaving on a plane for San Francisco within the hour. She has a teenager with her, a Korean kid. She is taking him illegally and she has to be detained."

"I'm sorry, Sir. That's outside my jurisdiction. You need the Security Officer."

"I know that. I've been trying to reach him forever."

"I can page him for you. Will you hold?"

"Yes! No! Can you page the passenger? Maybe she'll answer and in the mean time you can find the security officer and get him to stop her from leaving."

"We don't usually page passengers, Sir. Unless it's an emergency."

"I just told you what she's doing. It's a kidnapping, for God's sake. What could be more of an emergency?"

"I'm sorry, but I don't really know who I'm talking to or what this is about. I'm trying to help, but you're not making it very easy."

"Oh, Lord, I know. It's a very long story and there's not much time. Can you please page Feyhe Baumann and see if she responds. Can you just do that, please."

"Hold on. I'll see what I can do. What was that name again?"

On hold, Billy imagined the sound of a loud-speaker voice crying out Feyhe's name, asking her to contact the help desk using a "white" phone. He saw her in his imagination, sitting quietly in a pre-formed hard plastic chair, over in a corner, near a window looking over the docking bay. He saw her gnarled hand, discolored by the cigarettes that ultimately burned her fingers, holding the puffy, childlike hand of Danny Kim. He saw her smile the quirky smile she showed when she knew she was winning a battle that no one else knew they were fighting. He almost heard her pathetic chuckle and her whispered words to Danny to ignore the summons. He heard the boy laugh out loud. He saw the door opening onto the gangway that would lead the two of them onto the airplane that would take them out of reach. He heard the stewardess announce the boarding procedure, and he saw the two of them rise, their early boarding passes held high, a sickly grandmother with a youngster, needing to board ahead of others. He saw them leave the waiting area, saw them board the plane, saw the airplane's hatchway sealed, saw the plane pull away from the gate.

"I'm sorry, Sir, there's been no response to the page. Shall I try again for you?"

"I'm sorry too, Mr. O'Donnell. Perhaps they're at Kennedy or LaGuardia."

"Perhaps. Thank you for calling Newark International." The phone went silent.

Billy waited for a call from Owen, hoped he had better results to share. He sat and waited, not knowing if Feyhe had managed to escape with her grandson or had been stopped. Not knowing. Not knowing anything.

At ten-past-midnight the phone rang and Owen picked it up before the second ring could rouse an exhausted, and finally sleeping, Billy.

"We're here," Feyhe said. "We've arrived and we're happy here."

"Where are you, sweetheart?" Owen asked nicely.

"Our new home, our California paradise."

"What's the address there? Feyhe, where are you?"

"San Francisco. Home of the free spirits, the talented madmen, the genius-savant."

"I know. Where in San Francisco? Be exact."

"My apartment."

"Which is…?"

"Which is where it should be…on a hill with glorious views of the city, the bay, the hills."

"You're not going to tell me, are you?" Owen's voice sounded tired, depressed.

Feyhe heard the tone and giggled. "No. And my phone number isn't listed."

"Feyhe, this is wrong. You know it's wrong."

"It feels so right, Owen. And I'm all right. I'm taking my pills. I'm eating the right foods and the atmosphere is just so special, so perfect for me."

"Feyhe, you are on a high. I can hear it. You have to change the medication now and bring yourself into that middle place where you are healthy."

"I like the place I'm in, Owen. And it's not the pills. And I'm not high. Or if I am, it's due to this place, this wonderful place."

"Feyhe, the boy, is he all right?"

"He's in the hot tub. The hot tub, Owen."

"But he's all right?"

"He is my delight. You know that. He's my child and I will nurture him."

"Feyhe, I'm worried about you."

Billy stirred, the sound of Owen's voice finally rousing him from slumber. He sat up and blinked a dozen times or more, listening to the one-sided conversation.

"We'll be fine. Someday you and Billy must visit us here. You'll love it, too. I know you will. You'll want to come here. Gay people are so easily accepted here. I think it's the fault line or something. No one cares what you do or who you are."

"Can I speak to her?" Billy whispered. Owen shook his head.

"Feyhe, it's not about being Gay. It's not about the San Andreas fault. You did something you shouldn't have done. You're an outlaw, now."

"Owen, that's silly. I just took my grandson home."

"That's not how the courts will see it."

"He doesn't need to be in court again until next month. I'll bring him back and he'll tell them what they want to know, within reason, and then we'll come back here to live again. It's so simple."

"I want to talk to her," Billy said a bit louder. Owen shook his head again, more violently and put his hand over the mouthpiece.

"She's not rational. I have to talk her into some sense."

"Is Billy there?" Feyhe asked him. "Can I talk to him, please."

"Just a minute," Owen responded, then giving the phone to Billy, he turned away, got up and went into the bathroom. He turned on the light, but didn't close the door. Instead he sat down on the toilet seat lid and slumped forward, his chin in his upturned hands, his eyes on Billy.

"Feyhe? Billy."

"Leave him," she whispered hoarsely. "Leave him and come to me here. You'll love it here."

"Feyhe, I—"

"Danny loves you. He'll be good to you. He's good to me, Billy. Leave that old man. I hate him. I hate what he's done to you. Leave him and come and join us. We'll be a commune, Billy. We'll enjoy free love and sunshine."

"Feyhe, you're not being rational."

"I'm a bird, Billy. I'm a bird and you're a beetle. Come out here and find us and join us." She hung up the phone. Billy hung up the phone. Owen stood up and moved into the open doorway.

"What did she say to you?" he asked from a distance.

"She hates what you've done to me."

"What have I done to you?"

"I don't know." He looked at Owen, still a short distance away. "I don't know, actually."

"I've loved you."

"Yes, you have."

"I've helped you…in some ways, I hope."

"Yes, you have."

"Is that a bad thing?"

"I never thought it was. Feyhe…Feyhe, though…"

"She's beyond our help, Billy. She's out of our hands, now."

"I have to think about this, Owen. I have to think."

He turned away from Owen, flopping back down on his own side of the large double bed. After a minute, he felt Owen's weight on the opposite side, heard the man lie down, felt Owen's hand on his thigh. Still trying to get his thoughts together, Billy fell asleep and, before he woke again, dreamed of open skies and birds and flute music and smiling faces that said sweet-toned syllables of airy nothingness.

20

"Billy?" He heard the voice, hesitated, then responded. "Yes?"

"Billy, Hi," she said. He still didn't recognize the voice. He waited.

"It's Sandy." Billy still didn't respond. The voice and the name didn't ring true, somehow.

"Sandy Ryan, Joe's daughter. Don't you remember me?"

He did, of course he did. "Of course I do. I do," he said into the receiver. "You sound different, that's all. I didn't recognize the voice."

She laughed. "I'm a lot older than the last time we talked," she said. "My voice matured."

"Did you, too?" He asked her without thinking about his words. He was talking to a teenager, a girl of seventeen, and he wasn't considering that at all.

She giggled. "I did. You'd be surprised how much I did." She laughed outright.

Billy tried to conjure up an image of Sandy Ryan in his mind, but the only picture that emerged was of a child of ten, her red hair braided and long, her face clean-scrubbed and freckled, her legs long and thin and slightly rubbed where she had skidded into a wall on her skateboard.

"What must you look like now?" he said to her, again without thinking.

"Come and find out," she responded instantly.

287

"Wait, what do you mean? Come where?"

"I'm in a play. I'm the romantic lead. Come and see it, Billy."

"What school are you at?"

"What?" She sounded confused by the question.

"Where's your school, Sandy? Where the play is—?"

"Oh, no. This isn't for school, Billy. It's a new play. At the Cort Theatre on 44th Street."

Billy sat still, holding the phone a few inches away from his face, staring at it. The news had altered his thinking, confused him, set him ablaze with confusion, actually.

"I don't understand…"

"I'm acting now," she said, "professionally. This is my third show on Broadway and I'm on television, too. On a soap opera. Guiding Light."

"This is Sandy Ryan, right? Joe Ryan's daughter?"

"Yes, Billy. It is."

"And you're a kid. You're a teenager."

"Well, I am nineteen, Billy, so technically, yes."

Nineteen. Billy exhaled almost to a whistle. *Nineteen*, he thought, *nineteen. Has it been nine years since…*"

"It's been almost ten years since you last saw me," she said, echoing his thoughts. "I'd really like you to come to the opening. I'd really like to see you. I can leave a pair of tickets at the box office."

He thought about Joe, about their last days together, all in a jumble in his mind. He almost couldn't recall Joe's face, but he suddenly smelled the odors of the man in his nostrils, the breath, the body, the hair of the man he had once lived with and loved.

"Billy, are you there?"

"Yes. Yes, Sandy, I'm here. The opening, you said. When is it?"

She gave him the details and he agreed to come. He hung up the phone, still feeling the total unreality of the conversation. Sandy Ryan, the thought of seeing her, seeing her as a young adult, gave him chills once again. He couldn't even envision that pigtailed child as a woman, couldn't make the corporeal transition happen in his imagination.

And Joe Ryan, he thought…*will Joe be there and will I know him and will he know me and will he care to know me?* He saw the New York

Times, the Sunday edition, still slopped on the floor near Owen's end of the couch. He retrieved the Arts and Leisure section and opened it out on the coffee table, looking for an advertisement for the play. At first he couldn't find a reference to it, but then he spotted the display ad in the inside left-hand lower corner of page seven. He lifted the page up to get a close look at the faces in the photograph.

There were two women, both young and pretty, both fair with light hair and open smiles. There were three men, two of them also young and one considerably older. The older man was a star, someone Billy admired, whose work he had seen many times in the past twenty years. None of the younger people's faces rang a bell.

He read the copy, the list of credits and couldn't find Sandy Ryan's name. There was a Sandy, but not a Ryan. He assumed that she had taken a stage name and had just forgotten to mention it to him on the phone. He noted the opening date in the ad and was glad to see it was the same performance Sandy had asked him to attend. As he replaced the newspaper page to its section on the table, it occurred to him that he had never once asked about Joe, about Sandy's grandmother, about anything. He suddenly felt very lonely. He went to get a pill.

Owen had no interest in seeing the play. He suggested that Billy invite someone else and Billy couldn't think of anyone to ask. Feyhe would have been a natural choice, but they had not heard from her in a long while and weren't sure if she was in New York or San Francisco or someplace else. His few clients were not the right choices and he couldn't really call any of his old friends friends any longer. He decided to go alone.

He dressed in an Edwardian style suit, tailored and trim, pale beige wool with too-wide lapels. He left the apartment early and walked to mid-town, a three-mile hike that he handled in just over a half hour. He found the box-office, retrieved his tickets, and went back out onto the street to walk some more. Billy recognized his nervousness for what it was, an edgy, take-no-prisoners fear of confronting his past, tinged with an eagerness for information about the present state of affairs in the lives of people he had cared about for so long a time. Outside the theater he recognized no one, so he ventured over to 6th Avenue, the current site of construction and changes, meandered for a block or two, then turned back toward Broadway and the theater.

A crowd had gathered outside the Cort for the 6:15 opening. From his vantage point he could read the large marquee, see the crowd and the open doors of the building. There was still no one he recognized. He felt a quiet and a safety that appealed to him. He moved forward.

Once Again, Henry, Billy read on the marquee. Written by Sven George. Directed by Bobby Aaron. Starring Raymond Rogé. With Alain Arbus, Mindy Lewis, César Mingus, Sandra Robbins. He stopped reading the words. She must be Sandra Robbins, he thought. Why Robbins? Why not Ryan?

People were surging forward through the late afternoon sunlight, streaming into the lobby, past the ticket-takers, into the cavernous old theater. He joined the crowd, handed his two tickets and took the stubs. He was given a program and directed to the center aisle where an usher escorted him to the fourth row. He excused himself, pushing past five people already seated and found the chair with the number of his ticket stub on it. He sat down, opened the program and began to read it. Sandy's bio in the Who's Who was easy to spot and, as he read it, he knew that she was indeed now Sandra Robbins.

Trained as a dancer, Sandra Robbins has been appearing on Broadway since she was twelve years old. She was seen as Euphemia in Edward Albee's *Three Young Women*, as Alex Five in *The Importance of Being Alex* and, most recently as Brenda in Walter Wyler's autobiographical play, *Brenda*, at the Far-Out Festival at Lincoln Center. She is currently also appearing as Judy French on *Guiding Light*. The daughter of a New York City policeman, she proudly dedicates this performance to the memory of her grandmother.

As Billy read the bio, he felt himself swell with pride at her accomplishments, then felt himself diminish at the mention of Joe and the death of Joe's mother. He hadn't known about her death, he told himself. He wasn't responsible for that. No one had contacted him. No one had told him. No one had…

He touched the place over his heart with his free hand. He could feel it pumping in his chest, could feel the extra pressure there. He reached into his pocket and took out the small pill-case he carried for such moments. He opened it, took out a blue pill and a yellow pill and popped them both in his mouth at once. His own saliva was enough liquid to carry them safely into his throat and down into his system. He closed his eyes and took several deep breaths. He felt himself calming down. God bless the pills, he whispered inside his own head. He opened his eyes, feeling instantly better, much calmer.

The theater was filling up. Billy checked his watch. It was already 6:30 and the ticket said the performance was starting at 6:15. He hadn't been to a Broadway opening in many years, but he remembered how flexible they tended to be in these instances. He knew they were holding the curtain, anticipating critics who had not yet appeared. The theater has too many divas, he thought, and he smiled at the concept. He tried to picture the large photos outside the building, see the cast's faces, fix Sandy's new face in his mind. He looked at the program again and found her name in the cast list. She was the fourth person listed. Her character was called Belinda Fairchild. He was ready for the show to start.

Apparently so was the house manager and so was the stage manager. The lights began to dim and music played through the speaker system. It was a familiar tune, but Billy couldn't place it. Before he could think too much about the music, the curtain rose and the play began.

"I don't believe you'll find her, no," said a character on the stage, talking into a hole in the wall, one that Billy realized was intended to be a wall speaker, probably a door buzzer intercom. It was poorly rendered, he thought. He made a mental note about that, then checked the set's decor. It was all right, he supposed, but not the sophisticated space it would seem to be intended to represent. "You can wait, if you want, but...oh, come on up. I don't care." The man moved away from the wall and came into the central portion of the set. He flung himself down on a couch that seemed to swallow him up. The actor's visible hand picked up a magazine and the sound of sluffing pages could be heard. A doorbell rang. "It's open, Henry. Come in," the same actor called out from somewhere in the center of the couch. The upstage door opened and Raymond Rogé entered grandly. Billy felt a groan welling up inside his mouth. The old stage star was showing off, being foppish, being too grand, he thought.

"Richard. How kind of you to let an old man rest among your lovely things," Rogé intoned. Billy did groan, then caught himself and slumped down an inch or two in his seat. Someone was moving past the people to his left, heading for an open seat two chairs to Billy's right. Billy sat back up, pulling in his legs, to let the person pass.

On stage, the two men were conversing, the younger actor now standing up so that he could be seen again. The dialogue was wispy and not very intelligent. There was a laugh now and then, a snicker or two mixed in with the other reactions from the audience. A woman entered, coming down a spiral staircase upstage left.

"You two are so noisy," she laughed from about four steps above the stage deck. "And you say so little of consequence." The literary quality of the dialogue was depressing Billy in spite of his pills. He started to look at his watch, but restrained himself. He was here for the duration, a guest of an actress, he would wait it out, think of something nice to say later when he saw her.

Then, suddenly, she was there. She came in the same door that had admitted Rogé. She turned, Loretta Young-like, swirling her dress and her coat. She was carrying packages and she dropped them noisily when she saw the other three on stage. Billy recognized her instantly from the startled look on her face. She was Sandy, all right, the Sandy he remembered. She was older, prettier, lovelier actually, than he had imagined, but she was Sandy.

The person who had entered late and pushed past Billy burst into applause as Sandy finished her balletic turn. A few other people joined in and Billy added a single clap to the sound, but the actors on stage took no notice and went on with the scene as though there had been no audience reaction to Sandy's entrance.

"Belinda, won't you—" Rogé's Henry said, but she stopped him with her first line.

"What are you doing here? You can't be here, Henry. You're not allowed to be here. This is *my* home, these are *my* friends, and *you* are not allowed." Her delivery was sure and true and honest. Billy felt her anguish, felt her fears.

"So, once again, Henry, once again bounced from Belinda's life," Rogé responded in dark, despairing tones and the plot thickened.

At intermission, as the lights came up to relieve the tensions the audience felt over the dilemma on stage—play and not the plot—Billy glanced over at the man in the seat next to Billy's empty second seat. It was a casual glance, not meant to intrigue or antagonize. It managed to do both. The man was Joe Ryan. He turned and saw Billy, saw his expression, saw his sudden fear. He glowered at Billy. He turned away. Then he turned back to find Billy finally moving in the opposite direction. He reached for him and took him by the shoulder. Billy stopped where he was, waited for something, then jerked his shoulder away and moved out into the aisle. He wasn't sure if Joe was behind him or not. He was moving slowly through the crowd, surging up the aisle like nearly sleeping lava, hot and deterred by obstacles. He wouldn't allow himself to look back, glance over his shoulder. He just moved forward.

At the head of the aisle, he found Joe waiting. He stopped to look at the policeman, paused for just a moment to let his eyes meet Joe's eyes, then he turned toward the lobby and kept going. This time Joe did follow him. They went out onto the sidewalk and moved east, away from the marquee. There was still a vestige of sunlight in the early evening sky. There was the all-too familiar scent of car exhaust fumes. There were tears in Billy's eyes and he didn't want Joe to see them.

"Billy, wait up," Joe said from behind him. "Don't leave. Don't go because of me."

"It's a terrible play," he called out without turning. "I don't think I can see the second act and talk to your daughter afterward."

"Billy, please." He put his hand on Billy's shoulder and they both stopped walking. Billy turned and saw Joe, the same Joe, the old Joe he remembered so well, standing there in front of him. He let the tears flow and he moved forward into Joe's welcoming embrace.

They sat together for the second act, their grip on each other's hands taking its toll on blood flow to their fingers. At times they turned and looked at one another, neither believing that the other one was actually there, sitting there, grasping a hand and staring into the other one's eyes. When the curtain fell on the second act they reluctantly let loose their taut and frightened grip and used all four of their hands to applaud the entertainers on the stage. For Sandy's bow, Joe rose to his feet and cheered; Billy bravoed from his seat, then slowly rose to join Joe in the standing ovation. The cast moved upstage, finally, and the curtain fell as the house lights came up. Already standing, Billy and Joe began to move tentatively toward the aisle. Joe moved close to Billy, his lower body pressed gently against Billy's. They were both excited and Billy knew it.

Over his shoulder he said to Joe, "We have to behave, for Sandy's sake." Joe nodded and took a half step back, then moved against Billy one more time. Billy smiled and sighed and Joe heard, and felt, the reaction. He laughed, agreed with Billy, and stepped away. As they moved out of the theatre, slowly, they both relaxed.

"Where do we go?" Billy asked. Joe pointed down the street and set off and Billy followed him. The stage door was an unusual one, not easily accessible from the street. They moved quickly through the mid-evening crowds on Broadway and finally turned the corner, one street north of the theatre and headed back toward 6th Avenue. Billy was a pace or two behind Joe and when Joe suddenly darted down an alleyway, Billy hesitated, not sure why Joe had gone this way.

"Come on, will ya," Joe shouted, grabbing Billy by the oversized lapel and dragging him into the darkened by-way. "The stage-door is down here." He let go of Billy and headed down the twisting alley, Billy in hot pursuit. There was a door at the end of the stretch and Billy knew that Joe was not merely trying to seduce him in a public place. This was the Cort's door. They entered the tiny vestibule and the doorman, looking up, nodded at Joe, clearly familiar with him as a presence and was about to stop Billy when Joe indicated that they were together. The older man nodded and returned to his seat, an old round-bottomed wooden chair, one leg slightly shorter than the other three.

Joe led Billy up two flights of stairs to a doorway with the name Sandra Robbins on it. He knocked and, without waiting, entered. Sandy was there, in a lightweight, short, Oriental silk robe. She nearly leaped out of her seat and into her father's arms. Then she saw Billy. She reached out for him, took his hand and pulled him close to the already engaged twosome. As he approached she let go of his hand and put her arm around his neck.

"This is the gift I wanted for my opening," she said. "The three of us, just like this."

"It was great, baby," Joe said to her. Billy merely nodded.

"Don't lie, Daddy. It's a piece of crap and we all know it."

"It's a Rogé show," Billy said. "That's all."

"And it will run, guys. It's already got a seven week advance and we've been placed on run of the show contracts."

"That's terrific," Joe said. Billy could see the pride in Joe's eyes, the selfless pride that Billy had always admired, loved, and partially resented.

"And you've got the soap, too, Sandy. I'm so proud of you," Billy added.

"It's work. I love it."

"And you're good at it. But I didn't know you ever even wanted to act."

"You've been away for a long time, Billy."

"Too long," Joe said. "We've missed you a lot."

"Well, thanks." Billy ducked his head and lowered his eyes.

"Are you all right? Are you with someone?" Her questions were vague and left lots of openings for conversation.

"I'm fine. I'm not busy so we can chat and I'm alone," Billy said. "That is, I came alone tonight."

"Then you are with someone?" Joe asked.

"Sure. Aren't you?" He was sorry he asked the question even before he'd finished asking it.

"Sure am," Joe said. He put his arm around Sandy. "We've been together now for a year. And I love it."

"And no men," Sandy said. "Not for either of us, no sir."

They both looked at Billy, waiting for an understanding response.

He just smiled at them. "It's good to see you both, see you both looking so well, so happy."

"It's great to see you, Billy," Sandy said. "I'm so happy you came."

"And I'm happy you came, too," Joe added. "I've wanted to call you so often, but I didn't have the nerve."

"You didn't?" Billy laughed. "You have enough nerve for all of us."

"Not where you're concerned, kiddo. You steal my nerve."

"Well, you always said I did," Billy said, and he smirked.

"Watch it. There's a child in the room."

"A young adult, if you please."

"Yes, nineteen, Joe."

"You remembered that, Billy," Joe said. "I'm impressed."

Sandy gave Billy a knowing look and a nod, then she winked. Billy chuckled.

"You both meant so much to me. You still do."

"Why don't we all go out to the party? The opening night party." She looked at them both; they both quietly nodded. "Great! Now out in the hall. I have to dress." She shooed them both outside and shut the door behind them. She gave herself one long look in the mirror, so grown up, so gay and intelligent and she giggled, hugging herself for joy.

It was morning when Billy returned to the apartment. He tiptoed through the door and down the hallway to his room, hoping not to awaken Owen whom, he assumed, was still asleep in his own bedroom. Billy's head was swimming with mixed emotions bulking up like waves surging against the hull of a decrepit fishing boat. Had anyone he knew suggested that he would spend a night with Joe he would have slapped them silly and told them to get help. In spite of that, he had done the unexpected and now had to confront the consequences. Not that he knew what they could be as yet, but bobbing around in that sea of confusion were options, none of which seemed to be attached to life preservers.

As he passed Owen's door, ajar and far too wide at that, he paused to look inside. Owen was not in bed. The blinds were up. The room was well lit by the morning sun and showed the lack of any human presence. Owen's bed was unmade, which was not like him, and Billy immediately forgot his need for subterfuge and he stepped inside. The door to Owen's bathroom was open and it was obvious that he wasn't inside that room either. Billy stepped back out into the hallway and walked more confidently down to his own room.

He hesitated a moment before pushing open his door, sure for the instant that Owen would be there, waiting for him. He girded his loins and pushed his way in only to find that this room was empty also. He flung his jacket onto the bed, stepped into his own bathroom and took a look at himself. He was presentable, he seemed rested and fine. He went out into the hallway and headed down to the living room and the kitchen to see if Owen had left a note of some sort.

He wasn't surprised to find that Owen had done just that. He read it quickly.

Billy,

Feyhe called from an airplane last evening. She is heading back to New York and she sounds terrible. Apparently the earthquake happened just after her plane took off and she witnessed the distressing sight of San Francisco from the air. That was when she called.

She really wanted to talk to you, of course, but you were already on your way to the play. I am going to the airport to wait for her. I know there are still a lot of hours to go, but you're not here, you're probably going to see your young friend afterward and I need to be somewhere else, somewhere the news may be good.

I will call you from the airport and let you know what we're doing once Feyhe touches down.

I love you.

Owen

Billy checked the phone machine next. The light was blinking and as he pushed the playback button he knew he'd be hearing Owen's questioning voice. He was right.

"Billy, where the hell are you?" Owen's voice called from some other borough of the city. "Feyhe is here. She is in a terrible state, an emotionally and physically exhausted state. I am taking her to Columbia Presbyterian Hospital right from the airport. Meet us there, please." There was a pause. "Billy, it's one o'clock in the morning. Where are you?"

There was a second message that followed Owen's first.

"Billy, this is Owen. I hope you're on your way up here to the hospital. I really need you here. It's two o'clock. I'll be watching for you. Love you, kiddo."

And there was a third message.

"Billy...what's going on? We're at Harkness Pavilion. Room G-151. It's an isolation room in the psych ward. Get up here, now."

Only silence followed. Billy stood still for a second or two, then he twitched once and turned to grab his coat from the hall closet.

Billy spotted Owen immediately. The elevator door wasn't even completely open when he saw the man's legs and arms in the distance. He was seated on a bench opposite the nurse's station, his hands supporting his chin, his knees supporting his elbows. He looked very old, older than Billy has ever anticipated Owen looking. Owen never looked up as Billy proceeded down the wide corridor in his direction and when Billy stopped and sat down next to him, Owen still didn't look up at him. He just continued to stare forward.

"Tell me about it," Billy was calm and he kept his voice low.

"Where were you?" Owen asked him.

"Later. Tell me about Feyhe, first."

"Where were you? I needed you. She needed you. Where have you been?"

"Did she ask for me, Owen? Really?"

"She always does. You know that."

"I know."

"So where were you?" He sat up and turned a half-turn, giving Billy an up-and-down once-over. "You look terrific."

"We went out after the show, to the cast party and then to a bar and then...it was late and I took Sandy home...and she wanted to talk... and...."

"You're not telling me everything," Owen said.

"No. No, I'm not."

They looked at one another and said nothing. Owen ultimately broke the silence. "When she came off the plane, Billy, I thought she was dying. She had no color in her face, she was staring indifferently, lost and utterly confused. I went to her and she recognized me after I said my name a few times. Then she started to cry. I took her over to one of those little phone booths for two, and settled her in there where she could let go and cry in privacy of a sort. I held her. She asked for you. I told her you were coming. Then she broke down and held me, and that's a first for her in all these years."

"Owen, I'm so sorry I wasn't there to—"

"She saw the quake happen. They had literally just turned back over the city after taking off maybe four minutes earlier. She saw the highway crack and fall. She saw the city tremble and buildings crumble. She saw the turbulence in the bay. She watched the bridge shiver and shimmer. She says she saw Danny Kim crushed under a falling fenestration from the top of a building in Chinatown. She was hysterical, Billy."

"Owen, I couldn't know that she'd need—"

"When she phoned us from the plane it was to tell us that Danny was dead and that she was dying. Dying, Billy. That was what she said on the phone."

"I'm sorry, Owen."

"I couldn't just sit there. I had to go to the airport."

"I know."

"I waited for hours, Billy. Hours and you didn't come. I knew you were at the theatre. I knew you were out having fun. I needed you and I couldn't find you."

"I know. And the play was awful."

"Is that supposed to be funny. Am I supposed to feel sorry for you, Billy?"

"No. Of course not."

"I told Feyhe that she should come here with me and she agreed. She agreed, Billy, just like that. There were no arguments. There were no protests. She said yes and came along like a two-year-old."

"Oh, God, Owen—"

"They admitted her and examined her and the results are horrible. She is severely dehydrated. Her vagina shows signs of extreme sexual abuse. Her body is covered in scars and teeth marks. Her mental state is even worse. She can only talk about you and about Danny. She calls out for him with an agony that is unbearable to hear. When she says your name it's different, calmer, more even. Where were you?"

"What could have happened to her, Owen?" Billy asked his question, avoiding Owen's. "Isn't it obvious? Some California pervert has had her in his clutches and taken every advantage of his position. I'd kill the bastard if I knew who it was. I'd kill him!" Owen shouted this last. Two nurses looked up from their chairs across the hallway, behind the counter. One of them clucked and then shushed him. Billy put his arm around Owen's shoulders, but Owen pulled away, not willing to be touched.

"I can smell him on you, Billy. I can smell the other man."

"Owen, I was going to tell you. It's not the right time."

"You should see her, Billy. You should just see her, see the state she's in."

"I will, Owen."

"You should see her." He gestured toward the counter and returned to his former slumped over, face-in-hands position. Billy waited for a moment, then rose and went to the counter. He explained who he was to the nurse who seemed to already know his name. She stood up, taking a key from a hook on the wall in front of her and came around the counter to join him. She walked past Owen, turning to him as she did. "Anything else, Mr. Khanzadian?"

Owen shook his head and the nurse kept on going, Billy right behind her. He glanced over his shoulder at Owen, hoping to see some new movement, new attitude, but there was nothing.

The nurse turned a corner and Billy found himself in a hospital cul-de-sac. There were two doors, one on either side of the short, dead-end hallway. There were bars on the windows at the far end of the little side passage. The nurse stopped at the door on the left and opened it with her key.

She went in and Billy followed.

Feyhe, or a smaller version of the Feyhe he expected to see, was lying in the hospital bed, her wrists twisted in gauze and attached to the bed frame. She was staring up at the ceiling and seemed not to notice their entrance into the room. She wore no makeup and her face looked delicate, old and translucent. Her pale eyes were even lighter than he remembered. Her hair was disheveled and gray and thin.

"Don't stay too long," the nurse said in a hushed tone. "She's very tired, but she's been asking for you." She gave him a nod and then handed him the key. "Lock the door when you go, please and return the key to me." She left the room.

Billy felt peculiarly uneasy, alone with his cousin. He approached the bed slowly, expecting Feyhe to say something, but she stayed absolutely still, unmoving and seemingly unaware of his presence. When he was a foot away he whispered her name twice, "Feyhe. Feyhe."

Her head snapped around in his direction. "Untie me," she demanded. "Untie me, Billy. I hurt."

"I don't think I'm supposed to—" he said, but she interrupted him.

"I need to leave here. Untie me."

"Where would you go?"

"Home."

"Home where, Feyhe?"

"My home. East 82nd Street. Untie me."

"The nurse said—"

"Untie me. Now. Please."

"I can't Feyhe. You're in the hospital. You need care. Medical care."

"Untie me."

"Feyhe, I can't." He was sounding mournful, not receptive. He hated the way his voice sounded.

"Untie me. I have to go home."

"Feyhe, you have to stay here," he said. "It's for your own good."

"Untie me. Danny is waiting for me."

"Danny?"

"It's morning. Danny always has me in the morning. I have to be home. Untie me."

"Danny…Danny isn't here."

"Untie me. Danny will find me."

"No, Feyhe, I can't do it."

"Untie me."

Billy looked at her, thoughts cascading the way thoughts do when they can't be connected easily. He took a step back from her.

"I love you, Feyhe. We'll do what's right and we'll make you well. I have to go now."

"Dammit, untie me, Billy. Please. Please." Her final word was drawn out and whined. His ears hurt from the pathetic sound of it.

He moved quickly from the room and out into the hallway. His head was throbbing and his hand hurt badly. He looked at it and saw a key clutched tightly against the soft tissues of his palm. There was tiny spot of blood where one of the jagged edges had driven itself into his skin. He couldn't remember for the instant why he was holding a key, and then he recalled the nurse giving it to him with instructions.

From inside the room, Feyhe called out to him one more time. "Untie me. Danny wants me now." He locked the door and moved very quickly out of the cul-de-sac. He returned the key to the nurse who gave him a knowing look as she took it from him.

"Not what you expected?" she asked, already knowing the answer. He shook his head. "You could use some coffee, I think. Cafeteria is open. Basement elevator." She looked away, going back to her paperwork. Billy shifted his position and headed back to Owen, still on the bench.

He sat down and took Owen's hand. Owen looked at him. He looked better this time.

Billy squeezed his hand.

"Danny Kim did this," he whispered to Owen. There was no response. "Danny."

"Feyhe did this," Owen said. His voice sounded normal, sounded reasonable. "I won't blame anyone else. It was Feyhe."

"She's the victim, here, Owen."

"She's the victim, sure. She's also the perpetrator. She's the adult. She's the one who should say 'no' when that word is appropriate."

"You knew about Danny before I got here?" Billy asked him. He nodded. "Why didn't you say something?"

"You had to see for yourself," Owen responded.

"What do we do now?" Billy asked. Owen took his other hand. Their bodies were half twisted on the bench, their faces half facing one another.

"For her? Or for ourselves?"

"Yes," Billy said.

"I'll tell you what I already know, Billy, and you tell me what you already know. Then we'll answer the questions."

He stood up and dropped Billy's hands. Starting down the corridor toward the elevators, Owen looked older and older with each step. Billy finally lifted himself off the hard wooden seat and followed him carefully down the hallway.

J. PETER BERGMAN

21

Thirty minutes a day with Feyhe. The schedule was taking its toll on Billy, a visible toll at that. His hair was graying, his face was growing pale. The drugs she ingested daily, combined with the rapid mood swings left a smoothed out facade on her face, and Billy could never tell when he entered her hospital room which version of his cousin he might be confronting.

The subway ride to the northern extreme of Manhattan where this new hospital was located took forty minutes. The waiting room experience, each day, added another twenty minutes to his anxiety. During the trip north he would plot a way to remind the charge nurse that he was the same man who came each day. He had been through dozens of rationales and nothing had made the daily load any easier. He still had to fill out the same paperwork every time he went. He still had to wait for an attendant to escort him to her locked room. He had to be patient while Feyhe was prepared for a visitor. Then he had his thirty minutes.

He had been bringing a pad and pen with him to take down notes for all the things she wanted him to do for her. Most of these chores were undoable, but Feyhe didn't seem to realize that. Many of the remaining wishes were unachievable by Billy and anyone else he could think of to enlist in their service. Then, once the dictation and the impossible conversation had been completed, there was the search he went through as the same guard who had escorted him to Feyhe's room tapped him down, looking for anything he shouldn't be carrying away with him.

This was followed by the consultation with the nurse or the attending physician or the psychiatrist, when she was available, to plot the next steps in Feyhe's care. And, of course, there was the forty-minute trip back to his West Side office afterward, time to think about the whole package and how to get out from under this burden of responsibility.

"It's the guilt, I guess," Billy had confided to Joe when he told him about his new relationship with Feyhe. "She did so much for me when I was building my business, I really feel I owe her."

"You're too Jewish," Joe had laughed. "All this guilt stuff."

But it was truly how he felt about the way things had worked out. Feyhe had been there for him, now he was doing the same thing for her. She had supported his dreams and his work with her East Side friends as his clients. He had a lot to be grateful for and he was paying it back in spades.

After a few weeks at Columbia Presbyterian's Harkness Pavilion, Feyhe had been transferred to this largely inconvenient location by the psychiatric team at Columbia. There were many reasons for the move. Columbia didn't have the room to accommodate her for very long. They also didn't have the people needed to deal with her particular problems.

"Feyhe's condition is delicate at best," Owen told him over dinner a few nights after Feyhe's sudden reappearance in their lives. "Her manic-depression has been complicated by the abuse she's suffered at …" and here he paused to gain control over his own emotions, "…Danny's evil little hands. I could kill that kid. If I ever see him, I don't know…"

"Get a hold of yourself, Owen," Billy said to him.

Owen took a deep breath and started again. "Her manic-depression has been complicated by the abuse she's suffered. It took her over a precipice, Billy. She can't climb back up this hillside any longer. She's in a deep gully, so to speak. The walls are steep, slippery, slimy. That's her perception now of the world she inhabits. We're not really there with her when she's down in this place of hers. She's alone and we're only existing in her imagination. Does that make any sense?"

"No," Billy said. "I can see what you're drawing, but I can't imagine it. It's not real."

"That's right," Owen insisted. "That's exactly right, Billy. Feyhe lives something not real. It's only real to her. Not to the rest of us."

"How does she see us?"

"We're not the same people we see. She sees us the way she used to see us. We haven't changed much for her. We're also not really there when she sees us. She hears us as though we were on a speaker phone or in the next room. At least, that's how she sees us when she's in the depressive end of her limited spectrum. When she's on a high, when she's elated, it's different. Then we're too real. She sees us as looming over her, dominating her, capturing her in some strange lair that she doesn't understand. We become evil, in a way, to her. We become something she's conjured up and can't dispel."

"Wow!" Billy blew his nose to keep Owen from seeing the tears in his eyes. "I don't like being at either end of that world of hers."

"No one does, Billy."

They had talked out the details of visits and work. Owen was doing nights and weekends and Billy was taking the weekday shifts. Between them they visited Feyhe at least nine times a week. It was hard on them and it was taking an emotional toll on their own relationship, already a strained friendship at best.

After three months of Feyhe in their lives again, they took stock and found their warehouse of emotions had quickly emptied, so quickly they hadn't really noticed the depletion. Over a late supper on a Saturday night, they finally talked about it. Billy was emotional, Owen rational, at least at first.

"It's exhausting, Owen, absolutely exhausting."

"Take a day off from her, then. Just don't go."

"She'd be miserable. She'd feel I deserted her."

"She won't even notice. To her all days are the same day right now."

"And what if that should change? Suddenly? What then? She wakes up and she waits and I don't show up. That's not right."

"You don't have to be there every day. That's all I'm saying."

"I don't want to be there, Owen. That's the trouble. I really don't want to be there at all, but I have to be. Isn't that clear?"

"No. Billy, it's not as clear and rational as you imagine."

"I don't know what else to say, then."

"Say what's good for Billy."

"Billy has to repay his debts, somehow, some way."

"Crap!" His voice had risen a decibel or two and Billy's followed suit.

"It's not crap. I told you. I owe her." He stood up and stared down at Owen.

"You owe it to yourself, Billy, to find some personal happiness. And this isn't it." He was up, eye to eye with Billy, now.

"You're absolutely right this isn't it. You don't make me happy. I'd rather be back with Joe. That's what I want!" They stood staring at one another in silence. Billy turned away, but stayed where he was. Owen reached out and touched Billy's shoulder, touched it lightly, gently. "There. It's said. You've said it. Finally." Owen sounded calm, much calmer than Billy expected after his outburst had revealed his secret desires.

"I didn't mean—"

"Don't say you didn't mean it, Billy. We both know that you meant every word of it. I don't make you happy. I don't even make you well anymore."

"It's Feyhe, Owen, not you. Feyhe always makes me a little nuts. Not you."

"Not me. That's right. And yes, Feyhe does make you crazy. She affects us all badly. But she takes a stronger, deeper toll on you. You have to break away from her. You can't help her now, so make the move. Move away from her, and from me. I'm too much a part of her. You need to be away from all of this. Make the break."

Billy wanted to grab Owen, hold him, clutch him close and hold him tight. He was suddenly very much afraid of being alone, lonely, old. He had not felt this much tension and fear in a long time, not since he had fled from the Village, left that horrid life behind and gone to Feyhe for comfort and solace. At this moment, this moment here and now, he wasn't even sure when that had been, how long ago it had happened. He looked into Owen's eyes and he saw the tears there that he knew he had caused. He felt no remorse, no love, no sorrow. He felt loneliness, only loneliness.

"I don't want to leave you," he whispered.

"I don't want you to leave," Owen responded, "but you must. It's time. I'm too old for you, I'm too involved in all this nonsense with Feyhe. You don't have to be trapped in it also."

"You've been kind to me, good to me," Billy whined. He caught himself mid-whine and pulled back the emotional tone into something more adult.

"Billy, sit down again." He gestured and Billy sat immediately, taking the suggestion as an order. "It isn't love when it becomes subjugation. It isn't love when it's just obligation. It's love when it pours through you like sugar, firm and sweet, and flowing white and clean. We're in obligation, you and I. I'm obliged to help you and to love helping you. You're obliged to accept my help, my guidance, my love and to love me for what I can give you. But it's not the sugar between us."

Billy nodded, but remained silent. He understood and he agreed.

"And with Feyhe its subjugation. You are indebted, in your mind, for favors granted long ago. You feel there is no other option for you but to be there to do her bidding. She uses that to keep you doing those things that you shouldn't have to be doing. That's not love. That's a salty, bitter pill, not even a sugar-coated one."

"I see," Billy said.

"Is there a chance? Is there a real chance you might go back to Joe?"

"I don't know."

"Have you seen him? Spoken to him?"

"I've seen him." Billy stared at the floor. "Since that night at the theatre, the night Feyhe came home, I've seen him for lunch a few times and we went to see Sandy again in that awful play. You remember. It was the night after they transferred Feyhe uptown. You spent the night up there with her."

Owen nodded this time.

"We've talked and it's been good being with him, Owen, but I don't know if we have a shot or not."

"Billy, you can stay here for a while longer. That's the best I can offer. But this has never really been your place. It's always been mine and you were here because I wanted you to be here. But you need a place you can really call your own. A place that belongs to you. A place that brings you security and happiness. This isn't it."

"I know." They hugged and after the release, the look, the light kiss, Owen bolted out of the room. Billy stayed where he was until he heard Owen's door close, then he turned and reached for the telephone.

He followed the attendant down the hallway toward Feyhe's room. He had gotten into the habit of not paying attention to his surroundings; it made things easier. If he didn't hear the sounds coming from the rooms he passed, then he didn't have to worry about what was going on behind those closed doors. If he didn't make eye contact with the attendant, then he didn't have to feel that explanations were in order. If he didn't make anyone else too visible, then he wouldn't be so very much noticed by others in this place. That was Billy's strategy, and it was working.

They reached her room. The attendant unlocked the door. "I know the drill," Billy said. "I've been here before."

"Yes, sir," the attendant said in a soft, almost whispered, voice. He stepped back to let Billy into Feyhe's room. As he moved through the portal, Billy sensed something familiar, something in the air, but he couldn't get a grip on it. He let the thought pass, because Feyhe was sitting up in her bed, looking nice, looking almost happy. It took his breath away.

"Hello, Billy," she said. "It's nice to see you."

"Feyhe!" he said. "You're looking so well."

They hugged and Billy took the chair from near the corner and moved up alongside her bed.

"Owen told me you've been to see me every day. He told me I've been asking you to do stupid things for me and that you've done them."

"I only tried to help."

"I love you for it."

"Owen didn't tell me anything about this recovery, Feyhe. I wish I'd known."

"I wanted to surprise you. I wanted you to see for yourself."

"What's changed?" Billy asked. "I don't understand."

"I don't quite understand it myself," she said, and then she laughed. It was the light laugh that Billy recalled from their earliest days as friends. He lit up inside. He felt wonderful.

"When I left San Francisco, the day of that awful earthquake in Oakland, I wasn't myself. I was fleeing from my life, trying to find something older, earlier, something good to cling to, but when I looked down and saw that earthquake right there below me I panicked. I actually felt like Lot's wife leaving Gomorrah with that deadly, salty, backward glance."

She shuddered, licked her cracked and dry lips. Billy instantly grabbed her water bottle with the flex-straw and handed it her. She took a long, deep sip of the water and handed him the bottle.

"Thanks, honey," she said. He tried to recall if she had ever said that to him before, called him *Honey*. He couldn't remember. "I remember thinking, as I looked out that window, that Danny Kim was down there, alone, frightened as he always was, and that the buildings were toppling around him, catching him, crushing him. I was so scared, Billy, that Danny was dead. I phoned you from the plane, called to tell you what had happened, what was happening. That's the last thing I actually remember about that day. I don't even remember arriving in New York and finding Owen. I don't remember that."

"So Danny's all right?" he asked her.

She bit her lip before responding. There was no blood, but her teeth marks remained visible for a while on her lower lip. "I don't know for sure, but I don't think so."

Billy waited to ask a question, then finally asked it. "Have you heard from him? From any of them, the Kims?"

She shook her head slowly. Drool sprayed from her open mouth. She was beginning to look, again, like the mental patient she had been only the day before. "I don't want to talk about them," she said.

"Okay. What should we talk about?"

"You," she said. She smiled, practically grinned as she said it. She reached for his hand and when he took hers into both of his own he was aware of how thin she had grown, how translucent her skin was, how cool her flesh, how discolored her fingers were from smoking, and how blotchy her hand was from the combination of medications and malnutrition.

"I want to talk about you. I want you tell me about your work, and about Joe Ryan and his daughter and about your plans and about … things. Just things, Billy."

Billy laughed at her good spirits and was about to launch into a quick menu of events that involved him, when she spoke up again.

"And I want you to telephone my cousin Mireille, in Paris, you never met her, but she knows your name. You'll have to speak with her in French because she doesn't understand any English. I want you to tell her that I'm all right, Billy. She's so much older than I am and I don't want to shock her. You'll find her number in my book, over there in the nightstand. Then I want you to call Kim and Ni-Na and tell them where I am and tell them that Danny is all right. Make sure they understand that I'm just sick and that Danny is fine. Tell them to visit me. Next I want you to call my cousins—I know you don't like them—and tell them the same things. After that I want you to go to the apartment and have everything packed up. I really only came back here to close it up and put it on the market. I don't want to live out my years in New York. I like California. It's always sunny and pleasant and the people there are remarkable. Next I want you to—"

"Whoa, Feyhe, hold on a minute," Billy said, his voice rising. "You're going too fast. I can't get this all down." He looked up at her, and the subtle change that had come over her face made his heart stop and miss a beat. The good color in her cheeks was gone, replaced by a reddish pallor. Her eyes were slightly glazed over and she wasn't looking at him at all. Her mouth moved slightly, though she wasn't speaking. One hand touched one cheek and the fingers thrummed there against her weakened jaw. "Feyhe…no…"

"What? What?" she asked him repeatedly. "What? What? What? What? What?"

Billy stood up and went for door. He rapped four times, Feyhe creating a distinct counterpoint to his physical rhythm with her verbal repetition of her single syllable question. The attendant opened the door, allowing him to exit, then snapped it tight behind him. He didn't wait for his escort, but moved hastily down the corridor, back toward the locked entry door. Once there, he waited for the door to be opened. Then he passed through it, passed out of the horror and into the medical stillness of the greater hospital.

The couch in Owen's living room seemed crowded with just the two men sitting there, the void between them emphasized by the extent of empty cushion. Owen fidgeted with a throw pillow that seemed to need constant fluffing. Joe, whose long legs and arms seemed constricted by the fussy, Edwardian sofa's high back and awkwardly down-curved arm, looked terribly out of place. Billy, hovering in the archway behind them was hardly even in the room, nowhere near the couch, yet seemed to fill in the upholstered hole that gaped its ungainly depths.

Owen's face was taut, his skin seemingly polished. His eyes glowed darkly. Joe, by contrast, was almost too relaxed, almost too self-assured and content. His lips curled into a smile that Billy, when he could see Joe, thought a bit sadistic, a bit forced.

"Billy belongs with you," Owen had said, opening the conversation with a direct assault on the topic.

"Being with you has been good for him," Joe had said. "He's stronger, more in charge of himself."

"You're the right age for him. You have the strength he lacks."

"You're emotionally attuned to his entire being. He's a very complex man. I'm a simple one."

"The simple answer," Owen stated his case, "is Billy loves you."

"Excuse me," Billy interjected. "Does anyone care what I want?" Both men looked over at Billy.

"You're not here," Owen said.

Billy hesitated, then turned his back on them both and went to his room. They returned to their argument over suitability. Neither one faltered for a second in his statements regarding the other one's qualifications.

"I don't think I can give Billy the attention he needs. I have a daughter and I have my work."

"You won't die young, Joe," Owen said. "Your end of police work is not dangerous.

You'll grow old with him. I've preceded him and, frankly, I could die any day."

Death in the conversation threw an additional pall on the proceedings. The two sat and fidgeted, neither one commenting on the thought of Owen dying, Joe dying.

"We should talk to Billy," Owen said, finally breaking the silence.

"What would we say to him?"

"I don't really know."

"I think I do," Joe said. "Let's call him in." Owen rose from his corner of the sofa and left the room. Joe watched him go. *He is old*, Joe thought. *He is so very old.*

Less than one minute later, Owen was back, Billy trailing him. Joe was sipping coffee when they entered the room and he staggered to his feet awkwardly, one hand clutching the half-empty coffee mug and the other outstretched for balance. Billy took Joe's available hand and accidentally tipped him in the other direction. Coffee spilled onto the sofa.

"Oh, God, I'm so sorry," he mumbled, but Owen just shook his head. "Scotch-guarded. No fear," he said quietly.

"I'm so sorry," Joe repeated, louder this time. No one responded. He sat down, his leg grazing the small puddle of dark brown liquid.

"It's okay," he said to Owen and Billy, gesturing toward his pant leg, "it's scotch-guarded." Billy laughed, then squeezed himself into the wide space between Owen and Joe's spilled coffee.

"I don't know how much you overheard, Billy—" Owen began, but Billy jumped into the conversation and silenced him.

"So, does anyone actually want me?" he asked, half in jest and half serious.

Owen and Joe looked up at Billy. He was no longer sitting between them on the couch, but now stood before them. "It's not a matter of wanting you, Billy, it's a matter of what is in your best interests," Owen responded.

"We're not being fair to you, are we?" Joe asked.

"My time with you, Joe, is always special now," Billy began. "It's always good and fun and comfortable. The sex is excellent! And, for the first time, maybe, our conversations are good, too. We actually talk about stuff that matters."

Joe blushed with pride.

"On the other hand, my hours with Owen have always been all of that. He showed up when I needed someone. And he's always there for me when I need him. I'm not something everyone can handle."

Owen's face matched Joe's for color and complexity.

"I think we should continue like this. That's what I think." He sat down again.

Owen took Billy's hand and held it, squeezed it, released it. He smiled and the patina of composure that held his face in perfect check cracked a bit. Instantly the look of age grabbed the skin, eyes, features. Billy saw a much older Owen than he had seen in recent weeks.

"I'm too old, Billy," he said. "You think I'm trying to get rid of you, but I'm not. I'm trying to release you from your own bonds. You've tied yourself to me and it isn't cozy anymore."

Billy watched the older man's face as he spoke. He could see the credible sense in Owen's eyes that matched the honest appraisal in his speech. He choked and coughed without saying a word, then he looked away, not at Joe, but in some neutral direction away from both of them.

"The restraints in this relationship are hurting you, now," Owen continued. "You need the space that only a real intimate relationship can allow you. I want you here, Billy. Of course I want you. You opened up something in me that must have been dormant for half a century. I didn't look for it. I didn't expect it. You brought it life and you nurtured it through your needs. Now you don't need me, you don't."

"I was never happier, never more miserable than when we were together," Joe said. "You let me be me and then, well, you didn't like all that I was. You weren't comfortable, Billy and I understand that. I can't say I've really changed much in this time we've been apart. But you have. Maybe what I am isn't something you'll really be happy with in the long run. I don't know."

"You two are making me nuts," Billy said. "And, genetically speaking, I don't need your help for that." He laughed. After the briefest pause, so did Joe and Owen, the former heartily, the latter awkwardly.

""I won't pretend I like it, but you still stand a better chance with Joe," Owen said. "I can't deny it's how I see things."

"I think I'm your best shot too, Kiddo," Joe said. "And I don't anticipate it being any easier this time around. That doesn't thrill me."

"I don't know what to do."

Owen leaned forward and kissed Billy on the cheek. The touch of his cracked lips irritated Billy, although he wasn't sure just why it did.

"I don't want you to stay here much longer," Owen said. "Does that help?"

Billy shook his head. The place where Owen's lips had touched him now stung as though heavy salt had been suffused into the open pores of his skin.

"My apartment is just too small for us both," Joe added. "I can't really have you there. It's not for not wanting you there, Billy. You just need more room, more space than I can provide. It's killing me, kiddo."

Billy nodded. He leaned over to Joe and, as Owen had kissed him, he kissed Joe. Joe's skin was hot to the touch. His skin was firm and taut and youthful.

"You guys don't leave me many choices, do you?" Billy said. "Not many choices at all, really. I guess I have to go out into the wide, wide world and make a place for..." He stopped mid-sentence and his mind went instantly blank, then filled up like a movie screen coming through a fade-in.

Feyhe's face loomed up in front of him, emerging from the deep darkness. It was Feyhe younger, smarter than she was now. It was Feyhe ten years earlier, maybe even younger. In his film's-eye view of her she was walking down the long, familiar hallway of her apartment looking smart in a cocktail dress. She was smiling and nodding and he could feel himself entering the picture, smiling also, nodding also.

He turned to look at both men again, taking them in with his eyes, his mind, his heart. He smiled. They smiled back, hesitant, unsure. He laughed. They looked on, helpless, clueless.

When he finally got control of his laughter, he held out his arms to both men. Neither one moved a muscle.

Billy stood up, walked to the window in much the same fashion that his vision of Feyhe had walked, paused, then dramatically turned back to face Owen and Joe, both still seated. As he turned, Joe stood up, his coffee mug still bobbling about in his hand.

"I'm throwing a house-warming party, fellas," Billy shouted. "You're both invited. Bring a sweet!" And he laughed again.

22

The instant he entered Feyhe's apartment, Billy knew what was wrong. The air inside the long-shut-up suite of rooms lacked the staleness that should have greeted him. His first thought was "intruder." He glanced to his right, through the kitchen arch, checking to see if the window had been broken. It looked fine. He took a step into the living room and once again surveyed the windows. They were intact. But there were signs of life in evidence.

Several pieces of furniture had been moved from their more familiar places. The old couch had been stripped of its cushions, long soaked in Feyhe's urine and cigarette ashes. In their place were new cushions in a loud, crimson satin fabric that he knew Feyhe would have hated instantly. There was a large television against the far corner where her old Victrola had stood proudly, its external horn, painted with woodland scenes, constantly in view. The television seemed so wrong there, so incongruous. The drapes had been replaced by window shades.

He moved down the hallway. The first room, the dining room, was unchanged, but there were papers on the table, seemingly inviting him to peruse them. He entered quietly, reached for nearest stack of papers and picked them up. These were Feyhe's bank statements from the past several months. They had been opened, flattened and placed face up, in ascending order, the most recent one on top. He read it quickly and was horrified. Her balance showed at $253.77. This was her checking account, the account into which her various royalty, pension, and social security checks had been automatically deposited for years and years. Billy couldn't believe what he was seeing. He knew there should be more than this in her account. Her lawyer had kept him and Owen abreast of the deposits and the various bills paid out of her accounts. They had needed this information in order to maintain her health care. This was impossible!

He moved out of the dining room and went on down the hall, passing the bathroom first—nothing really wrong there except for the shaving brush in one of her best Royal Doulton teacups. That disturbed him, but he let it pass.

The guest room, his old room in less happy days, was empty and seemingly a box storage room once again. He let it go. He moved to the door to Feyhe's bedroom. It was closed. He reached for the doorknob, hesitated, his hand in mid-air burning with an odd mixture of desire and fear. He clutched it, felt the coolness of the crystal knob, turned it and let it drift open, inward, away from him. The room was…

A sound behind him made him turn instantly. He expected a demon, a horror, a something he couldn't quite grasp. There was nothing there. No one there. He took a step in the vague direction of the sound and then he could clearly identify it. It was the refrigerator door. It had been opened and now it was slammed shut. He wasn't alone in the apartment. Whoever it was that had made these changes, that had invaded Feyhe's privacy by opening her mail, was in the kitchen. He moved stealthily through the hallway until he was just outside the kitchen door. He looked around for something to grab, to use as a weapon if he needed one. There was nothing useful in the vicinity. He decided to be butch, to brave it out, to make his presence known.

"Who is it?" he belched out, but his voice was only a hoarse whisper.

There was a scream. He jumped backward into the cloistered hallway. The scream persisted and he moved into the bathroom to avoid the screamer. He slammed the door and turned the lock sharply, caging himself in the most inconvenient room in the place.

"Who are you?" he shouted out this time. "Who is that?"

"Who are you?" came the reply in a voice he didn't know.

"Who are you? I asked you first." Suddenly this was becoming a game and there didn't seem to be any posted rules.

"I'm calling the super," said the voice, a woman's voice, one he didn't recognize. "Feyhe?" he shouted. "That can't be you!"

"She's sick!" said the voice, a little bit quieter this time.

"Who are you?" he asked again.

"Who are you?"

"Stop it," Billy screamed. "You're making me crazy!"

There was a silly sort of silence punctuated by a scratching sound outside the door. Billy stood his ground, halfway back into the room. The new sound was a strangely familiar sound, but he couldn't really place it.

"Ah hah!" said the female voice from outside the door, but somehow clearer, sharper, from much lower down.

Billy's inner ear cleared up one form of confusion. The sound had been the lock guard on the old-fashioned door. The female person was looking at him through the wide-open keyhole.

"You know me?" he whispered.

"You are Billy Duncan," she said.

"And who are you? Who the hell are you?'

"Open the door, please."

"No," he said. "Not until you tell me who you are."

"Open the door." Her voice was familiar, so familiar. "Please, Billy. You know me." He did. He knew he did. He knew the voice.

"Ni-Na?" he asked tentatively, knowing he knew the right name, the right words.

"Please, Billy. Yes, Billy."

He unlocked the door and opened it slowly and firmly. He looked at her and he knew her instantly. Ni-Na. Kim's wife. Danny's mother. They both stood and looked at one another.

Neither one spoke. He moved past her, out into the hallway and back up the short companionway to the living room. He heard her follow him. Without turning to look at her, he addressed her again.

"Were you here when I came in?"

"Yes, Billy. I hid in closet when I heard the door key."

"Why on earth—?"

"I was frighten. You are not expected."

"But I am. The super was informed that I would be here."

"I am not super."

"Well, why would you expect me to tell you?"

"I am daughter-in-law of Feyhe."

"That doesn't give you any rights here. This isn't Korea."

"I take care of apartment. I clean. I clean up."

"Clean up from what? What's going on here? So much is so different."

"From San Francisco comes things, boxes, television, couches."

"How...?" but he stopped before he continued. Feyhe's things from her apartment in San Francisco had been shipped east, of course they had. He remembered that now. Her possessions not ruined by the earthquake had been sent here by neighbors, or by someone acting for her.

"But why you?"

"I am daughter-in-law. It is fitting for me."

"And you sleep here, too?" he asked her. She blushed a moment, then nodded. "Without Kim?"

She nodded again. "Kim not come here no time now," she said. "He will not be part of anything that is to do with Feyhe, he says. She betray him, he says."

"She gave him everything," Billy said before he thought about it.

"She give too much, take too much."

He sensed her tears without seeing them. He held out his handkerchief and she took it delicately. She turned her back and he heard what sounded like a muted sob. Then she turned back to him and returned his still pristine cloth.

"Feyhe is generous with love and with Feyhe," Ni-Na said. "She save me from Danny's anger. She save me from Kim's anger."

"At what cost, Ni-Na? Have you seen her?" Ni-Na shook her head in silence.

"She is destroyed, Ni-Na," Billy continued. "He took what was left of her sanity and stole it from her."

"Please, Billy Duncan, sit and talk with me," Ni-Na said. She gestured to the garish red cushions and he moved around the re-angled couch, sat and waited for her. She joined him quickly. "I will tell you what I know of this," she said.

"Don't, if you don't want to," Billy told her, but she shook her head, biting her lower lip as she did so.

"If you want, please."

"After Feyhe has taken Danny away to California my husband becomes so furious that he beats me and his other son in anger. We are not at fault, but he still beats us. It is only then I realize that he loves her as he has not loved me. I am curious, but I am also very angry for myself now. I mean only to ask questions, but no, this is not how things happen between us. Instead I accuse him. He is almost honest and he tells me much of what has transpired with Feyhe. I tell him about Danny and his attacks upon me. He beats me again, Billy Duncan. I flee from him, meaning to take my young child with me, but he has pulled the boy from my arms and so I ran from him alone. I came here."

"You've been living here ever since?"

"No, no. I return to New Jersey, to my husband and my son. I live there today, but I come to New York each week to clean and care for Feyhe's home."

"Why? You have to hate her?"

"No, Billy Duncan. She has been my savior from attacks by my boy. She has put herself in harm's way for me. I will care for her all of my life."

"But who's been living here?"

Ni-Na was silent. There was no answer escaping her lips.

"Ni-Na? Is someone else living here? I need to know, because I am planning to live here for as long as possible. So, tell me, please."

She looked at him and her dark eyes shone with her tears and her pride. Her lip shuddered and her nose quavered. She slowly lowered her eyes, then her head.

"Danny Kim is sleeping here, is living here," she said in a voice so small that he wasn't really sure she had spoken, that he hadn't imagined the words, hadn't created the awful thought.

"Danny Kim is sleeping here, is living here," he repeated, hearing the words in his own voice, knowing for sure that she had said them, that he hadn't fantasized them. He was up, moving away from her, approaching the clean, gleaming windows.

"Danny Kim, yes, Billy Duncan."

"We thought he was dead, that he died in the earthquake." That had been Feyhe's excuse, her words, her thoughts, he realized. They had never known, never seen proof, had only accepted the truth they wanted to hear.

"My son, yes, Billy Duncan. With the boxes came my son and my son could not return to our home. My husband, his father, would surely have murdered him."

"Well, this is…" Billy stopped, not knowing how to express his feelings. "This is…terrible. This is a situation. This is…terrible."

"Each week I come and clean and cook for him," she said. "I do this because he is a boy and cannot do this for himself. I do this because he is my son. You will not harm my son, Billy Duncan. You will not harm him?" She had followed him to the window. He stood looking down at her, so pretty still, yet not so young anymore.

Billy looked more closely at her, not sure how to tell her all that he felt at this news. He and Owen had sworn to kill the kid who had destroyed Feyhe so completely. Their fury had never abated. Now, they had him. Now, he was here at the ready, waiting for them to finish what they had sworn to do. How could he answer Ni-Na, this sweet, pathetic woman, his mother. How could he tell her that he would not hurt Danny, her son. How?

"I'm confused, Ni-Na. He lives here, has been living here for a while. Why didn't we know of this?"

"He would not have you know it."

"How does he live?" Billy asked, and he knew the answer before he had finished the question. "He uses her accounts, doesn't he? He steals her money, isn't that right?" Billy heard the indignation in his voice, was unable to control it. "He's been an abuser and now a thief, hasn't he, Ni-Na? And you help him? You help this monster you gave birth to? How? How can you do that?"

"He is my son, Billy Duncan. He is not monster!" She recoiled from him and raised her hands, palms out, as if to protect herself. The quick gesture turned into coiled fingers and claw-like fingernails hurling back in Billy's direction. Surprising himself, he caught both her wrists only inches from his face and he shoved her backward. She fell to the floor and was rising, ready to come at him one more time, when the door to the apartment opened and the sound of a man's gasp stopped them both. They turned to look at the newcomer and Ni-Na cried out in Korean just as Billy realized that the man in the doorway was Danny. He lurched past Ni-Na and around the couch, just as the front door hit its frame and locked itself into place. He turned the knob and yanked open the door. Ni-Na was sobbing loudly now and he could hear both her throaty noises and the whirring of the elevator as it descended.

He ran for the stairwell door and found it bolted. He hit it hard, but its metal toughness never budged.

"Damn!" he shouted loudly enough for doors to open on the floor above. He could hear the apartment dwellers up there edging forward, timidly, wondering what might be going on down there on the twelfth floor. The door to Feyhe's apartment slammed shut again, for the second time in a minute. "Damn!" he whispered as he moved back in that direction.

He opened the door, stuck his head and shoulders inside and called out to Ni-Na. "I am moving in tomorrow," he said. "Have his things out of here by then. Only his things, Ni-Na. If there is one thing of hers touched I will come to New Jersey and I will tell your husband what you have done. I will hold you while he beats you. I will do that. I will. I will do that."

He stood upright, in the hallway outside the vestibule. He shut the door, turned and rang for the elevator.

Feyhe sat upright staring out the window of her room which overlooked a baseball diamond, the vast expanse of marsh beyond it and the Hudson River access of the Spuyten Deuvil Kill, the wide stream that connected the Hudson to the East River and separated Manhattan from The

Bronx. No one was playing ball on the field. A New Haven-bound train was crossing the narrow railroad bridge. A barge, pulled by a tugboat was lazing its way up the River to Yonkers. Feyhe was staring after the train, Billy assumed. He was standing in the doorway watching her watch the world.

She heard him, or sensed him. She turned to look at him. She smiled a vague smile, a grin actually, or a grimace that filtered itself into a half smile. She nodded at him, moving her head only an inch or so, then returning it to its former position. He nodded back at her.

"How are you today?" Billy asked her.

"I'm fine, thank you, Sir. How are you?"

"I'm okay," he said. "You're wearing a black scarf," Billy added.

"My husband's dead. I'm in mourning."

"I'm sorry about that, Feyhe. I liked Owen so much."

"Oh, did you know my husband?"

Billy coughed before answering. "I did. Of course I did, Feyhe. I'm Billy."

"Oh." She still stared at him. She hadn't blinked or moved a muscle since they had started the conversation. "Billy. Yes."

"You do remember me, don't you?"

"Yes."

"Who am I?"

"Billy."

"How do you know I'm Billy?"

She looked at him, her expression unchanged. "You told me."

"And who is Billy? Think a minute. Don't answer until you know."

They were both very quiet for several minutes as she continued to look at him, then out the window, then back at him. He stayed where he was. He tried not to breathe too loudly. He didn't want to distract her for an instant. He wanted her to concentrate.

The nurse had alerted him a few weeks earlier that Feyhe's mind had been slipping, that she had to be prompted over and over again.

"You're Miriam's boy," she said suddenly, breaking the silence. "How do you do?"

"That's right."

She smiled as he spoke. She was pleased with herself. He was just as pleased as Feyhe. "I do just fine, thanks," he said. "Have you had any other visitors today?" It was a question he asked her every day, had asked her every time he saw her since he had seen Danny lurking in the doorway of her old apartment.

"Why yes, I have," she responded. "A very nice man in a white suit came in."

"That was probably your doctor, Feyhe."

"Am I sick?"

"Yes." He gave her a smile. "You are sick."

"I feel fine, Sir."

"What's my name, Feyhe?"

She stared at him, no answer coming. She nodded again. Nodded once more. "Billy."

"Yes, that's right."

"Why are you standing so far away?" she asked him. "Come over here where I can see you better." He walked around her bed, putting himself between her and the window.

"I was watching the train, you know. It was going somewhere not here. I like that, you know."

"I know," he said. He remembered the day they had gone to West Point, had stood near the fortress wall watching the train meandering up the eastern shore of the Hudson. "You always liked to watch the trains, Feyhe."

"You wanted to know something, Billy."

"I did?" He sounded confused, was confused.

"About visitors," she said. "He was here. That's the question you wanted to ask me."

"Yes, you're right. I did."

"You always ask me. I never tell you. But I'm telling you now. He comes to see me every day. He comes to see me at night."

"He can't, Feyhe. There are no visiting hours at night here."

"He comes to me in the darkness, and he stays with me until the dawn."

"He doesn't Feyhe."

"He does. You should see him. He's beautiful. He wants me to buy bibles and to give them to people."

"To who?"

"People. He wants me to present Bibles to the nurses and the doctors and the other patients. He made me write down a list of Bibles—different Bibles for different people, Billy. You have to go to the American Bible Society to get them and you have to bring them here to me and I have to wrap them myself. That's what he tells me in the night."

"Who, Feyhe?"

"God." It was a simple answer.

"God comes to you, to see you, every night and he wants you to give bibles to people."

"Yes, of course. Who else would I be talking about?" She sounded miffed. He knew the sound because he felt miffed and knew how he must sound.

"And who pays for the Bibles?" he asked her.

"I do. I will. When I can get to my banks. In the meantime, you can lay out the money. You'll be repaid, don't worry."

Billy let his mind wander to Owen, wishing that Owen could see this, hear this new nonsense. He wished that Owen had lived just a few months longer, had not given up the way he had, let himself go, let himself die.

"I don't have the kind of ready cash to—" he stopped as she handed him her list of Bibles and people. Without meaning to he let out a low whistle of amazement.

"Feyhe, there must be two hundred people on this list. Two hundred bibles?"

"It's small, I know, but it's a beginning." She smiled at him again. Nodded at him again.

Smiled.

He smiled back at her and nodded, not sure how else to deal with this. "I'm counting on you, Billy."

"Okay, Feyhe. Let me work on it." He folded the list in half, half again and then put it in his pants pocket. She had turned away from him and was staring out the window again, past him, toward the north,

The Bronx, the future perhaps.

He moved away from her, toward the door, preparing to leave for the day, when she spoke to him once more.

"Don't I get a kiss before you go? He always kisses me."

"God?" he asked. "God kisses you before he goes?"

"No," she laughed. "Danny."

Billy handed the list to the man behind the counter at the Bible Society building on Broadway and 61st Street the following morning. The man ran his index finger swiftly down the side of the hand-written sheets, humming a tiny tone that Billy could barely hear. Still, it was a distinctive noise, different from what was issuing from the white-noise machine that effectively drowned out the traffic din from outside. The showroom was completely glass enclosed and semi-circular, and the tinted glass altered the exterior just enough to make it look like an animated Doré illustration. The man's humming stopped. He looked up at Billy and let a perfectly avaricious grin suffuse his face.

"We can provide all of these," he said with a smarmy tone that made Billy edgy. "I can give you a good price for buying in bulk, Sir. Shall I run a tally for you?"

Billy nodded and the man moved away into an enclosed area behind the stalls of books. Billy wandered through the room, waiting for the man's return and counted the number of titles he could find for *Good News Bibles*, finally winding up with nine different editions in seventeen different sizes and bindings. At least three of those appeared on Feyhe's list, as he recalled, and maybe even more of them. He saw the clerk re-emerge from behind the desk and he moved out of the aisle to meet him.

"Well, Sir, we can let you have this lot for $1300," the man said. "And if you need them delivered anywhere in Manhattan, there's no charge."

Billy had paled at the price. He nearly choked before he spoke. "I'll have to let you know," he said. "I need to check with my cousin, who's the one buying them, before I commit. Is that all right?"

The man agreed, handed Billy his card and moved off much more quickly than he had approached. Billy suppressed a desire to snicker and just as quickly left the showroom. The change in light hit him instantly, the lack of serenity, the lack of peace was amazing. He walked up the street, heading toward Lincoln Center. He was supposed to meet Sandy for lunch at O'Neal's Balloon and the time was already on him.

He spotted her outside the side-street entrance. He waved and she waved back. She took his arm as he passed her and together they swept into the restaurant. She snuggled against his arm and shoulder, and the head-waiter, seating them, assumed them to be a happy young couple. He said as much while handing them the oversized menus and grinned as he walked back toward the front door. Sandy broke first, giggling irrepressibly. After a moment, Billy joined her in enjoying the situation.

He told her about the bibles. She laughed. She told him about the play she was going into at the Vivien Beaumont Theatre at Lincoln Center. He stifled a yawn. It sounded like a long, pretentious play, the kind that would leave the audience totally cold. He said so, finally, when she had finished telling its tale.

"It's not so bad. I just don't tell it right," she offered.

"I hope that's it, sweetie," he said to her. "If not, you're going to be out of work pretty soon again."

"No. Wrong. Subscription audience. Nine weeks guaranteed." She laughed again. "Then, if you're really wrong, they could move it downtown for an extended run."

"Well, don't expect to see me opening night," he said.

"Why not?"

"Well, Joe will be there, for one thing, and I don't want to see him."

"I thought you and my dad were getting along now."

"We are. At least as long as we don't spend any time together."

"When did you see him last?"

"Owen's funeral. Three weeks ago."

"Oh, right. I'm sorry about that. I should have come."

"You were working. You're an actress. You work when you get it."

"I should have been there." She looked genuinely sad. He believed the look and the tone of voice. He forgot that she was an actress. He only knew she was Sandy.

"Well, anyway, you were busy. It happened. It's over. Joe was there. He was kind, the way he can be, and he was sincere. I needed that, then. I don't need it now."

"You don't like sympathy, do you, Billy?"

"Not for myself, no."

"So…what do you like?"

"Meaning…?"

"Meaning in your life, what do you like? What are you looking for? What would make you happy?"

He reached over and touched her hair, shoved it back off of her face. He wanted to see her eyes more clearly.

"Why are you asking?"

"No reason," she said, sounding far too snippy.

"Oh, yes. There is. I can tell. Confess, girlie!"

"Well, I met this man," she started, but before she could continue, he had placed his hand across her mouth.

"That's enough! Not another word. No more match-making, Missy."

"Bt, mtchmkknng i' wht I duh," she said through his muffling fingers. He moved his hand away. She exhaled and broke into a smile. "It is."

"Not with me, please. Set your father up, if you want, if he lets you that is. But leave me out of it. I don't want or need anyone. I'm doing just fine on my own."

"Oh, are you?" she burbled. "Really?" She held up her right hand and wiggled its fingers in his face. "Dating your digits, are you?"

"None of your business, you impertinent brat!" He slapped her fingers away, not hard, but not merely in fun.

"Well, if you are, we're dating cousins," she said, as she waved to the waiter who was approaching their table. "Can we order, please?"

"Sorry. Not my station," he said, hurrying past.

"Have a little patience, Sandy. Our waiter will be here. You'll see."

"That's fine for you, Billy. All you ever order here is steak tartare. What does that take?

Cold meat, an egg, some capers. I have a meal to plan."

"Oh, all right. Waiter!" Three good looking men, dancers and waiters, turned to look in his direction. "Well, now," Billy said to Sandy, "if that was all it took to turn a man's head I should have tried it sooner."

The two of them were still chuckling when their own waiter appeared at their table, moments later.

He handed the list back to Feyhe on his next visit to see her. She looked at it without any apparent curiosity, never even picking it up off the bedspread.

"$1300, Feyhe," he said. "Where's the money for that?"

"I beg your pardon?"

"You asked me to lay out some money for you to buy these books. I want to know where the money's coming from to pay me back?"

"I have it."

"Where?" He waited. "What bank?"

"I have it. I'm a very wealthy woman."

"You had money, once, Feyhe. Now you don't."

"You don't know everything, Doctor." She sounded strong, but she had lost color and strength, couldn't even sit up without the support of the hospital bed's upright end.

"I'm not the doctor, Feyhe. Who am I?"

"The bible salesman."

"Wrong. Try again."

"Are you … I don't know."

"Who did you give that list to? Who did you promise to repay?"

"I don't know. That's not my list."

"Of course it's yours. Look at it. Pick it up and look at it."

"No. I don't want to touch it. It will make me ill."

"Just look at it, Feyhe."

"How do you know my name? Are you my doctor?"

"No. Who am I?"

"I don't know you. You're a crazy man. A Stranger. Leave my hotel room this instant or I'll call the front desk."

"Who am I, Feyhe. Look at me. Think. Tell me my name."

"You don't know your own name. You're pathetic." She spat at him, still too far across the room to be affected.

"I know my name. I know your name. You're the one with recognition difficulties."

"You're going to hurt me. Like the other man. You're going to hurt me." She was whimpering now, huddling against the bed pillows, pulling her legs up, her knees protecting her chest.

"I'm not going to hurt you, Feyhe. I love you."

"That's what he always says. But he hurts me."

"Who, Feyhe? Who hurts you?"

"The Japanese boy, Billy."

"I'm Billy. I don't hurt you."

"The Japanese boy, Billy." she said it again.

"That's Danny. He's Korean."

"That's the one. Billy, the Korean."

"I'm Billy. I'm Billy!" he shouted at her.

"Don't hurt me." She took a deep breath and let out a scream that made his ears nearly burst. He stepped back, opened the door and left her room. Two orderlies and a nurse came racing past him, bursting through the door and into Feyhe's room. They would restrain her, he knew, and they would inject her with more tranquilizers and she would calm, she would forget, she would settle in a torpor that would protect her from him, but not from Danny. Somehow Danny always eluded him, always managed to move past him. Danny was never going to leave them alone. He knew that now. He knew it with a certainty that made his blood boil with rage. He turned away from Feyhe's door, turned toward the elevator, and made his way out of the place that served only to calm, never to quell, never to protect.

23

It was his first big job in several years and he was nervous. He knew he had gotten the work through one more Feyhe-related fluke. It bugged him. He wanted to say no, to turn the business away, deflect the deeply felt reaction that tasted of gall, but he needed the money. Billy really needed the money.

For the first time since his mother had died he was facing a new set of challenges alone, without a support system in place. His father was dead. Owen was dead. Joe was out of his life, except for those rare occasions when Sandy managed to get them all together for a brunch or a dinner or a movie. Feyhe was absolutely no use. Her mind wandered into places Billy couldn't, or wouldn't, accompany her to in spite of her persistent invitations. Billy was truly on his own.

When Ostendorf had phoned him about the work Billy had expressed his surprise at the offer. The man, now in his late eighties, had been out of touch with Billy and Feyhe since the Kendalls had taken Billy under their sick, double wing.

"Billy, dear boy, it's Frederick Ostendorf," the voice on the phone said, "and I'm not sure you'll remember me. I used to know you."

"Well, of course I do," Billy had said. "How nice to hear from you, Frederick."

"Is it? That's kind."

"I hope you're well."

"For a man of my uncertain future, and that's my age talking, Billy, I am remarkably active." He coughed a few times. "If you know what I mean." He chuckled and Billy was sure he knew what the man was referring to in his less than oblique fashion.

"How can I help you?" Billy asked him.

"Well, do you remember the statue that Feyhe designed for me, then destroyed at my party?" Billy did. He said so.

"A dear friend of mine remembered it also and he was wondering if you had access to any of Feyhe's unsold pieces. He is opening a new gallery in SoHo and wants to permanently display something of hers. Not to sell it, understand, but to celebrate it."

"Well, there are a few things here and I know she has some in storage."

"Could he contact you for this, Billy-boy?"

Billy blushed at the use of the nickname, then let go of the emotions that brought on the color. "Please," he said. "Give him my number and I'll see what I can do."

"You are a dear man," Ostendorf chirped into the receiver. Billy's eardrum throbbed at the sound. "So nice to chat with you again." He hung up. No mention of Feyhe, no questions. Either he knew about her condition and didn't care, or he assumed she had died. Billy didn't know.

When the phone call came from the art dealer, Billy was ready to chat. He had gone to the storage room that Feyhe had always maintained on the upper west side of Manhattan and had spent the better part of a Tuesday inventorying the contents. There were five full male nudes, seven females, four groups of figures, slightly larger than life-size, a collection of busts and nearly forty abstract pieces, all curiously specific in style, all clearly Feyhe's work. In the apartment he added another seven pieces to the list. One in particular, a very late work, was clearly a bust of Kim.

"Mr. Duncan," said the man on the phone, a deep, lush baritone voice that washed over Billy, soothing him and intriguing him at the same time, "this is Adam Beck-Wright. Freddy Ostendorf tells me you have access to—"

"Yes, I do," Billy said, rushing into the conversation, taking a moment to seat himself before continuing the chat. This voice, this man's voice, was erotic, arousing, annoying. "I have a complete catalogue of what's available and I'm sure we can arrange something from my cousin's holdings that would work for your new gallery. I'd like to see the space before I make any suggestions. Is that possible?" He breathed a sigh, relaxing, distancing himself from that voice.

"There's nothing to see yet, actually," Beck-Wright continued, his voice once again penetrating to Billy's loins. "Right now it's merely 22,000 square feet of empty space in SoHo. I'd happily show it to you, but I haven't decided on a plan for it."

Billy choked back a furtive giggle that was attempting to break loose from the middle of his throat. He nodded, squirmed and physically wrenched himself into the conversation. "That would be great." He named a time when he would be able to journey downtown to the arts colony below Greenwich Village and Beck-Wright agreed to it. He gave Billy the address and they hung up simultaneously, without even a "goodbye" to end the chat. Billy sat very still until his heart stopped racing. Then he stood up slowly, straightened out his clothing and went to the bathroom where he turned on the shower. The water turned hot quickly and the room began to fill up with steam. Billy breathed in and out as slowly as he could, leisurely regaining his composure.

The space on Vesey Street was off the main drag of SoHo. West Broadway, running north and south, cutting through the heart of the district, was where most of the important galleries were located. The better wine bars and restaurants either graced this avenue or stood, highly visible, on the intersecting side streets. Vesey was two streets east of the main drag and Billy headed that way, cutting across Grand Street, not sure of the location of number 224. He spotted it easily. The Ironstone building was a classic, its first story glass windows rising sixteen feet, braced by ionic columns of gray marble. The three floors above the street-level gallery also showed large, high windows, each marked in the style of the late nineteenth century that had brought it into being. He let his eyes roll up the building, taking in the height and breadth of the construction. The exterior had been recently cleaned, and the marble and concrete structure gleamed in the half-light that the autumn afternoon allowed onto Vesey Street. He took a long step backward, his hand shielding his eyes from the glare off the top floor glass, hoping to get a good look at the roofline. The light defeated him and he felt his eyes begin to squint before he lowered them once again. A man was standing in front of him, braced against the column that bordered the first gallery window. At first glance, Billy couldn't tell if the man was inside or outside. He stepped forward and the light altered and the man waved. He was behind the glass. He smiled at Billy and pointed to his right, Billy's left, and disappeared in that same direction. A moment later, the large oak door swung outward and Billy moved forward, ready to see the inner sanctum.

"Welcome, Billy," the man said. "I'm Adam."

The second half of the introduction had been totally unnecessary, Billy said, as he knew the man from the sound of his voice. Adam Beck-Wright laughed when Billy said the words.

"People tell me all the time that I should be on the radio," he said.

Billy looked at Adam before speaking. He realized that he was shaking his head, indicating a "no" before he spoke, but he still said the word. "No. With your looks you should be on television."

Adam laughed again and took Billy by his upper arm, leading him into the space that would someday soon be his new art gallery. Billy was amazed at the size of the room they stood in. He said so.

"Behind that wall you see," Adam remarked, "there is a duplicate of this. I want to open it up with a large, wide graceful archway and join the rooms. There'd still be the second gallery, but it could accommodate a single artist if I needed that."

"I like it," Billy said.

Adam pointed toward the far left wall. "That comes out," he said. "This first room becomes half a *T*, an upside down *L*, if you will. And that's where the new stairway will go to the second floor galleries. I want to have five separate rooms on the second floor. One of those rooms is where I want the Baumann statue."

"Can I see it?" Billy asked. Adam nodded and led him to a ladder that reached up the seventeen feet, through a hole in the ceiling and on into the second floor space. Billy sprang onto the second rung and dashed up the ladder much more adroitly than he would have believed possible. Adam, equally agile, followed him up.

The second floor had a very different feeling to it. The ceilings were only ten feet high and the windows, smaller and narrower, brought in a different version of the light. Billy moved through the first and second rooms, already marked with struts and partially exposed wiring, and into the third room. This was a large, square space with no exterior lighting. This was a totally enclosed room with three large openings for doors or archways.

"This is her room," Adam said quietly. His voice was almost unbearably sweet, echoing slightly, an effect brought about by a large oriental gong that occupied a corner of the space. "I thought her work would look wonderful here. We can control all of the elements in this space. Nothing natural can interfere with it."

"This isn't a museum, though," Billy said. "You're creating a gallery. Selling art."

"I want this for her."

"Why?" He looked at Adam and for the first time saw that the man's perfect face was flawed. His head was oval, with his eyes set high against an angled brow that fled from his eyebrows into his widow's peak hairline. His nose extended the line forward, perfectly bisecting the face and shadowing his upper lip as it flared equally left and right. Adam's mouth was full, sensual, and slightly curved into a simple, casual smile. There was a scar under his left eye, almost two inches long, that cut along his high cheekbone and nearly connected with the tiny crow's feet at the outside extremity of the socket.

"When I was young I saw her work," Adam replied. "I could never forget it. I found something in it that touched me, made me hungry for art, hungry for the exquisite. When I met Frederick, many years later, he told the story about her mad destruction of her work on principles, principles he could never comprehend, Billy. I think I fell a bit in love with her that day. I was leaving New York, knowing I could come back only to do this, to do what I'm doing, and that I had to celebrate the artistry of the person who brought me to this. That's why."

"Where did you go?" Billy said, mesmerized.

"That's a story for after dinner, in front of a fire, with a brandy, don't you think?"

Billy nodded.

"Let me show you the apartment," Adam offered, taking Billy's hand. Billy nodded again and Adam led him to the freight elevator that Billy hadn't even noticed.

As though he'd known that Billy would stay for it, dinner was already prepared. Twilight played through the windows on the west side of the building, bordering this large open living room on the fourth floor of the building.

"You own the building?" he had asked in the elevator.

"No," Adam said. "My mother owns it. She'll give it to me under certain conditions, which I intend to meet."

Billy didn't ask the conditions. He was sure Adam would tell him when he wanted to, and not a moment before.

Dinner was simple. Cold potato soup, accompanied by an excellent Pinot Grigio, pot roast with root vegetables consumed with an Australian Shiraz, flan and coffee. Adam set and lit a fire in the large fireplace trimmed in green Portuguese-fired tiles. He tossed large embroidered cushions onto the deep pile carpet and offered Billy a place before the roaring flames, then offered him a snifter of a dark, rich, florid liquid. Billy took his place on the floor and Adam joined him after a moment.

"This is what heaven must be like," Adam said, giving voice to Billy's own thoughts. "Don't you agree?" Billy just nodded. He took a sip of the brandy, held it in his mouth, letting the aromas invade his nostrils from the inside out.

"This is lovely," he said.

"German," Adam said. "Asbach Uralt. I'm glad you like it."

"Asbach Uralt," Billy repeated, letting the words invade his mind as the spirits had done to his senses a moment earlier.

"I have such plans, Billy. May I share them with you?" Billy nodded again.

Adam went on to tell him everything. Every few minutes Billy nodded, sipped, nodded. He hadn't felt this alive in a long, long time.

CEMENT DUST

He was beginning to savor it.

It took Billy only three days to draft a concept for Adam's galleries. He was lucky, he knew, that so much had been planned already. He had started with the second floor, internal gallery that Adam wanted to dedicate to Feyhe's work. There were three pieces he wanted to feature there and he placed them expertly, lit them—in his drawing—from three vantage points each and gave them a depth and strength they certainly weren't exhibiting in storage. The first was an abstract piece, one he felt clearly represented her art at its best. It was a female breast emerging from a solid coarse piece of marble, beige and red and rough, with the exception of the breast itself which gleamed white, polished, perfect. The second was another of the abstract pieces, this time a man's genitals and part of his ass. Carved in a green Tuscan stone, this combination seemed to be pressing upward, out of a centuries' old stone tomb. There was an evident force behind the portion of male anatomy in the work. The third piece, also from the abstract group, was of the top of two human heads, seen from the eyes of each, the two forms pressed together, as lovers heads might be. Their eyes and their hair melded, yet separate, came out of a piece of blue-veined yellow stone that was soft to the touch, warmer than marble, cooler than flesh. There was something decidedly, if spookily, real about all three pieces.

Next he found a series of sketches left over from Feyhe's Korean experience, nature studies and human heads, that he wanted to place in specific locations around the room. He drafted them into place. Finally, the central figure for the gallery emerged from the middle of Billy's memory banks. He chose one of the groups of figures, again left over from the Korean experience. This was a group she had chosen not to include and so it had survived the slaughter of so many hard-hewn figures. A plaster sculpture, it portrayed two serving maidens, one kneeling, one groveling, offering their material wealth to the Emperor who seemingly was paying no attention to them, his eyes riveted on something unseen elsewhere. Perhaps, Billy wrote in his explanation of his choices, the Emperor was hearing the first sounds of the disruptive thieves who would end his reign in so short a time.

Once he had finished his work on this room, Billy absently sketched

341

a few ideas for the rooms that surrounded the Baumann Gallery. He hadn't thought as much of the layout as Adam had while presenting it. He had seen other ways to make the various spaces on the second floor really pay off. He had appended his sketches and sent them all off together. He hoped that Adam would like his choices and perhaps take his other suggestions in the way they had been meant.

When the phone jangled, he received his answer.

"You're a fucking genius," Adam said without introducing himself. "I never thought about using the inner window concept. What are you, Billy, a Shaker magnate or something?"

"No, not at all," Billy responded. "I saw that once in the brick residence at the Hancock Shaker Village in Massachusetts. I was impressed with the idea of transporting natural light into an interior space that way. I thought it might be a way to really use the vastness of that back gallery of yours. That's all."

"Well, you really took on a lot, didn't you?"

"I'm sorry, Adam. I didn't mean to be presumptuous here—"

"It's okay. I liked it. I just wish I'd thought of it."

They chatted a while, talking about nothing, then made plans to meet for a drink later that day. Billy hung up the phone and leaned back, relieved and almost overjoyed at the reaction his ideas had garnered. Once again his brief talk with Adam had left him elated. He got up, went to the bathroom and turned on the hot water tap in the shower, waiting for the steam to start rising.

He liked this method for controlling elation. He liked the soothing, hot steamy air. He liked the feeling of calm that came over him after just a few minutes of this unusual treatment he had learned from Owen. He also liked that it was Owen's idea. He missed the man, admitted to missing him when anyone asked him about it. He had hated leaving him, but knew that Owen had been right about the need to part. They had been too close, too dependent on one another.

Owen was dying and, apparently, he knew it long before Billy did. He had created a special distance that ultimately made it easier for Billy, a final gift from the man who had saved him from despair. And there was still this treatment for the unnatural highs that came with his illness.

He had one thing left to do before meeting Adam. He had to see Feyhe and tell her the plans for the gallery devoted to her work. He had left this for the end of the work, not wanting to jinx the project, hoping that she would be amenable to it. She still had to grant permission for the display of her work and Billy wasn't sure how she would take this news. He was right to worry.

In her private room at the Mary Magdalene Home on upper 5th Avenue, Feyhe was sitting up in a chair near the window when Billy entered. She didn't look up at him. Instead her attention was riveted to something in Central Park, directly across the street. She beckoned to him, as though he had been there for a long while, and he moved silently to join her at the window. He looked out. Nothing seemed to be different than any other day.

"Do you see him?" she asked in a whisper. "Over there, behind that double row of oaks. Do you see him?"

"See who, Feyhe?"

"Danny. That's Danny down there."

"I don't see him. I don't see anybody."

"It's him. I've seen him there every day this week. He watches my windows, Billy, hoping to see me. I always stay here, to the side, near the blinds. I don't think he can find me."

"I don't think it's Danny Kim, Feyhe. We're only a few streets south of Harlem and people of all types walk around up here. It could be anyone." He had glanced again out of the window and seen no one who even remotely resembled Danny. "Can we talk for a few minutes, Feyhe?" he asked her. "I need to discuss something important with you."

She nodded, turned her wheel chair hard and quickly pushed herself over to the door to her room. She beckoned him silently and hustled her chair out into the hallway. He caught up to and grabbed the handles at the back of the upright seat, but she waved her right hand at him, indicating that she didn't want his help. He followed her through the corridor, around two corners, past the bank of elevators and, finally, into a large open room filled with a long banquet-style table and a set of unmatched, industrial chairs.

"Sit," she said. He took a chair, pulled it away from the table, and sat down instantly. A woman in the room beyond this room, a woman standing at a sink, her arms deep in the sudsy waters that filled it, looked through the open door and shouted. "Room's closed."

"Yeah, yeah," Feyhe replied. She waved at the woman, looked up and smiled her most charming smile, then turned back to Billy. "Okay, we're alone and we're safe here."

"What do you mean, safe?" he asked her.

"No one can overhear us in this room, Billy."

"Why is that a problem?"

"It's a concern." She smiled at him this time, that same charming smile. "Communists." She nodded her head three times.

"Communists?" She nodded again.

"Here?"

"You may think this is a religious order, nuns and such, but its really dyed-in-the-wool commies. I know. I was married to one once."

"I thought Owen was a Socialist," he said.

"Owen was a commie. He was a good commie, don't get me wrong, but he was still a commie. I think he was a spy and I think he might have been training you as one, too." She smiled at him again. "Was he?"

"No."

"All right. We're alone. What's on your mind?"

He told her about Adam, his adulation of her, her work. He described the gallery in SoHo, the tribute gallery he had planned for Adam and about her work being permanently displayed. As he spoke, he watched her for reactions. He had no idea how this would affect her, how she might react. When he finished telling her about the room and had brought out his copies of the sketches, which now lay on the table between them, he sat back in his chair and waited for her to respond. He didn't have to wait long.

"Is he a fag?" was her first question.

"Yeah, he is," Billy said.

"Do you like him?"

"Yeah, I do, I guess," he answered.

"Will he hurt you?"

"I don't think that's a matter to discuss. I'm just helping him with this gallery."

"I know you, Billy," she said. "You'll fall for him and then it will be too late."

"I'm not the same guy you used to know, Feyhe. I'm different."

She shook her head. Her face was no longer lit by the charming smile. It had darkened with her expression.

"You'll always be Billy Duncan. Like me. Always the same Feyhe Baumann. I can't change me and you can't change you. Stuck."

"I have changed. I have, really," Billy insisted. "Don't you want this tribute gallery?"

"I'm not dead!" she shouted at him, the last word far too loud for her own good. She clutched her chest immediately after crowing it.

"It's not that kind of a tribute, Feyhe. This guy kind of worships the work you did, says he owes his artistic understanding to what you achieved. He just wants to celebrate that."

She leaned forward, getting so close to Billy that her breath, onion and old meat inflected, nauseated him when she spoke again. "Can I go to the opening?" She smiled again.

Billy took both her hands in his own, and stood up, putting some distance between their faces. He nodded. "Of course you can. I'll arrange it."

"I want a chauffeur to pick me up. I want a good dress. I want to have my hair done, dyed maybe. I want to not use the wheelchair, maybe the walker instead. And I want ribbons. All of them blue."

"Whatever it takes, Feyhe," Billy said. "Whatever."

Adam was overjoyed to get the news about Feyhe and her work. He was even happier to learn that she might be well enough to attend the opening. Over cocktails at Le Bernardin he informed Billy that he would do everything he could do to make the opening an occasion about Feyhe. Billy was reserved, but pleased.

"I won't let her come unless she's ready for it," he promised Adam. "I certainly don't want to see another scene like the one she made all those years ago at Ostendorf's."

"I'd pay ten thousand bucks to witness that," Adam said. "That must have been really something."

"It shocked us all. Terribly."

"I still think it would be worth it," he said, laughing about it again.

They talked about the drawings that Billy had sent along with his draft for the Gallery. Adam was even more impressed by the Duncan concepts than Billy had realized on the phone. They talked about the way light would be conducted and the sort of work they could display in such a light. They settled on watercolors and pastels and other types of drawings that would benefit from the infusion of natural, outdoor lighting. Neither one of them realized that they had slipped easily into "us" and "we" as they talked, the singular Adam having been left behind in the early stages of their planning. It wasn't until they realized that there was no longer any outdoor light intruding on their table, that candles and low soffit lighting had replaced the waning daylight, that they began to hear their conversation and the direction in which it had gone.

Billy was the first to notice. "I'm sorry about that," he said, changing the mood with the variation in topic. "I'm presuming an awful lot."

"You are, actually, but I'm not objecting to it."

He reached for Billy's hand, on the table. Billy pulled away.

"Why did you do that?" Adam asked him, that voice of his once again deepening and penetrating into Billy's senses.

"I don't think I'm ready...to answer that question."

"I didn't think I was ready to ask it, Billy."

Their waiter advanced on them, bringing them two oversized menus. Billy spoke to him first.

"No, thanks, really, I think we're about done here."

"Stay. Have dinner with me."

"No, I—"

"My mother is joining me in about twenty minutes. Stay. Meet her. Dine with us."

"I shouldn't, Adam. Really, I shouldn't."

"Shall I take those glasses, now," the waiter asked. Adam and Billy both nodded, agreeing. The standing man took the empty drink glasses, the two menus and silently departed.

"Really, Adam, I shouldn't," Billy said once more.

"I'd like you to meet her. Actually, I'd like her to meet you. It would help me, Billy." They sat in stillness. They started at one another.

"Why would it help you?" Billy finally asked him. "I don't understand."

He smiled. "I told you at dinner, the night we met at the gallery, that my mother owned the building and that she had agreed to give it to me under certain conditions."

"Yes, I remember that."

"These are the conditions," he began, but Billy stopped him.

"This is between you and your mom. I don't need to know any of this."

"You do," Adam said. "Just listen for a moment."

"Okay." Billy picked up his replacement drink and took a sip, found he had lost his taste for it, and put it back on the table.

"My mother's family has owned this place for over a hundred years. They ran their factories there, then later they leased the floors to sweatshops, then let them go for fancy residences—A.I.R. spots, you know 'artist-in-residence.' Well, those days are done. Not enough artists can afford those floors. They're enormous. I don't qualify for one, Billy. I'm not an artist. I have no talent whatsoever. Part of my mother's credo, when it comes to that building, is to establish one artist in residence. She told me that if I could do that, she would let me live on my own floor and manage my gallery, my dream gallery. I'm not an artist, but I appreciate good stuff. I know it when I see it, and I think I can market it."

"Okay, I see all that. So what do I have to do with this."

"You're the artist."

"No, I'm not."

"Yeah, you. You're the artist for the third floor."

"I'm not an artist."

"Of course you are."

"I'm not."

"I've seen what you can do. You can't convince me that you're not an artist. The layout of the Baumann Gallery, the concept of the inner window for natural light to the gallery, the Kendall house…"

"Excuse me, what?…the Kendall house?"

"Yeah, you designed that, right?"

"The Kendall house. In the village? You've seen it? You know them?"

"Sure, but—"

"I'm sorry, Adam, Mr. Beck-Wright, Adam, but I'm not staying around for—"

"Don't go, Billy, please," Adam implored. "Don't do this!"

He could feel the fear charging up his spine, through his gut and into his lungs. He needed to get clean, clear air. He needed his steam. He needed Owen. He stood up, his left hand clutching his napkin. He took a step away from the table and he heard the tinkle of glass followed by the crashing of more glass behind him. He turned to look and saw that he had grabbed the table cloth and not the napkin, that he had brought down the entire table, drinks, bowls, crystal candleholder, everything. Adam was still sitting, but had pulled himself backward into the hard surround of his chair. He was staring up at Billy, a horrified look on his face.

"All right, go," he said, his voice much lower than its normal volume. "Just don't make another scene about it. Go."

"It's just not right, Adam. Not the right time for this. I don't know what else to say to you."

"Billy, just go. Please." The look on his face was one Billy couldn't grasp. It wasn't anger. It wasn't pity. It was something else, something he recognized but couldn't identify or name.

Billy moved away, his hand still clutching the cloth. He wouldn't turn around again, couldn't turn around again. He walked into the reception room and out the door of the restaurant. He didn't look back, couldn't look back. He never stopped for his coat at the checkroom. He kept moving forward. His arm brushed against the arm of a woman who had just emerged from a taxicab. She stepped back, recoiled from him. He kept walking, forward, away, forward.

24

When Billy arrived at the Mary Magdelene Home on May 9, Feyhe had disappeared. He was fairly sure he knew what had happened, but he had no way to prove it and no one to prove it to. His parents were long gone. Feyhe's old friends had melted away into the deep shadows cast by New York City's smaller buildings. Joe was out of his life. Owen was dead. There were only Feyhe's peculiar cousins on her father's side of the family to talk to about her disappearance.

Billy had his theories, but there was nothing he could do about them. She had removed herself from his presence somehow. After twenty years in his life, she had disappeared and might be dead, might be alive somewhere doing who knows what.

Technically she was too weak to leave on her own and too close to destitute to have gotten beyond the greening trees in Central Park any way other than on foot. She hadn't even had bus fare. It was a mystery, to be sure, how she had gotten up from her modified hospital bed, put on clothes that couldn't possibly fit her any longer, got down a long and windy corridor to the elevator, rode down three floors, passed the front security desk, got out onto the circular drive that graced the old mansion the building had once been, down the walkway to the street and off to somewhere else. And on a rainy Thursday in May.

Billy could rattle off the many excuses he'd been given by the staff at the Mary Magdalene home. They ranged from the simplistic, "We're sorry, nobody noticed her, I guess." to the more fantastic, "Perhaps she disguised herself as a nurse."

Billy's own answer, easily distilled into one word, was "Feyhe." He could say this to himself out loud because he knew her, had made himself know her.

He called Joe. Joe sent a detective who took notes, took a photo that Billy had in his wallet, took a hike. Billy didn't expect to hear much from him again. He sat in Feyhe's room, her phone in hand, and called her cousins, told them the news. As usual they were of little help, only wanting him to answer questions about her money and her apartment and her possessions. He didn't enlighten them about the new exhibit. He wasn't even sure there would be a new exhibit now.

He finally called Kim and Ni-Na. He had resisted this, but knew it had to be done. Kim told him to stay at the hospital, that they would drive in at once and meet him there. Billy had wanted more, but he agreed to wait.

They came to the room an hour later. Billy's patience had long-since flagged. He was tired and hungry. He was angry, angrier than he'd been in a long, long time. When the Koreans entered Feyhe's room, he wheeled on them, physically and emotionally.

"Where the Hell have you been?" he demanded. "You make me wait here when I should be out in that park searching for her body. How dare you!"

"Billy, please remain calm for this instant," Kim said quietly. "We have, perhaps, news that will enlighten you."

Ni-Na said nothing, merely bowed her head, avoiding his eyes. She turned away slightly, almost as if fear of his intensity had made it impossible for her to participate in the conversation. Billy noted her actions, remembered their last encounter at the apartment and turned back to talk with Kim.

"What are you talking about? Be specific, Kim."

"You are thinking this is work by my son, Danny. Is that not what you have in your mind, Billy Duncan?"

Billy looked him the eyes, directly and unblinking before he answered. "He's been stalking her, Kim. We know it. Feyhe was afraid of him. She would sit here, behind the blinds, staring at the park, identifying every man she saw as Danny, afraid it was him."

"This is nonsense."

"I beg your pardon?" Billy knew his voice sounded the confusion in his mind.

"Nonsense. Every night Feyhe has called Danny and talked with him for many hours."

"That's nonsense."

"It is true. You can check with hospital records of phone use. Every night, Billy Duncan. She has kept him close to her."

"Why would she do that? She was scared shitless that he'd try something."

"She loves him."

"She fears him."

"So does his mother," Ni-Na said suddenly from within her former silence.

"You fear him, too?" Billy asked.

She nodded, then said, "but I love him. Feyhe love him also."

"He's a maniac and he ought to be locked up, Ni-Na."

"He is a boy, my boy, Feyhe boy."

"He is not harmless, Billy Duncan," Kim added. "He is cruel and he is short-tempered, but he is also loving and respectful."

"You know what he did to Feyhe and you call him loving and respectful?"

"I know what he do to all of us, and yes, I say he is loving and respectful. He cannot hurt more than he has done. He believes in an afterlife that will not allow him to participate. He is loving now. He is respectful now."

They were at a stand-off, now. Billy hadn't been left an objection, had barely survived with a question. He asked it.

"You said you knew something about Feyhe's whereabouts. You asked me to be calm. I am calm now. I have no anger left, Kim. What do you know?"

The Korean stared directly into Billy's eyes. For the first time in many years they were face to face and for the first time Billy felt neither a threat from this man, nor a jealousy. He only felt a deep humanity and a mutual sense of loss.

"Feyhe and Danny are together, Billy Duncan. Danny has fetched her and taken her to a safe place. She will not suffer more medical madness. She will not suffer more inhumanity from cousins. She will not suffer."

Billy gulped twice as he listened to Kim's litany of sufferings. "What do you mean, she won't suffer? What does that mean?"

"She is past suffering, Billy Duncan."

"She's dead, you mean."

"I not say dead. I say not suffer."

"I don't know what that means." He heard his own voice rising again, knew that his artificial calm had left him.

"Feyhe is now at peace in her heart and her mind. She is with Danny who love her and keep her warm and well."

"Danny couldn't keep a cockroach warm and well!"

"You not a nice man, Billy Duncan," Ni-Na screamed at him. "Not nice to Danny or to me."

"What I am or am not is hardly the issue. I want to know where Feyhe is."

"Feyhe far from you," she replied. "Feyhe happy at last."

"How would you know? Have you seen her?"

"I know." Ni-Na looked almost haughty as she said the words. Kim moved to stand next to her, put his arm around her waist.

Billy hadn't seen the man in several years and he was struck by the tableau he and his wife made, their very western clothes and her make-up, his hair and moustache, made them seem incongruously American. He blinked a few times, forming his next question, his renewed pursuit for information, real or otherwise.

"Where is she?" he finally mustered. "Tell me or I will call the police and you can tell them. It's your choice."

"She is safe. She is happy. Why must there be more?" Kim asked him.

"She is not well, Kim. Her physical and mental states are highly unstable. She needs medications, many medications. She needs attention."

"She has love. That is all she need."

"That is not all she needs. She needs her medicine."

"She has love."

Billy reached for the nearby, bedside telephone, dialed the operator and asked to be connected to the police. Kim and Ni-Na stood where they were, his arm still around his wife's waist. They both stared defiantly at Billy who never took his eyes off them.

When he was finally connected he asked for Joe. Through the second waiting period, he kept Kim and Ni-Na always in his sight. They had not moved, seemed to be planning no escape from the room. Finally, he had Joe on the line. He quickly explained what had transpired and then he listened as Joe told him what to do. He hung up the phone and moved around the hospital bed, closer to Kim and Ni-Na.

"The police are coming. You are to wait for them and go with them and tell them what you know. You can avoid telling me, if that's what you want, but you will tell them. You will tell them everything."

"I will not betray my son," Kim said. "For Feyhe I betrayed my wife, my family, my country. I will not betray her again, nor will I do so for my son."

Billy stepped as close to Kim as he ever had, closer than he remembered ever being to the man. He could feel the hot breath escaping from Kim's nostrils as it played against his cheek.

"You will rot in jail, Kim, rot in jail. And no one will care."

Standing like that, they waited for the police.

Sandy was sitting in her dressing room when the phone call came from Billy. She had already put on her costume and done her makeup and the fifteen minute call had come over the backstage PA system. When the doorman paged her with a phone call she was stunned. It defied protocol, but feeling sure it was an emergency, she went to answer the call.

"I've had Kim and his wife arrested," Billy said without even a "hello."

"I have to go on stage in a few minutes, Billy."

"They helped their son steal my cousin from her room. They won't say anything about where he's taken her, so I've had them arrested."

"That was the right thing to do, Billy. I have to go, now."

"I just had to tell someone."

"I understand. You did the right thing."

"Don't you think I know that? That's not why I had to tell you."

"Okay."

"I just had to share this. That's all."

"It's shared, Billy. Bye."

She hung up the phone and went back up the two flights to her dressing room. She didn't close the door, didn't sit down. She just stood there and looked at herself in the mirror. She couldn't see her own face, but she could see her body, her maturity, her self-assurance. She could almost see Billy's head, his face, floating above the mirror, smiling sweetly with a different sense of himself. She laughed. She had misjudged his call. It was just sharing. It was a choice, an adult choice. She laughed again.

Joe was waiting at the police station when Billy arrived, twenty minutes after Kim and Ni-Na had been taken into custody. He stopped Billy as he entered and ushered him into a small interrogation room just off the main offices. He looked worried and Billy saw it at once.

"Don't do this, Billy. You'll regret it if you do."

"I'm having them charged, Joe. That's what I'm doing."

"Don't. They don't know anything. I'm sure of it. They're only trying to protect their son."

"Their son is a criminal who kidnapped my elderly and feeble cousin. They know where he is, where he's taken her. I want them charged as accessories."

"Don't, Billy, really. Think about it rationally. You'll see I'm right."

"Joe, they've behaved badly. They've aided and abetted him. They're as guilty as he is."

"Of what? Loving him? It's not a crime."

Billy gave Joe a short punch, just hitting him slightly in his ribs. Joe flinched, but stood his ground.

"If loving is a crime, Joe, then we've been guilty of it ourselves."

"We have. According to the law."

"Well, the law is shit."

Joe smiled at Billy but he refused to return the sweet gesture. "Billy, get over this, please.

Let them out of this. They stand to lose a lot more than you do."

"Feyhe is missing, Joe. What don't you get about this? Danny Kim kidnapped her, took her by force, is holding her somewhere for some reason I don't even want to interpret. What's wrong with holding his parents as—?" He stopped mid-sentence.

"Exactly," Joe said. "You get it now?"

"This is revenge, isn't it? My revenge."

Joe nodded. Billy stood very still, unsure how to proceed. Joe stepped forward and embraced Billy, who let himself relax into the embrace, then pulled himself out of it.

"I have to go make this right, Joe. I have to make something right."

He turned and left the room. Joe sighed a bigger, longer sigh than he ever had before. It seemed to him as though someone had turned off the lights in this room, that it had darkened and that he was alone in the center of a space that had no definition. A tear formed in his eye, but he rubbed it away before it began its trek to his cheek.

Adam was in his top floor studio, sipping a buttery Chardonnay when the doorbell sounded. He hadn't been expecting anyone, so he didn't rush to answer the clanging bell. The ringing persisted; the ringer was convinced Adam could hear, that he was home, that he would be there. Finally, he put down the glass and walked toward the elevator door where the response bell and talk-box was located.

"Yes! Who?" he said curtly.

"Adam, it's Billy Duncan."

Adam gave a quick look around the room, for reasons he wouldn't have been able to explain had anyone asked him. His hand was still poised over the talk button. He hesitated, then shifted its position and without another word, he pressed the door release button instead. He heard the faint sound of the door opening, the door closing, its heavy metal clanging as it shut. The elevator whirred into movement and, without waiting for the full round-trip, he wandered back to his kitchen, removed a second wine glass from its shelf and filled it with the rich, yellow wine. When the gate snapped open, he was ready, the wine in his hand, his hand extended in welcome.

It took only three days for police to finally come up with an answer. Ridiculously simple, it was an embarrassment to them, to Billy, to the home itself. Feyhe had been taken for a ride in a wheelchair by one of the nursing attendants, a young Korean boy who had worked there since a week after Feyhe's arrival. The boy, Danny Kim, had been employed under another name and no one had paid any attention to him.

At Billy's insistence, the police widened the scope of their investigation to discover that Danny, under the same assumed name, had worked at both the mental hospital and at Columbia Presbyterian also while Feyhe had been a patient in both places. Danny had never been away from Feyhe; Feyhe had seen him daily, just as she had indicated.

Billy wanted to kick himself.

"How could I have been so stupid, so blind not to realize…?" he said out loud more than once to more than one person. No one had a good answer for him. It was Adam who came up with the only sane solution to Billy's internal monologue.

"Forget it, sweetie," he said bluntly. "It's like in the *I Ching*. No blame. At the bottom of so many readings in that book of knowledge there is the line 'no blame.' That's where you have to get to now, to the bottom of the reading."

"I don't know what you mean," Billy said.

"With each reading in the book of changes," Adam continued,

"there is a philosophical structure followed by an interpretive picture followed by a moral command or stance." He reached over his shoulder to a small jar on the counter and dumped out a group of small, oriental coins, circular with square cuts in them. As he spoke he tossed them six times, each time noting on a piece of paper the result of the throw. "You start with the philosophy—like this—a number nine, for example, Hsiao Ch'u, the taming power of the small."

"How do you know about these things?" Billy asked him.

"Please, sweetie, I've been throwing the Ching coins since I was eleven." He gave Billy a healthy example of smiling, then continued. "The taming power of the small—the judgement reads the taming power of the small has success. Dense clouds, no rain from our western region."

"What the hell gobble-di-gook does that mean?"

"You know, Billy, with that attitude, my mother will love you. It means a lot of different things. First we look at the image, okay? It has to do with the state of affairs in China at a particular time and it has relevance to today. The wind drives across heaven—that is the image of the taming power of the small. Thus the superior man refines the outward aspect of his nature. Get it?"

Billy shook his head, a definite *no* even if unspoken.

"Look, wind, it's all air. Nothing about it is permanent or great. So, nothing such an individual does can have a long-lasting effect on anything. Look, here's how this looks when you diagram the throw. A nine on top, a nine in the second place, then a six, then three more nines." Adam drew the lines as he spoke them—two unbroken ones, a broken line and below them three unbroken.

"Now, at the bottom a nine means *return to the way; how could there be blame in this? good fortune.* The book interprets that as being the nature of a strong man to press on, even with obstructions, and to achieve something worthwhile. The second nine, going up the structure here is interpreted as *he allows himself to be drawn into returning; good fortune.* Sometimes just pushing forward isn't enough, or isn't possible. You are advised to turn back, revisit the past and that's also a good thing."

"Okay, I get that," Billy said. "What else happens here?"

"The third nine reads as *the spokes burst out of the wagon wheels; man and wife roll their eyes*. Now I admit that's a bit obscure, but the book tells us that force was used to push forward and the pressure of such an ill-advised act has caused pain and torment and the people involved don't know how to proceed. See, it's not so confusing when you read each aspect.

"The six in the fourth place means *if you are sincere, blood vanishes and fear gives way; no blame*. See, no blame. I quote the book here, sweetie, *the power of disintegrated truth is greater than all obstacles*. Do you get it: *dis-integrated truth*—not disintegrated or falling apart, but not integrated, lies, half-truths, meaningless confusions. Okay?"

Billy just nodded.

"Now, a nine in the fifth place means *if you are sincere and loyally attached, you are rich in your neighbor*. Loyalty, sweetie, it leads to firm ties like yours to Feyhe and that means you complement one another. In the weaker person we're looking at devotion and in the stronger it consists of trustworthiness. I think you see where I'm going with this one, right?"

Billy looked at Adam and shook his head again, another *no*.

"All right, let's just move up one more rung and then we'll talk about it all. Nine at the top means *The rain comes, there is rest. This is due to the lasting effect of character*.

Perseverance bring the woman into danger. The moon is nearly full. If the superior man persists, Misfortune comes. A biggy, no? Look, success is so close here. The wind, down here at the bottom has driven up the rain here at the top. It's been a hard, unsteady climb up this ladder, and it follows that you have to exercise caution, you need to rest. The woman, the weak element has won the battle, but she can't flaunt it—it's too dangerous. Now the dark power of the moon is at its height when the moon is full. It was a full moon when Feyhe disappeared, right? Right. But when it's up against the sun, even the full moon wanes. There's an eclipse or something. Under these circumstances both parties have to be content with what they've achieved. To move forward now—too quickly, too soon, would be a disaster. And that's the Ching."

He sat back, letting the message settle into Billy's brain. Billy still looked confused.

"And how do you know these things?" he asked Adam again.

"I learned them at my darling mother's knee," he replied. "I know it's all strange and a little bit vague, but when you read the coins and read the words and read the interpretations over and over, you come to realize that there are patterns and we fall into them. We don't have to be controlled by anything more than our own wishes, but we do have to pay attention to those wishes and understand them for what they really are. We know who we are, Billy. We know it from the time we're born. We just don't have the tools to understand what we know, not from birth any way. That comes with experience, with finding the source of information. I find it in the Ching."

"So you think, from this Ching thing, that what happened to Feyhe was supposed to happen. You think my closeness with her was unavoidable and had to lead to this?"

"In a way, yeah," Adam said. He poured them both some wine.

Billy took the glass from him and sniffed it, stared at its deep, richly glimmering red color. He looked through the glass at Adam to find Adam staring back at him the same way.

"If we threw the coins about us, what would we find? What structure? What sense? No blame?"

"I don't know. Should we do that now?" Adam grabbed the coins again.

"No. Billy quickly stopped him. "I'd rather take my chances without knowing too much."

"You showed up on my doorstep, Billy Duncan, three night ago, like a demented visionary, hair wild and eyes wilder. I took you in and held you for a long, long while and when we moved apart you said something to me, do you recall the words?"

Billy didn't. He tried to think back, such a short time past, and he couldn't even see the picture Adam had described.

"You don't, I can see that," Adam said softly. "Let me tell you what you said." He took a sip of his wine. Billy could see one drop, caught in corner of Adam's mouth and he reached across the small teak table to where Adam was sitting and he wiped the drop away with one finger. They smiled at each other. "You said, Billy, 'My only friend in this world is gone forever.' Those were your words to me as I held you."

"I'm sorry," Billy said.

"No, don't be. You were perfectly right. I'm not your friend. I've lied to you about knowing you in the past. I did meet you. I lied to you about a few other things as well. I did pursue you. I did pursue you for my own purposes, but you did something to me that I hadn't anticipated. You made me like you. So I've not been your friend and your words were correct."

"I'm still sorry. I was upset and I shouldn't have let things go so far."

"I'm still lying to you, Billy. I don't like you. It's more than that for me. I can't get you out of my mind, day and night. I don't know why. I don't know how to handle it. I only know that it's real."

"Are you talking about love, Adam?"

Adam laughed a harsh, single burst of sound. His inescapable smile followed the laugh. "I don't know what that word means. I don't." His smile turned into a frown. "I understand obsession. I comprehend submission. But love? Perhaps one day."

"I loved my cousin. I still do. I can't explain that either, Adam. I want to know where she is, that's she's all right, that she's not in pain. I'm afraid I'll never know it all."

"When you know anything, you must share it with me, Billy. We'll learn some of these things together, won't we? Can we?"

Billy leaned across the table and gave Adam a short peck of a kiss on his cheek.

"If you'll let me be a part of your life, Adam, we can teach each other many things, I think."

There was a sudden cry from outside the loft, so sharp and shrill that it disturbed both men at the very same moment. Billy snapped his head around in the direction of the sound, and Adam leaned forward, sitting up on his bent and crossed knees. Then he laughed. Billy turned to him.

"That was the wind, Billy, the first step in your Ching reading. *The superior man refines the outward aspect of his nature.* We're on our way to understanding."

25

S andy lifted her glass to the others, receiving their birthday toast with grace. Billy was standing in the doorway, Adam behind him holding his mother's hand. Joe was seated on the divan in the larger gallery.

"To your legitimate years," Billy said loudly, his voice purring a bit as he said the words.

Then he giggled and Adam joined his laughter with Billy's.

Joe rose instantly and took his daughter by the hand, pulling her close to him. He kissed her lightly on the forehead, raised his glass in a similar gesture to Billy's and drank fully half its contents. "And welcome back to New York."

"That's quite a slog, Daddy," she said to him.

"Leave the man alone, Sandy," Billy called out to her. "He can't believe you're twenty-one and neither can the rest of us." Adam laughed again and his mother shushed him. He quieted down instantly. "And we're all so glad that Hollywood let you out of its clutches and that you're back to Broadway," Billy concluded.

"Or at least West Broadway," Adam added with a wink.

They were all in the Feyhe Baumann gallery, surrounded by her work, her visions made solid. The exhibit had been on display for just over a year; Feyhe herself had been missing for fourteen months. Nothing had been heard from her, nothing of her. Nothing, that is, except the superb reviews of her work by the critics who had attended the opening of the gallery. She was suddenly the hit of the city, the hottest thing on the art circuit that year. Money had been literally shoved through the transom of the building as peopled clamored to obtain an original Feyhe sketch, or etching, or carving. Every penny had been carefully accounted for, deposited in an account administered by Billy. Oddly, with all the money coming in, Feyhe had not been in touch with him and, equally oddly, Danny Kim had not been found or heard from either.

"I really thought it was all about money," Billy had confided in Joe a few months before this party. "I really thought that when the news hit about her sudden popularity, she'd be back, or he'd be in touch about her money. But I've heard nothing. No one has."

"Maybe they're not reading the same papers you are," Joe said.

"I let Kim and Ni-Na know, so if they had been in touch with him, he'd know and then she would, too."

"And Kim hasn't asked for any of this?" Joe wanted to know.

"No. He's been very distant, very apart."

"He is the heir, isn't he? She did adopt him."

"She did, but he sent me a letter claiming he wouldn't profit from her new success. He feels guilty about Danny, I guess."

"All right, then."

Adam joined them, his mother trailing behind a step or two. She was an inch shorter than her son and equally striking to look at. Like her son, her head was oval with the same dark eyes set high against an angled brow. They had the same widow's peak hairline, but her hair was a perfect black while his was dark brown with reddish highlights that intruded without warning.

Her nose perfectly bisected her face and shadowed a full, sensual mouth, not unlike her son's mouth. Seeing them together often gave Billy the impression of an original work of art and a fine copy that managed to slightly improve upon its source.

"I think it must be time for Sandra to open her gifts, William," she said softly. No one had ever called him William, but Virginia Beck-Wright insisted on the less familiar form of everything. "Why don't we repair to the apartment?"

As though commanded, the elevator door stood open and waiting.

The small group of celebrants boarded the large, rustic conveyance and ascended to the loft above. As they exited the lift, Billy heard Sandy's exclamation of surprise at the spectacle set before her.

Billy and Adam had constructed a gazebo in the center of the living room of their loft, built entirely of 8 by 10 glossy professional photos of Sandy taken from her album. They showed her from childhood through a sitting just a few days before for new glossies that she needed for auditions. In all, Billy had used just over six hundred photos for the structure. Its floor was covered with gift-wrapped boxes, each of them enveloped in photocopies of Sandy's reviews.

"I don't believe this," Sandy was shouting. "How did you do this? How?"

"Adam helped," Billy said.

"But where did you get these pictures? And…oh, my God, the reviews, how did you…?"

"I've saved them for years, honey. And Xerox makes a wonderful copier."

"But Billy," she threw herself into his arms and hugged him as tightly as she could manage. She was crying and kissing him and laughing, all at the same time. Then she whispered into his ear, "I couldn't love you more if you were my mother…or my father." Billy just hugged her back and tried to not blush.

When she finally loosened her hold on Billy, Joe was there to support her. She felt weak. She turned from Billy to Joe, then back to Billy, then to Joe again. As she moved she could see the sweet smiles of the others.

"You are my family, now," she said to them all as she moved. "Each of you has a part in my life and in my heart. I'll never forget this."

"Sandra, you are such a talented young thing, I should hate you, but I don't," Virginia said. "I have a special present for you. Let me get it. Shall I?" She hesitated for a very brief moment before breaking the contact and moving toward the gazebo. She picked up a box and turned back to the group, handing it to Sandy who took it with shaky hands.

"What is it?"

"A gift. Open it."

"Should I?" she asked the room, no one in particular but Billy and

Joe, in fact. They both nodded and she sat down on a cushion that Adam had placed on the floor for her. She held the large box in both hands and it landed on her lap as she crossed her legs, sitting. First, before unwrapping, she glanced at the reviews that had been blown up and multiplied and used as gift paper. A smile broke out across her face that promised to light up the building-front across the street.

"These are from my high school play," she giggled. "Even then I got better notices than my fellow players. How embarrassing!" Everyone joined in with their own laughter.

Sandy carefully unwrapped the paper from the box, obviously wanting to preserve it.

Adam left the group to fetch another bottle of Segura Viudas champagne. Joe followed him to the kitchen and when Adam turned to the counter, he found himself face-to-face with Billy's former lover.

"Oh, Joe, I didn't realize—"

"Not to worry. I just wanted to thank you for everything you've done for her."

"She's special to Billy. That makes her special to me, too."

"He wanted to be her other father, you know."

"I know."

"I couldn't let that happen for some reason. I still don't get it."

"I know."

"But thanks. This means so much to us both."

"I know, Joe. You don't have to keep thanking me."

"Okay, thanks." He moved away, hurrying back to see what Sandy had discovered in the box. Adam followed after a moment.

Virginia's gift turned out to be gift certificates for seven different, rather posh, stores located on 5th Avenue.

"This is so generous, Virginia. So very generous, how can I thank you?" Sandy said, sweet, genuine.

"Just use them in good *taste*, dear." Virginia gave her the benefit of another moneyed smile. Sandy impulsively moved forward to the couch and gave Virginia a kiss.

Billy reached into the gazebo and pulled out another box. "This one is from Joe," he said. "Oh, dear," Joe whispered a bit too loudly. Adam poured him another glass of champagne and moved away from him to refill other glasses.

Sandy opened this box as carefully as she had the first one, reading the reviews, commenting, carefully prying loose the tape and ribbons. Joe had given her several things, one of which was in this box. It was a bank book with an accrued balance of over fifty-six thousand dollars.

"The interest hasn't been adding much these last years," he said to her, "but in the early days compounding was pretty great."

"When did you start it?" she asked.

"I opened the account the day your mother told me she was pregnant. I put in fifty dollars, which wasn't so easy to do back then. I added to it every paycheck."

The crying and kissing that followed allowed the others to finish the bubbly in their glasses and get a refill from Adam.

Adam's gift was a simple one, a painting he had commissioned of Sandy from one of her portrait stills. Painted by Romaine Hartung, it was an excellent representation of the spirit and the polish of the young woman who held it close to her breast.

Billy's gift was next. It was in the largest box and that box contained another well-wrapped box and then another and another, until Sandy had opened nine boxes, each one smaller than its predecessor. In the final box there was a key.

"What's this for?" Sandy wanted to know. Her voice, demanding but soft, betrayed her impatience.

"You'll have to wait to find out," Billy said.

"Wait for what?" she demanded.

"Wait for the right moment, that's all."

"And when is that, pray?"

"When I say it's so," Billy said, pressing his forefinger against the bridge of her nose. She grabbed his finger and twisted it slightly. "Oh, no, you don't. I'm not a child any longer, remember?"

"Ow! I know." He pulled his hand loose from hers. "I'll tell you when I tell you." He quickly moved away from her but, before getting too far, she called after him.

"Wait a minute. What about the other box?"

Billy turned back to look at her, then at the gazebo. There was, indeed, another box in the structure, although this one was not wrapped in the same sort of paper. He moved forward and picked it up. It was clearly weighty, wrapped in plain brown paper, an extended cube with a mailing label on the side he held away from himself.

"It's addressed to you, Billy," Sandy said, reading the label upside down, her head turned awkwardly to see it. The brown paper-covered box's label was without a return address, but the postmark, clearly readable, indicated it had come South Carolina. "It's for you, not for me."

Billy turned to look at Adam who just shrugged. The others seemed equally unsure about it. Then Virginia spoke.

"I put it there, actually. When I came in tonight it was in the hallway and I just thought it was something for Sandra. So I brought it up here and added it to the others. All right?"

Billy took the package, the oddly heavy package, and brought it over to the kitchen counter. He pulled a large carving knife off the magnetic rod that held it, along with a host of others, on the wall above the counter. He slit the paper and released one end of the box. This allowed him to slip another box out of the first one.

"Looks like your own idea's following you around," Joe laughed.

"I don't think so," Billy responded as he slid out the second box. It was a plain, black plastic container with a latch in the center of one side that slipped over a hollow sprocket that inserted itself into the latch and looped halfway to the right to form a tightly closed lid. The new box sat there untouched as they all looked at it. It was an oddity. None of them had ever seen anything quite like it before.

Billy was still holding the shipping box and he looked inside it, now seemingly empty, checking for anything else, a note, a card, some explanation. He shook it once, hard, with a violent, jerking action. A piece of paper fell out of it and landed on the counter. Billy reached for it. It was folded in half and then in half again. He carefully unfolded it, while the others waited. They watched his face as he read the contents of the page now spread before him. He paled, then turned red, than paled again as his eyes seemed to twist in their sockets.

"What is it, boy?" Adam said to him.

"Billy?" Joe said instantly. "Are you all right."

Billy held up his right hand, the note still clutched in his left hand, pausing, then thrusting them back into silence. He swallowed hard, twice, then he took a deep breath, letting it out slowly after holding it in for as long as he could. Then he forced a smile, which instantly faded from his face.

"It's Feyhe," he said so softly that no one was sure he'd spoken at first. He spoke louder the second time he said the words. "It's Feyhe. She's dead. These are her ashes. In the box. Feyhe."

He turned away from them. The knife he used to cut open the shipping box was suddenly in his hand again. He looked at it, not understanding how it had gotten there, whether he had picked it up a second time or hadn't put it down at all. His confusion threatened to expand, to overtake all else, when he acted without choosing to do so. He raised his arm to its full extension and, using every ounce of force in his arm and shoulder, thrust the knife straight down into the counter-top. Virginia jumped back to avoid the angry man's vengeance and Joe did the same, pulling Sandy with him. Adam grabbed Billy's arms and turned him quickly away from the knife, which had not penetrated the hard, Corian-covered shelf, but lay there, bent and distorted instead.

"Billy, get a hold on your emotions. Now. Do it." Adam called to him.

"Get your hands off me, Adam," Billy snarled.

Adam slapped him across the side of his face and Billy, startled, began to cry. In the midst of friends, of family, he stood alone, solitary, trembling, then fell forward into Adam's arms and allowed himself to be held as he let the sobs he had stifled for so long wrack his body. Words poured from him that made no connections, no sense. He babbled and he laughed, and the crying, which dominated all else, lessened with each twist and emotional turn he took. Adam held him through it all. Sandy had turned to be held by her father, shaken at the sight of Billy crumbling this way. Joe led her back to the couch where her gifts stood and the special gift papers lay neatly folded.

Virginia finally broke the silence.

"And the package was from whom?" she asked. Her question, so uninformed, brought a very self-conscious chortle from Billy, followed in echo from Joe.

"Probably the boy," Joe said, speaking quickly, speaking first.

"Yeah, probably," Billy conceded. "He must have gotten this address from Ni-Na, his mother."

"This is the boy who stole your cousin from the nursing home?" Virginia asked him.

"The very one," Billy said. "One and the same."

"Why would he do this?" Sandy asked.

"He found out there's no money," Billy said. "It's really all that simple. What could he do with her ashes? Nothing. So he sent them to me." He laughed again. "It's probably the first unselfish act in his life." He laughed once more. "He's spent more on her in death than he ever could have in life. Cremation and a shipping label. That's his gift to her."

"Well, I think we should add those ashes to the room downstairs," Adam said. "What could be more fitting?"

"Don't be morbid, Adam," his mother said instantly.

"Morbid? I think it's right," Billy responded. "I think it's just perfect."

"How do we change this morbid mood? It is a birthday party, guys," Sandy said.

"Let's find out what the key fits?" Virginia suggested. "Even if we have to tickle it out of Billy." She took a mock-menacing step in his direction, her hands extended, fingers parted and crooked.

"Wait! Don't! I'll tell!" Billy shouted, his mood altered by the mere thought of being tickled. "Sandy—the apartment, upstairs, here—yours," the words tumbled out of him surrounded by giggles at the thought, the concept, of being tickled into submission.

"You angel!" Sandy leaped on him and Adam joined her in the effort. Virginia backed off and joined Joe watching the three younger people at their game.

"I like it," she said softly. "He's good for both of them, and your daughter is good for them as well. And Adam, he's going to be just fine."

Joe said nothing. He just watched and grinned.

It was six weeks later that the truth became evident. Billy had contacted the Mary Magdalene Home about Feyhe's death and they had requested permission to conduct a small memorial service to their most famous, former inmate. Billy had agreed, given them a list of addresses, relatives, and a few old friends, and they had sent out invitations. He prepared a short eulogy, and discovered that one of Feyhe's cousins, one of the "other side" folks, had done the same. That seemed like a fitting tribute, two eulogies and an invitation to others to speak if they cared to. He felt they were doing the right thing. He even agreed to bring the ashes along.

The day dawned bright. It heated up intensely by early afternoon and when four o'clock rolled around the air inside the community room on the first floor of the Mary Magdalene Home was slightly rancid. The room was cold in spite of the day's unusual hot weather, the gray linoleum floor and the metal folding chairs adding their own chill to the place. One large potted palm stood in a corner, its own health seemingly tied to the physical condition of the occupants of the building.

Feyhe's other cousin had asked to speak first, and Billy agreed. He was in no great hurry to stand up in front of so many strangers and speak.

The girl, who had stayed with Feyhe for a short time before the flight to San Francisco, was dressed in quiet shades of green. The color didn't flatter her, but Billy knew that telling her that wouldn't help anything, so he remained silent on the subject. She introduced herself and began to speak.

"My cousin Feyhe was a special sort of woman, an inspiration to my mother and to me."

"She had a strength that we so admired." Billy put a hand discreetly across his lips, hiding the out-of-control smile that had spread instantly at her opening statement. "She had a clarity that we aspire to. She had the foresight to predict her end and she took the proper steps to assure that we would not be left without something of her. In her will, she left my father, my mother, my brother and me samples of her best work. To each of us she gave a personal piece of art that expresses her hope for us and for our future." Billy smothered an actual guffaw, then gained control of his face again. "Such an amazing thing to do, to pick out and deliver to us, so very much of her best self. She was good to me, kind to me when I was younger and so very needy. She was sweet with her advice and her help. She loaned me money and refused repayment when I was working. She prepared the way for me and my brother as we grew up and she never failed us by showing us her own values and making them our own. My father knew her best, of course, knew her the longest. They were devoted. Always in one another's company, they shared intimate secrets and discoveries from childhood until shortly before her death. He will miss her the most, I know, of anyone." Billy stifled an impulse to raise his hand, wave it about and interrupt. "As her executor, he will be the one to bring her back to prominence in the world of art and he will be the one to share in the glory that is, really, hers alone. Feyhe, without you we wouldn't be who we are today and we thank you for that. Rest well in eternity."

She sat down in a short blaze of limited glory, applauded by her parents and her brother and by one or two strangers who had come with them to the memorial. A few elderly inmates of the home applauded as well. As the mini-furor died away quickly, Billy stepped up to the podium.

He surveyed the small group of mourners, nodded to the few he knew, acknowledged Kim and Ni-Na, Joe and Sandy, Adam and Virginia. Then he drew out the prepared statement he had brought with him, unfolded the pages slowly and carefully, and looked up at the group before speaking. He found himself smiling, holding onto a secret that he shared with Joe, with no one else but him. Then he began.

"For over twenty years Feyhe and I have fought with one another, loved one another, been the person that each of us sought out in times of need, times of trouble, times of great success. Without her help I might never have achieved some of my goals, created some of my best work. Without her guidance I might never have had the friends and associates whose closeness helped make me the man I am today." For a moment after this statement he paused, his mind inexorably equating this opening with his bar mitzvah speech. He looked around the room at the faces turned his way. Then he continued. "But even so, without

Feyhe in my life I might have actually had a life. She was an exhausting person, exasperating to the N'th degree. In devotion to me she was stellar, always turning the best occasions in my professional life into her personal moments. That was frustrating. She should have been better behaved." There was an audible gasp from the female cousin. Billy shot her a quick glance, as if saying *I was quiet for you and your nonsense, now you shut up for me.* Instead he just looked at her, looked away, and then continued. "But the thing we need to remember about Feyhe was that no matter how awful she behaved at times, she was always genuine and sincere. When her drugs no longer controlled her moods she could be insulting and even dangerous, but there was a certain strange charm about that danger, that insult. You hated it at the time, but you never forgot it and, over a period of days or weeks, it became less hateful, more inspiring in an odd way. That was her real value to me and to so many others—she inspired. She suffered from manic-depression, suffered greatly and we all suffered along with her. Still, she managed to teach me many things in both stages of her mania.

I learned how to be honestly expressive from her depressed states, how to enjoy the smallest details in anything I do from her manic ones. It may not seem like a lot, but it was a gift. I won't miss her very much. She took a lot of time, a lot of care, a lot of worry. I know you heard her cousin here talk about the time she and her family spent with Feyhe and how much they meant to one another. Frankly, I never saw that. But I wasn't with her twenty-four hours a day, so maybe their perceptions are absolutely correct. What I know for certain is that she touched their lives as she touched mine and probably all of yours in some way. That's really the best thing a person can do in this life—touch someone else's life. That Feyhe did."

He sat down again and waited for anyone else to step up and take the podium. When no one else did, he stood up again, thanked them all for coming and announced that cookies and punch were being provided at the back of the room. When he looked over at Feyhe's cousins, he saw them glowering at him. He gave them a jaunty wave, and turned away, but the female cousin was behind him immediately, tapping on his shoulder.

"That was a terrible eulogy," she said to him without so much as a hello preceding it. "How dare you say such terrible things about her?"

"These moments are for painting pictures, telling truths, remembering the person," he said.

"Well, she's ours again," the girl responded. "We were nicer about her and we want her ashes."

"No thanks," Billy said. "They were sent to me and I'll take care of them."

"We deserve them," she insisted. "My father wants them and he'll sue to get them."

"Why does he even want them?"

"They represent her to him. He wants them."

"Well, you know what represents her to me? I'll tell you and you can tell that mean old fuck, your father, what I said. What represents Feyhe to me is spirit, not ashes. She had spunk, she had spirit, she had nerve and an intensity that took hold of your mind, your imagination. She wasn't a pile of ashes, she was a personality, a force. If he wants the physical remains, he can sue me for them. What he'll never possess is the woman she was, the energy, the inspiration, the incredible personality. In the meantime, here, give him this," and he reached into the box he was carrying, took a pinch of Feyhe's remains and tossed them at the young woman, who was instantly flailing at the front of her dark, silk suit, brushing away the drifting remains of Feyhe that had dotted her clothing for a moment or two.

"Oh, you're hateful!" she spat at him.

"It's a family trait," he said smiling at her. "I get it from Feyhe."

He moved away from her, leaving her fuming. He got about ten feet away when one of the inmates of the Home stopped him with an odd gesture.

"Yes? How can I help you?" Billy asked the elderly, fragile woman.

"Feyhe was supposed to leave me money," she said to him in a high, barely audible voice, more than a whisper, but only just a bit more. "My name is Ellen Rubinsky and I knew her here. She promised me thirty thousand dollars if she died."

"Why?" Billy asked, astounded at the sum mentioned.

"I used to read her the newspaper," came the reply.

"And that gets you thirty grand?"

"It's what she promised me."

Billy pointed toward Feyhe's cousin, deep in conversation with his still miffed daughter. "See that man. He's the executor." She nodded at him and began to shuffle off in the direction of the "family."

Without even a single breath for a break, another elderly soul was approaching him. "Did she get her thirty thousand?" asked the old person, gender to be determined, Billy thought,

"'cause I want what she promised me, too."

"Excuse me, but my cousin promised you money, also?"

"Twenty-two thousand dollars and a pocket watch from France," said the old man, now a man for sure, Billy realized.

"Why? What did you do for her?"

"I made the phone calls," he said. "I called the boy every day and told him how she was doing."

"What boy?" Billy asked.

"Billy."

"I'm Billy. You never called me."

"No. The boy, Billy."

"There is no boy Billy. Just me. The man Billy."

"I want my money and the watch."

"There is no money. There is no watch."

"She promised me."

"I'm sorry. I don't know any more. See that man," he said pointing again to Feyhe's other cousin. "Talk to him."

"She promised."

"Apparently she promised a lot of people a lot of things, but she shouldn't have because there isn't anything. I'm sorry." He moved away before the man could speak again. He felt he had to get out of this place, and fast, because he was going to burst if he didn't. Adam grabbed his arm as Billy hurried past the row of seats where he and his mother, Joe and Sandy had been seated.

"Where're you going, boy?"

"Out of here. Now. Come on."

"I take it, it's over, then?"

"It is. Come on. Everyone, let's go."

He gathered his group and headed for the lobby. The director of the Home was waiting there, a bill in her hand for day's event. Billy indicated Feyhe's other cousin and shepherded his friends out of the building. At the end of the driveway he turned around and addressed Joe, the others as witnesses of the statement.

"Can you do me a favor, Joe? Something's not right about this."

"Sure, what?"

Billy opened the box containing Feyhe's ashes and, using a small pillbox he normally used for his own medication, scooped out about two inches of the fine, powdery substance inside. He closed the box and handed it to Joe.

"When I reached in and got some to toss at that little bitch in there it didn't feel right, didn't feel like ash. Can you just have your crime lab analyze it for me. I don't know why, but I'm suddenly suspicious of this stuff. Suddenly this whole thing feels so wrong to me."

Joe took the container, put it in his pocket, hugged Billy and left the group, heading for his car parked around the corner on East 116th street. Billy gave the others a wan smile, then took Adam's arm and headed across 5th Avenue toward the park. They entered through the gaping entryway in the old stone wall and walked into the glade that Feyhe had always liked to stare at through her window. He headed for the tree that Feyhe had claimed Danny hid behind and he stood there looking at it, Adam clutching his arm. Sandy and Virginia joined them in a moment. The four of them studied the tree, the bushes behind it, the vague pathways that filtered through the century old greenery. No one spoke. No one had to speak.

At three in the morning Billy pulled himself out of bed, leaving a sleeping Adam snoring quietly on the other side of their king-size sleeping quarters. He pulled on his trousers and a sweater, picked up his shoes, and quietly left the room. At the top of the stairs he turned to look back at Adam. Some quirky light danced above his head, flashing on the subtle red streaks in his hair. *He is a beautiful soul*, Billy thought, the words slipping out from beneath his clenched lips. Then he moved on down to the next floor below.

He pulled on his shoes over his sockless feet and then continued on out to the street. It was a cool night, but clear and crisp and healthy. Securing the door behind him, he headed over to West Broadway, then south to Canal Street. From there he headed west, crossed the wide expanse of The Avenue of the Americas and then 7th Avenue South. It was the repeat of a journey he had made so often when he was younger, when his apartment and studio on Thompson Street was still his own.

He crossed Canal Street and wended his way through still familiar night streets until he saw the lights of the old diner on the horizon. He wondered for a moment if Andrea still worked the night shift there, if she would look as he remembered her, if she would remember him. When he climbed the four steps and entered the place, he was shocked at the transformation of the place. New Naugahyde seats at both the bar stools and the booth glared a harsh animal red. The countertops and tabletops had been redone also in a strangely patterned yellow and gray combination that fought for the poor taste award with the seats. The lighting was brighter than it had been in years past. It was a new sort of place, but even so he decided to stay.

He took his place, the stool he had used so long ago, and picked up the large, plastic-enclosed menu. The pancakes were still there. A waitress, not Andrea, burst out of the kitchen and stood, chewing gum, waiting for him to order. He asked for coffee and pancakes. She snapped her gum in response and went back into the kitchen.

When she brought the plate of pancakes out and put them down in front of Billy, she smiled and asked if he needed anything else. She had already deposited the familiar pour-jar of syrup when she brought the coffee. He thanked her, said no, and set about eating what he hoped would be the same as he remembered.

To his joy they tasted exactly like the griddle cakes his memory clung to. He had noticed a young couple sitting in a booth at the far end of the diner, but had paid no attention to them. While he ate, he heard them get up, come to the counter and pay their bill. As they finished he turned to look at them. They were so clearly in love, she clinging to his arm and looking at him with a look that was unmistakable.

"Enjoy the day," he said to them. They moved on as though they hadn't heard him at all, and perhaps they hadn't. Still, he felt good about saying it. A minute later, with one pancake to go on his plate, he heard the diner's door open behind him. Half expecting Joe, he looked at the pie case expecting Joe's reflection there, but the man who came in had moved down the counter and, of course, it wasn't Joe at all. Billy wasn't disappointed. Had it been the New York City cop he had met in this place that would have been too curious a coincidence. It would have been too romantic a moment to endure. His depression might have flared up, his elation might have overwhelmed him. He finished his pancakes, laid down some cash for the bill, and decided to go home to Adam. Home where he belonged.

Joe telephoned three days later with new news. Billy wasn't surprised a bit when Joe told him what the lab had reported, although the news was startling.

"The box, Billy, it doesn't contain Feyhe's ashes. You know we had her DNA from her hair on her brush that we found in her room."

"I'd say the DNA wouldn't be a match," Billy commented.

"You'd be right, because we didn't even have to try and match it, Billy. There are no human remains in that box of yours. It's crushed stone, crushed cement. What we call cement dust. Nothing cremated is in that box, just dust."

"It didn't feel right, Joe, when I reached into it. I knew there was something wrong."

"We're re-opening the investigation, Billy. As far as the NYPD's concerned, Feyhe is still a missing person. We'll check on the death certificate, of course, and try to retrace the steps of the person who mailed the package, but that was more than a month ago and he's probably no longer anywhere near that place."

Billy lowered his eyes, fought the momentary depression and re-emerged healthier. It had been a sudden thing, and the fact that he wasn't emotionally swayed by Joe's expressed plans pleased him.

"We'll find him," Joe said. "And maybe we'll find her, too."

"You won't, Joe. It's Feyhe. She's not meant to be found, discovered, uncovered, whatever. It's right, somehow. Cement dust, crushed and crumbled stone, so right, so like her."

"Billy, are you okay?" Joe asked him, the concern in his voice clear and sure.

Billy paused before responding, a smile holding strong on his face, in his arms and shoulders. "I'm fine. Thanks."

"We will keep on this, Billy. If she's alive, we'll find her."

"Joe, she is alive, best seen in her work. That's where she lives. The rest is just this...cement dust."

"Billy, you're not making much sense."

"Joe, if I've ever made sense in my life, I'm making it today. You think we're left with questions and I think we have answers. Sure, we don't know everything, and maybe we never will, but we have an answer like no other. One sure answer to a hundred little questions."

He hung up the phone before Joe could say any more. Then he took the stairs down to the gallery and went to look at Feyhe's work. He had left the rest of the box of her "ashes" there and he now went to it, picked it up and opened it. The gray, dusty crumbled fragments were so obviously not human ash, now that he knew this for sure. They were a choice, an obvious choice for her to make, to have had made for her, he would never know for sure which, or how. He would never know how conscious a decision had been made by Feyhe about any of this, but he knew what he had to do with what had been sent to him. The "ashes" needed their place, the viewing point.

At the base of a newly added self-portrait in gray marble that he had come across in the storeroom, Billy placed the crushed gray stone in its black plastic box. He left the box open, at an angle, its contents visible.

"Self-portrait, indeed," he said aloud. Then he laughed and, for the first time in over a decade, he felt alive and free and whole. He felt in control. And unafraid.